REVELATION

Tree gazed upon a city so lovely she shook her head to be sure she was not lost in a fever-dream.

Waxed paper lanterns with brightly-coloured silk banners hung from street poles along broad avenues lined with cherry and mimosa trees. Persimmon and plumtree gardens, fountains and half-moon foot bridges bedecked the medians. All these were mere settings for the architectural jewels: ornate temples with wrap-around verandas supported by spiral columns; palaces with red-enameled pillars outside and inside their spacious open-air rooms; upthrust pagodas of seven, eight or ten octagonal floors, each storey wearing its scarlet pantiled roof like a skirt of flames; a stupa as big as a planetarium, its dome of hammered gold; double and triple roofs of glazed shingles – blues, yellows and reds – swooped and dipped like sea waves and at the crest of each swell a bronze lion-dog perched. Tree's eyes followed colonnades that led to other streets and palaces, temples and pagodas in a multi-layered web of splendour.

The avenues radiated from a city hub towards which the soldiers carried her. At the hub's centre, a dense grove of banyan trees embraced a many-petaled temple. The building seemed to blossom out of the earth like a white lotus. It was as if some time-magician had gathered master-craftsmen from the Forbidden City, Angkor Wat, the Taj Mahal and Kyoto Gardens and challenged them to wed their great styles into a new architecture to outshine the others . . .

Also by Mark Canter in New English Library paperback

Ember from the Sun

About the author

Mark Canter was born in Kentucky in 1952 and moved to Florida when he was twelve. Dropping out of university in young adulthood to travel in the western USA and Canada, he later worked at a variety of jobs, from dishwasher to bloodmobile driver for the American Red Cross. He paid his way through the University of Florida School of Journalism by working as a stagehand for rock bands, theatrical shows and the circus and went on to become a feature writer for a Florida newspaper and senior editor at *Men's Health* magazine. He is married with two young sons. His first novel, *Ember from the Sun*, was published in 1995.

Down to Heaven

Mark Canter

NEW ENGLISH LIBRARY
Hodder and Stoughton

First published in Great Britain in 1997
by Hodder and Stoughton

First published in paperback in 1997 by Hodder and Stoughton
A division of Hodder Headline PLC

A New English Library Paperback

A CIP catalogue record for this title
is available from the British Library.

ISBN 0 340 66042 2

Printed and bound in Great Britain by
Clays Ltd, St Ives plc

Hodder and Stoughton
A division of Hodder Headline PLC
338 Euston Road
London NW1 3BH

To Margaret,
delicious and nutritious

ACKNOWLEDGMENTS

The author thanks Adrian Mendez, naturalist guide, for a senses-opening trek in the cloud forest of Monteverde, Costa Rica; Bob and Marcy Lawton, botanist and biologist, respectively, for pointing me toward research on the biogeography of tepuis and human hermaphroditism; Roy Bamfield, massage therapist, for erasing a stubborn hand pain that interfered with typing; Danny Baror, literary agent, for top worldwide representation, and Nick Austin, my British editor, for his astuteness and good nature. Without their assistance, this novel would not be in the reader's hands.

In a Countrey that hath yet her Maydenhead, never turned nor wrought, there bee a mountaine that hath the bewtey of a white Church towre. There falleth over it a mightie river which toucheth no parte of the side of the mountaine, but falleth to the grounde with a terrible noyse and clamor, as if 1000 great belles were knockt one against another. It bee tolde that diamonds and other precious crystales encruste the mountaine toppe, and the common soldier shal find there more riches and bewtifull cities, more temples adorned with golden images, then either Cortez found in Mexico, or Pizarro in Peru. But what it hath I knowe not, neyther durst any of my men ascende to the toppe of saide mountaine, the way to it so impassible.

1

Mason Drake awoke and saw the pilot burning. Flames climbed up the dead man's flight jacket, red nylon melted, forearm hair shriveled and smoked.

Mason had been thrown, strapped in his seat, through the helicopter's windshield. The seat now tilted on its side, gouged into the muck of a swamp. Mason choked on fumes of aviation kerosene; he wanted to fling himself from the crumpled aluminum and shattered Plexiglas but it was too much strain to force open his eyelids.

He blacked out.

A woman's screams jarred him alert. He spat out a clot of blood, sucked the sooty wind into his lungs, and his body jolted from its first shock of pain. His right arm had been wrenched out of its shoulder girdle. A dozen yards away the licking flames now consumed the pilot's body as if it were a tallow candle. Mason flinched at the sight, turned his head. The reek of oily fuel and charred flesh triggered a memory of napalm burning. Burning children. He bucked against the seat's shoulder harness and retched.

The woman yelled for help. Mason recognized her voice and suddenly he knew he was not in Vietnam. In Vietnam there had been no angels – no Tree Summerwood.

He unclipped his shoulder belts, slid from the seat into the cold black ooze and waded to the wreckage, lunging ahead with each step as he yanked his boots out of the sucking mud. The emergency exit handle on the helicopter's sliding door wouldn't budge. He kicked it once, twice. Harder. The door sprung open and a belch of black smoke stung his eyes. A body propped against the inside of the door spilled out into his arms: A dead woman. Mason's heart lurched.

'Tree?'

Bandoliers of film cartridge crisscrossed the woman's chest. *Lisa, the photographer.* He sighed with relief and shrugged off the body; it flopped into the swamp and flecks of mud splashed his face.

'Tree, where are you?' he shouted into the smoking gut of the wreck.

'Mason, oh my god, back here. I'm pinned.' She coughed violently.

Mason moved in a crouch, groping with one hand along the left wall of the aircraft, now its floor. His fingers found a slim arm, slick with blood. He tugged. The arm slid toward him with a sickening looseness, not attached to a body. He nearly retched again.

'Goddamit, Tree. Where are you?'

'Here. Jammed against the bulkhead – Barry's on top of me, they're all dead.'

Mason crawled to the back of the cargo area, shoving video equipment and cases of canned foods out of his path. His left hand touched a man's hairy legs. Barry was huge. Mason heaved with one arm until the veins popped out on his forehead and his right shoulder blared a trumpet of pain. He dragged the body part-way off Tree.

'Grab my hand.' He reached for her in the dense haze.

'Can't, my hand ... it's bad.' She convulsed into another coughing fit.

Mason gave another awful tug and Tree squirmed out from underneath the corpse and scrambled to her feet.

'Let's go, let's go,' she said.

Mason staggered back out of the cabin, tugging her along. He turned and hopped down into the swamp and spun to help her.

2

'Hurry.' He stretched his hand toward hers. Her left hand was mangled, missing its thumb. 'Oh lord,' he said. A vivid image intruded: Fourteen-year-old Teresa in a white chiffon dress playing Brahms on a big black piano. He grabbed higher up her arm and steadied her as she jumped.

The two slogged through the marsh away from the flaming wreckage. An explosion thudded behind them and knocked them to their knees.

'Cover your head,' he shouted and shielded Tree with his body.

Chunks and shards of aluminum, steel and fiberglass strafed the water around them. Something charred and smoking splashed down inches from where they crouched: A woman's Gore-Tex hiking boot. Mason spun to gape at the orange fireball. The thunderclap was still echoing around the mountain top when the hiking boot gulped water and sank.

At once, the noises of the landscape hushed. In the silence, Mason's ears rang and his heart thumped in his throat. Tree's eyes locked on his. He hoped his gaze did not reflect the fear and pain he read in her face.

Abruptly a million insects, frogs and birds resumed buzzing, chirping and trilling. Nine thousand feet below the mountain top where he and Tree held each other, Mason imagined barking howler monkeys and squawking macaws swinging and gliding in the rainforest canopy as growling jaguars padded its mulchy floor.

Way down there, raindrops sizzled through the jungle foliage, turning to steam. But up here, icy rain mixed with grit scraped at his skin. It had taken Mason years to adjust to the tropical swelter of the lowlands; now he stood shivering on a towering island in the clouds.

Tree Summerwood buried her face in the wet denim shirt that clung to Mason Drake's broad chest. With sinewy fingers he gently traced her apricot braids. Atop the giant mesa called Cameleon-tepui, her sobs added to the Amazon ambience a tiny human sound.

2

The swamp stretched into the distance but was no wider than a soccer field, and in minutes the two had waded to solid ground. They stood, resting, on sandstone gravel, coated to their waists in purplish-black sludge that exuded the sweet stink of decay. Mason turned to examine Tree's injured hand and found it gloved with mud. His stomach churned. *Not good.*

'When I fell,' she said, and checked his eyes. He hid his reaction.

'Let me take a look,' he said. She held out her left hand, cradling it in her other. He picked up a smooth flat pebble and gingerly wiped off the slimy coating. She winced and sucked air through her clenched teeth, fidgeting as red flesh appeared from under the dark mud.

He tossed the pebble aside and inspected her injury. The severed bone at the base of her thumb jutted from crushed muscle tissue. Delicately, he turned her palm over. Fire had seared the wound, which in her case was lucky, because the heat had cauterized torn arteries. But experience told Mason that infection in the tropics was a given – even when you don't go bathing in muck – and bone infections were a deadly mess. He wanted the first aid kit that had been stowed under his helicopter seat, now scattered over the mountain top in smithereens.

'We need to wash this wound,' he said, frowning. 'Sounds repulsive, but the best thing we can do now, medically, is to wash it with urine.'

'What?'

'Fresh urine is sterile—'

'Pee on it?'

'We got to get it clean somehow.'

She glanced at the swamp. 'How about—'

'Swamp water? It's squirming with germs – that's what we've got to rinse off.'

She looked away.

'Come on, Tree, this is critical. Pick a better time to get embarrassed on me.'

She shook her head. 'I'm not embarrassed – that's not it . . .'

'Well, I am, so let's get it over with.' He unzipped the fly of his canvas shorts. 'Okay. It's gonna sting like hell.'

Tree gasped and jerked back her hand when the stream of urine splashed over raw flesh.

'Try to hold still—'

'*Ow*, it burns, it burns.'

'—Could save your life.'

'*Yeow!*' She yanked her hand away again.

He gripped her wrist. 'Sorry. A few more seconds.' The last of the black slime rinsed away. Tree closed her eyes and shuddered.

Mason zipped up his shorts. 'What you really need is a big dose of tetracycline and morphine,' he said, 'and I should suture a skin fold over the bone.'

'And I should be at a spa soaking in a hot tub. But here we are, stranded on a tepui.'

Mason nodded and swept his eyes across the plateau. The tepui was an immense mesa, shaped like the sheer-sided tabletop mountains of the south-western American deserts but on a far grander scale. The mesas of Monument Valley in Arizona and Utah zoomed straight up to a thousand feet; the tepuis of the Amazon basin were ten times taller and jutted high above the clouds that hid the emerald roof of the rainforest.

More than a hundred tepuis, half of them never explored, were strewn over a vast area that stretched from south-eastern

Venezuela to just across its border with Guyana. Only the deep trenches of the world's oceans had seen fewer humans than these remote, unscalable jungle mountains. And each tepui, because of its eons-long isolation, had evolved a unique ecosystem, with types of flora and fauna found on no other tepui and nowhere else on Earth.

Mason squinted against the blowing rain. In every direction sandstone boulders loomed, some as small as huts and others as large as cathedrals. The rocks had been sculpted into organic shapes by winds that had scoured them for two billion years.

He and Tree huddled in the lee of a moss-draped reddish boulder with oval windows at its top and a scooped-out archway at its base. They crouched on a sandstone shelf that had been thrust up out of the Pacific Ocean floor before trilobites swam in those waters. Silver lichens etched the rock like graffiti, punctuated by clumps of green air plants. Ruby-throated bromeliads and spiked grasses poked from every patch of gritty soil at their feet.

Mason reviewed their predicament. Tree's smashed hand was not hemorrhaging, so the immediate medical concern was his dislocated shoulder. He had bitten completely through his left cheek and the swollen gash felt to his tongue like raw beef, but it would not be a problem unless – *until* – it festered. More critically, they lacked a medical kit, food, potable water, rain gear, shelter, and the means to start a fire. They were soaked and the wind-chill factor was bound to be in the teens tonight, which added hypothermia to the worry list. All wild cards that could kill them before germs got their chance.

The Raft is our only hope for survival.

'We gotta make it to the Raft,' Mason said. 'It's gonna be slow moving, but—'

'I know. We have to find it before nightfall. Period.'

The Raft was a portable biological research station that looked like a giant inflatable life raft. It had been designed and built in 1981 at Halcyon Pharmaceutical Corporation in San Diego, California, and shipped in sections the next year to Canaima, Venezuela, where it had been reassembled and inflated. The Huey had flown it to the mountain top and parked it atop a group of boulders that upheld it like columns. Two

Venezuelan team members, Domingo 'Domino' Cruz, a zoologist, and Lynda Loyola, an entomologist, had stayed with the Raft while the helicopter returned to its base at Canaima to ferry the rest of the biologists to the site.

In addition to its state-of-the-art biology lab, the Raft was outfitted with radios, sleeping shelters, food, clothing and enough medical gear to cover just about any emergency a seven-person science team might encounter during a four-month-long field project on Cameleon-tepui. The Raft was even equipped with a hot-air balloon system for short hops to other parts of the mountain in order to focus on each microclimate and ecosystem.

The research team's mission was to collect and analyze unusual species in order to find new organic compounds that might prove useful as medicines. Just before the relentless winter rains, the Raft was to be hauled by helicopter back to base and, later, carried to a different tepui for another season of research, with a fresh team of scientists.

Mason dug a compass out of his pocket. Its glass face was cracked but the needle spun freely and it appeared to be working.

'We turned south to get a closer look at that valley, but I don't think we veered far off our course,' he said, 'and when we went down we spiraled straight in. So my guess is we're still pretty much due west of the Raft, no more than a few miles away if we're lucky.'

Tree cushioned her wrecked hand against her belly and gently rocked her torso. 'Domino and Lynda may have seen the chopper go down,' she said. 'They surely heard the explosion.'

'Yeah, but they won't know if there were any survivors.' Mason nodded toward the afternoon sun. 'They'd be unwise to try to search for us on foot this late in the day. If they're smart they stayed put and radioed for help. When we get there I can patch up your hand until we can get another chopper up here to evacuate us to a hospital.' He glanced down at her wound and set his jaw.

'You're thinking what I'm thinking,' she said. 'It could take a week or more to get us off the mountain.'

'That's the problem. Closest chopper now is probably Venezuelan National Guard, at the base at Luepa. They'd have to fly in their fuel by stages to Canaima, just like we did. Seven or eight hops.'

'But if I get antibiotics at the Raft I should be okay.'

He nodded but turned from her gaze. Bone infections scared him. He had lost a number of his Indian patients that way. *Staphylococcus aureus* eating its way through the marrow – one of the jungle's more gruesome ways to add you to its compost.

The drips fell more slowly from the rock eaves overhead. 'Rain's almost stopped,' Tree said. 'Let's go.'

He shook his head. 'My shoulder. You're going to have to reset it or I'll never make the distance.'

'Tell me what to do.'

'Won't be easy with just one hand.'

She grabbed his corded forearm and squeezed hard. 'Hey, it's me, remember? I'm just as strong now . . .' Her eyes flashed with feeling.

In that instant, Tree's look cracked open in his heart a carefully sealed vault of memories. An image escaped: Mason was nineteen, Tree, eighteen, chasing her to the top of the abandoned lighthouse on Indian Mound Beach; both laughing as she dashed up the spiral steps above him. Their footsteps on steel clanged and echoed in the brick tube while his heart banged in his chest. Her linen dress billowing like a red sail; the shock of white cotton underwear against her summer thighs. They hadn't reached their romantic sea vista at the top, but made love standing on the stairs as she clung to the rusted railings, their cries of pleasure amplified as if in a megaphone.

Mason managed a smile. Tree was still as shapely and muscular as when their marriage had broken up after he'd returned from Vietnam. She was twenty-four then. They hadn't seen each other for eight years, until one week ago and his bombshell surprise when he'd found himself face-to-face with her at Canaima. Again he wondered if she had joined the research project only because she learned he was the team medic. *I hope for her sake she doesn't love me as much as I still love her.*

The ache in his shoulder snapped him out of his reverie. 'All right Lie down on your back opposite me, your left foot toward my shoulder.'

They positioned themselves on the rain-soaked bed of gravel.

Tiny pink mushrooms sprouted everywhere between the pebbles and their squashed caps gave off a strong musky odor.

'Okay,' Mason said, 'brace your right foot in my armpit and pull the arm toward you, slowly, at slight angle away from my torso.'

'Like this?'

'Ow, ow, yeah. Like that. Oh, dammit.' He sucked in his breath. 'Keep the tension on it . . . Ow.' He groaned. 'Pull harder, till you feel the bone start to shift – *OW* – stop, stop, stop.' The pain made him gag. He screwed his eyes shut and tears squeezed out from beneath his eyelids. 'I don't think,' he whispered, chest heaving, 'don't think I can do this.'

'Mason, you're the toughest man I've ever known.' She was breathing hard from her own exertion and pain.

He took a deep breath and blew it out slowly through pursed lips. 'Okay. All right. Once more,' he said. 'This time, tug twice as hard as you did before, and just keep pulling even if I scream for you to stop. When the top of my shoulder lines up with my collarbone, keep your foot in place and swing my arm in toward my side.'

She gripped his right wrist with her right hand. 'Ready?' she asked. He gulped and nodded. Tree braced her foot against his armpit and pulled down, hard and steady. Mason screamed and butted the back of his head against the gravel.

'It's coming,' she shouted, 'it's sliding down. Here goes.'

He gritted his teeth. Tree swung the arm inward and it made a loud *pop* as the upper condyle of the humerus snapped back into the glenoid cavity of the scapula.

Mason lay panting for a long while. Then he let out a loud, low whistle. 'I felt like an astronaut – I saw stars, galaxies.' He sat up with a wince and rubbed his reset shoulder. 'But what a relief.'

'Is it going to be all right?'

'It'll heal. Takes a month or so.' He reached out and touched her arm. 'Thank you. You're brave, same as ever.' The way she looked at him then made him swallow hard. He dropped his gaze. Spatters of blood from her wound had crusted on her gray wool hiking socks. 'Wish I could do something more for your hand.'

'We're alive. That's what matters now.' Tree stood and pulled him to his feet. '*Vamanos.*' She turned toward the fading eastern sky that silhouetted the gnarled horizon.

The two trudged in a cold drizzle without talking. The wind had died but occasional gusts whistled and swirled through the rocky labyrinths. Every jutting surface was thickly coated with moss, lichens and fungi. Mason's eyes followed a wide glistening ribbon of blue-green algae that snaked along a canyon wall like a painted river. Here and there a stubby banyan adorned with dangling yellow orchids or a dwarf jacaranda waving showy violet flowers stood out among the endless contours of rock.

Mason checked their bearing with the compass and touched Tree's elbow. 'This way, I think.' They squeezed through a corridor that led upward to a more open patch of terrain. 'Now we can make some headway.'

The ground was littered with chunks of rose-colored jasper and shards of obsidian that shone like black glass. Tree stepped over a brick-sized quartz crystal. 'Geologists' paradise,' she said.

Mason studied her for a moment. She coddled her injured hand by holding it close to her midriff so it wouldn't bump things, but occasionally it brushed her thigh as she scrabbled over a rock and she'd let out a moan. Her skin tone looked pasty – he knew that was from the pain – but she was keeping up with him and she didn't appear to be falling into traumatic shock. Not yet, anyway. Tomorrow would be an ugly day if they didn't make it to the Raft tonight.

'How you holding up?' he asked.

'Throb, throb, thob. My hand feels like lava bubbling in a crater. How's your cheek?'

He ran his tongue over the deep cut and grimaced. 'Could use a dozen stitches, inside and out. Mainly, I want to get lots of tetracycline into both of us.'

'Mason, what happened up there? I was staring down at the valley, Lisa was shooting video of the waterfall. Next thing, people and equipment were flying through the cabin, bouncing off walls.'

'A goddam bird,' he said. 'Huge. Must have been an eagle.' He started to spread his arms to show its wingspan and he winced from his stiff shoulder.

'Harpy eagle, maybe,' she said. 'Biggest species in the Amazon. They can hover like hummingbirds, snatch monkeys out of trees.'

'Yeah, well, this one shot straight up out of that valley like a surface-to-air missile, and then it dove on us . . . I swear it was attacking. Must have hit our tail rotor. I felt the impact, then Juan lost control.'

They trekked onward for a while. 'I went to Harvard with Lisa,' Tree said, 'met Barry in Monteverde.'

Mason nodded. 'Juan flew me up the Orinoco half a dozen times to set up village clinics. Helluva good pilot.' In his mind he saw his friend engulfed in flames and felt grateful that Juan had apparently been killed instantly. 'I knew Lisa from when she shot a story for *GEO* about my work with the Wawajeros.'

Tree sighed. 'When I saw you on the cover . . . I burst into tears in the middle of Barnes & Noble. That was the first I even knew you were still alive.'

'I'm sorry.' He shook his head. 'I actually did write you. Dozens of times over the years. I saved most of them for a while, hoping one day the words might evolve into the perfect epistle.' He rubbed one hand through his thick black curls. 'Even wrote you once in Spanish,' he said. 'Eventually tore that one up too.'

Tree shot him a glance. 'English, Spanish, what's the difference? Letters you don't send say *nada* to me.'

'You're right. I know that. They don't count unless I mail them. But, the point is, in a hundred languages I'd never find the right words to explain why I had to leave.'

They hiked on.

'We had so much love, Mason . . . a love like people hope for all their lives. You used to tell me that yourself.'

'Tree,' he said softly. 'Something happened . . .'

'Oh, here we go. 'Something happened in Vietnam.' You've said it again and again. And I hear you. I really do. I know it must have been something horrible beyond imagining for you. But you never tell me what it was . . . You're haunted by the past, ashamed of something that happened years ago, and you won't let me help you. You broke my heart, Mason. Eight years . . . and it still aches over you . . .'

He stared straight ahead and swallowed hard. 'Some things I

can never make up to you. But . . . well . . . I guess I've said it: I can't make it right. Some wounds just can't be healed.'

They weaved and detoured among the boulders. Mason heard Tree quietly crying. He wept too, but silently, inside a secret room in his heart. Since he'd returned from Vietnam he had never shed a tear. Not the real kind that stream down your face and cleanse your soul. Inside a sealed room he could feel his tears welling up now with nowhere to go. No outlet. No release. No one was allowed to enter that heart-vault anymore. Not even Tree. Not even himself.

One thing is certain, Teresa Diana. If you knew what I did in 'Nam, you'd never forgive me.

They squeezed sideways between two head-high boulders. On a flat hunk of granite ahead of them a large dead bird lay sprawled. The bird's legs were chopped off at the thigh and its dark blood had sprayed the orange fungi that mottled the gray stone.

'My god, it's the bird that hit us,' Mason said as the two hurried forward. 'Look at the wingspan – must be seven feet or more.'

'It's a harpy, all right,' Tree said. 'A female, they're bigger than the males.'

'Why did it attack us like that?'

'I'm not sure,' she said. 'We must have invaded her territory – they're fierce when they defend their eggs and young. You're looking at the world's most powerful raptor.'

'I believe it.' He hefted the carcass. 'Weighs about twenty pounds and she knocked down a helicopter that weighs two-and-a-half tons.'

'Twenty pounds plummeting at a hundred-fifty miles an hour, with talons bigger than a grizzly's claws,' Tree said. 'Her legs were sliced off when she spun feet-first for the kill.'

Mason nodded. 'The collision must have snapped a tail rotor blade, then torque from the main rotors spun us in like a maple seed.'

With grim respect, he placed the eagle back on the rock.

'Let's move on,' he said. 'New moon tonight. When the sun drops below the mountains it's gonna be black as squid ink up here.'

They trekked eastward a half-hour more and came upon a tall narrow rock with stair-like ridges that led up to a flat platform at its peak. The steps were so regular they looked as if they might have been hand-carved.

'Perfect,' Mason said. 'Erosion built us a lookout tower. Let me see if I can spot the Raft from up there.'

When he reached the top, he immediately saw the fluorescent orange Raft against the purpling sky.

'Tree!' he called down. 'I see it. It's not far – less than a quarter-mile.'

'Oh, thank God,' she said.

He cupped his hands and shouted from the bottom of his belly in the direction of the Raft. 'Hey! Domino! Lynda! We're coming! Put on the coffee, *mis amigos*.'

No response. *Why haven't they turned on the floodlights for us?*

Mason whistled piercingly between his front teeth. 'Lynda! Domino! It's Tree and Mason. We're on our way.'

'They can't hear you,' Tree yelled. 'Hurry down, we're losing daylight.'

From his vantage he turned a full circle and surveyed the horizon. Due west the sky was turning an ominous velvet black and anvil-shaped clouds roiled and surged toward the mountain. At this altitude sinister weather had a way of sneaking up fast.

He clambered down and grabbed Tree by the hand. 'All right, we really gotta move now. Quickly. There's a big thunderhead rolling in behind us.'

She glanced over her shoulder. 'Uh-oh. Where'd that come from?'

'Looks like straight out of hell.'

Scrambling over and around boulders in the menacing gloom they reached the Raft. The inflated neoprene structure formed an octagonal ring with eight spokes connecting it to an enclosed hub. Nylon webbing between the spokes supported sleeping shelters. On the outer ring, a number of observation platforms upheld frames that could be rigged with fine mesh nets for collecting insects, birds and bats. The fiberglass building at the hub contained a fully-outfitted lab complete with two gasoline-powered electric generators and a rack of wet-cell batteries.

The word **HARVEST** was emblazoned in bold white letters on each of the Raft's sides and beneath it, HALCYON AMAZON RESEARCH VENTURES, ECOLOGICAL SURVEY, TEPUIS. On the underside of the central lab was posted a hand-lettered sign: *Welcome Summer Science Team: December thru March 1982.* A nylon ladder with aluminum rungs dangled below a trapdoor.

Tree called up from the base of the ladder. 'Lynda! Domino!'

Mason cupped his palms and yelled. 'Guys! I need your help to get Tree up the ladder, she's hurt.'

He turned to Tree. 'Why won't they answer?'

'Shhh. Listen,' she said. 'The generators aren't running. I don't think anybody's up there.'

Mason tried Spanish. *'Necesitamos su ayuda! Mueven sus colas!* We need your help! Move your butts!'

Tree scrunched her eyebrows. 'Nobody's home. Probably out looking for us.'

The sky began to fall in lumps. The precipitation smacked the rubber Raft loudly and bounced off like marbles.

'It's hailing,' Tree groaned, and huddled next to Mason.

'Damn. Okay. Let me go up,' he said. 'I'll bring down a shot of painkiller and we'll get you up there somehow.'

'Bring down a couple headlamps, it's getting too dark to see the rungs.'

'Good idea. And I'll aim a spotlight down from one of the collection platforms.'

Mason scrambled up the ladder, stiff shoulder flaring painfully. He pushed through the trap door and entered the lightless lab. Groping along the wall above a folding workbench, his hands came to a large utility flashlight clipped into a recharging unit. It came free with a loud *click* and he swept the room with its bright beam.

What he saw made his pulse thud in his ears along with the first crash of thunder.

3

Bloody handprints groped a path across the far wall of the lab and slid to the floor in a reddish-brown smear that guided Mason's flashlight beam to the body. Lynda Loyola was sprawled face down with her hands covering her head as if to protect herself from attack.

'Lynda!'

Mason crossed the octagonal room in three bounds and knelt next to the body. A lightning bolt outside the room's high windows lit the walls with a blue-white flash. Thunder rumbled and vibrated through the aluminum floor and hail beat a furious drum roll on the roof. He gingerly turned Lynda's head upward to face him. The flashlight beam shone to the back of the dark caves of her empty eye sockets. Deep gouges raked her forehead, cheeks and neck, and in places the flesh hung in flaps exposing yellow fat, red muscle, white bone.

Mason involuntarily let go and the head thudded on the floor. '*For chrissake!* What happened?'

Tree called up from below. 'Mason, what's wrong?'

Lightning exploded into a nearby jumble of boulders, sending stones clattering down the sides. Shapes and shadows in the lab leapt out in sharp relief. Mason swung his light around the room seaching wildly.

'Domino?'

The bright circle at the center of the beam was trembling. Mason took a deep breath and steadied his hand. The room was in chaos. Shattered lab equipment was strewn around the counters and floor and smashed radios were heaped in one of the room's eight corners.

'Mason,' Tree shouted, 'talk to me.'

One, two, three lightning spikes split the blackness and a startled owl screeched from a nearby nook.

'Just stay put, Tree,' he called down. 'We, uh, we've got a problem here. I'm checking it out.'

'What kind of problem?'

'Uh . . . the worst kind. Just watch out down there. Looks like there might be some kind of wild animal . . .'

'Are you trying hard to scare me or are you just a natural at it?'

'Hang on,' Mason said. He hoped that somehow it *was* an animal. He didn't want to think of the other explanation: Domino Cruz had gone berserk and mutilated their colleague. He walked around the lab. A video camera had been crunched to plastic chips using a steel microscope as a sledge. *No animal did that.*

No sign of Domino. One of the sliding doors was wide ajar. He eased his head out and swung the flashlight beam over that half of the Raft. The built-in video tripods and spotlight trees at the collection stations, the mushroom-domed sleeping shelters, all the cubbies and dark spaces sucked up the light one by one. Empty.

He crossed the lab to the opposite door and swept the beam over the other half of the Raft. 'Domino?' he called. Hailstones in the rainwater collector made it look like a bucket of golfballs. He saw no one.

Lightning blasted into a pagoda-shaped stack of rocks a couple hundred feet from the Raft and the aluminum floor panels buzzed with the rumbling thunder.

'Mason?'

'Still here,' he said. He rummaged through a cabinet and found a bright yellow flame-retardant drop cloth. 'Domino's not aboard.'

'What about Lynda?'

He draped the cloth over Lynda's body. 'She's had an accident.'

'She okay?'

'Better let me come down, we'll talk.'

Mason climbed down the ladder. When he saw Tree shivering, her eyes big with fright, he grabbed her to him and held her close for a long moment. Hailstones clunked against the gravel and an icy gust tossed her braids like whips. Mason told her of the mayhem in the lab; he didn't mention mutilation, only that Lynda appeared to have been murdered.

Tree gasped. 'But what would drive Domino . . . ?' She shuddered. 'This morning on the radio he seemed totally himself. He even came on to me.'

'That's Domino. Never liked the guy.'

'Well, now that it's confession time: I can't stand him. I almost turned down the offer to be on the team when I found out he was a member. Eight months with Domino panting in my ear – but that's just his *machismo* thing – I never imagined . . .' She grimaced. 'What made him pop his laces?'

'Lynda told him his *pinga* was tiny?' he said. 'Don't know. But our rescue hopes are looking damn bleak.'

Lightning shot out of the dark and forked across the sky; the thunder bounced around the boulders for more than a minute.

He glanced up the ladder. 'We gotta get ourselves up there out of this storm and get some sleep. Tomorrow we can see if there's any tetracycline in that mess. We've got rain collectors for drinking water – we'll just have to see what's left of our gear, try to sort this whole thing out.' He gave her shoulders a squeeze. 'You go up first. I'll steady the ladder and spot you from the ground.'

'You're gonna catch me if I fall? I'll squash you.'

'No, you won't.'

'I'm a hundred and forty-five now.'

'Looks good on you,' he said. 'You were skinny before. Now go.'

'I'm worried about how it's going to look on top of *you*.'

'You won't fall. Let go with your hand and lunge for the next rung, use your legs to push yourself up. Go on.'

Tree started up the ladder and Mason pulled down with his

full weight on the ladder's nylon backbones. He kept his eyes on Tree as she moved from rung to rung, grunting with pain when she jostled her wounded hand. She paused at the top to catch her breath, then she dragged herself through the trapdoor.

When Mason crawled into the lab he saw that Tree had collapsed on the floor, too exhausted to budge. He stepped outside with the flashlight and returned from their sleeping shelters carrying a couple towels and two rolled sleeping bags wrapped inside a rain parka. He helped Tree wriggle our of her sopping clothes and towel herself dry. She crawled into a green nylon sleeping bag, keeping her injured hand outside. He zipped the fiber-filled bag around her like a cocoon, and folded a towel beneath her head for a pillow. Then he sat down hard, his back against the wall, and hung his head in his hands in the darkness.

Lightning flickered on the far horizon and thunder pounded like distant tom-toms; the storm receded over the moonless jungle below. On the mountaintop the treefrogs, cicadas and crickets resumed their engine of noise, but their two human guests remained silent for a long while.

'Mason, please hold me,' Tree said at last.

He furrowed his brow as he moved toward her voice in the blackness. 'You still cold?'

'Just scared.'

'I'm right here.' He sat next to her and laid his hand on her shoulder for comfort.

'Will you hold me? Just for tonight. Please. I need you right now.'

He sighed. He did and did not want this to happen. Reluctantly, he took off his chilly clothes and squirmed into her sleeping bag. At six feet, she was two inches taller than him. Her elongated body was smooth against his furry chest and legs. No, she wasn't cold, but warm and warm. Summer-warm. He thought of the many times they had melted together during the hot sunny days of their romance. He realized in that moment he had not once felt warm since their divorce. Not even in the lowlands with sweat dripping from his chin as he vaccinated a Wawajero child.

Tears swelled to the brim of the hidden well of his soul. *I don't deserve to ever feel warm inside again.*

Mason pressed his hand over his eyes and sleep swallowed him whole.

4

Tree awoke before dawn when Mason unzipped the sleeping bag and scooted out. In spite of her throbbing hand she quickly fell back asleep. When she woke again the sun had climbed a quarter way up the sky. Clean dry clothes from her personal stores in her sleeping shelter were folded neatly on the floor beside her head.

Tree sat up. 'Mason?'

'Right here.' He stepped into the lab through a sliding door. A deep blue wool sweater lent to his gray eyes a sea-colored hue. She watched his eyes, like a camera in a portrait studio, record her nudity in one focused take.

She felt suddenly shy and pulled the green nylon up over her small breasts. *His hands and mouth once made love to these breasts. Why should I hide my body from him now?* She took a breath and made herself stand up. The sun streaming in through the high windows gilded her willowy form. The blonde delta between her thighs caught the light like spun gold.

Mason blinked and swallowed. He turned around toward a worktable that had been folded down from its wall stowage. Transistors and circuit boards from several broken radios were spread before him.

'You never told me you used to think of me as skinny,' she said to his broad back.

'Never really thought of you that way.'

She pulled on her underwear. 'But you said last night—'

'I just . . . you look more beautiful than ever,' he said. 'It's obvious you've been working out.'

She smiled behind his back as she stepped into a pair of black denim jeans and tugged them to her waist with one hand.

'Gold's Gym, three days a week. Half-mile swim on the off-days.' She winced as she eased her injured hand through the sleeve of a green-and-black checkered flannel shirt.

He glanced over his shoulder. 'Here, let me help you button that.' He stepped forward and began buttoning up the shirt. Freckles covered the upper curves of her small breasts, '*like sprinkled cinnamon*,' he once had whispered between kisses. She searched for his eyes but he kept them fixed on his fingers as he closed the flannel over her bosom.

He crossed to the worktable and came back with a granola-and-raisin bar for her. 'Breakfast. Found a whole case of these in Barry's sleeping dome.'

'Thought you hated granola.'

'*And* raisins. Don't remind me. Looks like our only food for who knows how long. This morning it actually tasted good to me. "*La salsa mejor en el mundo es el hambre.*"'

'"The best sauce in the world is hunger,"' she translated. 'Marquez?'

He shook his head. 'Farther back.'

'Borges? Neruda?'

He brushed his hand through the air. 'Way back.'

'Oh,' she said, 'Cervantes.'

He nodded. Tree tore off the granola bar's wrapper with her front teeth and took a bite. 'Mmmm.' She chewed with her eyes closed.

Mason smiled. 'I remember. The original granola-girl-earth-momma.'

Tree took another bite and held the wrapped end of the bar in her teeth while she gingerly slid her injured hand through the sleeve of a raw wool sweater. She groaned.

Mason's brow furrowed. 'How's your hand?'

'Terrible.' The puffy flesh had bruised to purple-black. 'Won't stop throbbing.'

'Actually, that's a positive sign. Means you've still got circulation to the trauma site.'

'So, not to worry, as long as it hurts like hell?'

'Well . . .' He ran a hand through his black ringlet curls. 'I've got good news and bad.'

'First the bad. I like to end on a cheerful note.'

'Okay. There's no tetracycline. No morphine. No aspirin, even. The whole medical kit is just plain gone.'

She shook her head, stunned.

'And a lot of other stuff is missing, too. No fire extinguishers in any of the brackets, no hatchets, knives, machetes—'

'What about the stuff that's left?'

'Smashed and trashed, most of it. The gas generators are kaput. So are the batteries. Emergency transponders are in little pieces. The Dacron bag of the hot air balloon is shredded.' He paused.

'Oh boy . . . and now the good news.'

'I guess it's good news – Domino didn't do it. Or at least I don't think he killed Lynda.'

'What do you mean?'

'It was another goddam harpy. I found a dead one in the bat collection net this morning.'

'A coincidence?'

'No. Her face,' he said, 'I can't tell you . . . it had to be the harpy.'

'That's too bizarre.' She looked at the spot where Lynda's body had lain last night.

'I zipped her body up in her sleeping bag inside her shelter,' Mason said, 'till I can find a safe time to lower it to the rocks and bury it.' He held out a long white feather. 'Look at this. I found it under her.'

Tree took the plume. 'Flight feather, primary covert. Broad wing. Raptor. This bird was an albino.'

'Harpy eagle?'

'Not sure. Could be.' She shook her head slowly. 'Mason, I'm not believing this.'

He nodded toward the sliding door. 'See for yourself. I'm certain the harpy wasn't in the net last night. It's not an albino – but I think it was coming to attack us, broke its neck in the mesh.'

'Eagles don't smash radios.'

'Well, that's damn straight. Something deadly weird is going on here, and it's got me spooked. I don't know how Domino fits in. But there's nobody else on this mountain top – or is there?'

'Good grief, Mason.' She came and stood close to him; goose bumps rose up on the back of her neck. 'You're the expert on Amazonian tribes. Could there be a native hunting party up here – Yanomorduro?'

'Normally I'd say, no way. The Yanomorduro fear these tepuis – especially this one. They say yellow witches live on it, raid their villages to capture boys. But . . . unless Domino trashed our equipment himself, somebody else did.'

'Where *is* Domino?' she asked.

He shook his head. 'Beats me. Was your hand bleeding last night?'

She held up the seared flesh in the daylight. 'Don't think so.'

He touched the leathery scab on his cheek. 'I don't think I was bleeding either. This morning I noticed spatters of dried blood all over the rungs of the ladder. Domino went that-a-way.' He pointed down through the trapdoor.

'Fleeing from the harpy, maybe,' she said. 'Then he's hurt, too. Should we try to find him?'

'I gave it some thought, but I don't think it's our best plan. Especially not in your condition, and when we don't know his involvement in all of this. He knows where the Raft is, he'll probably try to return on his own. I think we should stick right here where we'll be safe inside the lab if any more birds try an Alfred Hitchcock on us. With luck, I may be able to salvage enough parts from these junked radios to build a working one.'

'All right. Sounds reasonable.' She pocketed the uneaten granola bar in her jeans and slid open the door. 'I'll go have a look at the harpy. There's got to be an explanation.'

His hand caught her shoulder and she turned. 'Tree,' he began; his mouth opened and closed, but no words came. He sighed.

'That's the most romantic thing you've said to me these past eight years,' she said.

He lowered his eyes. 'Sorry . . .'

'Hey. I'm teasing.' She squeezed his hand and stepped out the door.

'Just be careful. No, wait, I'm going with you.'

He unscrewed the barrel of a microscope and hefted it in his hand, wielding it like a steel club. Then he followed her out onto a bouncy rubber tube that ran from the lab to a juncture of two sides of the outer ring. The orange neoprene smelled like a giant wetsuit. On one side of the tubular spoke a nylon cord threaded through a series of aluminum stanchions to form a hand railing.

Ahead at the bat collection station Tree saw the harpy hanging by its neck, its wings flopped open behind it. The eagle's head had rammed through and tangled in the fine nylon mesh and it had apparently broken its neck. Mason had been right. The beak was blood-caked. The fiberglass net poles sagged under the weight of the carcass and the harpy's legs drooped over the side of the Raft, hidden from view.

Tree reached the dead eagle and pulled up its legs to examine the talons for blood. Attached to each leg was a leather cuff with a half-foot-long strap ending in a brass ring. Her eyes grew big and she recoiled with a gasp. *It can't be.*

Mason arrived. 'What is it?'

She scanned the horizon, turning a complete circle. Nothing but rugged terrain, like a moonscape, with moss and flowers and noisy bugs tossed in among the battered bones of rock.

Mason held the eagle's legs, staring down at the leather straps. 'What the hell . . . ?'

Tree felt a mix of equal parts wonder and terror. She whispered, 'Now I know what we've stumbled upon.'

5

Tree unfastened the leather straps from the harpy's legs and a third, smaller cuff that held a thimble-sized gold bell. Her green eyes shone in the mid-morning light. She tinkled the little bell and shook her head with amazement.

'My father was right,' she said. 'It's true. They're here. But he never in his wildest dreams expected the colony to be alive.'

'Who?' Mason said. 'Who's here?'

She glanced skyward and rolled the oiled leather between her fingertips. Gray clouds scudded low across the horizon to the west. 'Let's get back inside.'

'Right behind you.'

As soon as he followed her through the sliding door, she turned and held up one of the straps with a brass ring. 'This is called a jess.' Then she dangled the cuff with the bell. 'And this is a bewit.'

He reached for the trappings.

'Mason, it was a trained hunting bird, trained by handlers to hunt for meat. See the rings? The jesses stay on permanently and attach by a leash to a perch.'

'Falconry?'

She nodded. 'Invented in China four thousand years ago.'

'But . . . who trained these birds?'

'Chinese falconers.'

He shook his head. 'You lost me.'

'El Dorado. The Chinese. My father had it figured out.'

'Whoa, back up. Start at the beginning.'

Tree began pacing back and forth in the lab, her words tumbling after each other. 'Okay. Right after my mom died, my father moved us from Oxford to Nanjing so he could study the Ming Dynasty records. He was sifting through roomfuls of scrolls for information about a sea explorer named Zheng-He. Remember Zheng-He? I've told you about him.'

He nodded. 'He was like the Magellan of China.'

'Exactly. Did I ever tell you why my father moved Gib and me from Nanjing to Indian Mound Beach?'

He flinched at the mention of her brother's name. Gibraltar Summerwood. The best friend any man could hope for. Mason swallowed and squeezed his sorrow back inside.

'I just assumed your dad was there to study the artefacts at the mound,' he said.

'But not the Native American artefacts. The Chochomoc were traders like most of the coastal tribes. They traded blocks of salt for emeralds and turquoise with tribes as far away as the Incas of Peru.'

'I'd read that. They paddled big canoes up and down the Gulf, met with other traders from all over. Pretty remarkable.'

'Well, an archeologist at the site had read my father's work and wrote to him in Nanjing about some mound artefacts that looked Chinese in origin. We were on a plane to Florida the next morning.'

'Artefacts all the way from China?'

'No. All the way from South America.' She held up the gold bell and jiggled it. *Ting-a-ting-a-ting.* 'See? The ancient Chinese made a voyage to the New World. That's the premise my father was working on.'

'Let me see that,' Mason said. The bell felt heavy for its inch-long size; possibly it was cast in solid gold. The sides were etched with an ornate script that was much more fluid than the few hundred Chinese ideograms that Gib had taught him to read. The calligraphy swirled like oil on water. He felt his heartbeat race to keep up with his thoughts.

'In the early fourteen hundreds Zheng-He commanded the

largest fleet in the world,' Tree said, 'the Grand Treasure Fleet – more than two hundred ships sailing together.'

'That would dwarf the Spanish Armada.'

'Not just in number,' she said. 'His flagships were easily the biggest for centuries to come: nine-masted junks, four-hundred-fifty feet long, each carrying five hundred soldiers and sailors.'

Mason let out a low whistle. 'The *Santa Maria* would've looked like a dinghy alongside those.'

'Zheng-He's mission was to contact foreign civilizations in order to exchange gifts with the Chinese emperor. On his first voyage, he rounded the African cape – a hundred years before Magellan – and returned to the emperor with a giraffe, lions, leopards, Arabian horses and an elephant.'

'That must've impressed the imperial court.'

'More than you might imagine. They mistook the giraffe for a celestial animal called *qilin*, one of the four sacred creatures – along with the dragon, the phoenix and the tortoise – from Chinese mythology. The emperor funded six more expeditions. Zheng-He explored the Arabian Sea and Indian Ocean and returned with more exotic treasures. He made it all the way to Australia, three hundred years before Captain Cook. But all along, his secret mission was to find the Islands of the Immortals and bring back Ling-Chih, the Mushroom of Immortality.'

'Ah. That's why the emperor was putting up the cash.'

'Right. But listen: On his final voyage, Zheng-He sailed to India and died at sea. The Treasure Fleet split up and explored Sri Lanka and Indonesia, then the ships sailed home the next year to China.' She made a half-smile. 'All but *one*.'

Mason nodded. 'Now I'm getting the picture.'

'Ko T'ung Jen was its commander. He caught the Black Stream – what we call the Japanese Current – and sailed on toward the fabled Western Lands. His ship carried soldiers and sailors, plus goats, pigs, chickens, herbs, seeds, fruit trees – and young maidens.'

Mason sensed that his face reflected her look of wonder. 'Enough to start a colony.'

'The year was 1432. Some archeologists are convinced that

he made it all the way to the New World – sixty years before Columbus. A few artefacts have turned up to support the notion, but no one has ever found traces of a Chinese colony. It was my father's lifelong ambition to discover it.'

Mason turned the bell over in his hand. 'A Chinese settlement in South America,' he muttered, 'pre-Columbian . . .'

'My father's unique theory was that the legend of El Dorado, which the Spanish conquistadors kept hearing from the natives, was not just about a golden king in a golden city hidden in the Amazon – El Dorado was a golden *race*.'

'Ko T'ung Jen and his people.'

She nodded. 'My father spent years narrowing down the location of El Dorado, based on records from more than two dozen expeditions from Pizzaro to Humboldt. He concluded El Dorado lies here, in the tepui range, between the Orinoco and Uraricoera rivers to the north and south, and the Paragua and Caura rivers to the east and west.'

'But surely not on *top* of a tepui. We're at nine thousand feet.' He swept his arms around him. 'Nothing but crags. This is no place to start a colony. What would they have eaten – moss?'

'How else can you account for this?' She took the bewit and bell from him. 'The rectangular bell design is classical Ming. See the writing? It's called *t'ien-shu*, means "cloud script."'

'What's it say?'

'Don't know. Cloud script is a mystical text used only by Taoist priests. Even my father never learned to read it.'

'Could Gib?'

'Yes.'

'Of course. Doesn't surprise me.'

Mason had been thirteen when he and Gib had met. Gib was two years older and eight inches taller, and Mason had immediately found out, to his great relief, that he was not the smartest kid in the universe, nor even, any longer, in Dixon County.

Gib spoke several dialects of Chinese and his English was charmed with a British accent. Until Gib, Mason hadn't known a single boy who had read a book that wasn't assigned at school, or who preferred the real thing over *Cliff's Notes*. Gib devoured books like a seagull gulps oysters. He cared about ideas; what was more, he could talk eloquently about them:

27

scientific or poetic, mystical or earthy, they sparked through his open mind like summer fireflies. The afternoon they'd first met in the town's meager library, he and Gib yakked, perched on cool marble stairs, for three hours. Mason had felt as if he and Gib were reunited twins, never mind that they'd been delivered into the world through different wombs – a shipping error – they were definitely spirit brothers.

And then life got even richer. Gibraltar's best friend was his gracefully tall and slender sister, Teresa. She read books, too. Spoke Chinese fluently. Played grand piano grandly. Sang Joan Baez better than Baez, and danced to Marvin Gaye as if she were calling down the moon. Before long, Gib, Tree and Mason had formed a society of three.

It took until Mason was seventeen for the third and deepest surprise to strike. One evening he had sauntered toward the porch steps of the old stone mansion where Tree sat strumming a Baez tune on her gypsy guitar. She had looked up in the soft ruddy glow and smiled with aquamarine eyes. And all at once he knew that one beautiful girl in a yellow summer dress made all the difference, forever.

Mason jerked back to the present moment.

'. . . my father was searching only for its ruins,' Tree was saying. 'Maybe some mixed-race Indians who speak a native tongue sprinkled with Mandarin or Han – not a living, viable Chinese culture.'

'I don't see how a group of people could survive up here without food and supplies,' Mason said. 'Not even for a month, let alone – what? Five hundred years.'

'But the trained harpy is proof . . .'

'Could have flown up from the lowlands.' His eyebrows shot up and he snapped his fingers. 'Of course – that's it.'

Her face lit. 'The valley.'

'That first eagle zoomed up out of the valley. That's got to be it. That's where the colony is.'

'Good God.' She plopped down on a stool and the bell in her hand jingled. 'We've found El Dorado.'

Mason pictured the ribbons of flesh that were all that remained of Lynda's face. 'I'd say that they desperately don't want to be found.'

He stepped to the sliding door and peered out the window. The wind whipped grit against the fiberglass with a hissing, scrickling noise. He looked back at the radio parts on the countertop, and then at Tree.

Come on, Mason, quit fooling yourself, he thought. Even if he managed to put together a working portable radio, the main antenna was trashed and there was only a next-to-zero chance a walkie-talkie would have the range to contact Canaima so that the short-wave operator there could relay the message to the National Guard base at Luepa. And if he did make contact it would be a week or longer before a chopper could fly them off the mountaintop. By then, Tree's hand would turn into a bag of pus and the infection would burn up her brain.

He dragged his teeth back and forth over his lower lip. *She's going to die if I don't think of a way to save her.*

He'd considered maggot therapy. It had been a common treatment for infected wounds during the First World War, before the development of antibiotics, and the Wawajero *brujos* worked a similar debridement using tiny caterpillars. When Tree's wound began to rot, he could expose her hand to flies, cover it, and allow maggots to grow and eat away the dead and infected tissue. When the blood turned right red, it would mean the little bastards were invading healthy tissue; then he'd wash them out. Worms could save her from gangrene – but she might die from malaria or some other plague introduced by the flies.

Yeah, right, he told himself. *Teresa Diana with squirming larvae gnawing her hand. She'd probably fling herself off the edge of the mountain.*

He gazed at her and rubbed his stubbled chin. 'I once read the ancient Chinese mixed goldenseal and other herbs with honey and garlic to use as an antibiotic.'

She nodded. 'They had the Old World's most sophisticated pharmacopoeia.' She wrinkled her brow. 'Hold on, Mason. I know that look. You're not seriously thinking—'

'It's the only way we're going to survive this damned discovery of ours.' He held up the bell between them; sunlight glinted from the gold and the tiny clapper chimed a treble note. *Had*

Lynda heard the music of the ripping talons? He closed his fist around the bell and stifled the tone.

'We've got to make it back to the valley,' he said, 'and ask our would-be killers for their help.'

6

Tree and Mason departed the Raft in a pink dawn and headed westward toward the valley they had spotted two days earlier from the helicopter. They reached the lookout rock as the sun cleared the craggy edge of the tepui. Mason climbed to the top and peered into the distance.

'I can just make out the rim,' he shouted down, pointing west-south-west. 'Looks about three miles. We can make it there by dark if we don't slow down.'

Tree's injured hand had swelled like a puffer fish and the throbbing pain had kept her from sleeping all night. Mason had cradled her in his lap while he sat propped against a wall. Sometime after midnight, fever swung her on a pendulum from shivering to sopping. Mason gave her water from the melted hailstones, mopped her brow and cooled her body with soaking towels. Neither of them had said much, but Mason's presence and the rhythm of his breathing had buoyed her through the dark sea of hours.

Before dawn Mason had lowered Lynda's body wrapped in a sleeping bag down the ladder, dragged it to a shallow dip and heaped it with stones as the Southern Cross twinkled over the horizon.

Then he'd managed to truck Tree piggy-back down the ladder. Now she was sweating in the cool mountain air from fever and ache and exertion, but she dreaded how it would hurt to tug off her wool sweater, so she left it on.

The air smelled and tasted mossy and wet. Gravel crunched beneath their boots. Birds called and sang, interrupted by a low-pitched yodeling that rose through the octaves to a series of sharp yelps: a New World monkey of some type, but not a call that Tree recognized. Crimson and indigo alpine blossoms, no bigger than dimes, softened the rock faces here and there, interspersed with pastel pink and blue mushrooms. In spite of her dizziness and weakness, she found she could still marvel at the largest shelf fungus she'd ever seen, a six-foot semicircle, thick and orange, like a big wheel of Cheddar cheese.

Her boot toe snagged a ledge and she stumbled; Mason caught her arm and steadied her. 'We can rest here, just for a minute,' he said, and supported her weight while she eased herself down beside a clump of pitcher plants.

He had brought along the last of the water in a plastic specimen jar that he now passed to her. The water had picked up the flavor of polystyrene, but she didn't care; she felt thirsty deep down in her cells. She savored two slow swigs and handed back the jar.

Mason swished around a mouthful of water before he gulped it down. 'I was wondering just now,' he said, and took another small sip, 'how close did your father get to his goal?'

She nodded. 'You read my thoughts . . .'

'Did he make it to the mountaintop or did it end for him down in the jungle?'

'The Yanomorduro?'

'I was thinking more of malaria, typhoid, dengue . . .'

Tree pictured her father: white-haired, dignified and rarified; the quintessential British scholar-explorer. Dr Huxley Summerwood had quit his post as Dean Emeritus of the Department of Oriental Studies at Oxford to pursue his quest to locate El Dorado. When she was twelve, he'd left her and Gib in Indian Mound Beach, Florida, while he tramped through the Amazon basin searching for traces of a Chinese settlement. He'd been gone six months on that first expedition and she and Gib had to put up with creaky Ms Thurmond as live-in housekeeper and surrogate grandmother. Tree had sorely resented her father for abandoning her and missing her junior high school pageant and she'd tried hard to maintain her wounded mood when he came back. But she loved him too much, and had melted into tears at the sight of his emaciated frame limping through the arrival gate at the airport.

A year later her father left them again for a second El Dorado safari. From that journey he'd never returned.

Did a harpy eagle kill him? Here, within sight of his dream? Did he even realize he'd found El Dorado? Or did it find him first?

Tree took a deep breath and stood up. 'I'm ready. Let's keep moving.'

The sun was past its zenith when at last they gazed over the rim of the valley. The sides plummeted almost vertically several thousand feet to a lush green roof. Halfway down a granite wall a waterfall shot out of a rock fracture under tremendous pressure, as if from a giant burst water main. The frothing white gush cleared the face of the rock by twenty feet and arced with a thunderous pounding to the floor of the valley far below. Rainbows in pairs and triplets played in the dazzling mist.

'It's breathtaking,' Mason said. 'Look at all that green – a thick rainforest down there.'

'A cloud forest,' she said, watching patches of green open and close through the swirling vapors. 'It's a different ecosystem altogether, always cool and misty instead of warm and wet. This is big news – makes number four.'

'Four?'

'There are only three other cloud forests known in the world: two in Costa Rica and one in Nicaragua. We've only scratched the surface of all the odd species in them. And each cloud forest is one-of-a-kind.'

'Then this one should be especially rich in unusual species.'

'Why do you say that?'

'Certain geologic clues. This valley is a volcanic core. Quite ancient. Look at the cliffs, so steep they make the forest down there a kind of genetic island. It's likely there are species that have evolved in that ecosystem for millions of years in virtual isolation, like the marsupials of Australia. Who knows what an eco-survey team could discover down there?'

'If we still were a team,' Tree said, and pushed away a sudden wave of sadness and fear.

Mason crouched on his hands and knees and leaned over the edge. 'Trouble is, how do we get down without parachutes?'

'There's got to be a path – the colony is down there.'

A shrill whistle and screech made them both look up.

Keeee-yawk! Kee-yee! Kee-yee!

'It's a harpy!' Tree yelled.

'Get behind me.' Mason's eyes darted around the ground and he scooped up a baseball-sized rock.

The bird climbed into the sun.

Mason shielded his eyes with his hand. 'I can't see it.'

'There!'

The bird dived on them.

Mason cocked his arm and hurled the rock at the last instant. The eagle veered from the rock and missed its attack. It climbed again in a tight spiral toward the sun.

Tree scanned the terrain for shelter. A table-shaped boulder squatted near the ground to form a low overhanging shelf. She grabbed Mason's arm. 'Under there.'

'Okay, go, go. I'm right behind you.'

She ran toward the shallow cave and heard the eagle's war cry behind her.

Kee-yee! Kee-yeeeeeeee!

She flattened out on her back and scooted into the cave by pushing with her feet.

'Get in! Get in!' Mason yelled, looking over his shoulder. He dove headfirst as if sliding into home plate.

The eagle swooped by the cave mouth and slashed with its talons, shredding the loose cloth at the back of Mason's baggy sweater. It hovered for an instant in the cave mouth and wind from its pumping wings blasted sand against their faces. With a fierce shriek that stabbed the air the eagle took off and flew a short distance to a sandstone perch.

It raised and flared its blue-gray crest feathers and its black eyes flashed.

'Squeeze in,' Mason said, shoving her with his shoulder and hip.

'Can't,' she puffed, feeling dizzy. 'I'm mashed against the back wall.'

The heavy bird jumped down onto the gravel and hopped toward them awkwardly, its muscular breast puffed out, its huge wings tucked behind. It came at them three short leaps at a time and its leg bell rang: *Tling tling tling. Tling tling tling. Tling tling tling.*

Tree gagged, remembering a cock fight she had seen in Juarez, Mexico. The roosters had strutted to the attack in the same awkward way and then exploded into a fury of screeches and ruffled feathers and spraying blood. And the roosters had been only one quarter the size of this female harpy eagle.

'*Zu kai!*' Tree shouted in Chinese. 'Go away!'

Mason reached down and undid the top three grommets of his hiking boot and yanked it off. He stuck his hand inside, clutching the boot by its tongue.

The harpy charged and leapt into the air, raking its talons. Mason struck out with the boot. Talons snagged it and tore it out of his grip. The eagle attacked the boot with beak and talons; leather flicked off in chunks. Then the eagle flew a few yards away and perched and turned. It pierced them again with bright black eyes.

Mason tugged off his other boot. 'Here.' He handed the boot to Tree. 'You get ready to throw this at him.'

'What are you going to do?'

'Tackle him. Here he comes.'

Mason coiled his body in a crouch and when the eagle assaulted the second boot, he sprang out of the cave and lunged for the bird like a fullback. The eagle lurched away and Mason missed and sprawled in the rocks. The eagle leapt up, beating its wings, its legs cocked.

'Mason, look out!'

He rolled and grabbed wildly for a leather leg strap that hung down. His hand closed around the jess and he dragged the bird to the ground and crashed his weight on top of it, pinning its body beneath him. The powerful wings bucked and pummeled him. Clutching the leg strap Mason raised onto his knees and drove his arm forward and down as if hammering a spike into the lip of the cave. The bird followed the arc of its tether and slammed into the rock. Mason stood and swung the eagle over his head and rammed it down again. Its skull shattered in a red starburst on the pale sandstone.

Mason staggered back, his jaw muscles twitching, his chest heaving. Tree squirmed out from beneath the rock shelf and rushed to embrace him. Her tight hug tipped him off balance and he sat back hard, nearly pulling her down on top of him. Then he flopped onto his back, still panting. Tree sat down next to him.

'How the fuck ... we supposed ... to talk ... talk to them ... if they keep—'

'Shhh.' Tree held up her hand. A fetid stench of rotten meat wafted in the breeze. 'What's that smell?'

Mason sniffed the air and grimaced. 'Stinks like death. Get on your feet.' They stood up warily. 'I don't like this one bit.'

'What is it?'

'Don't know, but I got a feeling it's not nice.' Mason glanced around furtively. He looked behind him at the sheer-sided walls of the deep valley. 'How the hell do you get down off this tabletop?'

Tree gasped and grabbed Mason's arm. A lizard the size of a bull gator had scrabbled to the top of a boulder and crouched above them. Its tongue raked in and out of its mouth like a slick red whip. It lowered its triangular head and grunted and hissed. A leather harness fit its shoulders and an iron choker chain encircled its neck.

'Holy shit,' Mason said, and backed up, scooping Tree behind him with one arm. 'Komodo dragon. I'm not believing this. They only live in Indonesia.'

'The Chinese sailed to Indonesia.'

'Goddam. What else they got – war elephants?'

The giant reptile peered down at them, eyes rolling like cue balls set in black hide the texture of knobby tires. It bared its teeth and hissed, broadcasting a stench of carrion from its saw-toothed triangular fangs. Nausea rose in Tree's gut with force and she choked back the urge to puke.

She looked behind her to the lip of the valley. 'Maybe we can lower ourselves over the side.'

'But you can't – your hand. I'm not going to leave you.'

The dragon slid and slithered down the rocks and spilled its length to the ground with a heavy thud. Tree and Mason backed within a few feet of the cliff's edge. Mason shielded her, muscles taut, arms like teak. She clung to him, her stomach knotted in terror.

The Komodo dragon crept forward in an ugly, shuffling gait, massive deltoid head bobbing, foot-long tongue stabbing at the scent of its warm-blooded prey.

7

A Chinese soldier stepped out from behind the wall of rocks. She bellowed a sharp syllable and the giant lizard hesitated. The soldier dashed forward and clipped a leash to the choker chain. She yanked back hard and the thick throat squeezed shut. The dragon sank on its belly and closed its eyes, then its handler loosened the choker.

Tree and Mason stared at the soldier. She wore crimson silk leggings under a knee-length crimson skirt. Movable plates of black lacquer-hardened leather armored her torso like the overlapping scales of an armadillo. An iron ax tucked into a braided leather belt that also held the scabbard of a double-edged sword. One fist gripped the Komodo dragon's leash and the other held an oval wood-and-leather shield half the soldier's height, a bright green Chinese dragon coiling over its shiny black lacquered surface. A two-foot-tall plume of scarlet macaw feathers topped a black acorn-shaped helmet. The soldier's smooth face wore at its chin a fake beard of wispy black hairs.

The woman stood transfixed, a dozen feet away, gazing from Tree to Mason and back again. Soon six other female warriors joined her. They froze, mesmerized by what they saw. Each wore a thin fake beard.

'*Wo men zai he pin li*,' Tree said in Mandarin, 'We come in peace.'

She raised slowly to her feet, stretching her empty hands outward, palms up. She had rehearsed their introduction: 'We two are scholars, not soldiers or scouts. We came to this mountain only to learn about its plants and birds and insects. We meant no harm. We most humbly apologize for upsetting your *fung shui* – your natural harmony. A thousand sorrows.' She held out her wounded hand. 'I was injured by my own unmeritorious *karma*. Now I seek your pardon and mercy. *Jiu ming a qu bu qu yisheng* – Help, will you take me to your doctor?'

The band of women parted and an older woman stepped through. Her mock beard was thicker and braided into a short whip. She looked at Tree and her eyes grew huge. '*Lung-Hu*,' the platoon leader whispered, then cocked her head toward her soldiers. '*Lung-Hu!*' she hissed.

The others shouted in unison, '*Lung-Hu!*'

The leader kowtowed, touching her forehead to the ground at Tree's feet. The lizard handler wrapped the leash several turns around her forearm and bowed deeply, dragging the reptile's head to the gravel. The other soldiers followed with a *clack-clatter* of lacquered armor and iron blades against the rocks.

8

The path led straight down into a fissure in the plateau. A thick hedge of bamboo surrounded the crack in the ground and Tree and Mason had hiked right past the spot earlier without seeing the teardrop-shaped hole.

Two soldiers supported Tree and helped her to step down into the chasm. Lumpy iron deposits in the sandstone walls had bled orange streaks of rust onto the natural stairs leading down the deep well. The platoon leader carried a fat candle flame inside a ceramic box; she took down from a wall hook a bamboo-and-wool torch soaked in pitch, lit it and walked on, bearing the yellow torchlight high above her head. The dragon handler brought up the rear; even at a distance Tree caught whiffs of the reptile's putrid breath.

Everywhere geodes studded the rocks. Tree reached out and touched a stone nodule as big as a basketball; it had broken open and torch glow flickered from purple amethyst crystals that poked from its deep bowl.

As the party descended, the hum of rushing water grew louder until it became pounding, thunderous. Blowing mist condensed on the cave walls, dripping, dripping. They came to an underground river near the fracture in the cliff where it exploded free of its rocky banks and crashed into the valley below. Daylight winked blue at the top of the split in the rock.

A natural stone bridge, formed when the rapids had drilled a hole in the sandstone eons ago, arched across the river. A soldier on either side of Tree steadied her as they led her over the bridge.

As Tree stepped down onto the far bank, her knees suddenly gave out and the women caught her as she slumped. Their leader hurried back and shouted orders into their ears over the roar of the rapids. One soldier placed her shield on the ground; it resembled a shallow turtle shell. She gestured for Tree to sit in the bowl of the shield. Then the two lifted her on this makeshift palanquin and the group continued down the sloping path.

Tree glanced back at Mason; his face shone with wonder.

When she had surprised him in Canaima and announced that she too was a HARVEST team member, she was sure she had read the truth in his eyes, behind his shock at seeing her again after more than half a decade. Not just a love still there. *The* love. The love that had penetrated to the bottom of her appetite and the top of her soul.

Her thoughts roamed back to Mason's letters from bases in Da Nang, Quang Tri, Phu Loc and Hué, to her dorm room at Harvard in Cambridge. His musings had been spiritual and lusty, tough and vulnerable, sad and funny.

Shoeboxes filled up with his soulful dispatches, which sometimes arrived two or more in a week. In June of 1970 he'd hinted at a big surprise. Then for her twenty-first birthday he'd mailed her a rice paper scroll covered with a love poem handwritten in Chinese – Gib had been tutoring him almost daily for a year, and with the conversational practice he got in Chinatown in Saigon, Mason had become nearly fluent in her second language. And that was only part of the surprise: Postscript to the poem, he'd asked her – in Chinese – to marry him.

She'd hopped up and down on her dorm room bed until the slats broke. Then she'd rushed back a letter with her own surprise: '*Mi amor, te llevo en el alma. Por supuesto te voy a casar* – My love, I carry you in my soul. Of course I'll marry you.' With a private tutor she'd been studying Spanish for a year, and she'd become halfway fluent in *his* second language.

That kind of synchronicity had swept their romance along from the day it first spread its wings and flew.

But later that summer Gib had been killed in combat. Mason's letters abruptly stopped.

Mason got back to the States six months later and they were married in the little library in Indian Mound Beach. But it wasn't really Mason. Not the man she'd made love with on the beach, nestled between the pontoons of a catamaran; or on the lighthouse balcony in the warm summer rain; or on the cool tile floor of the garden cottage where jasmine mixed with their own perfume; or any of a hundred times they'd drowned in fire.

And he was no longer the Mason she'd talked with until dawn about Whitman, Klimt, Ellington and Ailey; and the universal imperatives of poetry, art, music and dance.

She thought of the night they'd sipped from a bottle of her father's best Cabernet up in their lighthouse love-nest. The full moon silver-plated the sea; they watched dolphins spouting and diving. 'I believe dolphins worship God,' he'd said softly, his scratchy chin tickling her freckled shoulder. 'Their God has a blowhole atop Her Eversmiling Face.'

That was the real Mason Drake.

The man who had dragged himself back from Vietnam had clenched his heart against grief. He'd never shed a tear when they'd divorced, while she'd wept enough for both of them.

Pain yanked Tree back into the present. The burning in her hand flared with each *tock* of her pulse. The path dropped sharply before them. In some places, stairs had been hand-carved, but much of the trail followed natural ledges, steps and ridges in the stone. Shadows danced along the irregular walls. In one passage the trail snaked through a forest of gigantic white crystals the size of pine trees that resembled rock candy.

Tree had lost track of the time when they ducked through a stone tunnel and the ceiling opened to a false sky. They had entered a chamber that looked big enough to house the Eiffel Tower. The floor was flat and at the room's far end a bright ball of shimmering light lit the cavern mouth.

When they exited the cave Tree saw that they had emerged directly under the waterfall. But in its several-thousand-foot plunge, the river had almost completely blown off into clouds of spray. Here, at ground zero, the falls were no more than a heavy stinging rain. A soldier held a second shield over her head for an umbrella and they waded through a wide, shallow stream that frothed white under the downpour.

In the near distance loomed a massive stone wall, as tall as the hardwood forest that hugged it. The troop entered a fragrant green tunnel formed by overhanging elephant-ear plants with leaves as large as bathtubs. Bird-of-paradise flowers spread their wings in the swirling dewy mists. Wild orchids poked out low and high in a riotous rainbow, some as big as a milk pitcher, others tiny as a thimble. The trail led under towering mahogany, ebony and teak trees, and each tree was itself a garden, branches thickly draped with moss, ferns, bromeliads, begonias, philodendrons and lichens.

Tree felt intoxicated by the crazy colors and rich notes of fragrance, while the botanist in her cataloged species. Most of the flora she recognized: golden tower tree, purpleheart, green-heart, zebrawood, ironwood, satinwood, Flame-of-the-Forest, bird's tongue, ox's eye, monkey-tail fern, Job's Tears, passion flower. But many plants were new to her.

She scanned for the source of a high musical chirping and spotted a thumbnail-sized frog with brilliant red skin that glowed in the mist like electric neon. She named the new species in an instant: *Bufo rudolfensis* – the Rudolf frog.

After a time the footpath arrived at a small circular door fashioned from a solid plate of pink jade. The surface was deeply carved with the raised figures of a tiger robed in clouds and a dragon couched in flames; the creatures curled together, each head toward the other's tail, as if chasing each other in a circle dance.

The commander whistled piercingly a melodic chain of notes. A moment later the round door glided open. The soldiers bearing Tree set the shield on the ground; one woman squeezed through the portal and turned to lift the shield through like a stretcher.

Tree ducked her head. When she raised it again she found herself in heaven.

9

Tree gazed upon a city so lovely she shook her head to be sure she was not lost in a fever-dream.

Waxed paper lanterns with brightly-colored silk banners hung from street poles along broad avenues lined with cherry and mimosa trees. Persimmon and plumtree gardens, fountains and half-moon foot bridges bedecked the medians. All these were mere settings for the architectural jewels: ornate temples with wrap-around verandas supported by spiral columns; palaces with red-enameled pillars outside and inside their spacious open-air rooms; upthrust pagodas of seven, eight or ten octagonal floors, each storey wearing its scarlet pantiled roof like a skirt of flames; a stupa as big as a planetarium, its dome of hammered gold; double and triple roofs of glazed shingles – blues, yellows and reds – swooped and dipped like sea waves and at the crest of each swell a bronze lion-dog perched. Tree's eyes followed colonnades that led to other streets and palaces, temples and pagodas in a multi-layered web of splendor.

The avenues radiated from a city hub toward which the soldiers carried her. At the hub's center a dense grove of banyan trees embraced a many-petaled temple. The building seemed to blossom out of the earth like a white lotus. Its graceful, curving architecture astonished Tree. It wasn't traditional Chinese, nor was it Cambodian, Indian, or Japanese; all distinctive styles she admired. Here and there the shape of an archway, a portal, a minaret caught her eye and hinted at one of the classical Asian forms, but the building embodied a unique design. It was as if some time-magician had gathered master craftsmen from the Forbidden City, Angkor Wat, the Taj Mahal and Kyoto Gardens and challenged them to wed their great styles into a new architecture to outshine the others.

She glanced back at Mason and caught his eye. He seemed stunned with wonder.

'So gorgeous,' she mouthed. He nodded.

The soldiers carried her down a walkway of scalloped bricks, past manicured junipers and pear trees, and through a round door. The entrance opened into a short hallway that swelled into a large globular chamber, its concave walls gleaming with a flesh-tone porcelain. Cloud Script calligraphy, too elaborate and ornate for Tree to decipher, flowed over the wall tiles from floor to ceiling. Ankle-high couches covered with quilted cotton mattresses and heaped with embroidered satin pillows were spaced around the polished wooden floor comprised of planks of red, yellow, pink and brown mahogany.

A heady fragrance of sandalwood wafted through the room and Tree puzzled why the air was not smoky from the incense. Then she passed through a gateway into an inner courtyard and discovered the source of the aroma – a grove of miniature potted trees: sandalwood, clove, nutmeg and cinnamon – that surrounded a fish pond filled with brilliant orange and gold koi, white lilies and red lotus blossoms.

A dozen women in colorful kimonos sat on the grass listening to a quartet of shamosen players; none of this group wore faux beards. The soldiers set down the shield Tree rode. Strings stopped plinking as every eye turned to gape at the two strangers. Then a masked figure at the front of the group stood and Tree felt the force of authority broadcast like a signal over the courtyard. The troop of soldiers melted to the ground in a unified bow. Tree followed their example and touched her forehead to the moist grass. It smelled sweet and green.

A pair of hands clapped sharply and everybody raised onto one knee.

The woman at the front wore a ceramic face mask of a fiercely grimacing deity. Her breasts rose and fell beneath a yellow satin robe and Tree recalled that in ancient China none but royalty were permitted to wear yellow. The mask gleamed with black and white enamel bands swirling over its contours; one eye highlighted, the other eye closed and painted red.

The robe bore a white tiger motif: fur, fang and claw embroidered in exquisite detail. More tigers decorated the white jade sleeve weights of the flowing satin, and a tiger seal etched a bulky gold thumb ring.

Atop long black hair, the woman wore an elaborate tasseled headdress studded with hundreds of sparkling, faceted crystals. It looked to Tree like an inverted chandelier; if the gems were what she thought they were, the one hat could dent the Dutch monopoly on diamonds.

The squad leader addressed the masked woman as Empress, Mother of Sons.

'We found these two in the upper hell,' she said in the Mandarin dialect. 'Her skin is as white as alabaster, her eyes green as jade . . . is she not *Lung-Hu*?'

Tree was able to follow the words but she had no idea what the soldier meant by *Lung-Hu* – Dragon-Tiger.

'Green Dragon and White Tiger are only symbols,' the masked woman said. 'You should not regard life so literally, captain. Bring the woman before me.'

The captain stood and with a strong hand under Tree's arm helped Tree to her feet. The two stepped forward.

Tree was ready to repeat the introduction she had delivered to the soldiers, but something in the glare of the dark eye warned her to keep her mouth shut.

With a motion so fast it caught Tree by surprise the Empress flicked out a blade that had been concealed in her sleeve, grabbed Tree's sweater and slit it from waist to neck, exposing Tree's breasts.

'Hey!' Mason shouted behind her, then his voice was muffled with a grunt of pain. 'She is Tiger above,' the Empress said. 'But you won't find Dragon-Tiger below.'

Tree gulped, not knowing how to react. She made herself breathe as calmly as she could.

'Remove her clothes,' the Empress said.

The captain unsheathed her own dagger and reached out to cut off Tree's jeans.

'Wait,' Tree said, in Mandarin. 'Please ask me what you want to know. I will answer truthfully.'

A buzz went up from the soldiers and the kimono-clad women.

The captain grinned nervously. 'She speaks our tongue,' she said, 'as would *Lung-Hu*.'

The Empress shoved the captain aside, jabbed her knife inside the waistband of Tree's jeans and cut them to the crotch. The denim ripped with a loud *skrrrrrrk*.

The crowd tittered when they saw Tree's red cotton underwear. Even the Empress chuckled, lips grinning behind the scowling ceramic mouth.

'Clothes inside of clothes,' the Empress said, 'like boxes within boxes.' With two more strokes she cut away Tree's panties.

Tree stood in her ripped open sweater, jeans down around her knees, underwear in the grass. She felt more bewildered and afraid than bashful.

'You see?' the Empress said. 'She is an ordinary woman. Though her hair color is as rare as peaches from the moon, she is not *Lung-Hu*.'

Tree noticed all eyes in the room fixed on her apricot-blonde pubic mound. Now her face blushed hotly.

The Empress raised her hands to the crowd. 'Have I not told you? The Holy Hermaphrodite can appear only through me or my lineage. *Lung-Hu* will not suddenly arrive from the outer hells, but will be born to us, through my womb.'

The crowd shouted, 'Mother of Sons! Mother of Dragon-Tiger!' and again kowtowed as one. Tree swallowed her embarrassment, pulled her jeans to her waist, knelt and touched her forehead to the grass.

A handclap. Everyone raised to one knee.

'The male is much more useful to us,' the Empress said, and gestured for Mason to be brought before her. He stumbled forward, rubbing the back of his neck. When he stood beside Tree he shot her a glance that she knew was meant to communicate

47

Don't worry, but his jaw muscles twitched and gave his own fear away.

The Empress yanked Mason's mouth open and examined his teeth. Tears sprang to his eyes and the gash in his cheek began to bleed but he didn't cry out. Then the Empress made a hand sign and Mason was stripped to his waist. The women in the room gasped at the pelt of dark fur on his torso. The Empress squeezed the thick slabs of his chest muscles and ran her fingers down his corded arms. Then she nodded and the captain sliced through Mason's canvas hiking shorts and his underwear and left him standing naked.

The women squealed and gawked at his male anatomy.

'*Ta Hung*,' the Empress said, 'Great Stalk. Maybe he'll father my next sons?'

Again the crowd cheered. 'Mother of Sons, Giver of *Lung-Hu*!'

The Empress held up her palm and the crowd hushed. She jerked her head toward Tree and ordered the captain, 'Banish this one to the upper hell from whence she came.'

The captain nodded and gripped Tree's arm.

A booming voice filled the room. 'One moment, soldier.' Again Tree sensed the aura of authority. Even the Empress seemed to tense at the arrival of a broad-shouldered woman in leather armor; glued to her chin, a thick black beard reached nearly to her knees. She wore a crimson silk robe embroidered with a fierce green dragon. Not a European-style dragon as described by the Brothers Grimm, but the *Lung*, or classical Chinese dragon, with a camel's head, stag's antlers, bull's ears and cat's long whiskers. Its eyes were round, not slanted or almond-shaped, therefore, to the Chinese, they were the eyes of a demon.

The woman strode forward and stood in front of the Empress and made a perfunctory bow, not more than a nod. 'Empress Feng.'

'Commander Yu Lin.'

'Why was I not informed immediately of this situation?'

'It was certain your many eyes would report to you the swiftest. Have you not heard the news and come running?'

Yu Lin glowered and her eyes bored into Tree.

'Why be in such a hurry to discard a plum blossom?' Yu Lin said. 'With your permission, Empress, I will take this one as my slave.'

The Empress met Tree's eyes. 'If you think you can manage her, Commander, do what you like.'

'My Liege, you are Ever-Gracious.'

'And your compliments are as transparent as quartz.'

From a leather pouch Yu Lin pulled out a leash with a woven silk choker collar. She slipped the collar over Tree's head and tied the other end of the leash to her waist belt between her sword and dagger.

Tree felt dizzy and sick. *Do it*, she ordered herself, *take a chance*. But her guts froze. *I'd be betting my life on a hunch*. The stocky commander gently tugged the leash to draw Tree next to her. Tree stood fast, thinking. A sharp yank on the leash jerked her neck and the collar squeezed her throat like a fist.

Tree grabbed the leash and yanked down hard as she stepped back. Yu Lin stumbled backward and nearly fell, and as the leash slackened Tree pulled the collar open, ripped it over her head and tossed it down.

'I will not be anyone's slave,' she said loudly, in her clearest Mandarin Chinese. 'I, too, am a Mother of Sons.'

10

T he crowd gasped and drew back at Tree's words. She felt as if every person in the room was waiting for the Empress to react before breathing again.

Please be right about this, Tree prayed to her intuition, *oh please be right*. Her heart pounded so loudly she wondered if the Empress could hear it. Yu Lin glared and rested her hand on the hilt of her sword.

'Your barbarian world and our world are very different,' the Empress said. 'Here we must raid tribes at the mountain's base to capture native men and bring them to our city so that we may reproduce. But even when such men make many women round with child, the women give birth only to daughters.'

Only daughters. No males. A city of women. Female warriors. Tree nearly stumbled from the impact of her sudden realization. This lost city, which the Indians called Manoa, the conquistadors called El Dorado, and its own citizens knew as Jou P'u T'uan, was home to the greatest tribe in all of South American folklore.

Tree's eyes took in the courtyard full of Oriental women, the musicians and servants and soldiers, and knew she was standing among the legendary Amazons.

The conquistadors had heard tales of a great inland tribe of female warriors ever since Pizarro invaded Peru. Indians of the interior claimed that boys and men were regularly stolen for breeding purposes by a society made up solely of women.

Tree's father had told her about one Spanish explorer, Francisco de Orellana, who sailed down a broad and mighty river in 1539 seaching for El Dorado. His expedition encountered a band of light-skinned, long-haired women who shot arrows at his men with deadly skill. The journal of the expedition's friar, Gaspar de Carvajal, reported that the local natives called the women *Coniupuyara*, and he described them as tall and robust, 'doing as much fighting as ten Indian men.' The friar marveled, 'There was one woman among these who shot an arrow a span deep into one of our brigantines, and others less deep, so that our two brigantines looked like porcupines.'

The Spanish suffered heavy casualties in the assault and were driven downriver by the women. Don Orellana named the river *Amazona*, because the female warriors reminded him of the Greek legend of the Amazons. He and the other survivors sailed all the way to the Atlantic via the world's largest river, which the whole western world today calls the Amazon.

Tree now grasped the truth behind the legend of the society of the Amazons. She understood that its citizens were exclusively female, not by choice, but because of some mysterious problem of monosexual conception.

'Let me stay in Jou P'u T'uan,' Tree said. 'Not as anyone's slave, but as my husband's wife – and I will give you many sons.'

A noisy mumbling went up from the women in the room.

'Then you claim you are my equal?'

'No, my Empress. I am a worthless nobody. I stretch up my hands to touch your lotus feet.'

'But you claim you can give birth to sons? Even here, in this City of Daughters?'

'Yes, Your Highness. It is as you say: Our worlds are very different. From where I come, even meritless commoners such as myself can give birth to male children.'

The Empress stepped forward and gently ran her fingertips over the smooth skin of Tree's cheek, traced her graceful nose and the orbit of her full lips. A gem-studded nailguard, like a long, skinny thimble, protected the four-inch nail of her little finger, a sign of highest rank.

Tree sensed sorrow in her touch.

'You believe you will become a Mother-of-Sons – here – in Prayer Mat of the Body?' the Empress said. 'How do you expect to birth sons without paying the terrible price?'

Tree's mouth went dry. *How deep have I buried myself now?*

'Please forgive my disgraceful ignorance, Your Highness, for I am indeed a far-flung stranger.' She licked her paper lips with a cotton tongue. 'I do not understand your talk of "price."'

The Empress reached behind her head and untied her mask. A shiver ran through the crowd. She slowly removed it. Her face was a hideous battlefield of craters. Pink scar tissue had lumped and fused like melted wax sealing her left eye shut. Both ears were gone. What had been her nose was now only a bisected hole above disfigured lips.

Tree averted her eyes and fought back the impulse to retch. *What in hell is going on here?*

'No woman in Prayer Mat of the Body can make sons who does not sacrifice herself to the scissor-teeth. Only the Empress is honored with this sacrificial role.' She pointed a long sharp finger nail at Tree's face; it nearly touched her nose. 'Do you petition to become the next Empress?'

Tree fought the bodily urge to spin around and bolt for the exit. For a dozen long seconds she didn't know if her willpower would win the battle with her adrenal glands. At last she took a deep breath and made herself gaze at the ruined face.

'Your sacrifice is magnificent and brings honor to the great hall of your ancestors,' Tree said. 'Nevertheless, it is true that my insignificant self also can give birth to sons – even here, my Empress, even without duplicating your noble sacrifice.' She reached out her hand for Mason and he stepped forward and took it and drew her to his side. She wondered how much of the Chinese dialogue he was keeping up with. 'He is my husband. Together, we have made sons in every land we have visited' – the title of a fairy tale sprang to mind – 'from east of the sun to west of the moon.' She swept her hand in a broad arc.

The entourage murmured noisily. Tattered lips whitened on

52

a scar-reddened face. 'How many?' Her voice trembled. 'How many sons have you birthed?'

What should I say? Tree thought. *I've got to make myself non-expendable – a male-baby-making machine – but I musn't surpass her and cause her to lose face. How many sons has she had? I can't even tell how old she is.*

Tree cleared her parched throat. 'Four, my Empress.'

The Empress rocked back as if buffeted by a gust of wind. More loud murmuring rippled through the audience, then the silence grew dense, like a solid presence engulfing the courtyard.

Damn. Tree held her breath. *She's had less than four boys.*

'And tell me, barbarian, how many of your sons have survived into manhood?'

Okay, get this one right. 'Only one, my Empress.'

The Empress sighed and again Tree sensed the sadness that engulfed the woman like scar tissue enshrouds a wound.

'With your beauty whole and unrelinquished,' the Empress said, 'you vow to birth males in this land of females. How very odd. How prideful. Yet I learn we share a grim fact – death stole all but one of your sons from you.'

Tree lowered her gaze. 'Have mercy on a mother of sorrows,' she whispered.

A dazzling blue Morpho butterfly flitted between them and Tree imagined she could hear its wings puffing the silent air. Water tinkled and splashed over the rocks in the koi fish pond.

'Inscrutable are the workings of *Tao* . . .' the Empress said at last.

'Yes, my Empress,' Tree said, bowing her head low. 'The Rule of Heaven . . . unfathomable.'

The Empress slipped her mask back on. Tree nearly sighed with relief. The Empress looked around the room from face to face.

'I sense you have poked a splinter of doubt into all their hearts. You may stay. Indeed, you *must* stay, so that you and all my subjects will know that things are different here than in the world from where you came. In Prayer Mat of the Body you will find that you give birth only to daughters. Here, there is only *one* Mother-of-Sons.'

The commander, Yu Lin, removed her hand from her sword.

'Thank you, Your Highness,' Tree said. Her head swam and her limbs sagged.

'Yu Lin. Send a messenger to gather up the unmarried girls and bring them here at once,' the Empress said, and turned her gaze on Mason. 'The outsider must choose other wives.'

'What did she say?' Mason whispered.

'You must choose more wives.'

'Oh fuck.'

'That's the idea exactly.'

'Explain that you're my one and only wife.'

'I don't know how far we can push our luck.'

'Tell her.'

'But—'

'Tell her, Tree. You've got to. Otherwise, the game's over.'

Tree dipped her head toward the Empress and Mason followed her example. 'Celestial Majesty, Husband says I am his only wife,' Tree said in Mandarin. 'He wants no other.'

This drew the loudest reaction yet from the women present.

'Until my son Meng Po reaches manhood the women of Prayer Mat of the Body are husbandless. They need to mate to make children. Or is that not required in your world?'

'Yes, Empress, we must mate to make children.'

'At least some things do not vary under the sun,' the Empress said. 'Then what is the matter with this man? Your dark-skinned companion who arrived before you is like a peacock in spring. He has chosen sixty wives.'

'Domino?'

'Yes, Do-Min-O. He doesn't speak our language, he chatters like a monkey. But he was eager to possess many maidens.'

'What she say about Domino?' Mason whispered. 'He's alive?'

'He's *here*. He's got sixty wives.'

'Tell her again I only want to be with you.'

'Daughter of Heaven, Husband insists he wants only me. He doesn't want any other wives.'

'Why is he so selfish?' the Empress said, and the diamonds dangling from her headdress clinked together. 'It's unnatural. Does a bee in a cherry orchard reject all but one blossom?'

Tree shook her head. 'Yet it is our practice for each man and woman to wed only one mate.'

'But . . . no subordinate wives? No concubines? Slaves?'

'No, my Empress. Only one wife for each husband; one husband for each wife.'

'That's wholly uncivilized. How can a society survive such stinginess?'

Tree shrugged. 'Such is the custom of the barbarian world.'

'And is it also your custom to deny those in need? Our maidens are husbandless and my son is now only eleven suns.'

'What Prayer Mat of the Body needs most is males. As I promised, Husband and I will make sons for you.'

The crowd babbled angrily.

The Empress blew out her breath. 'As you wish,' she said. 'How else can I pluck out the doubt you've driven in?'

Tree placed her palms together as prayer hands and Mason followed her lead. They kowtowed and touched their foreheads to the grass.

The Empress clapped once and they stood.

'Hear me. If you are not pregnant in three moons, you will be banished to the hell above,' the Empress said. 'And if you become pregnant and then give birth to a girl, you and the infant will both be fed to the Scissor Teeth.'

Tree opened her mouth to protest but again the dark glint in the eye behind the mask kept her quiet.

'Also, it is obvious you both need education,' the Empress said. 'So, in spite of your arrogance, I will grant you an opportunity to become civilized. Tell your selfish husband he must take a second wife. Someone to socialize you. Surely just one more woman will not tax his manhood. Everyone who dwells in Prayer Mat of the Body must know her proper place, like a doll within nested dolls. In hierarchy there is harmony. The alternative to harmony is death.'

'Yes, my Empress,' Tree said and bowed her head.

Mason bowed and whispered, 'She talks too fast.'

Tree relayed the message to him.

'Oh no,' he groaned, 'how we gonna keep wife number two from finding out about me?'

11

The Empress spat orders and in a moment Tree and Mason were draped in robes of crimson silk. Tree's robe bore a white tiger; Mason's robe, a green dragon.

'Bring in the maidens,' the Empress commanded.

Women began to file through the courtyard in front of Mason. Some of the women looked as young as twelve or fourteen, most appeared to be in their twenties or early thirties. The women wore silk robes of many colors and styles: kimonos, saris, and sarongs; and a few wore flowing or draped designs that were new to Tree. Embroidered white tigers peered out from some part of each woman's clothing; big albino cats wrapped from front to back, or tiny ones as small as the designer emblems stitched on knit shirts. Fantastic hats of silk and paper, shaped like Chinese castles, adorned the heads of all but a few, who instead sported elaborate wigs or hairstyles.

Some of the women passed without looking up from the ground. Others ogled. Mason with wide eyes, while a few smiled enticingly or made provocative expressions with their eyes and mouths. As each maiden filed past him she walked around to the far side of the koi pond and stood waiting with the others at the back of the courtyard.

Tree gaped at the unrelenting beauty of nearly every woman in the group. Although most had almond-shaped, corner-folded eyes, their features struck her as more Polynesian than Chinese, a reflection of their multi-ethnic parentage: not only did all these women have local Indian tribesmen for fathers, but Tree recalled that Ko T'ung Jen had sailed with crewmembers from Persia, India and Europe, in addition to his Chinese sailors and maidens. Although a few women had lighter-colored eyes or hair, they all looked like sisters from one huge South Sea Island family.

Tree thought wryly that if her predicament were not so bewildering, not to mention dangerous, she might spare her ego the luxury of feeling threatened by this surplus of stunning females. Her share of approving gazes from men over the years had secured in her the confidence that she was far from boring to undress with the eyes – but those guys hadn't been surrounded by a population of exotic beauties.

She'd joined the research project to try her best to reawaken the volcano of passion that once shook her and Mason to the core. An assortment of lovers since their divorce had only reinforced her hunger for her ex-husband and a dream of togetherness that refused to wane. Disappointment, even heartbreak, were risks she had been prepared to take for the chance to win him back. But now she was risking death, while Mason was about to choose a resplendent Asian princess for his second wife.

The last of the maidens, about age sixteen and more curvy than most of her competition, strolled slowly past Mason, a white tiger riding the back of her silk robe atop sensually swaying hips. Other women who had not passed by in review now joined the throng behind the pond. From their plain shifts of thin unbleached wool and their demeanor Tree guessed that these were the maidens' handservants or slaves. Even these unadorned servants did not lack physical beauty.

One attendant stood out, and not just because she was a head taller than the other women, almost as tall as Tree. Straight black hair hung to her waist, so shiny it caught the daylight and tossed it back with a bluish sheen. The spilled ink of her mane framed the pale smooth skin of her angular face and a twin shock of deep blue Oriental eyes. Tree thought she was the most beautiful woman she had ever seen. Across the flowered water their eyes linked for an instant, then the servant cast her sight to the ground.

The gathered maidens stared at Mason awaiting his choice.

'Help me out, Tree.'

'I can't. You're on your own.'

'If she finds out, we're doomed.'

'We can't let her find out.'

'They await your decision, barbarian,' the Empress said.

'Mason,' Tree said, 'choose.'

Someone in the crowd tripped the blue-eyed servant and she lost balance and stepped one foot into the koi pond. The crowd howled with laughter. The blue-eyed woman stepped out of the water and drooped her head low so that her hair swept forward and hid her face.

'Ask her if I can choose anyone among them.'

'That's the idea.'

'Ask her.'

Tree asked.

'Yes, any one of them can be his wife,' the Empress answered.

'I choose her,' Mason said, and pointed to the blue-eyed servant.

The laughter trailed off to a total hush.

'I have no patience for jokes,' the Empress said.

'She doesn't like your choice,' Tree said.

'She said I can choose any woman to be my wife. I choose her.'

'It is my husband's desire to take the blue-eyed woman as his number-two wife,' Tree said. The tension in the room constricted as if oxygen were being wrung out of the air. Tree swallowed dryly.

It seemed like minutes before the Empress cracked the taut silence. 'Send the bride to her husband.'

Several women in the front of the throng gave the servant a vicious shove and knocked her backward into the pond. She hunkered in the water looking afraid. Her eyes darted back and forth between Mason and the crowd.

Mason walked to the pond's edge and held out his hand. 'Don't worry about those jerks,' he said in English. 'Come to me. I won't hurt you.' She waded to his side of the pond and he tugged her out of the water. She kept her head down and her body hunched. Mason eased her up by her shoulders to her full height. Now she stood head-to-head with him, her dripping wet hair daubed over her breasts like a black waterfall in a Chinese brush painting.

Tree strolled over and laid her hand on the woman's shoulder. 'What is your name?'

'Hsiang K'un-Chien,' the servant said, avoiding Tree's gaze.

'We are strangers to your world,' Tree said, 'but we mean you no harm.' She smiled warmly, then their eyes locked. Tree suddenly remembered the blue stained glass of Mother Mary's flowing robe – altar window, First Episcopal Church, Indian Mound Beach. That was the soulful blue of K'un-Chien's eyes. Exactly.

'Her name means Perfume of Earth-Heaven,' she told Mason.

'Yes, I understood.' He turned to the Empress. 'Hsiang K'un-Chien is Second Wife,' he said in Chinese, carefully pronouncing each word. 'K'un-Chien can teach us the ways of Prayer Mat of the Body, Your Highness.'

The wrathful mask nodded slowly. 'So be it – according to your self-chosen fate,' she said. 'But if both your wives are not with child in three moons, barbarian, both will be banished – and I'll personally make you into a eunuch.' She spun and strode away out of the courtyard trailing her entourage like colored smoke.

'What was all that about pregnant wives?' he asked Tree. 'This dialect's so damn archaic . . .'

'She said we're way deep in shit.'

'That's what I thought. Out of the frying pan . . .' He blew out a tense breath. 'How's your hand?'

'Fear's a good painkiller. I actually forgot the hand for a while.' She leaned against him heavily. 'But now I'm really feeling weak, Mason.'

He draped Tree's arm over his shoulders and supported her with one arm around her back. He turned to K'un-Chien. 'Please, can you take us to a doctor at once? First Wife is badly injured.'

'Husband, I am myself a doctor.' K'un-Chien clasped hands in front of her bosom and bowed her head low. Black hair spilled to the grass like nightfall.

'We're in luck,' Mason said, and gave Tree another effort at a reassuring smile.

Tree didn't rate their luck too highly. They were only buying time until she could get strong enough for them to escape. Pregnancy was not an alternative.

Ever since he'd gotten back from Vietnam, Mason had been sexually impotent.

12

The white velvety ant was as big as a mud wasp. It looked to Mason like the stinging ants the Wawajeros called *veinticautros* – twenty-four – because their venom caused a vicious fever for twenty-four hours. The Indians dreaded them more than scorpions. Mason had been stung three times over the years and each time the blood blister at the site had burned so furiously he'd marveled that he hadn't smelled smoldering flesh.

With chopsticks K'un-Chien delicately grasped the ant and lifted it from a wooden box lined with sweetgum leaves. Mason cringed, reminding himself that a *veinticuatros* was smooth black, not fuzzy white.

'I trust her,' Tree said. She sat crosslegged across from K'un-Chien and Mason on a woven rice-straw mat on the dirt floor of a bamboo hut. She nodded to K'un-Chien who placed the ant on Tree's ragged wound.

The ant wasted no time. It curled its abdomen beneath its thorax and stung the inflamed tissue again and again.

'Oooh. Feels cold,' Tree said.

Mason let out his breath. 'Cold? That's good.'

'It's getting numb. Oh, what a relief.' She smiled at K'un-Chien and the woman lowered her eyes. 'The pain's ebbing away. It feels like ... like cold icing oozing over my hand, and everywhere it spreads goes numb.'

'We call them cold-sleep,' K'un-Chien said, and caught the ant with the tips of the chopsticks, returned it to its box and closed the ventilated lid.

'That's terrific,' Mason said. 'I'd like to find out what the analgesic is in the venom. Halcyon would love it. Figure it's got to be a tiny amount – what, a couple milligrams at most? Maybe mikes. That's powerful stuff.'

'I'm so tired,' Tree said. 'I need to lie down for a little while.'

Tree lay on her back and bent her knees to fit on the mat. K'un-Chien knelt at her head and began massaging Tree's temples with long slender fingers; the facial tension visibly melted beneath her skillful touch. Mason savored the vision of two beautiful women from opposite hemispheres: one with dark blue eyes and straight-straight hair as black as licorice, the other with sea-green eyes and blond locks as frothy as champagne.

'Oh that feels so good . . . your touch is wonderful . . .'

A hint of a smile crept across K'un-Chien's face. 'You honor me,' she said softly.

The only furniture in the tiny room was a large mahogany chest honeycombed with dozens of various-sized drawers, each labeled with Chinese ideograms. Mason stood to browse its contents. He recognized the characters for *ginseng, lotus seed, bee pollen,* and found in those drawers what he expected. But most of the drawers held herbs unknown to him: *bat root, devil snail, night glow, dragon song, moon woman* and *fire moss* intrigued him; inside were various aromatic powders, twigs, leaves, roots, petals, pollens, mosses and dried mushrooms. Several drawers seemed to relate to human plumbing: *water start, water stop, bowel start, bowel stop.* One drawer the size of a postcard was labeled bluntly *vomit until empty.* 'Some other time,' he muttered. *Phoenix balls* turned out to be sticky green balls of powdered herbs rolled in crystalline honey. His fingers sifted a maroon chalk called *womb tonic*; it took a moment to realize it was dried menstrual blood.

K'un-Chien laid Tree's head on a curved wooden neck pillow and stood up to light a charcoal fire in a small iron stove with a grill. She poured water from a gourd into a blue ceramic teapot and set it on the stove to boil. Then she placed Tree's scab-crusted hand to soak in a bowl of milky sour-smelling liquid that looked to Mason like bleu cheese dressing.

'Pain's all gone,' Tree said dreamily.

'I'm so glad.' Mason knelt beside her and stroked her hair. 'Local anesthetics usually don't work well with infections because the pus surrounds the nerve endings and blocks the drug. But this stuff . . .'

'It's so fast,' Tree said, 'works great.'

'This is what HARVEST was meant for,' he said. 'A find like this—'

'It's not worth our friends dying.'

'No, of course not. No way. But . . . sorry . . . guess I'm always thinking of the Wawajeros . . . what I can do to make their lives a little easier. I was thinking maybe they could raise the cold-sleep ants and export their venom glands to the States.'

Mason had joined the HARVEST project with the goal of discovering and developing native drugs for Halcyon Pharmaceutical Corporation that could lead to cottage industries and income for the Wawajeros. With enough profits they could hire top lobbyists to defend themselves against the lumber industry. Then maybe their forest homes wouldn't be hauled away in trucks day after day, driving them farther into the dwindling jungle. He also needed funds to build a floating clinic to serve a string of Indian villages; something like the hospital ship H.O.P.E., but on a riverine scale.

But what he desired most of all, Mason admitted, was to find some way to do enough with his life, his skills, to atone for what he'd done in Vietnam. Something that would turn the tide of his guilt. But how much was enough? What would it take to repay Gib?

I'm not asking for pardon, he thought, *only redemption*.

Tree touched his crimson robe. 'I didn't mean to be nasty,' she said. 'It's just . . . don't get too excited, I know you, Mason. Remember, we've still got to live through this.'

'Right. You're right, lover.' Her eyes opened wider and Mason looked away. He'd called her that out of an old habit, but it was too late to retrieve the word. *Lover. The one for me, the only one. I'm sorry I let you down, Tree.*

He watched K'un-Chien work, fascinated by her skill with treatments he'd never seen. She poured the steaming water from the teapot into a wooden bowl over a stack of dark three-lobed leaves that were purple on one face and green on the other. While the brew steeped, she took a bristly weed stalk and began to debride the softened tissue of Tree's wound, stripping away dead and infected flesh and scrubbing down to the bloody red muscle.

'Doesn't hurt at all,' Tree said as the blood turned the milk-stuff bright pink, 'but sure looks god-awful.'

K'un-Chien tested the temperature of the whiskey-colored tea and plunged Tree's hand in the deep bowl and swished it around and around. The water darkened. When she withdrew the hand the wound looked clean and all bleeding had stopped. Then K'un Chien sprinkled an orange cloud of spores from a puffball fungus onto the raw flesh; almost instantly the wet surface hardened into a dry shellac-like film, protecting the tissue like a bandage.

K'un-Chien gave a satisfied nod. Then she unwrapped a square package of banana leaves that contained a black paste that smelled like road tar. She took out one of the sticky green phoenix balls, coated it thickly with the paste and gestured for Tree to swallow it whole. Tree washed it down with gulps of fresh water from a yellow squash gourd.

Mason whistled low. 'What I'd give to know the active ingredients in all this stuff. There's a whole pharmacy lying in that cabinet that the West has never heard of.'

'Yuck.' Tree stuck out her tongue in disgust and guzzled more water. 'Tastes as bad as western medicine – worse.'

K'un-Chien made a second tar ball for Mason. He put it far back on his tongue and gulped it down, then screwed his eyes shut and shuddered.

'Warned you,' Tree said.

'Rather eat a granola bar.'

Next K'un-Chien held Mason's jaw firmly and placed a cold-sleep ant against his cheek wound. When the anesthetic venom took effect she stitched the edges of the wound closed, outside and in, with silk thread and a very sharp curved needle made from a smooth black thorn.

In a corner stood a little shrine in the form of a roofed shelter fashioned of oiled purpleheart. The niche held an unmarked black lacquer box guarded by a *pa kua* mirror to reflect away evil. K'un-Chien opened the box and took out a container made from a jointed section of green bamboo dipped in candle wax. With a *pop* the lid pried off and the room instantly filled with the pungent, sweet smell of rotten compost. She dipped in a copper spoon and scooped out a glob of brilliant yellow slime.

'Some kind of slime mold?' Mason said.

'Same thing I was thinking,' Tree said.

'*Ling-Chih*,' K'un-Chien said.

'Mason, oh my god.'

'What – what is it?'

'Ling-Chih – remember? The Mushrooms of Immortality. What the Treasure Fleets were searching for.'

'Yeah, but . . . come on. Just a myth.'

'Of course. But an anthropologist would love this: A medicinal fungi and they've named it after an archetypal item from their legends. I wish my father had lived to see this kind of thing.'

He nodded. 'Let's just hope it helps your wound to heal cleanly. No more infection. As soon as you're well we gotta get the hell outta this valley.'

K'un-Chien gently touched Tree's cheek and her voice softened as if she were talking to a little child. 'So sorry,' she said. 'This will burn. Please don't be afraid. The flames soon pass and you will see most clearly.'

'But my whole arm is numb. How can it burn?'

'No, First Wife, it will not burn your flesh,' K'un Chien said. 'It will burn your mind.'

13

K'un-Chien coated Tree's hand with the chromium-yellow slime. Within seconds Tree tasted a dank earthy flavor, like wet leaves.

'I taste it in my mouth,' she told Mason.

'The molecules must be super-permeable,' he said. 'That explains the wax coating on the container.'

K'un-Chien lifted Tree's head and rested it in her lap. Tree closed her eyes. She felt an odd sensation of hollowness as she grew lightheaded.

Abruptly the flames arose.

The fire started as a budding red glow in the center of Tree's inner vision. She opened her eyes, half expecting to find Mason holding a candle near her face. He squeezed her hand. 'I'm right here.'

When she closed her eyes again the fire had blossomed into a crimson rose that flickered and sparked at its edges. Now she felt its heat, and her thoughts began to boil away in the brightness. She lost all sense of spatial orientation and her hollow body became a faint cloud of sensations. Then it vanished.

Tree moaned.

'Do not fight it,' K'un-Chien said. 'Allow the heat and light to take you; yield to it as to a lover.'

The fire bloomed, expanding in concentric blazing petals and, at its center, white intensity. Deeper layers of memory and imagery evaporated like steam.

'Yes, yes, release everything,' K'un-Chien whispered. 'It is not death. The Ling-Chih is uncovering your immortal essence.'

The more Tree relaxed the more completely the fire overcame her. At last she surrendered altogether in the expanding, humming light. The rose blazed throughout the height and breadth of her mind, dissolving limits, burning away the last traces of her personality, until all that remained of Teresa Diana Summerwood was luminous pure feeling, an infinite well of light and sound. She had become a singularity – a choir of brightness, a radiant chord.

Next came a sense of hurtling speed. Then a sudden, lucid vision:

Tree watched her hands strumming an unfamiliar rosewood instrument that resembled a sitar, held horizontally. Within its deep soundbox dangled rows of quartz crystals, pea-sized to finger-sized, which vibrated sympathetically with every string she played, creating multi-layered harmonics, a music of resonating gems.

She studied her hands and marveled at how well her left thumb had healed. She couldn't even find the scar. Then she remembered the thumb had been severed in the helicopter crash: There should be no thumb. *Yet here was a new digit deftly plucking bass strings as thick as a harp's.*

A beautiful mezzo voice sang out, clear and vibrato, like an oboe, and the crystals warbled with it, sympathetically. She turned to see K'un-Chien singing, accompanying her on the qin, *a classical Chinese seven-string zither. K'un-Chien smiled at her with a tender look, both vulnerable and intimate, and a current passed between them as if Tree were made of zinc and K'un-Chien, copper.*

Tree gradually returned to outer awareness, lying on her back with her head in K'un-Chien's lap on the rice-straw mat in the little thatched hut. She opened her eyes.

'Good nap?' Mason said. 'You went out like a light.'

Tree sat up and opened her mouth to speak, but only shook her head in wonder.

K'un-Chien nodded to her, knowingly. 'You have seen a vision.'

'Yes . . . a vision . . . but I don't understand it.'

'Before your vision, did you feel that you were flying very fast?'

'Yes, yes.' She looked at Mason. 'I felt like a signal zipping along a zillion telephone wires at the speed of light. But I haven't a clue how to tell her that.'

'Were you rushing outward,' K'un-Chien asked, 'or did it feel that you were imploding?'

'Outward. Exploding.' Tree threw her arms wide.

K'un-Chien nodded. 'When you fly inward, you meet your ancestors and the ancients. When you fly outward, you see your future.'

'But . . . my hand. I had a thumb again.'

K'un-Chien smiled. 'Very good. That means the Mushroom has married your *chi* – your life-force – and will give birth to a new thumb.'

'A new thumb . . . ?' Mason said.

Tree grabbed his hand. 'In my vision I was playing a . . . a sitar-like instrument. Not only was my hand healed, but I had a thumb. An intact thumb.'

Mason shrugged. 'It was a dream.'

'No, it had an entirely different quality than a dream. So real.'

'But your thumb . . . it's just plain gone.'

'First the Mushroom marries one's life-force,' K'un-Chien said, 'then it reads one's personal scripture to regenerate old organs or build new ones.'

Tree and Mason exchanged puzzled looks.

'K'un-Chien, are you saying that this fungus enables people to regenerate living tissue?'

'Yes, Husband. The Mushroom will awaken her *chi* to grow a new thumb, according to her personal scripture.'

Mason eyebrows arched. 'Is this real? What if . . . My God, if this is true . . .'

K'un-Chien lowered her eyes. 'Husband, I would not lie to you.'

'No, no, of course not. I believe you.' Mason turned to Tree,

'Explain to her that I meant no insult. It's just . . . nothing I've ever learned in my medical training compares to this. The ability to grow new tissue. It's . . . it's . . .'

'Have others regrown fingers and thumbs?' Tree asked.

K'un-Chien laughed. 'Legs, First Wife. Arms. Short of being dead, one can regrow anything.'

Tree's mouth fell open and Mason had to steady himself on the mat with his hands. 'My God,' he whispered. 'This is more . . . Tree, what have we found here?' He held up Tree's injured hand to inspect it. Most of the slime had been absorbed into the flesh, leaving a dull yellow film.

'You said the Mushroom reads one's personal scripture,' Tree said to K'un-Chien. 'What do you mean – "personal scripture?"'

'The most essential internal scripture that tells the body's parts how to repair and rebuild themselves.'

Mason snapped his fingers. 'DNA,' he said. 'Exactly what she's describing. Somehow . . . oh man, let me figure this one . . .' He jumped up and began to pace in tight circles in the small room. 'Somehow the DNA in the mushroom acts as a genetic switch—'

'It reprograms the DNA in the cell nuclei—' Tree said.

'And reactivates the same genes that led to the tissue growth in the first place. Yeah. Limb regeneration. Salamanders can do it. Even rabbits have been coerced to do it with electrochemical stimulation. How. Think about it.'

'I am, it's making me dizzy.'

'The cancer research guys have been studying slime molds for years trying to figure out how they reprogram their own genes to activate such different growth phases in their life cycle,' Mason said. 'Part of the time they're like an animal and can propel themselves along, part of the time they're a big one-celled blob with a whole bunch of nuclei, then at one point they turn into a fruiting body and stand up in all sorts of flowering shapes. Genetic switches. Slime molds can switch signals on and off like a kid with a Lionel Train set.'

Tree nodded. 'One of my profs studied them. He thought they deserved their own kingdom – not plant or animal. There are five hundred species.'

'Five hundred and *one*,' he said, and glanced at the bamboo
container that held the Ling-Chih. 'Oh, this is big. This is the
biggest, biggest breakthrough in modern medicine. It makes
penicillin look like . . .' He paced faster and his circles got
tighter and tighter and then he stopped, tilted back his head
and yelled, 'Waa-*hooooo!*'

K'un-Chien smiled. 'Husband is pleased?'

'Husband is . . . *Mason*, call me Mason. I am delighted.
Thrilled. Tree, how do you say "Far fucking out" in Mandarin?'
Mason knelt and grabbed K'un-Chien's shoulders. 'Ling-Chih is
a most wonderful medicine, doctor.'

K'un-Chien laughed, displaying perfect white teeth. 'Yes,
May-Son.'

Tree could still vividly picture her vision. 'Have I truly seen
my own future?'

'You connected with the web of life and followed its threads
to *a* future. What you saw is not fixed, like the sun rising in
the east and setting in the west. It is more like watching a
trickle of water carving a groove in the sand and knowing
ahead of time that in three moons that groove is going to be
a small gully.'

'Sounds like the kind of statistical model computers run
for weather forecasting,' Mason said to Tree. 'She's saying
you witnessed a highest-probability outcome, the most likely
culmination of the many possibilities that in this moment
extend from you.'

'So what I saw is very likely to happen?' Tree asked K'un-
Chien.

'Yes, First Wife. Unless the threads of the web of life are
restrung they will converge at a specific place and time to
make manifest your vision.'

Tree studied K'un-Chien's eyes, remembering the emotional
content of the vision. The rapport between them had been
unmistakably sexual. Tree felt confused, as if some shadow
of her psyche was waiting to betray her. *I'm not the type of
woman to fall in love with another woman. At least . . . good
grief, I never thought I was.*

Tree set her mind firmly to guard against that particular path
to that particular future.

'Why didn't the Empress use the Ling-Chih to repair the damage to her face?' Mason asked.

K'un-Chien frowned and drew back.

'So sorry, I said something horribly rude,' Mason said. 'Forgive me.'

K'un-Chien composed herself. 'I must remember that you don't know our ways, May-Son.'

'Please enlighten my ignorance.'

'Through her sacrifice the Empress is granted the power to produce male children. If she were to have healed the damage to her face, the sacrifice would have been nullified and no male children could have been born.'

'Forgive me again,' Mason said, 'but how does this sacrifice occur? How did she come to appear like that?'

'A river runs through a ceremonial chamber in the Prayer Mat Temple—'

'The temple we were in earlier today?'

'Yes. The Scissor Teeth live in the river.'

'Scissor teeth?' Mason said. 'How do they look?'

K'un-Chien knitted her eyebrows. 'With their eyes, May-Son.'

'Some idioms don't translate well,' Tree said to Mason. 'K'un-Chien, describe for us the appearance of the scissor teeth.'

'Fish. With shiny black scales, a jutting lower jaw and razor-sharp teeth like saw-edged triangles—'

'Piranha,' Mason said. 'Tree, she's talking about piranha. Sure – the Orinoco River Basin is the only place in the world they live. This is their habitat.'

Tree's stomach knotted.

'How big are these fish?' Mason asked.

K'un-Chien spread her hands to show a length of two feet. 'Fat and heavy.'

'Holy shit,' Mason said. '*Serrasalmus nattereri* – the deadliest of all piranha species. I should have guessed it when she said scissor teeth – their serrated teeth mesh so tightly the Wawajeros use their jawbones as scissors.'

'On the first new moon at the outset of her reign, the Empress must endure a ritual sacrifice,' K'un-Chien said. 'She is towed by a golden silk rope from one bank to the other. The fish churn the river. Her body tumbles from their strikes. The water froths with blood.'

'Goddam awful.' Mason muttered.

'But only her face is scarred,' Tree said. 'Her hands and what I could see of her arms looked normal.'

'The rest of her body is thickly padded with leather for protection. Only her face is exposed.'

'I think I understand,' Mason said to Tree. 'It's the Confucian theme of the loss of face – made physical.'

Tree nodded. 'It's about taking shame upon oneself to atone for a whole group – in this case, mothers who can't give birth to males.'

'The Mother of Sons must pay for her power by forfeiting her beauty,' K'un-Chien said.

'She once was beautiful?' Tree asked.

'Ah yes, extremely so. It is said that even while still a toddler she was the one most expected to be chosen. Only the most beautiful woman in Jou P'u T'uan can become the Empress.'

'Damn, that's perverse,' Mason said.

Tree sighed. 'Appeasement. Expiation to the powers that be. 'Eat the maiden, O Mountain of Thunder, just don't eat us.' You find some version of it – either by human or animal sacrifice – throughout history, in every culture.'

Mason nodded. 'Like I said – "Damn, that's perverse."'

'Every twenty years a new Empress is chosen,' K'un-Chien explained. 'The next selection is three moons hence, on the morning of the autumn equinox.'

Tree shuddered, imagining the emotional horror that must have shattered each of the young women who became Empress; transformed by savage injury from the city's most physically attractive person to its most physically repulsive.

Her eyes appraised K'un-Chien's flawless features as an art dealer might appraise fine sculpture. She worried about the teenager's ranking on any scale of beauty. *Were there women in this city who were even more lovely? And, my God, what if there were not . . . ?*

'The Empress,' Tree said. 'Now even her long hair is only a wig.'

'I have often wondered what she looked like when she was

my age,' K'un-Chien said. 'I never saw her face when it was not cocooned with scars. I am told I resemble her strongly.'

Tree and Mason spoke at the same time, 'What did you say?'

'The Empress is my mother.'

14

The bedroom's high windows held panes of translucent paper glued to ornate cherrywood trellises. The window frames formed a menagerie of shapes: birds, fish, flowers, crescents and stars. Moonlight through the bleached paper suffused the circular room with a silver-white glow thatched with soft shadows.

Outside a bell bird clonged and another answered from a distance. Crickets and frogs scricked and chirped and peeped. A howler monkey barked and set off a colony of parrots screeching. Underneath these treble cloud forest notes, the rolling tympani of the waterfall reverberated in the lush, rock-walled valley.

Tree and Mason lay facing each other on their sides on a futon mattress atop an elaborately carved bamboo bed. K'un-Chien slept on a straw mat unrolled on the floor at the bed's foot, bamboo dragon heads poking from stylized clouds that swirled above her head.

Tree and Mason wore silk pajamas: his green, hers white. They spoke in low voices.

'I think we'd better start again with the basic question,' she said, 'Why are only females born here?'

Mason shook his head slowly.

'Like you said before, could be some kind of environmental factor,' Tree said.

'Maybe, but I've been racking my brain—'

'What about your idea of acidic water?'

'Nah. Now I'm thinking it was a goofy hypothesis.'

They'd talked earlier about techniques for choosing a baby's sex by giving an advantage to one of the two types of sperm: *gyno*sperms, the girl-makers, which are stronger and longer-lived, but slower-swimming; or *angio*sperms, the boy-makers, which are weaker, but faster swimmers and more numerous. In conditions that support the sperm overall, such as a slightly alkaline vaginal environment, the angiosperms tend to win the race to the egg, because they are faster and more plentiful. But in a slightly acidic vaginal environment and over more hours, the gynosperms tend to win because of their superior durability and staying power.

Thus the formula was simple: To make boys, have sex at ovulation, with deep vaginal penetration from behind – the best position to deposit sperm at the cervical opening to the womb – and try to ensure the woman has an orgasm to boost the alkaline secretions of the vagina. To make girls, have sex in the missionary position two or three days before ovulation, skip the female orgasm, and try for shallow penetration at the moment of ejaculation so that the sperm must travel up the vaginal canal, eliminating most boy-sperms along the way.

Mason had said that using those methods gave couples the boy or girl they hoped for up to ninety percent of the time.

'So what I'm wondering,' he'd said earlier, 'could there be some universal factor at work here, like frequent bathing in water that contains a lot of dissolved limestone – in effect, an acidic douche – that would cause women to make only girls?'

But now he downplayed his idea.

'I mean, every woman who ever got pregnant here would have to have bathed – or preferably, douched – in the water just before having sex. Far-fetched, unless it's some kind of ritual they perform. Besides, if this water was acidic it would taste sour. Have you noticed any sour water?'

Tree shook her head. 'It's all been sweet and delicious.'

'Exactly.' He sighed. 'No, even if they douched with vinegar you gotta figure angiosperms would win out some of the time – there's a lot more of them than gynosperms.'

'I've been thinking along dietary lines,' Tree said. 'Some type of food—'

'That acts as a powerful inhibitor to angiosperms? Huh. What could it be?'

'Haven't a clue.'

'Y'know, there was a study I read where a female diet high in calcium and low in salt and potassium tended to produce girls,' he said. 'The boy-diet was the opposite: low in calcium and high in salt and potassium. The women were supposed to stick with the diet for at least a month before trying to get pregnant. Out of about three hundred women in the study, eighty per cent got the girl or boy they aimed for.'

'Hey. Maybe it's something like that.'

'I sure wouldn't call theirs a low-salt diet. Those pickled plums had me guzzling water like a cow at a salt lick. This whole mountain is full of salt, used to sit on the floor of the Pacific.'

'Could be something in their diet unknown to western science.'

He nodded. 'Back where we started from: Unknown.'

'Got an idea,' Tree said. 'Let's take a different approach. Try this: "What is it the Empress has or does, that no other woman in Prayer Mat of the Body has or does?"'

Mason looked up. 'Yeah, that's good. How come she, and *only* she, *can* make baby boys?'

'What does she eat that no one else eats?'

'Right. Or what is her exclusive sexual ritual?'

'What about those goddam scissor-teeth?' Tree cringed. 'Could there be something in their saliva – or, hey, something in *that* water – that's special?'

Mason sat up straighter. 'I don't think that's it, because she only gets her face chewed off once—'

'Ugh.'

'—and that sacrifice makes her capable of having sons the rest of her life. So, it's not that she's exposed to the water or the fish saliva, or whatever, before every conception.'

'True.'

'But I think we're on the right track. What does she eat that no one else eats?'

Tree nodded. 'Or what does she avoid that everyone else is exposed to?'

'K'un-Chien might know. But we'll have to be careful how we phrase our questions. She seems to believe firmly in her mother's martyrdom.'

The moon had reached its zenith and began to sink over the mountainside. Creamy light spilled from the bedsheets, slowly flooded across the floor and up the opposite wall before either of them spoke again.

'Getting out of the city is not the toughest part,' Mason said. 'Only the gates are guarded. We could figure out a way to scale the walls.'

'But what's the use of making it back to the "upper hell"?' she said. 'That's exactly where they banish you when they want you to die slowly. Or quickly – from the harpies.'

'I keep trying to come up with a way to repair the balloon,' he said. 'It's torn at its base, but the upper envelope is undamaged. If the lower envelope could be stitched or glued back together, we could fire up the burners and float the Raft off the mountain top. The prevailing winds blow northward – we'd stand a fair chance of making it to Wawajero land. The Indians would help us get back to the closest town with a radio.'

'But even if we whipped together some sort of glue from tree resin or whatever, we can't be sitting around patching the balloon while dodging killer eagles.'

'That's true.'

'Face it,' Tree said. 'I need to get pregnant.'

His eyes and mouth hardened.

'Really, Mason. We have to try. It would buy us several more months to plan an escape.'

He gazed at her in the dim light. His gray eyes darkened like clouds heavy with rain. Neither of them spoke for a few minutes.

'Look, this tepui is virtually unscalable,' Mason said, finally. 'There's no way Ko T'ung Jen led a stream of people, goats and potted plumtrees straight up those cliffs. That means there's got to be an inner passage leading up from the jungle floor below, some kind of deep rift in the rock, like the one that led us down here from the top. If we can find it and sneak the hell out of here—'

'What about the Yanomorduro?' Tree flicked her hair with her hand. 'I'm sure they'd treasure a shrunken head with wavy blond locks.'

'One threat at a time. First we find out how to get down to the jungle. Maybe we can carry a stash of robes and gems from the "yellow witches" to buy safe passage through headhunter territory. We'll need some weapons, too – bows, spears, knives . . .'

Tree shuddered. 'Scares me.'

'If we make it to the Caroni and travel north along its banks we're bound to run into some Wawajero villages,' he said. 'They can give us a dugout and food, and we can cross east when we get to the Paragua river, to La Paragua. Or better yet, if we're strong enough, keep heading north to Ciudad Guayana; it's another hundred miles or so, but they've got a small airstrip there.'

Tree sighed. 'Exodus, stage left.' To her it seemed so much easier for Mason to just push her back in the moonlit bed and make love to her. *That's the escape I need tonight.*

But she said nothing. It was no use. She'd learned her lesson years ago, when Mason had first gotten back from 'Nam: The more she'd pressured him to make love to her the more withdrawn he'd become. Back then, whenever they'd start to snuggle he'd get sick to his stomach, or he'd panic and be unable to catch his breath. Somehow they'd managed to have sex a few times, but it was a miserable parody of their former lost afternoons of passion. If nothing else, Mason had lacked staying power – Mason, the man who'd had so much sexual stamina she'd called him her Coast-to-Coast. Soon the problem worsened and he couldn't perform at all. Yet it was clear the damage that caused his impotence was emotional, not physical: even now, every morning he woke up with his famous erections the size of a toy locomotive – O-Gauge.

Vietnam had ruined the kind of lover that women conjure in fantasies while fiddling with the shower massage. That, of course, was the least of the tragedy. Vietnam had broken Mason's spirit, the sweetest masculine spirit she'd ever known. And Vietnam had killed her brother. And in some secret way, Gib's death and the death of her marriage were entwined.

She flopped onto her back and stared up at the porcelain

tiles in the ceiling of the round room. The tiles created a repeating block pattern of four swastikas that opposed and reflected each other with contra-rotating arms, interfitted with six-pointed stars made from two intersecting triangles.

When Mason had first seen the tile design, he'd said, 'What the hell? Nazis and Jews?'

'It's not that,' Tree had said. 'Remember, these people have been isolated since the fourteen hundreds. Never heard of World War Two.'

'Yeah, I know, but how? . . . weird coincidence.'

'Both figures are archetypes, been around forever,' Tree had said. 'Swastika is a Sanskrit word, means "welfare" – it's a good-luck symbol, an image of the solar rays. You see it in Hindu and Buddhist art all the time. Even the Hopi Indians used it.'

'And the Star of David?'

'Same kind of thing. Pops up in Asian art four thousand years ago.'

'Well, it'll take some getting used to. If Barry were here, he'd croak.'

'That's for sure.'

A while later, he'd said, 'Reminds me of Gib, the stuff you told me. That's the sort of thing that fascinated him.'

She'd smiled. 'Who do you think I learned it from?'

On their first night in the city, soldiers had arrived at K'un-Chien's hut and escorted the newcomers to their own private palace. The Empress had decreed that the two be treated as Most-Honored Guests of Prayer Mat of the Body.

'Honored until we screw up in some way,' Mason had said, 'which is what she's counting on. Then we'll be treated as piranha chow.'

K'un-Chien, as Mason's second wife, had been allowed to move into the palace with them. For the first time in six years she could sleep on a futon mattress on a wooden bed in her own room instead of on a wool blanket on the dirt floor of a cramped hut. Yet she had asked to sleep on a straw mat at the foot of their bed.

'Long have I been cast off and alone,' K'un-Chien had said, 'now I wish to sleep at the feet of my benefactors, where

I belong.' Beyond a brief try, neither Tree nor Mason had mustered the heart to talk her out of it.

These days, K'un-Chien could soak in a luxurious indoor spa. But instead, she preferred to continue bathing alone, beyond the city's walls, in rock pools near the mouth of the hot springs that fed the city's baths.

K'un-Chien was extremely private about her own nudity, which struck Tree as odd. It didn't seem to fit with the wide-open innocence in her eyes and smile, her body language, her love for the world. And such shyness was counter to everything the society expressed.

In the two weeks since she'd arrived, Tree had seen women bathing nude in the middle of the day in heated pools in the plazas; some of them had even kissed and fondled unabashedly, while other women sauntered past on the sidewalks going about their daily business with nothing more than a nonchalant glance at the lovers. It was as if, to the citizens of Prayer Mat of the Body, seeing erotic behavior in public was as natural as seeing a butterfly sipping nectar from an orchid in a garden.

But K'un-Chien was different. She seemed even more bashful about her body than some of the pubescent girls Tree remembered from her Girl Scout troop – ones like Tammy Smith, who had acted as if getting her period was a monthly relapse of leukemia.

On the other hand, K'un-Chien's modesty focused only on her own body. One morning Tree had secretly watched from a doorway while K'un-Chien stared at Mason's nakedness as he slept with the sheets kicked off – toy locomotive with a full head of steam. K'un-Chien had stood there relaxed, hands on hips, face lit with appreciation and no small degree of wonder. Not like a schoolgirl at the Louvre sideglancing at *David*, trying not to gape at his big marble cock. K'un-Chien had traced Mason's topography with slow eyes of pleasure; memorizing his lines and shapes like a mapmaker in new territory.

Meanwhile, lingering in the doorway, Tree had been feeling the *ooof* of jealousy knot up her gut. Then she began to wonder what it must be like to be a grown woman, nearly eighteen, and never to have seen a man's sex. No, far more than only his sex. The whole man. Forehead to chin, broad shoulders and chest, corrugated belly, thick cock, ropy thighs and calves, sinewy feet and toes: altogether *male*. Seeing Mason from K'un Chien's point of view caused a warm wetness between Tree's thighs. She sucked in her breath and K'un-Chien looked up, breaking the spell.

Mason woke, spotted his audience, and grabbed up the satin sheets. 'What the hell's this – The Good Morning Peep Show?'

But K'un-Chien didn't react as if she'd been caught doing something indecent. She'd only smiled – just so – without a trace of embarrassment.

All this made Tree suspect a terrible secret about K'un-Chien's intense self-modesty: *Maybe she bears horrible hidden scars like her mother – but disfiguring her torso, not her face.* The thought nauseated Tree.

A monkey's high-pitched yodeling outside in the moonlight snapped Tree back to the present, lying in bed beside Mason. He'd rolled onto his back and appeared lost in thought. She returned her gaze to the ceiling and the tile stars and swastikas began to blur and float as she drifted back into reverie.

Tree brooded over the drug-induced vision of her possible future with K'un-Chien. Those magnetic blue eyes had attracted her with an erotic force she'd felt before only with Mason. Resisting that emotion would be like trying to swim against a riptide. But apart from her one brief vision, Tree felt no sexual desire at all for K'un-Chien. She only felt confused and upset.

She pressed a warm hand over her belly to relax a trembling bundle of nerves.

Once, back at Harvard, she and a very close girl pal, Liz Julliard, had gotten trashed on Boone's Farm Strawberry Wine and had danced to a stack of Marvin Gaye and James Brown 45's until they had fallen on their asses, dizzy and laughing. Then they'd wailed along with The Best of the Righteous Brothers – '*I've hungered for your touch*' – and suddenly they both were lonely and crying, missing their boyfriends in Vietnam. Next, they were kissing away the other's tears. One thing led to another and they'd ended up rolling around on the carpet with their hands up each other's T-shirts and down each other's jeans.

'Mason's gonna do you, girl, when he gets back, just like this.'

'Sock it to me, baby. Been waiting for it.'

It had been a silly sweet night. Not hot and heavy. Tree had felt a bit foolish later, but not guilty. Not *wrong*. So far as she knew, Liz had never worried about it either. Last Hanukkah Liz had sent her a card with a photo of her newborn twins.

Tree dearly loved Liz and a small tribe of other spirit-sisters scattered around the globe. But she'd never imagined herself *hungering* for a woman. That aching down-in-the-womb desire, where her soul fevered to give her body to her lover. *Take me, fuck me* was the name of that appetite. And *Take me, fuck me* was aroused in her only by men – most of all by Mason – or so she'd always believed.

So what the hell was she to make of her vision?

It's up to me to avoid that wavelength with K'un-Chien. I joined this project to find Mason again, not to fall into some hopeless love affair.

The trouble with shunning K'un-Chien was that the woman was so winningly nice. Not fake. She was loving, and plain lovable. How do you armor your heart against such an an artless person?

And why do I feel so jealous? Ugh. I don't even like people who get jealous. I don't believe *in jealousy, dammit.*

Tree daily reminded herself that Mason was sexually impotent – nothing to get jealous about when your man can't possibly have sex with your competition.

Competition. Have I really slipped into junior high mode at age thirty-two?

On the other hand, Mason and K'un-Chien took to each other like a Mutual Admiration Society. And hadn't she spied K'un-Chien adoring his dawn cock? And wasn't K'un-Chien the most gorgeous woman she'd ever seen, even in magazines – Lord, even in paintings?

Hoo-boy, here I go . . . who's gonna save me from my headtrips?

She glanced at Mason. Muscular arms folded across his chest, eyes open but inward-turned. He was going to spend nearly the whole night lying awake again, trying to figure out a plan for their escape and survival.

Tree took in a deep breath and tried to shake out the worries from her skull.

Mason rolled toward her. 'I swear to you, Tree,' he said, gray eyes like smoke. 'I'm *gonna* get us out of here.' He reached out and rubbed her furrowed brow with strong fingers.

Tree swallowed against a sudden lump in her throat. She understood that for Mason, 'us' now included K'un-Chien.

15

Mason and Tree sat on a half-moon bridge over a slushing brook, legs dangling off the edge of bamboo planks. A breeze produced melodious whistling from a thicket of acacia where beetle larvae had bored flute-holes in green shoots that held bouquets of yellow flowers. Dozens of metallic blue morpho butterflies danced above the clear water with dazzling wingbeats. A purple-throated mountain gem skimmed the stream for a sip and flitted off, seeking frangipani.

The midday sun abruptly burned through the haze, its first appearance in weeks. As soon as the sun broke out, all bustle in the city stopped. Women shed their clothes to let the rare brightness touch their whole bodies.

'Great idea,' Tree said and peeled her kaftan over her head. Sunlight off the water threw plums of light over her face and breasts. Her eyes were lit to their depths, clear and green, like Caribbean sea. She tilted her face to the blue hole in the clouds. 'Oh, Mister Sun, where ya been? I was starting to feel like a fern in a Seattle coffee bar.'

Warmth caressed Mason's face; his cheek had healed well enough for him to shave smoothly with a bamboo razor. He crossed his arms overhead and tugged off the red silk mandarin shirt K'un-Chien had made for him. Tree touched his latt muscles as they rippled, her touch as good a balm as the sun. His own fingers longed to graze the golden meadow of her body but he didn't dare begin.

He looked down at the water. Rose jasper formed the stream bed and its narrow beaches, spiked by shards of purple amethyst and pink quartz. *My duty is to figure out this society, find the keys to survive and escape.*

'Tree, let's take it apart again, from the top,' he said, 'Keep trying to puzzle this thing out. What are we overlooking?'

She shrugged. 'I'm as baffled as you.'

Mason squinted at gold domes and pagodas and spires gleaming in the sunlight. 'What do you make of this *Lung-Hu* cult – Dragon-Tiger – what's that mean?'

'The dragon and the color green are traditional symbols for *yang*, the male energy of the cosmos,' she said. 'Tiger and white represent *yin*, the female power.'

'Green dragon, white tiger – the icons are everywhere.'

'The two forces, yin and yang, are thought of as complementary opposites in an eternal dynamic balance. One doesn't exist without the other – in fact, they're said to be cyclical: when yin ripens it turns into yang, and vice versa.'

He nodded. 'Dancing partners, not sparring partners. Yeah, I remember some of that from talks with Gib.'

'If you look at the symbol of yin and yang – like two interfitted raindrops – you'll see that the dark raindrop, yin, grows a bright spot of yang within it; and the light raindrop, yang, grows a spot of darkness.'

'Interconversion.'

'What?'

'Interconversion: the mutual conversion of chemical compounds, one into the other.'

'Right. On an all-pervading scale,' she said. 'The eternal interconversion of these dual energies is said to create and drive the whole material universe – all the various qualities and processes and seasons within it. Yin-yang is the cosmic engine.'

'So Dragon-Tiger – male-female—?'

'Would be the human embodiment of yin-yang. The Empress called it the Holy Hermaphrodite. Said Dragon-Tiger could only be born through her.'

Mason stared at the exotic skyline and shook his head. On the streambank sunlight kissed the ruby mouths of hot-lips plants; a saber-winged violet danced before them, its long thin tongue whipping at caffeine-laden nectar. The hummingbird buzzed from blossom to blossom spreading pollen along with a cargo of tiny mites – a sexually-transmitted disease of flowers.

'They all act like the Lung-Hu is some kind of messiah, a savior,' Mason said.

'Been thinking about that,' Tree said. 'If your population is threatened with extinction because male births are extremely rare, the perfect rescue would be—'

'A battalion of eighteen-year-old Marines who can each come eight times a day.'

'No, that's just it. That wouldn't help ultimately. It's a stop-gap, like stealing Indian men from the jungle to use for breeding. But even if they make hundreds of babies, it's still a baby boom of girls. The society remains endangered, depending on outsiders.'

'What are you getting at?'

'Hermaphrodites. Male and female in one. Don't you see? It would be a self-sufficient society if it gradually came to be made up of hermaphrodites. They could impregnate each other. No more need to kidnap men. Each member of the population would be a male *and* female being.'

'No way. You're talking fantasy.'

'You sure?'

'I happen to know something about this because I did some grad work for a professor studying genetics among Appalachian families. See, what most people would call a hermaphrodite is technically a *pseudo*hermaphrodite; usually a male who went through a messed-up sexual development as a fetus, although it can be a woman. Rather than complete male-and-female in one, they are in between the two genders – incompletely male and incompletely female. A male pseudo-hermaphrodite could never get pregnant – he has no ovaries, no uterus; and a female pseudohermaphrodite could never make anybody pregnant because she lacks functioning testicles.'

'Oh, I see.'

'Keep in mind the female form is a kind of biological archetype – it's the template for all human embryos.'

'Right, I remember that from college biology.'

He nodded. 'I'm sure you know most of this stuff.'

'No, go ahead. It's been years – I could use a review.'

'Okay, then: Embryology 101,' he said. 'The male form is a modification of the primary human form – female. If that conversion is blocked for whatever reasons, the fetus does not change from its basic form and is born as a female, by default. Sterile, to be sure, but a female.'

She nodded.

'Between the fifth and seventh week after conception, embryos of either sex develop generic gonads that later become either ovaries or testicles. It's been shown that if you remove these generic sex cells of a female embryo, the baby will still be born as a female. That is, perfectly female in appearance, but sterile.'

'No ovaries.'

'Right. No ovaries, no fallopian tubes, no uterus. But externally, a female.'

'With a vagina.'

Mason nodded. 'With a vagina that dead-ends,' he said. 'Now what's fascinating is that if you remove the generic sex cells of a *male* fetus, the baby will also be born as a sterile *female*. Vagina included. Therefore, the female form is recognized as innate.'

Tree drew a news headline in the air with her hand. 'EVE INTO ADAM: THE TRUE STORY OF GENESIS.'

Mason smiled.

'I love that,' Tree said. 'I'm tempted to put a metaphysical spin on it. When I first read about it, back in my flowers-and-beads days, I thought of it as a scientific affirmation of the Goddess, the Great Mother. She's the Original Form of us all, women or men.'

'Well, it also applies to raccoons, kingfishers, water moccasins, right on down the line – all vertebrate embryos are intrinsically female.' He paused. 'But of course, outside the lab we're *not* removing the undifferentiated sex cells, so things get a lot more complicated.'

'Okay, I'm with you.'

'If the Y chromosome is present, the generic gonads start turning into testes around the eighth week. But otherwise, they start turning into ovaries around the thirteenth week. Nothing is needed for them to change into ovaries – they do that by default. But something has to intervene – genes on the Y chromosome – to make the gonads change into testes.'

'And things can go wrong in the conversion process.'

'Not only at that step, but even when the testes develop normally. There's a lot more to a man than testes alone.'

'*That* I wish more guys understood.'

'In addition to the generic gonads, the embryo is equipped with other all-purpose tissues that can develop into a penis or a vagina and other sex organs. But these later changes don't switch on directly from the Y chromosome, instead they come from male hormones secreted by the testes. Again, without male hormones the female organs develop by default. You follow?'

She nodded. 'It's a long march of biochemical steps.'

'Yeah. And just one mutated gene is enough to trip up the process at any stage along the parade. Some male parts may develop okay because they rely on hormones that remain normal. But male parts that depend on a hormone that's defective either end up missing or replaced by their female equivalents. So you wind up with genetic males who show a mix of incomplete male and incomplete female structures: *pseudo*hermaphrodites.'

'I see.'

'In fact, there's one type of genetic male who looks exactly like a woman. No chest hair or masculine build, no deep voice, no penis. They're missing a cell receptor for testosterone, so although they have internal testicles making normal serum levels of male hormone, they never grow any of the male equipment that depends on the hormone for development.'

'They look like *normal* women, or a little odd?'

'Perfectly normal-looking in every way. Nobody suspects anything's the matter until they reach puberty and worry why they aren't menstruating. A trip to the doctor and they find out they have no female internal organs, just a vagina that dead-ends, and testicles hidden in the abdomen or groin.'

'God, what a shock: "Sorry, Tiffany, you're actually a Tom."'

'It's more remarkable than you might think. As it happens, these blocked-androgen-receptor types tend to be strikingly beautiful "women". They've got the long-legged height of males, large breasts, flawless skin – did you know testosterone can cause terrible acne?'

She nodded. 'Remember Rodney Blane? He took estrogen to control his zits.'

'Well, what I'm getting at – more than a few pseudohermaphrodites have turned up among female fashion models.'

'No kidding. Whoa. So some of those sleek and glossy babes are really men who can't respond to their own sex hormone. Outrageous.'

'Androgen-blocked males nearly always choose to continue their lives as women—'

'Sure, why not? If you look that good in a leather miniskirt . . .'

'—they get married to men and often raise adopted kids, as the mom. The vagina is usually functional for intercourse. Without the receptor for testosterone they *are* women, by default.'

'That's really something,' Tree said.

A foggy white curtain glided across the sun. Mason felt a fine cool spray blow across his face and torso and he could gaze at the golden temples now without squinting. In a flurry the scattered sunbathers donned saris and kimonos and sarongs and resumed their lives in the mists.

Tree shivered. Goosebumps textured her pale breasts and her nipples grew taut. She stretched up, firm muscles sliding over ribs, and slithered back into her kaftan.

Mason's eyes drank in her slender beauty but glanced away when her head popped up through the garment. He still loved her. But to show his depth of feelings would be unfair. It would only feed her hope that things could be the way they'd been when he was free at heart. No. He had to stay remote. That was the kindest way to love her now.

He took his shirt down from the railing, slipped it on and buttoned the mandarin collar with twin braided loops.

'Anyway, true hermaphroditism is extremely rare,' he said, 'Only a handful of cases in the literature.'

Tree's eyebrows shot up. 'Aha. So it *can* occur.'

'Yeah, but wait a sec,' he said. 'A true hermaphrodite is that one-in-a-million person born with one internal testis and one ovary. Doesn't mean the person comes complete with all the female and male genitals. That's what you meant, right? Someone who could impregnate others and get pregnant too.'

'Right. The sacred hermaphrodite.'

He shook his head. 'Hard to imagine.'

'But we know next to nothing about the human genome and its workings.'

'You got a point there.'

'Okay. Maybe we're getting somewhere,' Tree said. 'The mixed set of gonads in the true hermaphrodite – do they function?'

'Often they do, yeah.'

'So the rare human individual produces both sperm and eggs.'

'See, now that's the catch: The problem with true hermaphrodites making anyone pregnant is that while the androgens don't seem to affect the female cycle – these persons menstruate monthly – the estrogens do cause the testis to atrophy.'

'So you're saying it's impossible?'

'Well . . . I recall a case I read in my dad's veterinary journal – this was years ago, even before I was out of high school. My dad was flabbergasted. A domestic rabbit, a true hermaphrodite, had fertilized itself.'

'There you go.'

'Well, yeah, but—'

'Shush. Just think about it a moment.' She held up her index finger. 'Could there arise a perfect human hermaphrodite, a being with complete sex organs of both genders?'

He frowned.

'Is it possible?' she said.

He shrugged. 'It's *possible*. Sure. Nature is vast. But . . . well, the thing is, it would require an exquisite compromise of sex hormones, so that the testis didn't atrophy.'

'Like the dynamic balance of yin and yang.'

'There's an idea . . .'

'I've been musing about this all day,' she said. 'Harmony of opposites, the union of Hermes and Aphrodite.'

He rubbed his chin. 'But the pseudohermaphrodite is a single-gene mutation. Easy to pass that on,' he said. 'I'd guess that to create a complete male-female human being might require a cluster of mutated genes.'

'Your point?'

'Well, is the gene pool here really so restricted that it would lead to such major mutations? You know it's something of a misconception that having babies with your relatives is tossing the dice of genetic disaster. Statistics show that making babies with a first cousin, for example, is a lot less risky than most people assume.'

'That so?'

He nodded. 'Consider the pharaonic dynasties: the Egyptian royalty was so holier-than-thou, they could only wed members of their own divine family. Cleopatra – Beauty of the Nile – was the daughter of seven generations of brother-sister marriages, and she herself married her brother.'

'Now there's one thing Gib never told me.'

'The professor I worked with figured that the babies of first-cousin marriages were maybe twice as likely as other babies to have congenital defects. But in real numbers, it means only about two cases in one hundred births, instead of one. Or, to look at it in another species: By the time congenital problems become common with pure-bred dogs, the breeders have inbred parents and offspring and siblings dozens of times.'

'Yeah, but there's the time factor here – think about a progression of inherited traits over five hundred years. Plus who knows the level of consanguinity of the original colonists from Ming Dynasty China – a polygamous society.'

'Huh. Good point,' Mason said. 'Y'know, there's a case study, a pocket population of pseudohermaphrodites – ninety of them, in a remote Dominican Republic fishing village – all descended on at least one side from the same great-great-great-grandmother. There was enough intermarrying among cousins that soon a lot of the marriages had parents who *both* carried copies of the defective gene.'

'So the effect multiplied with each generation.'

He nodded. 'As I recall, it was something like one pseudo-hermaphrodite among the founder's children, three among her grandchildren, fourteen among her great-grandchildren, twenty-something among her great-great-grandchildren, and forty-something among her great-great-great-grandchildren.'

'And that's what? Just six generations. Think how a genetic mutation could replicate over time in an isolated community like this one.'

'But remember, this is not a totally inbred gene pool,' Mason said. 'They do get a regular supply of imported genes from the Indian tribesmen.'

'True. But the gene cluster – as long as it's carried on the mother's side – would be dominant.'

'I see what you're saying.' He dragged a hand across his scalp of thick black ringlets. 'Given the time factor . . . five centuries.'

Mason looked at Tree with tremendous respect for her intelligence. He tended to engage a problem analytically and linearly, like taking a constellation apart to examine its individual stars, then reconnecting the dots one at a time. Tree, on the other hand, preferred to gather a problem's components into a whole pattern: one look at a smattering of stars and she made intuitive stabs at the big picture, the constellation, predicting stars not yet visible. She usually came out right and way ahead of him. Yet as a team they were stronger than either one alone.

Mason wondered if a true hermaphrodite would be alive to both halves of the human mind. He would love to meet such an integrated person.

'Tree, you're brilliant,' he said, nodding slowly. 'Yes, I believe a Lung-Hu could arise here.'

She nodded. 'So does everyone else in Prayer Mat of the Body. They await the birth of their savior.'

16

K'un-Chien lathered her hair with a cake of ginseng soap perfumed with jasmine oil; her wet mane poured over her shoulder and down past her waist like a long draft of shiny black syrup.

Steam clouds hung over the gushing head of the geothermal spring that heated the bathing pool. Tributaries from waterfall-fed springs snaked in and out of the rocky brooks and pools of the hot spring, mixing icy and scalding waters. By choosing pools closer to or farther from the geothermal vent, she could select among a range of bath temperatures.

The valley floor sloped gently toward the city, an hour's walk away, and the springs gushed and gurgled downhill, then spilled into canals that ducked under the stone walls and became a city-wide system of running fresh water, hot and cold, diverted into homes by bamboo pipes.

K'un-Chien's routine was to steep like a tea leaf in a pool just a grasshopper's flight from the hot vent, then, when her skin blushed bright red, to dash to one of the icy ponds and plunge in; just before she began to shiver, she'd return to the hot pool and ease into the steamy water, inch by inch.

If other bathers were nearby she wore a brief cotton loincloth to hide her nakedness. The loincloth drew no attention to her because most bathers in the springs wore them to protect themselves from sliverfish, a toothpick-sized parasite that would swim up any available orifice and then painfully anchor itself with its set of sharp spines. Because the sliverfish lived only in tepid ponds, and K'un-Chien bathed in water far too hot or cold for them, she was free to bathe nude if she was alone. In any case, she always kept a sarong lying close at hand so she could snatch it up and wrap it around her if anyone approached.

Today no other bathers were in sight. A mile away, a team of honey-gatherers dangled on rope ladders halfway down the Western Face: three torchbearers to smoke out the bees from their hives, and one to scoop the giant honeycombs into a woven bamboo-strip basket. K'un-Chien told herself that even a hawk would not be able to spy her nakedness from that distance; even so, she stayed wrapped in her sarong while moving between the pools.

For as early as she could remember, her father had told her to hide her body from all others. He'd warned that she must never let anyone find out who she was.

'The Lung-Hu cult is madness,' he'd said. 'If you truly care about the people of Prayer Mat of the Body, you'll understand that revealing your identity would destroy everything Ko T'ung Jen and your ancestors have built here, and ruin all the generations to come.'

The meaning of his words she could never erase: *Simply being what I am would ruin all the generations to come.* She'd kept her promise to her father. No one knew.

Now in the hot pool, the fragrant soap softened and rolled slickly over her high round breasts and the subtle curve of her muscular abdomen. How good the hot water felt, and how alive the touch of her own fingertips when she thought of Tree. In spite of the humid heat, goose-flesh stood out on her breasts and her nipples tightened. Her hands roamed over her full bosom and slid downward. She marveled at the tremendous rush of strength and desire that surged below her navel. And from that belly-center the force of life spread throughout her body and soul, infilling her womanhood and manhood to bursting. She felt as if she could shout and her spirit would be hurled up over the rim of the valley and halfway to the stars. Her whole spirit. Complete. Not just its feminine face.

Oh, Tree. Closing her eyes she sighed like windblown grass, dreaming in green.

Abruptly she opened her eyes and scanned her surroundings. *I must not let myself get swept away on the breeze of fantasy. It only worsens the aching.* A painful lump constricted her throat. *Tree does not want me. She flings darts at me from her eyes. Oh, how am I to bear my longing when it is not possible she could ever love me?*

Tears welled up with sudden despair, but she bit her lower lip and blinked them back. *I must strap a breastplate of armor over my heart, or I'll surely be found out.* Then she admitted to herself that in moments like this, when her loneliness became suffocating, she *wanted* to be found out, so that the pressure of her secret could be punctured at last.

She hung her head in shame. *K'un-Chien, you are a fool and a danger to your people.*

Cobalt ore deposits on the rocky floor of the pool made the clear water reflect purest green. The depth of its color did not help K'un-Chien to forget Tree Summerwood's eyes.

17

T ree and Mason strolled along the crowded thoroughfares of the bustling marketplace. K'un-Chien followed at a few paces. Tree stood a head above the dark-haired throng; only K'un-Chien and Mason came close to her height, with K'un-Chien a half-inch shorter than Mason.

A woman with a squealing piglet under each arm squeezed between them, weaving her way upstream against a river of pedestrians in multicolored robes and kimonos. Others toted shoulder yokes dangling buckets of goat's milk, or cages filled with chickens, guinea pigs or chinchillas; others balanced baskets on their heads heaped with grapes, mandarin oranges, papayas, guavas, or the pastel cocoons of mulberry silkworms; women dressed in drab black pajamas towed rickshaws carrying women dressed in lustrous embroidered silks with yellow orchids and gold combs adorning their black braids. One pair of giggling sisters, identical twins, stuffed into a single-seat rickshaw, craned their heads in unison to gawk and point at Mason and Tree. Each girl had a lilac-crowned Amazon parrot perched on her shoulder.

Jou P'u T'uan – Prayer Mat of the Body. Sunk in a volcanic valley atop an inaccessible mountain, the fifteenth-century city sustained itself in cloud-hidden solitude. No radios or televisions; no computers or fax machines; no beepers, no car phones – no cars. The distant granddaughters of the colonists of Ko T'ung Jen went about their lives here as if the imperial sun had never set on the Ming Dynasty.

Tree reflected on what she knew of China of that era. The word *Ming* was drawn with two characters, sun and moon. The Ming, last of the Chinese dynasties, was the brightest period in the Middle Kingdom's history, a time when culture flourished and China was centuries ahead of Europe in the fields of medicine, sea exploration, the arts and technology.

Even before the Ming emperors ruled China, while Europe was still sleeping off its Dark Ages, the Chinese had invented glass, porcelain, ink, paper, moveable type, silk-making, fabric dyeing, acupuncture, gunpowder, clocks, star charts and magnetic compasses. And the geometric principles of the right triangle had been discovered by the Chinese centuries before Pythagoras slaughtered two dozen oxen to thank Zeus for opening his eyes.

Then, in the late 1300s, when the Ming emperors drove the Mongols back beyond the Great Wall and founded their new capital in Beijing, Chinese arts and sciences reached their peak and Zheng He sailed outward on his seven voyages of discovery.

After the ripening comes the rot, Tree mused. Just after Admiral He's final voyage, China entered its own dark period of isolation and slumber. It became a crime punishable by death to build ocean-going junks. Tree guessed that naval captain Ko T'ung Jen foresaw the upcoming political withdrawal and cultural decline and set out on a well-planned secret mission with men and women of similar ideals to found a utopia in a new world. This lustrous city was their legacy.

Couples strolled arm in arm, false-bearded dragon-women with tiger-women. Some of them openly embraced and kissed. Tree was perpetually startled by the absence of males. All the roles she'd come to associate with men were performed here by women: soldier, hunter, butcher, guard, stonecutter, builder, laborer.

She smiled as an upper-class woman strolled by with two servants; the woman wore the most exquisite satin kimono Tree had ever seen: deep red and covered with embroidered white chrysanthemums highlighted with golden threads. Yet even in their plain black pajamas, the servant girls were just as pretty as their mistress; one of them had light gray Asian eyes.

Tree reminded herself for the third time that morning that her life was in very real danger and time was running out; for unless she forced her attention to return to this threat, the splendors and secrets of the city seduced her into a mood of wonder. She gazed at the panorama of towering pagodas, brass bells at each corner of their octagonal roofs; golden-domed stupas and temples brushed by silver wisps; the long waterfall like a billion beads of pearls against the redstone cliff. *Intoxicating.* Every day some new experience or discovery tempted her to forget her predicament and to give in to the city's magic.

Ling-Chih – the Mushroom of Immortality – a perfect example of something right out of an Oriental fairy tale. She glanced down at the inch-long pink bud of her thumb. Both joints had already developed and she could see the faint beginnings of a thumbnail. Tonight she'd ask K'un-Chien to apply a cold-sleep ant to give her relief from the constant itching of the rapidly growing tissue.

Tree glanced back at K'un-Chien, the un-plain beauty dressed in the plain frock. Enigma enshrouded Second Wife as surely as mists wrapped the cloud forest. Tree knew she mustn't forget her unsettling vision and the need to shield her heart against this exotic woman. She didn't allow K'un-Chien to call her by her name, as Mason did. Tree was First Wife. Their relationship must remain formal.

Her jealousy had not waned with time, but had swollen as K'un-Chien's and Mason's friendship grew. And to make matters worse, Tree couldn't help but like her. That kept the vicious wheel turning: jealousy, anger at herself for feeling jealous, obsessive struggling to *stop* feeling jealous, feeling low and thus more threatened by the teenage goddess, creating more jealousy and more self-reproach. Stir in to that evil mix the threat of being banished to the upper hell. Beat well.

Ugh. Tree put her hand on her belly. She was fairly certain she was getting an ulcer.

Guess I can always ask K'un-Chien to heal me. It was an ironic thought, but true.

She watched K'un-Chien gliding with slow easy strides through the crowd, long black hair like an artist's broad stroke down unbleached cotton.

Hsiang K'un-Chien, Perfume of Earth-Heaven. She was kind. That, above all, was her healer's gift. In spite of the disgrace and rejection that were her lot, women from around the city came to her in secret for medical treatment and K'un-Chien refused no one, not even those who in public insulted her to her face. Hidden from view, at the wellhead of those spring-blue eyes, Tree sensed in her a formidable strength.

Mason looked back. 'K'un-Chien,' he called. 'We are lost without you.'

K'un-Chien smiled and caught up. 'Yes, May-Son.'

After weeks of steady improvement Mason's vocabulary in Mandarin had abruptly broken through into fluency. Now he easily conversed with K'un-Chien as they stood at a stall that sold mushrooms of every description – big white puffballs, tiny inky caps, morels, oyster mushrooms, delicate branched shapes – many of which Tree had never seen, not even in botanical reference books. She wished she had her Nikon, or the talent to sketch like Audubon.

'. . . it's the mists,' Mason was saying. 'If fungi are good, they get to come here when they die.'

K'un-Chien knitted her brow. 'You make strange proverbs, May-Son. Many times I wonder if you are teasing me.'

Tree sighed. *If I were Mason, I think I'd be falling in love with her too.*

K'un-Chien pointed out a huge orange shelf fungus like a wheel of Cheddar cheese – the same species Tree had spotted on the rocky surface high above the valley.

'So, it *is* edible,' Tree said. The vendor was a white-haired woman whose face and neck were as creased with wrinkles as the gills of her mushrooms. Tree asked her for a sample of the orange fungus. The tender flesh tasted sweet like a baked yam, but left a sharp coppery aftertaste.

'How is it?' Mason asked.

Tree flicked her tongue around. 'Like sucking on a penny.'

'I'll pass.'

K'un-Chien noticed the tone of their words. 'Good. I don't like them either. They smell up the kitchen with a sweet stink when you cook them.'

The next two shops sold woven blankets of alpaca and guanaco wool and chinchilla fur. Then the trio approached a line of food stalls whose cuisines – sizzling, roasting, baking, stir-fried – filled the air with a strange mix of appetizing aromas.

At the first booth, brown, segmented ovals the size of brazil nuts were sizzling in a work in a splash of peanut oil. With oversized chopsticks an old woman stirred in chopped garlic, ginger and whole chili peppers.

Mason gave K'un-Chien an inquisitive look.

'Silkworm pupae,' K'un-Chien said.

The old cook smiled, teeth stained reddish-black from chewing betel-nuts. 'Would you care to try a sample?'

'Why not?' Mason said, and took a crispy fried silkworm pupa from the woman and nibbled on its shell. 'Ooo. They got like oily custard inside.'

'Gross,' Tree said.

'You thought Moonpies were gross until you tried one.'

'Mmm,' Tree said, 'and an ice-cold RC Cola with peanuts floating in it – you taught me to appreciate Southern white-trash cuisine.'

Mason popped the rest of the silkworm into his mouth and chewed and swallowed it. K'un-Chien and the old cook each ate one and spat the shells on the ground.

'Oops,' Mason said. 'Should've watched the experts first.'

At the next booth, a half-dozen tarantulas as big as tortillas were roasting over charcoals on an iron grill.

'Now *that* is a spider,' Tree said.

'Biggest in the world,' Mason said. 'They eat birds and mice.'

'I believe it.'

'Let's get one.'

'You're kidding, right?'

'Don't knock it till you've tried it. The Wawajeros eat them all the time. They're delicious.'

The vendor plopped a bulky brown spider onto a folded

banana leaf and passed it to Mason. He held his mouth close to its hairy limbs and puffed hard. The singed hairs flew off in a little cloud. He tore off a finger-sized leg from the abdomen, cracked the exoskeleton with his teeth, tugged out white meat and chewed with relish.

'You don't know what you're missing, Tree. How can I convince you to try it?'

He handed a fat spider leg to K'un-Chien. She cracked the delicate shell and munched pale flesh that looked like crab meat.

Tree stuck out her tongue in disgust.

'Come on,' Mason said. 'You told me you once tried dog and rat in Nanjing—'

'I didn't know it was a dog. I'd never knowingly eat a dog – poor thing.'

'Well, this is just a lowly spider, no one's pet. Just one taste.' He held out a jointed leg.

Tree took it from him and blew off the last of the stiff hairs. She hesitated. 'Tastes just like chicken, right?'

'Actually it tastes like rattlesnake.' He grinned, then stuffed another bite into his mouth.

Tree nibbled a teeny bite of spider meat. 'Huh. To me it tastes almost like shrimp.' She handed back the spider leg.

'What's the matter?' Mason asked.

'I don't like shrimp. Remember?'

'Oh, right. Forgot.'

Tree felt instantly hurt. She spun and stalked away. That Mason hadn't recalled that she disliked shrimp took on great meaning. *He's forgetting who I am. He doesn't really care about me. I was a romantic idiot to join the research project. Mason will never be mine again.*

Mason caught up. 'Are you upset?'

She walked faster. 'Course not. Why should I be upset?'

'C'mon, Tree. Don't play games.'

She whipped around to face him. 'Look, unless I get pregnant in the next couple months I'm gonna be banished to starve to death. Got any bright ideas how we might accomplish conception? Or would you rather focus on making your other wife pregnant?'

Mason glanced back at K'un-Chien. Apparently she'd not overheard Tree's angry tone.

'See?' Tree said. 'You're more worried about her feelings than mine.'

'She happens to live in a culture where ordinary put-downs like we might bant about can mean a traumatic loss of face.'

'Well, she doesn't speak English.'

'Okay, but let's not yell.'

Tree looked away, disgusted with herself but unable to control the outburst of her pent-up emotion. The three-month deadline to become pregnant had dwindled to nine weeks and Mason had not even tried to make love with her. 'Gee, I'd hate to cause a rift between you newlyweds. That's be a crying shame.'

Mason touched her shoulder and she shrugged off his hand, turned her back to him.

'Do you love her, Mason?' she whispered.

He stepped around to face her. 'What?'

'Are you falling in love with her?'

'I *like* her. I like her a lot. She's a remarkable person. Don't you think so?'

'Remember how you used to feel toward me – before Vietnam – do you love K'un-Chien that way now?'

Mason sighed, and swallowed. Tears welled up. 'I fell in love with you when I was still a boy. You were my Initiatress.' He gently raised her chin with his fingers. 'Tree, you escorted me into a world where love and pleasure bloom everywhere – like clover in sunny fields. How can I ever love another the way I loved you then?'

Tree was crying now, softly. 'But do you *feel* it now, or do you only remember the way it used to be?'

He sighed again, deeply. 'To be honest, I'd have to say I remember the way it was. What I feel now is mostly . . . I don't know . . . *blocked*. I don't feel . . .' his voice trailed off.

'Keep talking to me. It's so good just to hear you share yourself.'

'My heart . . . it feels . . . caved in . . . like desert sand into a pit.' He took a deep breath. 'But I still care about you, Tree. And I'll never love another the way I loved you then.'

She began to cry harder and put a hand over her eyes.

'Look. I've decided you're right,' he said. 'We do need to make you pregnant.'

She opened her wet eyes wide. 'You serious?'

'Tonight. We'll try tonight. I'll do my best.'

'Mason! That's what I've been waiting to hear.' She threw her arms around him. His muscles felt dense and warm and he smelled deliciously male, the fragrance of a seashore that had once been hers to roam. *Does this mean I stand a chance?*

'The timing couldn't be better,' she said. 'I felt a little pinch in my left side last night – that means I'm ovulating. Tonight could be the night. Oh, Mason, this could work.'

Mason dried her tears with the glossy green sleeve of his silk robe. They hugged again for a timeless moment, until Tree felt her chest rising and falling with his. Wrapped in strong arms, in the roundness of breath, the world felt whole again without sharp edges.

She drew her head back so she could look into his eyes. 'I never got the chance to tell you . . . first all our troubles . . . then the divorce . . .'

'I knew,' he said. 'You didn't have to spell it out.'

'You knew?'

'That you wanted to have a baby. You kept it inside, like a message in a bottle. But I knew how much you loved kids; I saw the way you melted around them. It's just that I was in no position to help. It seemed like clearing out of your life was the most generous gift I could offer you – your freedom to start over, start a family with someone new.'

She shook her head. 'Mason. I wanted *your* baby.'

He looked down. 'And I still may not be able to help you.'

K'un-Chien caught up to Mason and Tree. Her woven grass bag held two black eggs bigger than grapefruits.

Mason stared. 'Emu eggs?'

'Told you Zheng-He's fleet sailed all the way to Australia,' Tree said.

The trio strolled past food stalls offering armadillos, pangolins, and turtles cooked in their shells; soybean curd and fermented soybean paste; bamboo shoots; water chestnuts; litchi nuts; mangos; persimmons; pomegranates; bananas; manioc; breadfruit; sugarcane; vanilla, kola and cacao beans; lotus seeds, hearts of palm, cattails and water lilies; along with a dozen or more unfamilar fruits.

Tree bit through the purplish skin of a star-shaped fruit and puckered at its astringency. K'un-Chien laughed and shook her head. She showed Tree how to split open the rind and pop out the bright wet center of the pentangle with her thumb.

'One shining star for another,' K'un-Chien said, and tried to place the juicy core in Tree's mouth. Tree refused her and took it from her fingers. K'un-Chien hid her look of hurt by turning away to prepare another fruit. Tree felt surprised at how it bothered her to hurt K'un-Chien's feelings. *It can't be helped if I'm to keep a healthy distance between us.*

Tree bit down on the fruit and slurped up the juice that gushed over her tongue. 'Mmmm,' Tree told Mason. 'Tastes like your mom's honey lemonade.'

Mason closed his eyes and let K'un-Chien feed the fruit to him. '*Wow!*' With his finger he wiped the juice that started down his chin. 'Even sweeter. Where're the ice cubes?'

K'un-Chien gathered a couple dozen of the purple star fruit into her bag and paid the vendor.

Next they passed meat shops with dozens of chickens strung upside down in rows alongside headless pigs and goats; iridescent bottle flies walked in circles on sticky blood. Tree didn't recognize one skinned carcass until she noticed its three front toes and four hind toes: a tree sloth. Stacked bamboo cages contained live guinea pigs, chinchillas, hedgehogs, anteaters, mice, kinkajous and fruit bats, ready for butchering.

Nearby, three wooden tubs the size of laundry vats held live fish with scales as transparent as glass; their muscles and organs were visible inside them like pastel noodles in a kitchen jar. Tree gaped, fascinated, at acorn-sized red hearts beating.

'K'un-Chien, are these fish from the caves inside the mountain?'

'Yes, First Wife. That is why glass-fish have no eyes.'

A dark-skinned woman with betelnut-stained teeth scooped up a foot-long fish in a net and plopped it, flip-flopping, into the water of a customer's hinged-lid bucket. Then she sold another customer a thick glass salamander.

In the next stall, water boiled in a cast-iron cauldron. A black hand with long fingers drooped over the rim. Tree flinched, even though as a girl in Nanjing she'd often seen food vendors in open-air markets boiling monkeys.

'I'll never get used to that,' she told Mason. 'They look so human.'

'I'm with you. Spider monkey.' He cringed. 'Awful.'

Tree felt glad that K'un-Chien used mostly grains, vegetables, fruits and nuts in the meals she prepared for them. Tree was a big eater, but not big on cooking. Mason had his specialties, like chili, but when he'd offered to help K'un-Chien make the meals she'd been so flabbergasted and embarrassed he'd decided to leave the cooking to her. Each of her meals was delicious gourmet fare.

Tree patted her firm abdominal muscles below a thin cushion of fat. Mason used to tell her she had an irresistibly sexy belly. Luckily it was hard to gain weight on Chinese vegetarian cuisine.

K'un-Chien gathered in her shopping bag figs, sugar plums and rose apples, bael fruit and goa beans, tropical yams, tamarind and sweet palms. She paid for the groceries with brilliant scarlet pods called love-seeds, the size and shape of string beans. Vendors seemed to prefer seed pods to rice paper currency, and K'un-Chien's love-seeds were favored above all, so that she didn't need to spend as many as did other customers. Tree had noticed that any pod blotched with pink mold was worth dozens of smooth pods, and all of K'un-Chien's pods were fuzzy with the pink stuff.

Weeks ago Tree had asked K'un-Chien about the use of seed pods as money and she'd answered with downcast eyes, 'Their value becomes precious in Prayer Mat Temple.'

Mason had shrugged. 'No stranger than wampum,' he'd remarked, 'or beads or kowpie shells or dentalia, or any of the other things that cultures have used as money.'

But there had been a message hidden in K'un-Chien's shyness that bothered Tree in the same way her vision made her uneasy. She wondered if the seeds had something to do with sex; a sexual ritual maybe, was that what K'un-Chien had meant? Those low couches and pillows in the inner chamber of Prayer Mat Temple – in a city called Prayer Mat of the Body – she doubted the beds were used for ceremonial naps.

Were the love-seeds edible or only symbolic love-food? Perhaps they contained a potent hypnotic or aphrodisiac. If so, perhaps the love-seeds could help Mason get over his problem with impotence.

Tree reached for Mason's hand. His grip was firm and good. Her body remembered his weight pressing down, his strength and heat and man-smell, the taste of his mouth and skin. Her belly tightened and a hunger deepened at her core as she imagined the purpose of the couches in Prayer Mat Temple.

'What are they so interested in?' Mason asked K'un-Chien, pointing to a group of women squeezed in a huddle. The women chattered and shouted excitedly, waving fistfuls of rice-paper money.

'Gambling.'

'That much I figured. But what are they betting on?'

'On which *taotie* will win the battle.'

'*Taotie?*' Mason looked at Tree.

'Monster face,' Tree said, and shrugged.

'Let's look,' he said, and pressed forward at the edge of the throng. Tree peered over silk-clad shoulders. K'un-Chien stayed away.

A cage of thin bamboo strips sat on a tall stool. Inside the cage two beetles, each bigger than her hand, circled each other like insect gladiators. Antlers like those of stag beetles jutted above pincers that opened and snapped, *click-click, click-click*. A white and black pattern on the thorax looked like a snarling monster face with round black eyes as big as nickels; the real eyes were pinheads set on both sides of a beaked mouth. Their folded chitin wingcase refracted light as the combatants scrabbled about, bending colors through red, gold, green and blue. *Click-click, click-click, click-click, click-click.*

One beetle lunged and dug his antlers underneath its opponent's shiny abdomen, seeking leverage to upend it. Some of the spectators cheered, others groaned.

The attacking beetle backed the other into the bars of the

cage, where the retreating fighter gained traction and halted the onslaught. Then the dominant beetle spread orange wings and with a loud buzz hopped into the air, flipping its opponent onto its back. The hovering beetle dropped onto the fallen bug, pried its pincers into the crack between the thorax and head and twisted sharply. The head popped off and smacked the far side of the cage.

Cheers, laughter and groans from the crowd. Wads of money exchanged hands.

Tree felt sick to her stomach. When the three had walked on, she realized she was holding her hand to her neck.

K'un-Chien looked at her with a mysterious, gentle smile.

'What?' Tree said.

'First Wife has a tender heart,' K'un-Chien said. 'You don't like to witness war, not even between beetles. Nor do I.'

'Thai people set betta fish against each other,' Tree said, 'Mexicans fight roosters, Koreans fight dogs – it's awful.'

'Sorry,' Mason said, in English. 'I was curious. That's not a known beetle species.'

'Unknown to us, anyway,' Tree said. 'Lynda told me once that seventy-five percent of all the species on Earth are insects, and fifty percent of all insects species are beetles. Might just be a species you and I have never heard of.'

'Not in this case. I happen to know the Goliath beetle is the largest species recorded; they weigh three and half ounces each – a hundred grams – and I'm sure it would look puny in the cage next to those two bulldozers.'

'Then Lynda's dreams would've come true,' Tree said, and thought of their entomologist colleague from Venezuela, killed by the harpy. Sorrow and fear churned with her nausea in the unpleasant pool in her gut. 'I need to sit down and rest a minute,' she said.

She strolled over to the shade of a kapok tree and sagged down on one of its three-foot-tall roots. Mason sat beside her. K'un-Chien knelt in front of Tree and took her right hand. She squeezed hard on the muscular web between Tree's thumb and first finger.

'Ow,' Tree said, but she didn't withdraw her hand. K'un-Chien gazed at her with the sweetest mercy written over her features.

'God, they should send medical students to someone like her to study the high art of bedside manner,' Tree said to Mason.

Mason smiled at K'un-Chien. 'Her face looks to me now like one of Raphael's angels. The ones with golden light spilling out.'

A tingling current passed up through the nerves of Tree's arm and down into the pit of her stomach and the nausea began to subside.

'Amazing,' Tree said.

'It's called *Doh-In*,' K'un-Chien said.

Tree was familiar with the Chinese term. It meant precise finger pressure, like acupuncture without needles. In a few more minutes, her sickness was completely gone.

'My father once took me to a doctor in Nanjing who practiced Doh-In,' Tree said, looking at the red spot on her hand where K'un-Chien had pressed. 'He cured my chronic headache problem, but no one ever explained to me how it works.'

K'un-Chien bowed. 'Allow me to try, First Wife.'

'Yes, please do.'

'There are subtle rivers of energy that flow along pathways throughout the body,' K'un-Chien said. 'If a pathway is disturbed or blocked, the energy is compressed or obstructed.' She contracted her hand into a fist. 'Pain results.

'By massaging certain key points, called *tsubos* – gateways – along the energy paths, one can reopen those channels, restoring harmony or natural flow to the whole system.' She relaxed her fist and danced her slender fingers like water. 'Pain erased.'

'That's fascinating,' Mason said. 'Wish I had learned that in medical school.'

K'un-Chien beamed at them with sapphire eyes. 'I would be delighted to teach you all that I know, May-Son.'

Mason grinned. 'Then I am your eager apprentice.'

Tree smiled too, and found it harder to renew her inner resistance to K'un-Chien. Second Wife was like the city itself: too lovely.

Tree closed her eyes. *Is it really possible I could fall in love with a woman?* She honestly didn't know. She told herself the question was irrelevant, because K'un Chien was not who she wanted to love. *I want to be with Mason.*

She remembered how, at K'un-Chien's age, she gave her heart away as easily and completely. But it had proved to be a perilous, crazy business. When Mason walked out of her life, she had felt as if her heart had been lost to her, trapped outside of her own center, bound to his distant life.

In the past few weeks, she'd begun to realize that she might not be able to win back the man she loved. His problems were deeply, privately, his own. That bit of honesty had left her feeling emptier than ever.

But now, opening her eyes again and taking in K'un-Chien's kindness, a hope arose in Tree that she might regain something more central than her love for Mason – her own wholeness, her light. The way she had once loved the world, perhaps naively – but deeply and truly – before she'd learned to hold back.

In the blue sky of K'un-Chien's eyes, Tree saw the world that way again.

It's not Mason, after all. It's me. I'm really here to find Tree Summerwood.

That insight gave her more courage than she'd felt in years.

18

Beyond the din of the marketplace Mason could hear again the white hum of the distant waterfall. Ahead, the brick sidewalk branched in several directions. One colonnade led back to Mason's and Tree's palatial residence.

The square ground floor of the small palace upheld a roof of bright blue ceramic pantiles that peaked and dipped like waves; atop that glazed sea, the second storey was round, with a cone-shaped roof of red tiles; a third roof, like a bright yellow parasol, crowned the cone, and twenty-foot-long rainbow ribbons fluttered from its tip in the breeze that spilled down the surrounding cliffs.

The three companions arrived at the round front door. Its lower leaf was solid mahogany to chest height; above it, delicate openwork woodcuts of goldfish swam among lotus pads.

K'un-Chien paused at the door. 'With your permission, May-Son, I would like to go visit my brother now,' she said. 'I can be home in the evening, Husband, to prepare your supper.'

'K'un-Chien, you do not need my permission,' Mason said. 'You are free.' He smiled. 'Do you understand? You are not my slave, or even my servant – you are . . . well, as it happens, you are my wife. But that does not mean I *own* you.'

K'un-Chien cast her gaze to her feet and said in a small voice, 'Do I not please you, May-Son?'

'Of course you do. I hope you have not misunderstood what I am trying to tell you.'

'If a husband does not own his wife,' K'un-Chien said, 'who does she belong to?'

'To the Earth . . . to life. To your own heart.'

Her voice trembled. 'Before you chose me, May-Son, I belonged to none but my loneliness. I was an outcast. It is good to belong to you and First Wife. Please do not say – her voice broke – 'you . . . do . . . not . . . own me.'

K'un-Chien lifted her hands to her face and wept. Mason and Tree stepped forward and wrapped their arms around her. 'Shhhhh,' Mason said. 'Of course you belong to us. Friends belong to each other.' He kissed her forehead. Her hair smelled like jasmine flowers

Tree combed loose black strands from K'un-Chien's face. 'Mason did not mean to say he rejects you—'

'Not at all,' Mason said.

'Nor do I,' Tree said. 'Perhaps I have been too formal with you . . . The fact is, I am grateful for what you have done for me.'

'First Wife has not been too formal,' K'un-Chien said. 'You have been most gracious.'

'K'un-Chien, you *are* mine,' Mason said. 'And I am yours. So I want you to feel completely free around me. Around us.'

K'un-Chien broke off from their embrace and bowed low. 'Thank you, May-Son, First Wife. With your permission, I will do my very best to feel free.'

Mason looked at Tree and sighed. 'Can you help me get across what I mean?'

'K'un-Chien, Mason is simply saying he does not want to constrain you or command you, to be your master. In Mason's view, we are as free to come and go as he is. You don't *need* his permission.'

K'un-Chien's brow furrowed. 'But . . . he is a man, and he is older than us . . . and we are his wives. Would he pay us the same honor he pays his parents?'

'Ha. My mom and dad would howl at that one,' Mason said in English. 'Remember how we knocked heads?'

'Don't confuse the poor girl,' Tree said.

111

Mason said to K'un-Chien, 'I confer to you the same honor I would grant any true friend.'

Tree nodded. 'Please accept our companionship,' she said, 'as an equal.'

K'un-Chien shook her head but a smile tugged at the corners of her mouth. 'Such strange ideas from you two.'

'It is because we are but uneducated barbarians,' Mason said. 'We were not raised in the etiquette of *K'ung Fu-Tse*.' He used the Mandarin pronunciation of Confucius.

Gib had once explained to him the rigid social hierarchy of ancient China, established by Confucius twenty-five hundred years ago. Confucius had decreed the proper manner for all family and society members to interact. He'd even gone so far as to classify strictly the suitable ways to feel affection: a certain degree of love was appropriate for a pet, a different degree permitted for a daughter, another for a son, an elder brother, younger brother, father, mother, and so on. To feel or show affection outside of those inflexible bounds was disgraceful, the philosopher wrote, and would cause the harmonic social order to collapse into chaos. His prescription for an ideal society: 'All under heaven, carriages have the same track, books the same script, and behavior the same ethics.'

America had been built on an antithetical vision: 'All the past we leave behind,' Walt Whitman insisted. Americans had always celebrated their nation as a land of opportunity, where droves of immigrants had changed their names, stations and destinies, remaking themselves without a backward glance. In America few people could trace their own lineage past a double set of grandparents, and few cared. By contrast, the ancient Chinese emphasized continuity and literally worshipped heritage – they strove to emulate the greatest, and the greatest was always *prior* – the golden age of the ancestors.

Mason smiled at K'un-Chien. 'Perhaps our unschooled behavior, while inappropriate, could be more spontaneous, more fun?'

K'un-Chien's smile now spread over her features. 'Yes, May-Son. Odd. But, I think, perhaps much more fun.'

'And now, with *your* consent,' Mason said, 'I would like to go with you to meet your brother.'

K'un-Chien's eyes widened.

'If you prefer to go alone . . .'

'No, no,' K'un-Chien said. 'I would very much like you to come with me. And I know Meng Po would be delighted to meet you both.' She nodded to Tree. 'He gets very lonely.'

'I do not doubt it,' Mason said. 'It is beginning to bug me not seeing any other men in this city.'

'You have lice?' K'un-Chien asked. 'I can treat that with an herbal powder.'

Tree laughed. 'No, "it bugs him" means "it disturbs him."'

Mason chuckled. 'I keep forgetting, idioms don't always translate.'

'It would be my pleasure to go with you to meet your brother,' Tree said.

'Good. Lead the way, K'un-Chien,' Mason said.

'*Lead?*' K'un-Chien shook her head again. 'Very strange.' She turned in the direction of her brother's residence and Tree and Mason walked after her.

After a few minutes, K'un-Chien paused and turned back to Mason. 'May-Son, thank you so much.'

'For what?'

'For asking my consent to accompany me to visit my brother. Before today – before you – no one has ever asked me for my permission to do anything.'

He shrugged. 'That is the way friends treat each other. It seems only natural that you and everyone else should deserve a say in what affects them.'

'Here it is most *un*natural to think that way,' K'un-Chien said. 'Even forbidden.'

'She's right,' Tree said, in English. 'For everybody's sake, Mason, let's keep our little social revolution secret. *Si fueris Romae, Romano vivito more.*'

Mason knew Tree was right. *If you are at Rome, live in the Roman custom.* 'In private, K'un-Chien, let us live freely. In public, we had better obey the norms of your society.'

'Yes, May-Son,' K'un-Chien said, and seemed relieved as she stepped several paces behind them.

They walked on and arrived at a half-moon bridge that crossed a gushing stream. On the far side a brick path led to a trefoil archway in a domed building. The little temple resembled an inverted turnip dipped in gold.

'Where rutabagas go to pray,' Mason whispered to Tree.

Straddling the archway stood a thirty-foot-tall statue of a wrathful female warrior in an armored breastplate and skirt, her head ignited in a halo of stylized flames, one giant granite fist raised to smash intruders. Alongside each colossal sandal an in-the-flesh female soldier stood guard. Their lances flashed down, crisscrossing the entrance while their eyes tracked the approaching trio. K'un-Chien raised her open palms toward the guards and glanced at Mason and Tree who followed her example.

'Greetings,' K'un-Chien said, and halted. 'I have brought the barbarian guests to visit my brother.'

One guard nodded. 'Approach.'

The guards withdrew their lances and the three visitors passed beneath the stone giantess. Mason glanced up under the skirt at the titan's crotch. Tree poked an elbow into his ribs. A carved granite cloth girded the Amazon's loins.

Pale jade pillars the color of green tea upheld the high-vaulted ceilings in the open room. At the room's center sat what looked to Mason like a giant gilded canary cage. Guards stood watch at each corner. Behind the vertical golden bars a Chinese boy in yellow satin pajamas and red silk shoes crouched on hands and knees atop a long paper scroll, carefully painting calligraphy with a long-handled brush.

Squatting next to the boy, daubing fat scribbles on its own scroll, was the most beautiful primate Mason had ever seen. Mason glanced at Tree. She was staring at the creature, enraptured.

Short cinnamon-reddish fur covered the tomcat-sized creature except for its face of bare black skin and its head festooned with bushy white hair. The exaggerated size and slight protrusion of its bright amber eyes made it look comical, like lemurs and bush babies, as if it were in a perpetual state of amazement. A drooping white mustache and beard ran together into a blaze of white fur on its throat and chest.

An undiscovered species, Mason was certain. Maybe a new lemur, although it lacked that family's bushy tail. Or maybe a cousin of the golden lion tamarin monkey, although, again, no tail. Mostly, it looked to him like a cross between an old Chinese sage and one of the liquid-eyed kids painted in Tijuana who haunt from the walls of tacky motel rooms.

'Little Brother, I have brought you visitors,' K'un-Chien said.

The boy looked up and his jaw dropped. He set down his paintbrush on a tortoise shell holder and waved them closer, smiling broadly. 'Welcome, welcome.'

K'un-Chien introduced the three and they bowed to each other.

'I have heard much about you and wanted very much to meet you,' Meng Po said, 'but I did not think I would be blessed with a visit so soon.'

Meng Po motioned to a couch with butterflies and hibiscus embroidered on its cushions; his visitors sat. The boy tugged a mahogany stool close to the bars and straddled it. He reached back. 'Kiki!'

The pretty animal plopped down its brush on the scroll, scampered over and climbed up to perch on Meng Po's shoulder.

Meng Po and his pet looked Mason up and down. Mason read the same innocence in the boy's wide black eyes as in the amber gaze of his furry companion.

'You are male,' Meng Po said, 'As I am.'

'Yes, we are a fraternity of two.'

'Ah, you speak the human language,' Meng Po slapped his knees. 'So I had heard. Good, good. There is so much I want to ask you about your faraway world.' He bounced in his seat. 'This is a great day.'

Mason smiled back. 'After drifting in a sea of women, I am relieved to meet another man, however young.' As the words came out of his mouth he wondered how it must feel to be an eleven-year-old boy who has rarely, if ever, seen another male. Who are the kid's role models? Aunt Cherry Blossom? Cousin Moon Blood? Who tackles and wrestles and gets tough with him? He felt sorry for the little guy.

Meng Po studied Tree. 'I have, of course, been told of your extraordinary looks,' he said. 'They said your eyes were crystal-green like topaz, with hair the color of sunlight through

115

honey. But now I see these words capture your beauty no better than a net draws water.'

'Well, thank you,' Tree said, blushing slightly. 'I have never received such a lyrical compliment.'

The lemur-like creature climbed down off the boy's shoulder and scampered across the cage to a flowering jasmine shrub potted in a Ming-style porcelain urn. Mason watched, fascinated, as it snipped off four fragrant yellow blooms with its sharp incisors and hurried back to its perch on Meng Po. Then the monkey stretched its long slender arm through the gilded bars, offering the blossoms to Tree. It blinked amber eyes the size of tangerines.

Meng Po ran his fingers through the tuft of white hair. 'Kiki wants to give flowers to a garden.'

Tree laughed and took the jasmine blossoms. 'Thank you, Kiki. Oh, you're so sweet, you're a little doll, aren't you?'

The creature turned around three times on Meng Po's shoulder and clapped its long fingers together.

'He likes you,' Meng Po said. 'He is rarely this forward with visitors. Only toward K'un-Chien have I seen him act so friendly.'

'Tree adores animals,' Mason said. 'Maybe Kiki knows that. Is it a "he"?'

Meng Po reached up and parted soft fur with his fingers, exposing the creature's maleness. 'Thank the ancestors,' he said. 'It is good to have one male friend.'

'What do you call the species?' Tree asked.

'*Jindaoki* – sage-monkey.'

'Ha. That is exactly what I would have called it,' Mason said. 'Kiki looks to me like a little old Chinese wise man.'

Meng Po smiled. 'His father's name was Lao Tzu and his mother was Guan Yin, so you see that others agree with you.'

The sage-monkey picked up a short bamboo staff, rested it on his shoulder as if it were a lance, and began strutting stiffly around his barred domain. Mason stared in astonishment.

Meng Po laughed. 'See, now he performs for your attention – he imitates the Captain of the Guards.'

Mason whistled low. 'Where I am from no one has ever seen such a creature – nor even heard of it.'

'No sage-monkeys?' Meng Po said. 'How colorless my world would be without my sweet Kiki.' The boy spread his arms and the little ape dropped the stick, bounded over and leapt into his embrace. 'He is my friend and confidante. When I am Emperor, I will make him my Minister of Play.' He kissed the bare black skin on the sage-monkey's cheek. 'Are we not like brothers, Kiki?' The animal chattered, flashing sharp white teeth, and kissed him back.

'He seems wonderfully intelligent,' Tree said. 'I know of no other ape, not even a chimpanzee, that is as smart as yours.'

'*Chimp-an-zee?*'

'A tailless ape, like Kiki, from a land called Africa,' Mason said. 'Because our people do not know about sage-monkeys, chimpanzees are regarded as the most intelligent of all the apes. I now think we've been wrong all this time.'

'Mason, look – those are fingernails, not claws,' Tree said in English.

'I noticed,' he said. 'Pottos and lorises have fingernails – and they also don't have tails. Could it be an unknown species of loris or potto?'

She shrugged. 'Beats me. He's just so beautiful. I can't get over how much he looks like a little man with a long white beard.'

'I wonder if Domino has come across these guys yet. He'll go nuts. This would be a major discovery for him – career-making.'

'Domino's probably too busy with his harem to play the zoologist,' Mason said. '*Sixty* wives.'

Meng Po cocked an ear toward their alien tongue. 'Your language sounds very gruff,' he said. 'As if you are speaking from your guts.'

Mason chuckled. To the Chinese ear, the Germanic-Viking tones of English must sound surprisingly harsh. Mandarin, like all Oriental tongues, was a tonal language in which pitch itself carried meaning, so that a single word might express a half-dozen different things depending on the way one bent the vowel sounds.

'I agree,' Mason said. 'Chinese is much more sing-song.'

'Little Brother, did you finish your scroll?' K'un-Chien asked.

'Almost. This will be the longest and my best.'

'What is it about?' Mason said.

'It is a book of poetry,' Meng Po said. 'Do they enjoy poetry in the land from which you came?'

Mason glanced at Tree. 'We two like poetry very much.'

'Give us a poem, Little Brother,' K'un-Chien said.

'It would be my delight.' Meng Po cleared his throat, closed his eyes, and spoke in a slow, melodic tenor voice:

> *Moonlight through gold bars*
> *Stripes this body dark and light*
> *Boy with tiger dreams*

'Lovely,' Tree said. 'Haiku.'

'So barbarians know of haiku?' Meng Po said. 'It came to the Middle Kingdom from across the sea, from the Land of the Rising Sun.'

'Some of us know haiku. Five syllables for the first line, seven for the second and five again for the third.'

Meng Po grinned and applauded and Kiki stood and clapped his hands and turned three circles. 'Excellent. Please make one for me.'

Tree put her hand on Mason's knee. 'Here is the poet.'

'All right,' Mason said. 'I've got a haiku for you.' He recited:

> *Butterfly arrives*
> *No written invitation*
> *White lotus blossom*

'Ahhh,' Meng Po said, with eyes closed. 'Very fine. Let us trade again.'

> *Squatting on dead leaves*
> *Saffron robe hoisted to waist*
> *Pooping Buddhist monk*

'I see you've got a sense of humor,' Mason said, and recited:

> *A crowded ferry*
> *Passengers smell a bad fart*
> *Only I know whose*

Meng Po giggled. 'This is fun,' he said. 'The guards sometimes trade haiku with me if I plead long enough, but their haiku is as weak as third-time tea.'

'I've always enjoyed playing with words,' Mason said. 'But I certainly wasn't as adept as you when I was eleven.'

'A fellow poet honors me.' Meng Po said, and dipped his head. 'Now I would like to pay honor to your lovely First Wife.'

Tree smiled and nodded. 'By all means.'

> *Sly kitten eyebrows*
> *Are they secretly stalking*
> *Your bright goldfish hair?*

'Ooh, I like that,' Tree said. 'Nice.'

Mason was astounded. 'You composed that just now, in your head?'

Meng Po grinned. 'Of course, as with the others. Haiku is intended to be spontaneous.' He arched one fine black brow over an almond-shaped eye. 'You mean your poems—?'

Mason blushed. 'I . . . uh . . .'

'Oh, I see,' Meng Po said, and frowned.

'Looks as if you lost the haiku contest, Mason,' Tree said.

Meng Po's shoulders shook and then he burst out laughing. 'I am only teasing you.'

'So you did not make up your poems just now?' Mason asked.

'Actually, I did. But I was only teasing about being disappointed with you. Though it is memorized, I think your haiku is quite good – for a barbarian.' He smiled. 'Please tell me another.' He closed his eyes and waited.

Mason recited:

> *A vast empty beach*
> *Who sees the lonely starfish*
> *Giving directions?*

'Ah. The best one yet.' Meng Po opened his eyes. 'I like poems about loneliness. Somehow they make it a little easier to bear. But may I ask one question?'

'You mean two questions. You have just now asked one.'

Meng Po chuckled. 'Yes. Two questions. You also can tease.'

Mason nodded. 'Ask me.'

'What is a starfish?'

'Oh, yes, I forgot that you have never been to an ocean.'

'Brother-In-Law,' Meng Po said, glancing around his square-edged world, 'from the age of five, I have not been outside this cage.'

Tree and Mason exchanged looks. 'Surely it is not what you have chosen?' she said.

'A child is not given choices,' Meng Po said.

'That seems sad,' Tree said.

'If you study the great poets, you will find that sadness inspired some of their best haiku,' Meng Po said. 'Allow me to compose a poem now to commemorate this very moment's bloom of sorrow.' He shut his eyes and gently stroked Kiki's white beard. Then he recited:

> *Quickly fading rose*
> *Petals drop into my palm*
> *Slowly fading hand*

Mason guessed that after Meng Po's brothers died he'd been imprisoned like a zoo specimen to keep him safe from harm until he reached manhood. He wanted to talk to the boy about it, but he sensed it was a touchy subject. He liked Meng Po. He planned to come back and visit again soon, trade more haiku. Maybe then he could ask the precocious kid more about the way of life in Prayer Mat of the Body.

Kiki vocalized a noise that sounded like a child trying to pronounce the Mandarin word for candy – *bingtang*. He held out his little black hands.

Mason raised his eyebrows. 'Did he just say what I thought he said?'

'Oh, he begs for food all the time. Pudgy little buddha.' Meng Po's fingers combed the white fur that hung like a beard and blended into a flash of brilliant white on Kiki's cinnamon chest. He tickled the sage-monkey's round belly.

'Bingtang,' Kiki said, 'bingtang, bingtang.'

Tree's jaw hung slack.

'That . . . is incredible,' Mason said.

Meng Po knit his brow. 'That he likes treats?'

'*He can talk!*' Tree blurted.

'A chimp-an-zee cannot talk?'

Tree simply shook her head, eyes wide with astonishment.

'Chimpanzees don't have the necessary vocal equipment to talk,' Mason said. 'The tongue muscles, the structure of the voice box . . . Researchers are trying to teach chimps to communicate with sign language. But this is unheard of.'

Meng Po smiled. 'Kiki, say hello to our new friend, May-Son. Listen, Kiki: *May*-Son. *May*-Son.'

The sage-monkey came close to the bars and reached his slender hand through. Mason took it with a huge grin on his face. 'You're the Einstein of primates, little fella,' he said in English.

'Kiki, watch my lips,' Meng Po said. The boy pressed his lips together and exaggerated the pronunciation of the *M*: 'Mmmmmmaaay-Son. Mmmmmmaaay-Son. May-Son.'

The animal pressed its lips together and made the *M* sound: 'Mmmmmmmm.'

'Wow!' Mason said. 'Fantastic!'

'Mmmmmm-mmmmm-mmmmmmaaaay-son,' Kiki said.

Mason and Tree jumped to their feet. 'No way!' they said together.

Meng Po laughed. Kiki screeched and did a couple pirouettes.

'Mmmmmmaaay-son. Mmmmaay-son,' the monkey said.

'Kiki, say hello to Tree.' Meng Po sounded out the phonemes: 'Ta-rrr-eee. *Tree*.'

The sage-monkey said, 'Ta-rrreee. Trrreeee. Trrreeeeeeeee.'

Tree slapped Mason on the back and they both laughed out loud. 'I can't believe this,' she said.

'Mmmay-son, Trrreeeee,' Kiki said. 'Bingtang.' He held out his hands.

'Here, give him one of these,' Meng Po said, and reached into a lacquer box and handed Mason a small raisin cookie. 'He loves rewards when he has done well.'

'Kiki, you deserve the whole bakery,' Mason said, reaching out with the cookie. The sage-monkey plucked the treat from Mason's big hand with slender black fingers.

Tree stepped closer to the cage. 'You are just the sweetest, cutest, smartest little monkey in the world,' she cooed. 'Aren't you, Kiki?' She reached through the bars and stroked the soft cinnamon fur of his back.

Kiki raised his head of tufted white hair and gazed at Tree with intelligent amber eyes. Its droopy white mustache crinkled as it sniffed her, black nostrils flaring.

Then it did something no animal could be trained to do. It gave Tree a loving smile that until that moment Mason would only have described as human.

19

Tree and Mason eased down into the deep hot water of the spa, sighing together, 'Oooo-ahhhhhhh.'

Round open windows ringed the high domed ceiling of the circular bathhouse at the rear of the palace. The windows held no screens, but at this altitude there were no mosquitoes. Beyond each portal stars winked through rips in the gauze that veiled a moonless nightsky. Palm-oil lamps lit the nude couple in soft flickering yellows and golds, perfuming the humid air.

Steaming water spewed from the mouth of a polished brass fish; a second metal fish spat a stream of icy water into the oval bath. Tree twisted the dorsal fins on the spigots and shut off the water. She turned to Mason and smiled. He made a crooked smile, looking painfully nervous.

'Relax.' She touched his hand. 'We were friends before we became lovers. We've made this passage before.' Her breasts bobbed in the water as she slid forward and wrapped her arms around him. 'I don't just love you, Mason,' she whispered in his ear. 'I *like* you. You'll always be my friend, first. That's important.'

He swallowed hard. She reached her right hand up and began to massage his shoulders and neck. 'Babe, it's okay,' she said. 'We'll just do our best. It doesn't hurt to try.'

His strong hands glided over the twin slopes of her back,

fingers caressing the contours of each vertebra, massaging the little pockets of tension.

'Mmmm,' she said, 'your hands always know where to go. It feels so good just to touch like this again.'

The two embraced and said nothing for a long while. The palm-oil lamps slowly burned their fragrant fuel while the hot soak and massage worked a healing magic. Tree could feel Mason's armor melting like solder. She began to kiss the side of his neck. A light salty sweat dampened his skin. Tree closed her eyes. 'God, it feels so right to kiss you. I was born to kiss you.'

Her kisses traced up his neckline until her mouth found its way home to his mouth, his sweet breath. Lips parted like petals and tongues played like hungry bees. Steam rose off the bath wetting the air, its hot breath mixing with their own.

She bent her head and kissed the soaked fur on Mason's chest.

'Tree . . .'

'Shhhhh. It's okay. Just be with me. Stay with the moment.'

Her tongue painted circles over his nipples until they swelled and hardened like red kernels of Indian corn. She pressed forward and rubbed her own taut nipples against his. The sensation of satin on satin made her shudder with pleasure.

'Tree, I'm not sure . . .'

'Hush.' She put a finger to his lips, then replaced the finger with her mouth, brushing his lips gently, gently – then pressing his mouth hungrily. Tasting. Savoring.

A tower of flesh rose between his legs.

'See?' she said. 'You *can* do it, lover.'

With her hands on his hips she urged him up out of the water until he sat on the bath's tiled ledge. He had never looked so big and thick, vein-rippled, to her. Her fingers caressed him as she lowered her mouth. Hot. Pulsing. She worked witchcraft with her lips and tongue and fingers. He danced lightly, under her spell.

Even standing in the water she felt slick between her thighs. 'I need you inside me.' She stepped up the bath stairs, took his hand and led him to a wide couch.

She pushed him firmly onto his back and held him down

by his broad shoulders, glaring into his gray eyes with the fury of her desire and intent. Water droplets splashed on his deeply muscled chest. She swung a leg over him and a string of clear lubricant dripped from her onto his rigid shaft. She eased herself down; the sweetest moan escaped her throat.

Her belly tightened as her inner walls clutched at what they wanted so badly. At the bottom of each slow-motion plunge their hair meshed – apricot and coal – and she sank her weight onto his pubic bone. 'God yes,' she said. 'Fill me up, I don't care if you bruise me. Just don't stop. I've been hungry so long . . .'

Abruptly he began to go limp.

'Babe, it's okay,' she said, and bent forward and kissed his lips. 'Feel the pleasure, forget everything but pure sensation.'

He continued to shrink like a leaky balloon. 'I'm . . . I'm sorry.'

'Don't talk. Don't talk.' She lowered her mouth onto his shaft again and her hair fell forward over his corrugated abdomen. He no longer felt heavy in her mouth, but hollow. She did her best magick, but he kept fading until he was soft as gel.

Mason put his hand over his eyes. 'Tree, I just can't . . . When I get close to you, you know – like this – so much sadness wells up in me I feel like I'm going to drown. Sex becomes the last thing on my mind.' His face had grown pale. 'I'm drowning, Tree. I can't breathe.'

Tree turned to sit on the side of the couch. 'But why? Why sadness now? We love each other, don't we?'

'Gib—'

'Gib is *dead*. I loved him too – he was my brother, Mason, my *brother*. I still love him, I miss him. But I've let him go. Why can't you release him? He wouldn't want you to grieve like this over him, not for all these years. He'd hate that. If Gib were here right now he'd kick your ass.'

Mason lowered his head, shaking it slowly. 'You don't know what happened,' he whispered hoarsely.

'I don't care what happened. That was then – a goddam war. This is *now*.'

He sighed and flopped his head into both hands.

Tree grabbed his chin and forcefully tilted it up to her face and mashed her lips against his. When Mason broke off the kiss, Tree pounded his chest with her fists. 'Make love with me. I need you now. Don't waste your soul on the past.'

Mason began to choke and gasp like an asthmatic. 'Move. Let me up. I can't breathe.' He pushed past her and stumbled out the door of the bathhouse that connected with the palace.

Tree stood up and stamped her foot and screamed.

'*I'd* be glad to make love to you, Tree. Been wanting to since I first laid eyes on you.'

She spun around and saw Domino Cruz in the other doorway of the bathhouse. Tree stood speechless. Domino stepped inside and a dozen teenage women in tiger robes followed behind. He wore a blue robe with a green dragon emblazoned on the chest, highlighted with gold and silver threads. From one pierced earlobe hung a gold chili pepper, and from around his neck dangled a *figa* – a fist with a thumb poking through the closed fingers, a Latin fertility symbol representing the penis penetrating the labia. Domino stood four inches shorter than Tree, but he was heavyset and muscular, with a square head, thick neck and a huge black mustache that drooped beneath a Mayan nose.

Tree snapped out of her shock and reached down and wrapped her kimono around her. 'How long you been standing there?'

'The door was wide open, amiga.'

'You didn't answer my question.'

'It's wonderful to see you, too, Tree.'

'What the hell. You scared me. What were you doing, spying on us?'

'Entirely unintentional, believe me. I apologize. But the fact is, I found out you've got trouble.'

'That's between Mason and me. Please honor our privacy in this.'

Domino held up his hands. 'Of course. Who am I to butt into your personal affairs?' He stepped over to the spa and peered down at the clear water. 'Nice. Real nice. I got one just as swank in my own palace.' He chuckled. 'Hey, how you like this little town?'

'We're trying to figure out how to get out as soon as possible.

Have you heard anything about a route that leads down through the mountain to the jungle?'

'*Mierde*. I'm not in such a hurry to leave. I'm like a god here.' He spread his arms toward his harem. 'This is a paradise for anyone with balls.' His black eyes narrowed. 'That's why Mason wants to get out, isn't it? He can't perform like a man. Servants have eyes; word is that he hasn't bedded you or the other one.'

Tree felt her face flush hot. 'Mason is more manly than anyone I've ever met, and that especially goes for machismo creeps like you.'

Domino's eyes flashed back at hers. 'Don't be so quick to insult me, amiga. Remember, I don't need you, but you most definitely need me.'

'For what? To borrow your earring?'

'As if I have to spell it out for you. Mason can't get it up. You need me to get pregnant. The only other male in this city is eleven years old.' He grabbed one of his consorts by the arm and dragged her forward. Her white robe bulged softly around her belly. 'Look. I've already made eighteen of my wives pregnant. *Eighteen*.'

'Just go,' Tree said. 'Go make some more girls pregnant. I'm not interested.'

He stepped forward. 'I wasn't exaggerating when I said I'm like a god here. I have the power to get anything I want. And I've been wanting you since Canaima.' He smiled through this thick mustache. 'Perhaps we should begin the beguine?'

She shoved him hard as he reached for her kimono sash, but he had more than a hundred extra pounds on her and he kept coming. She backed up until she bumped the couch. 'I told you,' she hissed. 'Not interested.'

He stopped, still smiling confidently. 'Think it through, Tree. Come on. Why delay the inevitable?'

K'un-Chien appeared in the doorway with a bow. The yew wood was bent in a deep C, bowstring to her nose, arrow tip pointing directly at Domino's chest. Her forearm rippled. The bow did not waver. Domino's harem stood transfixed, horror etching their adolescent faces.

'You are not welcome here,' K'un-Chien said in a low, even

voice. 'First Wife wants you to leave. Please do so. Immediately.'

Domino stepped back from Tree. 'Wait. Tell her I don't speak
chink too good.'

Tree smiled coldly. 'You speak bow-and-arrow?'

'Yeah, yeah. I'm outta here.' He spun and headed for the
bathhouse door trailing his harem. In the doorway, he stopped
and faced Tree.

'The way I see it, your time is running out. When the clock
ticks down near zero, you'll have to come and ask me to fuck
you. I'll think about it then. Maybe if you beg me, or pay
me . . .'

'*Get out!*' Tree yelled.

Domino turned around and left.

K'un-Chien lowered her bow and her eyes met Tree's. Nothing
shy or meek about the woman now. For Tree, it was like gazing
into bright, fearless masculine eyes.

Tree turned her back on K'un-Chien, breaking the powerful
current that surged between them. She slumped onto the edge
of the couch, dropped her head in her hands and sobbed.

Everything was going wrong and time was slipping away.
Mason couldn't make love to her. Domino – the pig – was
right: she *did* need his services in order to get pregnant. And
despite all emotional resistance to it, her disturbing vision of a
sexual bond with K'un-Chien was, mysteriously, coming true.

20

M ason knelt on the wooden floor practicing calligraphy strokes with a long brush on a silk paper scroll.

'Excellent,' Meng Po said. 'You are surpassingly good for a beginner.'

'Actually, this is not my first try, but I am long out of practice. I had a friend named Gibraltar – Tree's brother – he showed me how to create the basic strokes. Gib was a wonderful calligrapher, a great painter.'

'Two of the Three Perfections.'

'Oh yes, *and* a fine poet. He excelled at all three.'

'A man of high refinement.'

Mason nodded and sighed. 'My best friend. He was killed during a war in a land not far from China.'

'So sorry,' Meng Po said softly. 'Such is karma.'

'Yes, I suppose. Karma. His and mine.'

Mason had lain awake all night agonizing over his failure with Tree, his responsibility toward her. He'd hoped that time spent alone with Meng Po would help clear his mind so that he could think creatively, devise an escape from their predicament. He smiled at his young friend. The boy's company soothed like a balm.

Meng Po dripped three beads of water into the shallow dimple of an inkstone shaped like a lotus. He ground an inkstick made of pinesoot and lampblack mixed with animal glue against the wet stone until he had blended a smooth jet ink.

'You and Tree have journeyed all the way to *Chung Kuo*, the Middle Kingdom, my ancestral home.' He dipped a human-hair artbrush in the shiny puddle on the inkstone. 'I, myself, have never seen beyond the cliffs of this valley.'

With a swift dance of his brush over the field of white, he grew a stand of bamboo, applying the sticky ink in sudden strokes, painting the plants in the traditional order: stems, nodes, branches, leaves. Meng Po had taught Mason that classical painters considered black a most important color, and many landscapes were painted solely with black ink. His grove of bamboo was alive and swaying on the paper.

'Actually, I have never been to China,' Mason said. 'Tree and Gib grew up there, in a city called Nanjing. But most of my traveling has been through books.'

'That we have in common. I have read many accounts from the court historians of the various dynasties, Shang through Ming. I have learned about the seven voyages of Zheng-He's Treasure Fleets, and the great expedition of our founder, Ko T'ung Jen. Was not Nanjing his home?'

'Yes, Tree's father was fascinated by Ko T'ung Jen. He moved with his children from a land called England across the world to China to peruse the ancient court records in that city. He was convinced that Ko had sailed to the New World and founded a colony; but his colleagues scoffed at him.'

'A sage once said: "The problem is not that people simply do not know, but that they know so many things that are not true."'

Mason glanced around the palace room. 'I am certain a large school of know-it-alls would be duly humbled by the things to be discovered here in your amazing city.'

'And no doubt your world offers surprises that would strike our citizens dumbfounded.'

'Young scholar, may I ask you a question that is certainly no business of this foreigner?'

'Yes, ask me anything. That will free me to ask you anything, and there is very much I want to learn.'

'Why are you not allowed to venture outside of this cage?'

Meng Po sighed and laid down his brush on its enameled wood holder. He stroked Kiki's white shock of hair and shifted on the small couch just inside the bars.

Mason sensed the boy's discomfort, but he desperately needed to understand the workings of the society. 'I asked K'un-Chien, but she told me she could not bear to talk about it.'

'May-Son, let us agree that between us we can discuss anything, but what we say here must not spread like ink in water.'

'Understood, but I would ask a further permission – may I share what we discuss with one other friend?'

'Tree?'

Mason nodded. 'I have trusted her since I was a boy. She and I need to comprehend our situation here.'

'Her eyes show much affection when she looks at you,' Meng Po said. 'You have my permission to share our conversation with her – on one condition.'

Mason nodded.

'That she come here to visit me again soon. I want another chance to marvel at the colors of her hair, spun from the sunrise.'

'She will come for more of your poetry when I tell her you said that.'

Meng Po took a deep breath. 'You wanted to know how I came to live in isolation in a guarded caged inside a guarded palace. The answer is drenched in sorrow. I once had two older brothers. On the same terrible afternoon they drowned, along with my father. Their death left only one Great Stalk in all of this society.' His eyes misted. 'How I wish it were not me.'

'I am sorry for your loss,' Mason said. 'And I think I understand: Your brothers died and so you must be kept in this cage, secluded from all harm.'

'Exactly so. I was five years old when the tragedy occurred. The Empress ordered this lonely cage to be built for me that same day. No doom can befall me here, unless the Earth itself swallows up this palace.'

Mason whistled low. 'Six years.'

'Six years, two moons, ten suns,' Meng Po said. 'I keep track on my *suan p'an*.'

131

Kiki hopped down and returned with a Chinese abacus. The colored beads marked columns of ones, tens, hundreds, thousands, tens of thousands. 'Thank you, Kiki. I don't need it now. Please put it back.'

Mason marveled as the sage-monkey returned the suan p'an to its drawer in a carved mahogany desk.

'Soon, a new Mother-of-Sons will be chosen to replace my mother. Then, when I reach manhood, I myself will become Emperor. I will husband the next Mother-of-Sons to make as many boys as we can.'

'I see.'

'But until I reach manhood, I am not allowed to exit this gilded prison,' Meng Po said, and shut his eyes.

A silence ensued. Mason wondered at the boy's plight. It was sad enough to lose one's older brothers and to wind up the only male in a family of women in an all-female society. Added to that, Meng Po was imprisoned throughout his youth while awaiting the fate of being the sole husband to hundreds of maidens. Some men might think that sounded great, a fantasy come true. But fantasy and reality are distinct realms. The actual everyday living would surely grow wearisome – physically and emotionally exhausting. Yes, for a time it could be a sexual thrill, a power-trip. But in the end, Mason believed, boredom and loneliness would defeat the pleasure. It is impossible to shine as a male without fraternity, brothers in flesh and spirit.

'Tell me, Meng Po, what is K'un-Chien's history? Perhaps it is not a foreigner's appropriate concern, but the question still haunts me – how did such a beautiful person come to be held in total disgrace?'

'That is simple: K'un-Chien fell from grace because my brothers died instead of her. She was there, as was I, the day it happened. As a female, she was expendable,' he said. 'If she had died while trying to save them, she would have been buried without shame. Or much better, if she had actually saved them and died in their stead, she would have been buried with highest honors. Or best of all, if she had saved them from drowning and also survived herself, she would have been regarded as a great heroine. But to have survived when her brothers died was considered obscenely rude – contemptible.'

Mason sighed. The sexist reasoning was based on the ideals of Confucius – the Great Tutor. It turned his stomach.

'Now K'un-Chien is despised,' Meng Po said. 'You see, many older girls had already married my brothers in their minds and were waiting patiently for them to become men. My eldest brother, Yu Sheng, was older than I am now.' He bent his head and combed Kiki's soft fur with his fingertips; the sage-monkey snuggled in his lap, making a low sound in its throat like purring. 'I now see girls look at me the same way. They bring me gifts . . .'

'And K'un-Chien? How does she feel about what happened?'

'She feels terribly guilty for having lived. That is why she cannot bear to talk about it. I may be the only one who has never held it against her. She saved my life. She tried to save our brothers, but fate snatched them from her hands.' He sighed heavily. 'I love her. She is not just my sister – along with Kiki, she is my one other true friend.'

Mason reached his big hand through the bars and stroked the sleek black hair on the boy's head. 'Please count this barbarian as one more true friend.'

Meng Po did not look up, but gripped Mason's hand with both his own, pressed it over his heart and held it there tightly. Meng Po made no sound, but Mason felt the boy's heart thumping as the little shoulders shook and hot tears splashed Mason's skin. Kiki whimpered softly and kissed and patted the boy's head. Mason tried to imagine the tragedy's impact on Meng Po and K'un-Chien and the whole society.

'Remember what I said the day we met,' Mason whispered in a soft bass voice. 'You and I are a fraternity of two.'

Meng Po looked up at Mason, face streaked with tears. 'Yes.' He snuffled and dried his cheeks on a flowing yellow sleeve. 'A fraternity of two. Thank you, elder brother.' He squeezed Mason's hand and Mason smiled and squeezed back.

'Tell me how it happened – if you want to talk about it.'

'My father had escorted us outside the city walls to go swimming at a beautiful spring. The winter season is the drier season, and this was a particularly rare day when the sun stood out in the sky for several hours in the afternoon,' he said. 'Have you tasted the dark red honey they sell in the market place?'

'Best I've ever had, sweet and also very fragrant, like flowers.'

'Several honeybee hives are worked just beyond the city's walls. They yield golden honey – good, but not divine. Not like the dark red honey. According to the captain's journal of Ko T'ung Jen, these ordinary hives were brought on the voyage all the way from the Middle Kingdom.'

'China.'

'Yes. Shortly after arriving here, in the Year of the Rooster, our scouts discovered a celestial honey, made by local wild bees. But as with anything else that is supernal, one must overcome a challenge to obtain it.'

'How so?'

'The red honey is gathered from halfway up the Western Face, in a series of caves that have been made into massive hives by large bees we call *Guan Di* – Gods of War.'

'They sound dangerous.'

'Yes, extremely. The honey gatherers have learned to survive by becoming conditioned to the painful stings and not swatting the bees. To instinctively squash a bee is a deadly error.'

'What happens?'

'The squashed bee releases a potent odor that instantly alerts the others. Their soldiers then swarm in squads. They follow the alarm odor to their targets and they sting and sting until the creature, man or beast, stops screaming and squirming.'

'Is that what happened to your brothers?'

Meng Po shook his head. 'That is what would have happened to my brothers and me if K'un-Chien had not saved us. We were hiking along singing, anticipating the clear, refreshing spring water. The path to the spring passes by the foot of the Western Face.

'A thousand feet above us, on the sheer rock, a honey gatherer must have mashed a bee by accident. The hive swarmed over her. We heard a scream and looked up and saw her blanketed in bees, a dark struggling shape. She plummeted from her rope ladder and thudded a hundred feet from us. A few dozen soldier bees fanned out toward us and we dashed for the water. They overtook us and stung us, head to toe. We were yelping, but we knew not to fight the bees. We raced ahead. Almost at the water's edge my father began knocking the bees off us, smacking them on our backs and heads. K'un-Chien screamed for him to stop, but he didn't understand the danger. He was a barbarian, like yourself, from far away.'

'That's terrible.'

'The bees lifted off the dead honey-gatherer like a black storm cloud and swarmed toward us. The buzzing was furiously loud: I can remember the drone of a million beating wings vibrating through my chest. K'un-Chien grabbed a reed boat from the shore and dragged it into the spring as my two brothers and I leapt into the cold water. The dark shroud enveloped my father and he fell to his knees on the bank; he never screamed, but pitched forward, dead.'

'You could only hold your breath so long,' Mason said. 'How did you come up for air?'

'K'un-Chien flipped the boat over and we surfaced underneath it and breathed from the pocket of air trapped there.'

'Quick thinking.'

Meng Po nodded. 'But my oldest brothers had been stung worse than K'un-Chien and me; their eyes were already swelling shut and they began to panic because they could not see. The buzzing bees made a terrifying din outside the boat. K'un-Chien spoke to us in a strong, quiet voice and calmed us down. She explained that we were going to float down the river beneath the boat; after a few miles the bees would be gone and we could come out.'

'Good.'

'Yes, and her plan would have succeeded, except for the workings of our wretched karma. You see, the silk factory is located several miles downstream. It sometimes uses a waterwheel to turn its looms. When they open the sluice gate to power the wheel, it diverts the stream down a steep gulch until it spills over the big wooden wheel. K'un-Chien didn't realize what was happening until we were trapped in the rapids. We were swept along in the current toward the spinning waterwheel. K'un-Chien grabbed me and both my brothers and we formed a chain and fought toward the bank, but Yu Sheng and Hsiao Chu were the farthest from her and they lost their grip. They were both dragged under the wheel and crushed.'

'But none of it was her fault.'

'She was merely a woman. Therefore, she should have died in her effort to save her brothers.'

'But . . . she saved you. She couldn't have saved you and *also* died trying to save her other brothers. She had to survive to get *you* to shore.'

'That is precisely the reasoning that spared her life. Otherwise, she would have been banished to the upper hell.'

Mason shook his head. 'For her crime of living while her brothers died.'

'Instead, she was cast out of the society to live without face.'

'It is hard for me to accept that her own mother felt no more compassion.'

'Actually, our mother, the Empress, shunned K'un-Chien from the beginning. An old midwife delivered the baby and as soon as my father told the Empress it was a daughter, she turned away and said it did not belong to her. So he raised K'un-Chien himself, in his own palace. She was his special child and pupil.'

'But why? I don't understand this rejection. Do not even Mothers-of-Sons occasionally give birth to daughters?'

'Of course. But in every case, the daughters are likewise disregarded. *Every* woman in this society can have daughters. Only the Mothers-of-Sons can have sons. And my own mother is special among them all, because she is destined to give birth to Lung-Hu.'

'How does she know that?'

'She saw it in a vision.'

Mason thought of Tree's vision while intoxicated by the healing mushroom. 'The Ling-Chih?'

'Yes. The Empress is allowed to take the Ling-Chih for the purpose of making prophecies. Otherwise, it is used solely for healing.'

'But even when it is used for healing, the patient sees visions, is this not so?'

'Yes. Visions of the past as well as the future. But only the Empress is allowed to eat the Ling-Chih at the beginning of each of her pregnancies in order to foretell the future of her sons. It is considered critical to know this, as males are so desperately important to our society.'

The news stunned Mason. *Bingo! There it is: The one thing the Empress does that no other woman here does – she eats the mushroom each time she gets pregnant.*

'Then did she not foresee that two of her sons were going to drown?' Mason asked.

'No. The first time she took the Mushroom, she saw that it was she herself who was going to give birth to Lung-Hu, who had been foretold since the time of the very first Empress. But each time since, she has only returned to the same vision, that she will be the Mother of Dragon-Tiger. She did not foresee the tragedy that would befall her line.'

Mason sat in silence, digesting all that he'd heard. He felt eager to tell Tree. Somehow, they'd find a way to use this information, perhaps it was even a key to their survival and eventual escape.

'Obviously, the Empress must get pregnant again to give birth to Dragon-Tiger,' Mason said.

'Yes,' Meng Po said. 'That is why you and Domino are so important to her.'

'What?'

'The moon will be full in two more days. Then arrives the *Ho Ch'i* ceremony when everyone partakes of the love-seeds. There, in Prayer Mat Temple, you and Domino will have sexual congress with the Mother-of-Sons.'

21

Mason hurried back to his palace at a fast stride. He wanted to race at a flat-out sprint, but that would only attract more attention to himself. As it was, women passing by in pairs and groups gawked at the anomaly of a strapping male in the midst of their female homogeneity. He broke into a trot when he neared the palace's round front door. Through its openwork woodcuts he saw Tree inside, pacing. When he opened the door she pounced.

'You won't believe what I found out from K'un-Chien,' she said. 'I know where the passageway down to the jungle is, I know the secret of this whole dragon-woman and tiger-woman thing—'

'That's great news. I want to find out everything you know because we gotta get our asses outta here. Tonight.'

'What's the matter?'

'C'mon, let's go for a walk down to the gardens. I'll tell you about it. I'm too nervous to sit still.'

They stepped outside. A fine drizzle was falling and in the dampness Tree's wavy hair quickly frizzed into a thousand curls. They hurried along a colonnade that dropped off to steep stairs with a bamboo banister, its husk polished shiny by countless human hands. The steps led down to a garden no bigger than a tennis court that seemed to contain a dozen

distinct terrains within its green borders. In one portion, shrubs
had been hand-sculpted into curvy shapes that suggested the
bodies of snuggling lovers; another part held a five-foot-by-ten-
foot rectangle of fine gravel that had been raked into patterns of
parallel lines embracing rugged stones; near the middle of the
garden a brook surged and danced through a mountainscape
of miniature peaks and waterfalls, looking like a scene from a
Chinese landscape painting; the pond at the base of the little
mountains teemed with colorful lionhead and fantail fish.

Tree sat on a stone bench near Mason's favorite feature of
the garden: a bonsai forest of miniature tropical hardwood
trees. The Lilliputian woods looked to Mason as if at any
moment a half-inch-long jaguar would come padding out of
the gloom and scratch its coarse fur against the rough bark
of a foot-high oak.

Tree patted the sandstone bench streaked with red feld-
spar.

'No, thanks. I'll stand and pace like a madman, if you don't
mind.'

'Okay. Let me tell you what I've learned,' Tree said. 'I was
asking K'un-Chien some female questions. I'm going to be
starting my period in a few days and I was wondering what
women here use as tampons. She said they use slender rolls
of cotton cloth made by tiger women for other tiger women. I
thought it strange she singled out tiger women, so I said what
about the dragon women? She looked confused and then she
laughed, thinking I was joking. Finally she said, "Dragon women
don't bleed with the moon".'

Mason's mouth fell open and he stopped suddenly.

'Right,' she said, nodding. 'It hit me like a ton of bricks.'

'Holy shit, half the population *is* male. The dragon women –
no ovaries or womb, therefore no menstrual cycle.'

'I remembered what you told me about androgen-blocked
males,' Tree said. 'You said the innate human form is female,
so without a hormonal factor to alter that given form, every
fetus is born as a girl, even if it has XY chromosomes. You
said when men can't respond to their own sex hormones, not
only do they appear as women, they even tend to be tall and
beautiful.'

'The dragon-women – the soldiers – most of them are taller than tiger women.'

She nodded. 'And the soldiers are exclusively dragons, have you noticed? No tiger women become soldiers.'

'And only dragons and tigers marry. All the couples are dragon-tiger couples.'

'True. When kids here reach puberty, the separation into dragonhood or tigerhood begins, depending on whether they bleed each month or not.'

Mason walked in circles, grabbing the ringlets of his curls between his fingers, stretching them straight and letting go; they rebounded like soft springs.

'Okay, listen. The pieces of the puzzle are falling into place,' he said. 'I found out that the Empress ingests the Ling-Chih each time she becomes pregnant in order to foresee the destiny of her sons. None of the other women are allowed to use the mushroom in that way.'

'That's it, then. That's what she does that no other woman does.'

'Right, and I think I understand now what happens. The Empress carries the defective gene, same as every other woman here. But when she gets pregnant—'

'She eats the mushroom and it fixes the gene; the androgens kick in and male plumbing develops.'

'Yeah, or maybe it's just a defective switch – the gene itself is okay but switched off, and the Ling-Chih switches it back on.'

'Hey, maybe it's a viral infection – the fungus is only the host for a virus that modifies the DNA – and happens to be beneficial.'

'Could be. I like that. Whatever the mechanism, instead of being born as pseudohermaphrodites, the XY fetuses are converted to normal healthy males – Meng Po and his brothers.'

Mason felt a renewed sense of awe at the Ling-Chih's medical potential. 'Talk about a miracle drug . . . wow.'

Tree held up the thumb of her left hand like a trophy and wiggled it. 'Magic slime.' Her thumb was well on its way to full regeneration: bones, joints, thumbnail and all. The genes for growing new tissue – dormant in her case for a couple decades – had been reactivated.

Mason grinned. Then he remembered his plight and sat on the bench and told Tree everything he'd learned from Meng Po. Tears shone in Tree's eyes when she heard the story behind K'un-Chien's stigma. Mason told her that he and Domino were expected to have sex with the Empress two nights hence.

'I'm not up to studding for that dominatrix,' he said. 'And if she finds out I'm impotent . . .'

'Which leads to the other big news I learned from K'un-Chien,' Tree said. 'The passageway out of here.'

'Where?'

'A split in the rock at the foot of the Western Face tunnels all the way down to the jungle floor.'

'She didn't hesitate to tell you that?'

'She looked . . . concerned. But she answered my question and said nothing more.'

'I trust her. She won't betray us.'

'Lord no, I get the feeling she'd rather die than be disloyal to you or me.'

'But I'm scared that they'll do something terrible to her when they find us gone.'

'I assumed we would take her with us.'

'Really? You really want that?'

'Isn't that what you want?'

'Well, yeah, but – you've acted kind of cool toward her.'

'My feelings about her . . .' She sighed. 'It's hard to explain. I never told you about my vision of her. It was a sexual thing . . . an accord of energy. I've only felt that intensity with one other person in my life.' Her green eyes kindled.

Mason had to look away from the fire in their depths. 'Dreams can be so sexual,' he said. 'I once dreamed I was making love with a dolphin . . . the smell and taste of the seawater, a slick film on the dolphin's smooth skin, shiny black eyes with bright spots of flame . . . Dreams can seem so real, and they aren't required to show any logic.'

'Oh, this was no dream, Mason. No dream.' She shook her head. 'Kind of spooked me, to tell you the truth. I've been resisting K'un-Chien ever since.'

'But . . . she's hard to resist, isn't she?'

Tree punched his shoulder. 'It should make me jealous that you said that. But it doesn't so much now.'

'I . . . I just meant—'

'You don't have to apologize. You meant she's easy to love. She's enthralling. And it's unpracticed – she can't help being alluring any better than we can help being drawn to her.'

He nodded. 'If K'un-Chien is a seductress, she's not the devil of seduction – she's its angel.'

'There's something mysterious about her. I can't intuit what it is. It haunts my soul. She's unlike any woman I've ever met.'

'That's not so hard to figure. She was born and raised in a Confucian culture. Her world is utterly different than that of any of your women friends, even your modern Chinese friends. She's a daughter of the ancient Ming Dynasty.'

'No, no. That's not what I mean. For that matter, she thought it odd that I didn't know that dragon women don't menstruate – she grew up with Amazons, for chrissakes. But that's just not it.'

'What then?'

'I don't know.' She shook her head. 'Can't put my finger on it. But we have to take her with us, that's for sure. If she'll go.'

'She'll go if I order her to. She's my wife. According to Confucius, she's my property. We can sneak over the wall tonight and make our way quickly to the passageway. We'll need food and water. Torches for the caverns. Stuff to bribe the Yanomorduro with.'

'Mason, I'm scared.'

'Yeah, me too.' He hugged her. Her heart beat beneath her small breasts.

She laid her head on his shoulder and nuzzled her nose against his muscular neck. 'I bet Penelope used to smell the neck of Odysseus,' she said. 'It's reassuring.'

'Tree, you know we have to tell Domino.'

She pulled back and stared. 'I don't trust him. And I doubt he'll want to leave.'

'But I still think we're obligated to tell him. If we escape without him he might be punished or killed in reprisal.'

She sighed. 'I suppose you're right.'
'You know I am. If he wants to go, we have to take him.'
Tree wore the same look of distaste as when she'd nibbled the tarantula.

22

K'un-Chien straddled the chalk line on the floor with her bare feet planted shoulder-width apart, back foot parallel with the line and front foot at a forty-five degree angle. Using three fingers she drew the bowstring to full tension and anchored her thumb beneath her jaw so that the gut string pressed in a taut line against her chin, lips and nose. She eased out her breath, and with it, she let go of thoughts, images. Her visual field narrowed onto the straw target shaped as a wild boar. Fingers flew open. A hiss of wind. The arrow rocketed home and buried its shaft nearly up to the feathers in the boar's flank, behind its shoulder blade.

'Heart kill!' Meng Po shouted. 'Oh, I wish I were as skilled as you.'

'You're far better than I was at your age,' K'un-Chien said. 'Just heed what I told you: Snap your fingers open but don't jerk the bow upward as the tension is released.'

Inside his golden-barred room, Meng Po mirrored his sister's stance. He drew back his bowstring, locked his thumb under his jaw. Released the arrow. It shot several feet too high and struck the far wall of the palace with a *whack*.

He groaned. 'Forgive me, tutor, for being as straw-headed as the boar.'

'Nonsense,' K'un-Chien said. 'Did you see how fast your

arrow flew? Look, it pocked the limestone. That is a great improvement in power.'

'Yes, when I am Emperor, I will be renowned for stopping walls in mid-charge.'

She laughed. 'Little Brother, you must work on your concentration. Remember: Archery is a skill of the mind as much as of the body. You let the bow jump up again as the force left it. Now watch my bow, my arm.'

In one fluid motion K'un-Chien drew an arrow from her quiver, notched it on the bowstring, pulled it back to her chin and let it fly into the straw boar's heart.

'Splendid!' Meng Po clapped his hands and Kiki did his little circle dance.

'Have a seat,' K'un-Chien said. 'Let me tell you a story our grand aunt told me when I was her archery student. It illustrates the importance of concentration.'

'Good. I love your stories.' Meng Po sat crosslegged on the plush handloomed carpeting that covered the floor of his room; its woven scene showed a warrior woman driving a lance into a wild boar's neck. Kiki climbed into Meng Po's lap and snuggled under his heart.

K'un-Chien began: 'Two warrior-sisters desired to master their skills of archery, so they journeyed to the castle of the Adept Archer to ask for her instruction. After a long trip, they arrived at the master's gate, laid a tapestry on the ground and spread upon it their gifts of rice and plum wine, caged nightingales, a bow of polished yellow yew wood, and a hand-tooled leather saddle with matching reins and bridle. The eldest sister then grabbed a wooden clapper and struck the gate's brass gong – *kong-nnnnnnnnnng!* – it rang out, shimmering in the sunlight.

'In a moment, the Adept Archer's servants appeared and they carried the gifts inside the castle walls along with the warriors' polite request to study archery with the famous teacher. After many minutes, the servants returned bearing a stretcher with a feeble white-haired lady reclining upon it. The wrinkled skin of her face looked as aged as the parchment of a venerable *sutra* scroll, worn from the hands of ten thousand scholars. Through white hair, finer than cobwebs, the warrior sisters saw her pale smooth scalp, so thin it pulsated with each beat of the ancient woman's heart.

'"Forgive us, old teacher," said the eldest sister. "We did not realize that you were so advanced in years. Please keep our gifts in honor of your supreme reputation. Perhaps you'll give them to your great-great-great-grandchildren?" With a deep bow, she added, "By your leave, my sister and I will now be on our way."

'The Adept Archer lifted a bony finger, gnarled by time. "Wait," she said in a feeble whisper. "Indeed you have arrived at the very hour of my death. The priestess was bending her torch to light the funeral incense when the gong resounded. But perhaps I have sufficient time remaining to train one last student." She paused and rested, each ragged breath creeping faintly after the other. "Which of you two will qualify?"

'The sisters glanced sideways at each other and puffed out their breasts a bit. The eldest raised her arm and pointed across the river to a black spot against a white chalk cliff. "That crow at the top of that ledge," she said. "I will try to hit it." She locked her bow against her ankle, dipped its ends and strung it with a fresh gut bowstring. Then she notched an arrow, raised the bow at a steep angle and drew it back till it formed a deep crescent.

'"Tell me all that you see," the Adept Archer said.

'"I see a rough limestone cliff," the eldest sister said. "Wind-twisted pine trees growing sideways out of the cliff face at crazy angles. A rookery of crows in an outcropping above the pines. And one big crow perched on the ledge at the very top."

'"Let fly your arrow," the Adept Archer said. The eldest warrior shot the arrow and it arched high over the river and stuck in the jutting trunk of a pine.

'"With your gracious permission, Elder Sister, may your humble junior try?" the younger warrior asked.

'"Of course. Do your utmost. And hurry, your potential tutor is fading fast." Indeed, the hoary master was now wheezing more than breathing. The younger sister strung her bow, notched an arrow and drew the string to its fullest tension.

'"Tell me all that you see," the Adept Archer whispered.

'"I see only the crow. Fat and shiny, bluish black. I see its great red eye with a black pupil."

'"Let fly."

'The younger sister sent her arrow soaring over the river and it smacked the limestone at the big crow's feet and clattered down the cliff. The crow squawked and ruffled its feathers, indignant.

'"Hand to me your bow," the Adept Archer ordered. The younger sister passed her bow to the antiquated figure. "Stand me up," the Adept Archer commanded her servants. They raised her to her feet, supporting her where she stood.

'"Warriors, help me to draw the bowstring," she told the two sisters. One helped hold the bow, the other helped to draw the string, while the Adept Archer aimed the arrow.

'"Let fly!"

'The arrow sliced through the air above the river and pierced the crow straight through its eye.

'"Old Master," the sisters shouted, astonished. "How could you even see that crow at this distance?"

'"Crow? What crow?" the Adept Archer said. "I saw only a huge red circle with a black spot at its center."'

K'un-Chien smiled and bowed to Meng Po. He placed his upturned palms together and returned her bow.

'An excellent fable,' he said. 'Concentration is the key.' He stood and notched an arrow, drew his bow, steadied his gaze, then let fly. The arrow whizzed a fraction of an inch over the target's spine and smacked the far wall.

'Ah, see?' K'un-Chien said. 'Much better. Much better.'

'If only wild pigs wore monsoon clogs, eh? A thumbnail taller and tonight I would be feasting on straw ham.'

K'un-Chien laughed. She looked at her brother, yellow satin sleeves rolled high up on wiry arms. 'I love you, Meng Po – the way you make me laugh. I am glad I came to see you.'

'A friend notices when a friend is troubled,' Meng Po said. 'Do you wish to talk about it?'

K'un-Chien looked away.

'Does it have something to do with our fascinating guests?'

She nodded, shutting her eyes and pressing her lips together to hold back her tears. But even squeezing her breath to a standstill could not lock in her sorrow. The levee of her heart burst and tears flooded down.

Kiki reached through the bars and stroked K'un-Chien's hair. She took his warm black fingers and moaned softly with sobs. Meng Po laid his hand on his sister's muscular shoulder. 'Can I help?' he asked gently.

She shook her head and let out an aching cry. For so many years she had kept her heart armored against the pain. Now her armor was brittle and cracking.

'Pardon my weakness,' she said, snuffling. 'I am a faint-hearted coward.'

'You are the bravest, most powerful person I know. I am blessed to have such a wonderful sister.'

She read the caring in her brother's eyes and wept harder, his satin robe blurred into a yellow smudge. Crying gave her exquisite release from the heaviness of years of holding back her emotions. She felt that if she let go completely now she would melt beyond the boundaries of her body, float away on a bouyant sea of tears, and simply die. But she stopped her sobs by taking long deep breaths, long deep breaths.

'I . . . I believe May-son and Tree are going to try to escape,' she said.

'They expect to survive in the upper hell?'

She shook her head. 'I told Tree about the passage down.'

'But the headhunters, the dragons – did you warn them?'

'They already know about the headhunters. They are willing to take the risk. I have not yet told them dragons guard the exit, but I don't think that will stop them, either. Oh, Little Brother, I am in love and it hurts so keenly.'

'I am not sure I understand. You are in love with your husband? What is the problem? Go with him.'

'But I do not want to leave you.'

'Your loyalty is more precious than a mountain of jade. But I want you to go with the man you love. This is my command, as your future Emperor. And surely your husband also will command it.'

'It is much more complicated than you know. I am also in love – with Tree.'

He shrugged. 'Is this not commonplace?'

'Not in their culture. Not at all.'

'She has told you this?'

K'un-Chien shook her head. 'I have been afraid to talk with her about it. But I can read much in her face and eyes, the way she looks at women embracing, the way she shuns me. And Father used to tell me all about his world. Theirs is a land half-filled with men. No need for women to marry women.'

'How strange that must be, to see male and female couples every day, as commonly as one sees parrots flying, two by two.'

'Father taught that such is the natural order. The *Tao* to which we must strive to return.'

'Sister, may I speak freely?'

'With me, always.'

'Although you bleed with the moon, I recognize in you many qualities of a dragon woman. Witness your prowess in archery – even Yu Lin is not your equal. Therefore, I believe you and Tree could form a dragon-tiger union, blessed by the polarity of yin and yang.'

Tree sighed and shook her head. *How can he understand my dilemma without knowing my secret?*

'Please let me know what is troubling you, K'un-Chien.'

'How I wish I could reveal it.'

'You have always kept this mystery from me. Your central secret. And I have never pried, because I knew it was very important to you to keep your privacy. But for a long while now I have seen that your secret is destroying you. It eats you to the stem, like a silkworm on a mulberry leaf. I think you need to tell someone. Indeed, I insist that you tell me, so that I can share your burden.'

'But I promised father I would never tell. Only he and the old midwife, Zu Chou, have ever known. From my earliest days he stressed to me again and again that no other soul was ever to be told.'

Meng Po furrowed his brow. 'What could it be that requires such hiding?'

K'un-Chien clenched her teeth.

Meng Po stood to his full height. 'As your future Emperor I command you to tell me,' he said in his deepest voice.

'My own authority overrules your oath and the strictures of our father. For your sake, tell me now what you conceal.'

K'un-Chien gulped.

Meng Po's face softened and he smiled compassionately. 'It must be so lonely for you . . . In my own isolation your love has been my sweetest solace.' He kissed Kiki's smooth black face. 'Your love and his. Reveal to me what you need to uncover, sister. I'll do anything to simplify your karma, lighten your footsteps along the path.'

'A brother's kindness softens my steps as if I walked ankle-deep in cherry blossoms, yet there is nothing you can do to simplify my karma. Nevertheless, I will tell you – and thank the ancestors for this release from my vow of silence.'

She glanced around the palace room at the guards. The dragon women were at rest, but each had a sword, a bow, a lance. K'un-Chien leaned closer to her brother, and he toward her. She paused and took a deep breath.

'I am Lung-Hu,' she whispered. 'I am the Dragon-Tiger. I, Hsiang K'un-Chien, am the Holy Hermaphrodite.'

Meng Po's eyes grew wide. 'Is it possible?'

K'un-Chien glanced at the guards again. 'Bring your blanket.' He returned from his futon with an embroidered blanket and she grasped one corner. 'Hold your corner tight,' she said, and stretched the blanket behind her like a privacy screen. With her free hand she unwrapped the front fold of her sarong, revealing her nude body below the waist.

She was female, and above her womanhood, male.

K'un-Chien refolded her sarong. Meng Po dropped the blanket and bent low to kowtow before her.

'Don't, please,' K'un-Chien grabbed his arm. 'No rituals between us.'

'What are you two doing?' a guard asked.

Meng Po glared at the guard. 'Attend to your own boredom and permit your future Emperor what little privacy he can manage in a cage.'

'Of course, Great Stalk, my apologies,' the guard said, and looked away.

K'un-Chien held her breath. She had never felt more vulnerable in her life, as if she were a transparent being – a glass fish. *I could not bear it if he rejects me.*

Meng Po caught her eyes and his gaze did not let her go. After a moment, he said:

> *Fine wine from best plums*
> *In a mug or a goblet*
> *Tastes as sweet and good*

K'un-Chien inhaled again, clutching her hand to her heart.

'It makes no fundamental difference to me,' Meng Po said, 'you are still the one I love.'

Oh praise the ancestors. 'Thank you, dear brother.' This time she let her tears flow. For a long while they embraced as best they could through the vertical bars.

'Why did father insist that you keep the secret?' Meng Po asked at last. 'The Empress still awaits Lung-Hu, as does everyone. Why have you not stepped forward to replace mother as our monarch?'

'Everyone awaits Lung-Hu,' she said, 'but not everyone awaits eagerly. To some, the idea of a male-female being is repugnant, even evil. But because the Mother-of-Sons and her cult have so much power, the others keep their disgust to themselves. Father, for one, was adamantly against the way of the Dragon-Tiger.'

'He never told me that.'

'Does an adult discuss such things with a five-year-old?'

'No, of course not.'

'There was another school of thought here before the Lung-Hu cult became dominant. When you studied the journals of Ko T'ung Jen, you must have read about the Debate of Two Schools?'

'Yes, Ko T'ung Jen was very clear about which side he was on,' Meng Po said. 'The School of the Outer Alchemy sought physical immortality through a perfected human body – the Holy Hermaphrodite. Ko T'ung Jen's school rejected the idea of an immortal body and sought to purify the inner soul. He argued passionately against those who welcomed the Lung-Hu.'

'Our father agreed wholeheartedly with Ko T'ung Jen's teaching of the Inner Alchemy and tried to reinstate them.'

'I am confused. How did a barbarian know so much about the way of our founder?'

'Our father had always been drawn to the Middle Kingdom intellectually. He even taught Chinese history and culture at a large university in his western land. But after his wife died, he turned toward the East with a more urgent spiritual hunger. He had come across a rare book of the teachings of Ko T'ung Jen—'

'*The Sutra of the Golden Flower*? I have read it.'

K'un-Chien nodded. 'It became father's obsession to learn more about its author and the path he taught. In the process he discovered that Ko T'ung Jen had secretly planned a voyage to the New World with a crew of colonists who wished to found a utopia. Father journeyed to China to examine the ancient dynastic records for clues about Ko T'ung Jen's voyage. Later, he made two expeditions in search of this colony, and found us on his second try. But our culture was no longer following Ko T'ung Jen's teachings. The Mothers of Sons and the cult of Lung-Hu had become nearly all-powerful. Father did his best to restore the original way.'

'In other words, father worked to recreate the spiritual path he had come here to find,' Meng Po said. 'Do you see the karmic circle? Out of necessity the seeker became the teacher.'

'I see it clearly. And he saw it too. He believed it was his destiny to bring us back to the Way of the Inner Alchemy. He said he was called here to us to save us from a mistaken path.'

'But why is it mistaken? The Empress teaches that Lung-Hu is our savior—'

'I know the dogma: Lung-Hu will usher in an age of persons who are complete in themselves, and thus rescue us from our plight of dependence on the opposite sex.'

'Would not that be a good thing?'

'But that is only the exoteric teaching; there is an esoteric teaching that few have heard: The real motive of the cult of Lung-Hu is physical immortality.'

Meng Po frowned. 'But how?'

'According to the School of the Outer Alchemy, the marriage

of yin and yang in a single body generates a life-force that renews cells indefinitely. So although the Empress herself cannot escape death, she believes her legacy is to birth a race of Immortals.'

Meng Po looked at his sister with big eyes. 'Are you . . . ?'

'Immortal? I certainly hope not. No. But the alchemists were right about one thing: There is a constant generation of energy in me, as if my belly were a cauldron of power.'

'Oh, K'un-Chien – Lung-Hu. I never knew who I was relating to. Perhaps I have been too casual, disrespectful.'

'Do not start with that. We are best friends. I am K'un-Chien, same as always. You should not even think of me as Lung-Hu.'

'But I must. I was taught that Lung-Hu is a new order of human – *more* than human, a god.'

'My dear brother, in your years of knowing me, have I ever struck you as more than human?'

'Uh . . .'

'Believe me, dear heart, I am all too human. Did you not just witness my tears of sorrow and joy – my hopes and fears?'

Meng Po smiled. 'It is as you say. You do not seem to walk above the clouds.'

'Compare the views of the Empress with those of Ko T'ung Jen and our father. They saw the Lung-Hu as an abomination, a corruption of nature. They thought of a society of hermaphrodites as a society of monsters.'

K'un-Chien's face darkened. 'Father once told me that on the day I was born he had stayed awake all night deciding if he should take a pillow and smother me.'

Meng Po's eyes flashed. 'How dare he!' Kiki jumped off his lap, startled by the boy's anger.

'By dawn, he had chosen to let me live, but on the absolute condition of keeping my identity forever secret.'

'Dear sister, you must remember, our father was a barbarian—'

'And a lifelong scholar of the founder of our society. Ko T'ung Jen firmly believed that the advent of Lung-Hu signaled the beginning of the end for our people.'

'But . . .' Meng Po sighed. 'That was the past – centuries ago. How many feel that way now?'

'I am aware of at least one person in Prayer Mat of the Body who hates and dreads the Lung-Hu as much as father did.'

Meng Po raised his eyebrows. 'Name her. Send her to me, I will discuss it with her.'

His sister's eyes drooped with shame. 'Her name is Hsiang K'un-Chien.'

23

A girl of thirteen or so answered the palace gate and led Mason down a stone path and under an ornate arch into a high-windowed living room that opened onto a courtyard. A quartet of women were soaping and scrubbing each other's backs in a sudsy hot tub, a fifth woman swam naked in a rectangular pool. Domino Cruz, the Venezuelan zoologist on the HARVEST team, was seated on a low bamboo stool, his eyes half-shut; he wore only a raw silk loincloth. Three of his young wives attended him: one dressed in a pink kimono combed his black hair and beard with coconut oil; the other two, dressed in multicolored saris, massaged his feet.

Domino was short and solidly built, not fat, yet something about him made Mason picture a bulging hairy caterpillar, gorged to bursting on the soft petals of a rose.

'Amigo! Que tal?' Domino said, without rising. 'Welcome to Paraiso de la Cruz. You want some plum wine? A haircut? Massage? Maybe something more spicy?' He winked and squeezed the small breast of the woman bent forward to comb his thick beard.

'I came here to tell you something important,' Mason said, 'and I need you to pay attention. I don't have a lot of time and I'm only going to say this once.'

Domino shooed the women away with his hands and stood up. 'What is it? What's wrong?'

155

'Tree and I are escaping tonight. We think you could wind up in deep trouble if you don't go with us.'

'Man, you crazy? I don't wanna leave this place. Look around you.' He swept an arm around the green courtyard. A dozen beautiful young women were kneeling in a circle on the lush lawn, each brushing the long dark hair of the woman in front of her. Several of the teenage women looked pregnant. Like all the citizens of Prayer Mat of the Body, Domino's wives looked to Mason like Caribbean peoples he'd occasionally met who were a mix of European, African, Chinese and Indian roots the genetic emphasis here was clearly Chinese, but he discerned the multi-ethnic influence on hair and eye color and facial shapes. Variations on a lovely theme.

'I'm in Pussy Heaven – Tierra de las Conchas.' Domino laughed and grabbed his crotch. 'What I got to go back to that's better than this? I'm a Castillian king, here. A conquistador.'

Mason bristled. 'Lift your brain out of your cock for a damn second and take a good look at our situation. Tree's life is in danger here; I'm in danger, too. And if we escape and leave you behind, you're likely to be in danger.'

Domino shook his head. 'No. I don't think so. In this town, I'm the big bank director – the sperm bank. They're not gonna close me down. When you got a stable full of brood mares you don't get rid of your only stallion.'

'Well, let me give you some news. In two days, at some kind of temple celebration of the full moon, they're expecting you and me to have sex with the Empress.'

'Says who?'

'Just believe it. We're supposed to make her pregnant.'

Domino tugged on his mustache. 'Okay.' He rubbed his mouth. 'Okay. What the hell? I'll service the lady.' He shrugged. 'Long as she keeps that mask on – I heard her face is one big scar. But her body looked pretty fine beneath that yellow robe. Big mamitas.' He cupped his hands in front of his chest. 'Just so she don't scratch me with those long nails.'

Mason rolled his eyes. 'Were you always so romantic, or did it take years to develop your tender side toward women?'

Domino frowned. 'What's this shit? Who are you – San Francisco?'

'It's just that your macho act really turns me off. I can't understand, I guess, why you need to prove your manhood all the time, act as if women are your toys.'

'What you talking? I love women. Making it with a beautiful girl is one of the few pleasures I've ever known in my life. You call it a crime to like to fuck? Who are my victims?' He nodded to the circle of kneeling women on the grass; they had finished hair brushing and now were decorating each other's manes with white orchids and red lotus blossoms. 'Before me, these girls had never gotten laid. And let me tell you, they don't hate to ride a stiff cock, that's no lie. I give them pleasure, I make them pregnant. The way I see it – and *they* see it – I'm doing them a service. And for that you want me to feel guilty? Wake up, hombre. I don't speak much Chinese yet, but my antennae are buzzing – everybody in this city has heard about you and your measly two wives and they think you're unforgivably selfish.'

Mason took a step back, surprised by the anger in Domino's outburst. 'Guess I pushed your button.'

Domino stepped closer and Mason smelled the coconut oil that slicked his hair and beard. 'Y'know, you got that Anglo thing – that gringo *attitude* – like you're somehow superior to me in every way. Well, let me tell you a little something about Domino Cruz: I'm the only kid – from a family of fifteen – who went to college. I fought damn hard to get my degree and to rise through the ranks of the faculty – and for what? The street-corner drug dealers in Caracas – like my teen-age brother – make more dinero and have more prestige.' He looked around the courtyard. 'But now, amigo, I got my own palace. Now I'm living like a cartel boss. Better. I got my own harem of angels. And you expect me to want to escape? That'd be like diving off cloud nine to plummet back to earth.'

'Domino, seriously. I hear what you're saying, but for your own good, I think you'd be safer if you came with us.'

'Down into the fuckin' jungle with the headhunters and the blowguns – that's what you call *safer*? Mi Dio! Safer than rolling around a big bed with girls spread over me like warm honey? To hell with you. I'm staying. If the Empress needs some action, I'm her stud.'

Mason sighed. 'Have it your way. Good luck.' He turned to go.

'Hang on a minute, amigo,' Domino said, and laid his hand on Mason's shoulder. Mason paused and turned to face him. 'Thank you for coming to warn me. Okay?' He stuck out his hand. 'No hard feelings?'

'No hard feelings.' Mason shook Domino's hand; it was small, strong and hardened with calluses. Domino's thick Pancho Villa mustache crinkled as he smiled, showing sharp white teeth.

'Look, if they feed me to the piranha,' Domino said, 'I'll remember you warned me.'

Mason nodded and turned toward the door. Domino stepped after him. 'Hey, hombre. Let me ask you one question.'

Mason didn't stop walking.

'If you could get it up,' Domino said, 'woudn't you be staying, too?'

Mason spun on him, glowering. 'Who told you that?'

'A few days ago I dropped by to visit you and Tree, you two happened to be in the hot bath, and . . .' He shrugged. 'I overheard.'

Embarrassment overcame Mason. He suddenly felt small and weak and hollow. It was as if he and Domino had been butting antlers and then, suddenly, Mason's rack had gone as soft as boiled macaroni. He couldn't utter a word.

'Hey, no problem, man,' Domino said, clapping him on the shoulder. 'Tree is still your girl, no? She's prettier than all the women in this city.'

Mason hurried out into the evening mist and did not look back.

24

K'un-Chien guided Mason and Tree along the interior of the city wall and into a dense grove of tropical hardwoods. A massive banyan with a central trunk the size of a small living room towered beside the stone wall; elephantine branches sent vertical shoots down to the soil to form secondary trunks, like rows of columns supporting thick roof beams. In the bright moonlight its wind-tossed leaves flashed silver like schools of darting fish.

No one had spoken since they had left the palace an hour earlier, just after midnight. K'un-Chien seemed tense and sad to Mason. This morning, in his most formal and polite Mandarin, he'd asked her to help Tree and him to escape – and to accompany them. He knew it was painful for her to leave Meng Po behind, but she could not, by Confucian ethics, refuse her husband's request. Truth was, Mason had wanted to take her brother along too, but couldn't work out a practical plan to do it. He tried to read her face now in the ivory-white light, but she turned away.

K'un-Chien laid down her bow and slipped her knapsack and quiver off her shoulders. She shimmied up a secondary trunk of the banyan to its horizontal branch, then shuffled with sidesteps to the main trunk After scrabbling to the next higher level of branches, climbing the rest of the way to the tree top was as easy as ascending a ladder of fat wooden rungs.

Mason touched Tree's arm. 'You okay?'

Tree nodded, watching K'un-Chien scale the banyan. 'She looks so unhappy. I hope we're doing the right thing.'

'She's already an outcast. Do you really think she'd be safe here after they find out we're gone?'

Tree shook her head. 'No. This is the only way.'

'Besides, I don't think we could pull this off without her help.'

'I agree, but God, I know she's torn-up over Meng Po.'

Mason sighed. 'He's a terrific kid. If things were different . . .'

K'un-Chien dropped several ropes. Mason attached their supply bags and K'un-Chien hauled them up into the treetop. One heavily bundled package wafted a faint but obnoxious stench.

'What in hell did she pack in there?' Tree asked. 'Stinks like rotten fish.'

'Don't worry, it's not tomorrow's lunch. It's bait.'

'Bait?'

'You'll see when we get to the cliff.'

Then Tree and Mason followed K'un-Chien's route up the banyan's smooth black secondary trunk.

Mason put his Army Med-Evac training to work. Perched near the top, he hitched a sturdy rope to the trunk, looped it in a semicircle around his waist, ran the working end through a free-sliding slipknot, played out the full length of slack and slung the rope over the far side of the wall. He scooted backward on the limb until he was sitting over the far side of the wall, then he lowered himself down until his feet touched its vertical face. He pushed his body weight out over his hips and walked the rest of the way down the wall.

Mason stood on the ground and guided Tree's descent. K'un Chien followed.

As he had expected, getting outside the city's wall had been easy. The perimeter was guarded only at its two small round gates – and even those posts were more emblematic than strategic. The dragon women had assumed there was no possibility of attack from above the valley and very little danger of invasion from below: The Yanomorduro Indians had been afraid of the women warriors from the earliest days of the colony. But for extra measure the soldiers allowed Komodo dragons to roam and nest in clawed-out tunnels near the mouth of the passageway to the jungle. Like keeping a kennel of junkyard dogs near your backdoor, Mason thought, only the guard animals in this case were much more like junkyard dinosaurs.

In an hour's fast walking the trio arrived at the Western Face. K'un-Chien signaled for Mason and Tree to keep back. She approached the cliff, set the thickly wrapped package on the ground and opened it to reveal a large mound of bloody fish offal she'd gathered from several butcher stalls at the marketplace.

'Ugh,' Tree said, covering her nose as the smell drifted her way. 'Bait – for what?'

'Remember our little encounter with the Komodo dragon?'

Tree shivered and stepped beside Mason. He draped an arm across her shoulder. 'It's gonna be okay,' he said. 'She knows what she's doing.'

K'un-Chien stepped back near them and the three waited and watched. After a few minutes, K'un-Chien walked forward slowly, glancing all around. 'This is most strange,' she said, frowning. 'They should be here by now.'

'Maybe they don't smell it yet,' Mason said.

K'un-Chien shook her head. 'They have very poor eyesight, but from a league away they can sniff a dead monkey and follow their noses directly to the carcass.'

They waited in silence. Mason and Tree sat on the rocky ground to rest, while K'un-Chien moved closer to the cliff to keep her vigil. After a half-hour, she returned to them. 'Something is wrong,' she said. 'There are fourteen dragons, and not one has responded to the bait. I do not understand it.'

'Shall we move on?'

K'un-Chien stared ahead, blue eyes glowing softly in the pale light of the moon. 'All right,' she said, at last, 'but carefully. The dragons have scooped out many shallow caves in the sandstone near here. Usually, we count them to be certain they are all gorging on the bait before we enter the passage.'

She drew an arrow from her quiver and notched it on her bowstring. 'Stay behind me.'

Mason did not see the fissure at the base of the cliff until he was almost upon it. A thin crack snaked jaggedly along the ground parallel to the cliff and widened in one place to a snaggle-toothed mouth darker than the surrounding rock.

'Wait here,' K'un-Chien said, and passed her bow to Mason, arrow still notched. Mason grasped the weapon awkwardly. 'Eddie would love this,' he said to Tree, referring to his oldest brother, an avid bowhunter.

'Maybe he'd finally get over his black bear saga,' Tree said. 'He could brag to all his beer buddies that he bagged a *dragon* with a conventional bow.'

Mason tensed his jaw. 'I just hope my archery skills aren't called upon.' He tested the give of the bow by drawing back the gut string. His forearms bulged, and he guessed it to be a seventy-five-pound draw. 'Wow. She's got arms of steel.'

K'un-Chien lowered herself into the fissure and dropped down onto its first ledge. Her eyes just peeked above the lip of rock. 'Please hand me the torch.'

Mason reached for the torch, curious how she expected to light it. K'un-Chien took a tiny leather bag from her belt and in a swift action spilled its contents over the fishliver-oil-soaked rags of the torch. With a brilliant flash of silver light the torch burst into an oily yellow flame.

'Sodium,' Tree said. 'Pure sodium. It combusts as soon as it hits the air.'

'Pretty ingenious,' Mason said.

The torchlight threw shadows around the lumpy granite walls as K'un-Chien headed down.

Mason and Tree waited above, glancing around furtively for signs of ten-foot-long carnivorous lizards. Less than five minutes had passed when K'un-Chien shouted up to them from below. Her voice sounded urgent, a warning. Mason looked at Tree and drew the bowstring to its full tension.

Tree cupped her hands and yelled down into the opening. '*What?*'

No answer.

'*Are you all right?*' she yelled.

From below, another muffled cry bounced around the tunnel.

Mason handed the bow to Tree. 'She's in trouble, I'm going down.'

Tree shouted: '*Mason is on his way down to you.*'

Mason swung his legs over the rim and then he saw the torch glow, bouncing. 'Here she comes.' He snatched a knife from his waistband; its blade gleamed like a shard of moonlight. His whole body tightened like his hand around the knife handle, waiting.

Suddenly K'un-Chien's head appeared in the tunnel below his boots. She yelped in pain and in the same instant Mason heard the low drone of angry bees.

'*Guang Gong!*' K'un-Chien shouted, looking up frantically. 'Run for the water.'

Tree shot a look to Mason. 'C'mon!' She grabbed his arm. 'You can't help her. Run!'

He leapt up, seized Tree's hand and sprinted toward the water. A buzzing as loud as a power saw bore down on them. 'Don't swat them,' Mason yelled, 'and don't scream, they'll fly into your mouth.'

Mason glanced back. K'un-Chien had climbed out of the fissure. He heard more than saw the bees swarming around her. He resisted the impulse to race back to her and swat at the bastards that strafed her mercilessly.

But he held onto Tree's hand and they dashed toward the stream that shone like a white satin ribbon in the terrible distance. Now the bees had caught them and were nailing them with vicious stings right through their clothing. *It's not the whole hive*, Mason told himself. *Not the whole hive, just a few dozen. We can handle it as long as we don't swat them*. He wanted to shout encouragement to Tree, but he knew from the Wawajeros that attacking bees zoomed right into one's mouth and stung the tongue and throat.

Stride by stride the water's edge drew closer. At last, their boots slapped the damp mud and they plunged head first into the deep stream.

Mason still clutched his knife. He clamped his teeth flatly on the blade, spun around underwater and swam back toward the bank where'd he seen a stand of euphorvia. He sliced off three stiff reeds and swam back toward Tree. When he broke the surface to catch his breath the knife slipped from his mouth; he snatched at it underwater but it flicked away from his fingers and was lost.

Mason handed Tree one of the foot-long tubes, as wide as a piccolo, to use as a snorkel. The fresh-cut reed anchored between his lips tasted strongly of almonds. He raised his head to eye level with the surface of the stream and saw K'un-Chien running toward them, eyes clamped shut.

'*This way!*' Mason shouted, and received a forehead full of stings and another inside his upper lip. '*Head straight to my voice.*'

Black darts strafed K'un-Chien's face and torso. After what seemed a long moment, her feet splashed into the stream and she dove underwater. Mason handed her a hollow reed. He gripped her hand and the three of them dog-paddled, heads just beneath the surface, breathing through the hollow euphorvia reeds and drifting in the strong current as the army of bees hunted in sweeping orbits for an enemy to kill.

Twenty minutes later and a couple miles downstream, Mason cautiously lifted his head above water and scouted with eyes and ears for the bees. He tugged K'un-Chien up by an elbow. 'It's okay,' he said. 'We're clear. Are you all right?'

Her face was a puffy mask with swollen slits for eyes. She nodded, and tried to speak through fat purple lips, but only moaned softly. He head wobbled and she started to slide underwater.

'Shit.' Mason grabbed her under her armpit and flipped her onto her back. 'Tree, help.' He began towing K'un-Chien head first toward the shore, hand under her chin, her legs pointing downstream in the swift current. 'Tree! She's going into shock, help me to get her in, quick.'

He swept his eyes around. 'Tree? Where are you? Tree!'

'Mason!' Tree yelled. 'I can't hold on!'

Mason spotted her, ahead and to his left, clinging to the rim of the near wall of a wooden sluice that angled off from the stream and dipped steeply toward the city. The rapids surged over her, sending a fishtail of spray off the back of her head and forming an air pocket for her to breathe. Terror twisted her face. Mason stabbed the air with curse words. That sluice, he knew, fed the giant waterwheel that powered the silk looms.

He looked at K'un-Chien, her hands flapping in the tugging current. He glanced back at Tree, saw her sputtering and choking in the gushing froth. His heart cramped like a fist inside his ribcage.

He realized that, by the time he towed K'un-Chien to the bank, the rapids would peel Tree off the wall and drag her down the chute a half-mile to be crushed beneath the waterwheel. But if he let go of K'un-Chien now, swam with all his speed to the bank and raced along the ground to yank Tree to safety, by the time he could race back to rescue K'un-Chien, her body would be tumbling along the streambed, lungs sloshing with water.

Pain gnashed like teeth in his gut. *I can save only one of them.*

He froze. Time stood still inside his locked breath, and a night's agony from years before and far away ambushed his senses. He was holding Gib's body, head in his lap, surprised by its heaviness – as if the departed spirit had taken with it all buoyancy and nothing remained but sheer weight, an ingot of death.

In buddy flicks, a man's dying friend gets to look him in the eyes and stutter a few words. A last goodbye, one final soulful gaze. But that was Hollywood. In Vietnam, in the green dark, Gib had already been dead when Mason flipped him over. He could have stuck his arm through the slick wet tunnel in Gib's chest. The smell of blood, gunpowder and rain-rotted earth hung in the air strong enough to taste. His ears rang from exploding mortar shells and the staccato fire of automatic rifles. There, in the real fire and rain, his best friend didn't get to say a thing. Gib's body felt so heavy, gravity reeling it graveward. Gib was gone. And Mason had squeezed the trigger.

Mason snapped out of his flashback and, for an instant, he thought he knew the best way out of his dilemma. Sartre had said it: *'Not to choose is to choose.'*

He could simply do nothing. All three of them would slip away, one at a time gulped down the throat of the sluice. Then he wouldn't be left behind to grieve another loss.

No, goddamit, that's too selfish. I've got to choose: Save one and let the other die.

He vented another flare of curse words.

And let go of K'un-Chien.

25

'Mason! Stay where you are! I'll get Tree.'

Mason looked up and saw Domino Cruz sprinting toward Tree where she clung to a wall of the wooden chute in a torrent of whitewater. Mason spun back to K'un-Chien, whose head had slipped beneath the surface. He grabbed her up and towed her to the bank with powerful sidestrokes and scissor kicks. When he had dragged K'un-Chien onto the pebbles he looked over to see Tree lying safely on the bank near the sluice, Domino kneeling beside her. A dozen dragon-women soldiers circled the pair and another dozen surrounded him.

Mason turned his attention to K'un-Chien. With noisy wheezing gasps she struggled to breathe. He pressed his ear to her chest. No sound of water in her lungs. She had not begun to drown, he realized. Instead, her problem was anaphylactic shock from the bee stings – her airways were rapidly swelling shut. *Damn*, he wished he still had the knife. He had only had a few seconds to open an oxygen route to her lungs.

'Have you got a knife?' he yelled to Domino.

Domino shook his head.

'Is she breathing?' Tree called.

'Not for long,' Mason said, and turned to the group of soldiers. 'Hurry. Let me use one of your daggers.'

Yu Lin, the soldier's commander, started toward him, unsheathing her dagger. 'You will kill her?'

'Of course not,' Mason said. 'I am going to save her. I need to open an airway to her lungs.'

Commander Yu halted and returned her dagger to its sheath. 'Why trouble yourself? She is hopelessly disgraced. First, she let her brothers drown, then she tried to help you escape. She is without face forever.'

'K'un-Chien is my wife, I am not going to lose her.'

'You have already lost her. She is death's bride now.'

'You are mistaken, I can save her if you will let me use your dagger. _Please_.'

'No. She is meant to die, it is her evil karma.' Commander Yu turned her back and strode toward Tree and Domino.

Mason looked down at K'un-Chien's darkening face. Her eyes had rolled back in her head.

Think, man.

The ideal way to perform a tracheostomy is under local anesthetic and sterile procedure in a hospital operating room, using a bronchoscope, a scalpel, several retractors, a dilator, and a plastic trachea tube. But in emergencies, people's lives had been saved by cutting a vertical slit into the front of the windpipe with a penknife or razor blade – even a pointed fingernail file, for chrissake. Trouble was, he didn't have anything of the kind.

In the moonlight K'un-Chien's skin was starting to turn blue.

Think, goddamit.

He remembered an anecdote about a battlefield tracheostomy – the medic had simply shoved a large-bore needle through the windpipe, pointing down toward the lungs. The crucial trick with this method was to keep from puncturing the far wall of the windpipe or slipping off to the side and ripping the carotid artery or jugular vein.

Mason spun around and began snapping off nearby euphorvia reeds. The rigid stalk he'd used as a breathing tube had been sliced from its base at a sharp angle, the point had jabbed his tongue making it bleed. But now, breaking the stalks with his hands, he couldn't come up with a sharp enough point. He tossed down a handful of blunt-ended reeds and ran to another clump, frantically breaking them off in twos and threes. *Come on! Just one decent point.* Finally, a reed broke off with a sharp edge. He jabbed it on his palm. *Ouch.* Good and stiff.

He raced back to K'un-Chien, knelt beside her head and tilted her neck back to stretch the skin over the windpipe. With fingertips he felt for a dip between the rigid horizontal rings of the trachea. He took a deep breath to steady his hand, then he bore down hard with the stiff reed against the taut skin. Blood began to trickle, but the reed didn't poke through the tough elastic cartilage.

Do it, Mason. This is no time to be chickenshit.

He steadied the pointed end of the reed against her windpipe, angled downward toward her lungs. Then he balled his hand into a tight fist and punched down *hard* on the top of the reed. The punctured cartilage made a popping sound – *whup!* Mason winced and held his breath, half expecting bright red arterial blood to spurt from the end of the hollow stalk. Instead, he heard air whistling through the reed into her lungs. Within seconds, K'un-Chien's color began returning to normal.

'Mason, is she all right?' Tree called.

He swallowed hard. 'She's gonna be' – his voice broke – 'she'll be okay.'

'Oh, thank God,' Tree said. She stood, wobbled, and sat down again. Domino helped her to her feet and the two walked over to where Mason knelt in the pebbles beside K'un-Chien; her face was horribly swollen, but her breathing was strong and regular now.

Mason looked up at Domino. 'So, what brings you to us in the middle of the night, amigo?'

'Listen, you just better be damned glad I came.'

'Oh, I'm glad. I'm glad. But what the hell were you up to, following us out here?'

Domino cleared his throat. 'I got to thinking about what you said – about me being in jeopardy, getting the shaft if I stayed behind. Look, Mason, I told you I didn't wanna leave . . .'

Mason gave a tight, crooked smile. 'So you squealed. You ratted to the guards.'

'Like I said, you should be thanking me. Without me, she'd

be dead,' he nodded toward K'un-Chien. 'I saw you drop her and go for Tree.'

'Thus our betrayer becomes our savior,' Mason said. 'What a hero.'

'To hell with you.' Domino spun and walked away.

Tree knelt beside Mason and laid her hand on his shoulder. 'Mason, calm down. He's right, you know, he did save my life.'

'I was coming to get you, Tree,' Mason said in a low raspy voice.

She kissed him gently on his cheekbone. 'I know. I saw you.' She whispered into his ear: 'I know you struggled with a terrible choice, and you chose to rescue me. Bless your soul, I know how that must have hurt. Now I feel so foolish – I'll never feel jealous of K'un-Chien again.'

He looked at her and smiled weakly. 'But now we've got to go back.'

'Don't give up, Mason. I love you—' she hugged his broad shoulders '—*so much*. We'll beat this trap yet. You'll see.'

Mason shook his head forlornly. 'You're forgetting. Full moon tomorrow – I've got a date to have sex with the Empress.' He shivered in his wet clingy T-shirt and shorts. 'By this time tomorrow night . . .'

He couldn't say it aloud. The day they'd met, the Empress had threatened that if he failed to be *Ta Heng* – a Great Stalk – he would be castrated. He could picture the glare of her eye, black as volcanic glass, her ruined lips moving behind the garish mask. 'I'll personally make you into a eunuch,' she had vowed.

Her threat stung now as cold and sharp as a razor.

26

Mason sat on the futon bed and bent over K'un-Chien's reclining form. Her respiration and pulse were stable. He'd found a salve, labeled specifically for bee stings, in her medicine cabinet. The waxy green balm was stiff and he rubbed it briskly between his palms to heat it to a soft paste. It gave off a pleasant odor like warm beer. Gently, he smeared the salve on the dime-sized red welts that dotted K'un-Chien's face and arms. Then he sat back, wondering at the medicine's ingredients and hoping for the best.

Less than an hour later, the balloon of K'un-Chien's face had deflated and her features had resumed their exotic Eurasian beauty. Mason's curiosity about the herbal medicine now turned to amazement: As an anti-inflammatory the unguent made cortisone seem downright puny.

The swelling in K'un-Chien's airways had subsided completely. Satisfied that her breathing was strong, Mason removed the euphorvia reed that had served as a trachea tube. He carefully washed and bandaged her neck wound. With the hole drawn closed by the bandage, he felt confident the flesh would knit rapidly. Before he let her sleep he also gave his patient one of the sticky black Phoenix Balls that she'd made him swallow on the day they'd met, for he'd guessed the medicine was an antibiotic and K'un-Chien had confirmed it: 'It helps the palace guard repel invaders.'

The body as palace. He gazed now at the soft architecture of her face. Morning light filtering through mists painted her dreaming eyes with the brushstrokes of a master.

'A work of art, isn't she?' Tree said softly, walking up from behind.

He smiled. 'You can always read my mind.'

'She going to be all right?'

'Yeah. Just fine. She's strong as a Clydesdale.'

Tree put her hands on Mason's shoulders and massaged the thick muscles. He closed his eyes and sighed, leaning his head back against her firm belly.

'Thanks,' he said. 'Feels great.'

'How about the physician? You okay?'

He shook his head. 'Scared shitless about tonight.'

'Well, I think I've come up with a solution. Did you read all the labels on K'un-Chien's medicine chest?'

'What'd you find, "Instant Erection?"'

'Nope. But I found this.' She handed him a tablet the size of a bottle cap. It had been compressed from dried herbs, purplish-gray like sage. 'The label said "Vomit Until Dry".'

'Hey, that's good.' He sat up straighter. 'I take this, I puke all over the Empress, and instead of castrating me she just has me skewered on the spot.'

'You start throwing up and you're off the hook. Nobody wants to have sex with somebody who's sick as a dog.'

'Tell that to the frat boys. But yeah, it's worth trying, I've certainly got nothing else to rely on.'

'What about Domino? How's he feel about it?'

'About having sex with someone who's puking? Wouldn't slow him down.'

'Come on. I meant about having sex with the Empress.'

'Said he doesn't care as long as she keeps a bag over her head. He even mentioned her *mamitas* with a certain enthusiasm.'

'Figures.'

K'un-Chien opened her eyes wide and sat up with a cry of fear.

Mason leaned forward and gave her a hug. 'We are

safe, we are back in our home.'

K'un-Chien squeezed him tight. 'Oh, May-Son,' she whispered. 'First Wife. How wonderful that you are both well.'

Tree took K'un-Chien's hand. 'How do you feel?'

K'un-Chien smiled. 'So grateful that you are alive.'

'I meant, how does your body feel?'

'Sleepy, mostly.'

'Close your eyes again and get some more rest,' Mason said. 'Tree and I will watch over you.'

'Then perhaps I have passed on to the Great Hall of the Ancestors? To me, you two look as beautiful as guardian spirits.'

Tree smiled. 'You have not died. But you gave us a big fright at the spring. Mason saved your life.'

'Yes, but do not blame him for that. I know that first he let go of me and swam to rescue you.'

Mason felt a pang in his heart. 'I . . . I am so sorry. I had to choose—'

'Please do not apologize,' K'un-Chien said. 'There was no choice, of course. Tree is First Wife. I am second – expendable.'

'No.' Mason shook his head forcefully. 'No one is expendable.'

'It is written in the Analects of K'ung Fu Tse—'

'I do not care for his system of stacking people into a pyramid with the emperor enthroned at its peak. Human beings are not born to live in such a vertical arrangement – with some treated as doormats while others are made loftier than clouds. Do we not all enter the world by the same gate? We stand on the same ground, as equals. Equally worthy of life, and also equally mortal. No one is expendable.'

K'un-Chien only stared at him. Her hair fanned out over red satin and spilled off the mattress edge like black rain. 'First Wife, do you also believe in May-Son's way?'

Tree nodded. 'It is my way, too. Most of the people in our homeland believe this way, though it can be very hard to put such values into practice.'

'It is such a different view from the way I was raised,' K'un-Chien said. 'But I have been infected by it and I cannot seem to get it out of my heart. The idea of freedom for each person – the right to make one's own destiny – it has touched me like a magical spell for which there is no cure.'

'It is an irony,' Mason said. 'Many of the people of our own nation fail to appreciate the preciousness of the free society they are born into. But here you are, grown in the soil of the rigid doctrine of K'ung Fu Tse, and the ideal of personal freedom has taken root in you.'

'The Tao of heaven and earth is inscrutable,' K'un-Chien said, sleepily. 'With your permission, I will rest now.'

'With whose permission?'

She smiled and closed her eyes. Her thick lashes were like soft black combs. 'Yes, husband, I will rest now *because I want to.*'

The round moon hung above the city like a festive paper lantern when Tree answered the sharp rap at the palace door. Yu Lin and a half-dozen soldiers stood outside, their lacquer armor gleaming dully in the moonglow.

Yu Lin addressed Tree in a commanding voice: 'We are here to escort your husband and you to the Ho Ch'i ceremony as special guests of the Empress.' She looked over Tree's shoulder toward the bedroom. 'Where is he?'

Mason staggered out of the bedroom clutching a bamboo bucket to his pale lips. His gray face seemed drained of blood. He glanced up at the commander of the guards with bloodshot eyes and then retched loudly, spilling his stomach into the bucket with a sloppy splash.

Yu Lin grimaced and swallowed. Tree wrung out a cloth in a porcelain water bowl on a wooden washstand and pressed the cool cloth to Mason's forehead.

'What is wrong with him?' Yu Lin asked.

'I do not know. He has been vomiting for hours – now he is vomiting flecks of blood, and he has no control of his bowels.' She laid the cloth in the bowl and put a hand to her gut. 'I fear his sickness is contagious. I myself am beginning to feel most poorly.'

Almost as a unit the soldiers took a step backward from the open door.

Yu Lin scowled. 'Your husband is commanded to share the bedchamber of the Mother-of-Sons – the supreme honor. This will be regarded as a grave insult to the Empress. A most inauspicious moment to fall ill.'

Tree bowed with palms pressed together. 'So sorry. As you say, it is a black misfortune.' She wrung out the cloth again and reached to mop Mason's brow, but he pushed her hand away and vomited noisily into the bucket. 'My husband has eagerly anticipated tonight's blissful embrace but, alas, he cannot halt the cruel wrenchings of his gut.'

Mason coughed weakly, then said in a hoarse whisper. 'I . . . I . . . am most humbly regretful. I . . . oh, pardon me—' He clapped a hand to his belly, doubled over, and hurried in an awkward trot back into the bedroom. The sound of his violent retching echoed around the tall-domed main room.

'Is there nothing K'un-Chien can do for him, no medicines—?' Yu Lin asked.

K'un-Chien appeared from the bedroom door. 'If only we doctors were the absolute rulers of the body. But no, I already have done everything I can for him. He needs to rest or his sickness might overwhelm his *ch'i* – even kill him.'

Tree bowed again to Commander Yu. 'Please make our apologies to the Empress. Truly our karma has tossed us about on a sea of sad surprises.'

Yu Lin strode forward and grabbed Tree by the wrist. 'You can talk to the Empress yourself. I see no reason for you to avoid the ceremony. You also are commanded to attend. Come with me.' She towed Tree toward the door; the other soldiers exited ahead of them. Tree looked back at K'un-Chien.

K'un-Chien started after them. 'Then I must go too, to accompany First Wife as her proper maidservant.'

Yu Lin sneered. 'Ha. You are not invited. You have never been invited to Ho Ch'i and you never will be.'

Tree tried to break free of Yu Lin's grip but could not.

'Wait,' K'un-Chien said. 'According to tradition, upper-class women must bring a servant to the ceremony to display their rank appropriately.'

'We will find a servant for her,' Yu Lin said, and began to drag Tree through the round doorway.

'No,' K'un-Chien said, and squeezed around in front of Yu Lin to block her exit. 'I am her rightful servant. I am Second Wife.'

They stood face to face, without words. The captain was shorter than K'un-Chien, but built more densely. The captain's breathing was ragged and her face and eyes darkened. The soldiers spun around with the metallic *jang* of a half-dozen swords being drawn.

'You defy me?' Yu Lin spat. 'You goat's turd, you disgraceful stench! By what authority do you tell *me* what to do? I should have you butchered on the spot like the pigmeat that you are.'

'It is I who defy you,' Tree said, feeling blood pound in her temples. 'With the same authority by which I defied you the first time: I, too, am a mother of sons. And *I* select Second Wife as my servant – by my prerogative as a citizen of high rank. That is the proper etiquette. Tell your guards to put away their swords: it is they who disrupt protocol.'

Tree jerked her wrist hard and Yu Lin let go. Yu Lin grunted an order and the soldiers sheathed their weapons. But Yu Lin's charcoal eyes smoldered and Tree imagined she could see her own eyes reflected in them like jade flames.

Tree reached out and took K'un-Chien's hand and their long fingers entwined. They strolled toward the love-temple in a valley overflowing with silvery milk from the moon.

27

Perfume saturated the air of Prayer Mat Temple like an invisible liquid. Tree tasted the rich, sweet musk on her tongue as she entered a circular chamber lit with red paper lanterns. At the center of the room she spied the fountain of the fragrance: a single gargantuan bloom that resembled a white magnolia blossom. Tree had learned that nature's largest flower is the three-foot-wide, twenty-four-pound *Rafflesia arnoldii*. But the unfamiliar species that broadcast its scent throughout the temple surely weighed closer to 100 pounds.

Tree was still holding K'un-Chien's hand as they waded through the nectar-filled atmosphere to a low couch heaped with embroidered pillows. Staring down at the love-bed Tree felt suddenly overwhelmed, as if several versions of herself crowded the same body.

One self was the social scientist, fascinated by the opportunity to observe first-hand a sexual ritual that had been practiced for centuries in ancient China. She knew about the Ho Ch'i ceremony from her talks with Gib about Chinese history and philosophy. Ho Ch'i literally meant *unification of the breaths* and referred to collective lovemaking practiced by Taoist schools since the time of the Han dynasty. On the night of the full moon, the love-temple dancers performed the dances of the dragon and the tiger, then the participants began an all-night sexual marathon with as many partners as possible. But Ho Ch'i was not to be confused with the kind of oblivious group-grope one might find, say, at a motel keg party in Daytona Beach over Spring Break. The Taoists took their orgies seriously – sex was central to their mysticism. Taoists believed they could cultivate life energy through arousing and joining yin and yang, and thus stave off disease and live a long, vital life; and their ultimate purpose was even spiritual enlightenment – the transcendence of self through bodily ecstasy. By the time of the Song dynasty, Confucian moralists had squelched the Ho Ch'i ceremony and most references to it had been erased. But here, in a society named after a classical Taoist sex manual – Prayer Mat of the Body – Tree was certain tonight's Ho Ch'i would be the real thing.

Tree sat tentatively on the edge of the futon couch and another one of her selves took over: the shy, scared girl, as self-conscious as a teenage virgin. She didn't let go of K'un-Chien's warm hand, but she didn't dare look into those blue eyes. What was going to happen here? Was she crazy? Could she really go through with this?

Folded somewhere in her psyche between the scientist and the virgin was a body-hunger, a yearning to touch and to be touched. Her deeper sexuality had been on hold for years while she waited to give herself to Mason again. Tonight she felt a temptation more emotional than physical to just let herself go. Here, in this perfectly foreign environment, where no one knew her, she was free to go wild in ways too unreasonable to take seriously later.

K'un-Chien let go of Tree's hand and stood. Tree caught her arm. *Please don't abandon me now, I need you*, was what she meant to say. But she only opened and closed her mouth, suddenly too bashful to speak.

K'un-Chien smiled. 'I will return shortly.'

She came back into the room carrying a pot of steaming water and a teacup. Tree noticed other servants bringing the same to their mistresses. K'un-Chien reached into a fold of her blue kimono and dropped a love-seed coated with fuzzy pink mold into the cracked-glaze china cup. Hot water melted the pink fuzz. The naked bean pod looked dark and colorless, the crimson hue of its flesh canceled by the sanguine glow of the room's lanterns. Neither of them spoke as the love-seed steeped.

Tree's pulse throbbed in her ears. 'What happens next?'

K'un-Chien pulled the softened bean pod out of the tea cup and, to Tree's surprise, poured the water from the cup onto the floor tiles. Tinkling and splashing sounds circled the room as other attendants did the same. With her teeth K'un-Chien cracked open the pod to reveal a half-dozen brilliant white beans – at least, Tree guessed they were white, for under the red lanterns they shone like wet rubies.

'Do not chew the love-seed,' K'un-Chien said. 'Just put it under your tongue and allow it to dissolve.'

Tree's heart skipped a beat. She was tempted to ask, *What's the love-seed for?* and *Do you really think I should?* But she already knew the answer to the first question, and the second question was just the virgin in her automatically resisting the very thing she desired.

The oblong seed tasted bitter. But the longer she sucked on it, the sweeter it became, like a persimmon ripening under her tongue until her mouth filled with saliva at its sugariness. K'un-Chien held out her palm and Tree spat out the shriveled seed and sucked on a fresh one; bitter at first, then very sweet. After two more love-seeds, her mouth seemed to be growing hot. The sugary seed burned under her tongue. Then her attention shifted and corrected the sensation: It wasn't just her tongue – her whole body was burning with a gentle, easy fire. Tree giggled and realized she was feeling as relaxed and soft as a piece of sun-warmed taffy. But she didn't feel at all woozy. Rather, her senses were acutely heightened. She became attuned to the seashore rhythm of her breath rising and falling in the bellows of her lungs. Breathing in; filling with bright energy, accepting everything. Breathing out; surrendering down to her marrow, releasing everything. She was in awe at the deep and simple pleasure of respiration.

Four servants carried the giant perfume flower out of the room and a tall woman in a sleeveless tunic and short kilt strode to the center where the blossom had stood. The woman's arms and legs were sculpted with hard muscles; an embroidered green dragon wriggled down the chest of her white tunic, stained red by the lantern lights. Her hair was arranged in a thousand tight braids that hugged her skull like a black helmet; her fake beard also was a cascade of braids.

All eyes turned to the statuesque dragon-woman, and for a moment, Tree thought the woman had taken center stage to make an announcement. Maybe she was tonight's emcee: '*Good evening, Ladies, and welcome to the Fuck Room. And now – let the orgy begin.*'

Then Tree noticed the dragon-woman had already begun to dance. She was dancing with her eyes only. They flicked back and forth like a serpent's tongue and then her eyebrows shot up and her face opened into a look of orgasmic rapture. The dance was comprised of the tiniest movements, which made it all the more mesmerizing and Tree found herself leaning forward in order not to miss the subtleties of the facial expressions and postures of the hands. Gradually the dancer's neck, shoulders, arms were added into the choreography, and by the time the dance had moved down to her pelvis, Tree felt captivated by the dancer's erotic power and grace. The effect was hypnotic, like listening to a slowly building bolero in which, one at a time, each group of instruments adds another layer to the repeating motif until every voice in the symphony is imprinting the melody upon the listener.

The dancer suddenly leapt into a high spinning kick and Tree literally jumped out of her seat. The choreography became increasingly athletic and Tree understood the dance as an expression of male aggressive energy – the dragon of *yang*.

Abruptly the dancer dropped into a crouch and waited, motionless. In the ruddy light, beads of sweat stood out on her bare skin like drops of blood. Barely turning her head she scanned the room like a jaguar hunting for deer.

K'un Chien leaned close to Tree's ear and whispered, 'Now she will choose a tiger-woman from the audience to perform the Tiger Dance.'

With two swift strides, the dragon dancer bolted straight for Tree, grabbed her hands, tugged her to her feet and dragged her to the center of the room. Then the dragon-woman seemed to evaporate into the crowd, leaving Tree standing hot-faced as the new target of attention. She looked to K'un-Chien for help.

K'un-Chien nodded and waved her on.

'But I don't know the Tiger Dance,' Tree hissed.

A murmuring went up from the audience. 'The dance is according to you alone,' K'un-Chien whispered. 'You are a tiger-woman, it is your very own expression.'

Tree took a step to return to her couch but K'un-Chien shook her head in real alarm. Her big eyes said, *Don't you dare back down – it could get you killed.*

Tree gulped. *What the hell am I doing up here?* She'd never felt more self-conscious in her life. Beneath the red lanterns she could see all eyes in the room locked on her like compass needles pointing to magnetic north. All bodies leaned toward the center.

My very own dance. What I am supposed to do, act feminine? Act sexy?

She tried to think of some erotic moves. All that came to mind were the tacky stripteases she'd seen as a curious Harvard sophomore on visa to the combat zone of downtown Boston. But to bump and grind and lick her lips would be a ridiculous lampoon after the beautiful erotic dance she'd just witnessed.

In Nanjing, she'd studied ballet for eight years, beginning at age six; but all those graceful moves now also felt modeled and contrived. She breathed in and closed her eyes.

The tiger of *yin*. Spirit of woman. Tree realized she'd never stopped to contemplate just what it was to be a woman. In a society of two genders, females were the ones with vaginas; males had penises. Yet clearly women and men were a blend of the other. A blend of what forces, what qualities?

Here, in a society of only females, genitals didn't create a distinction. So what was it to be a dragon or a tiger? It was more than the fact that dragon-women didn't menstruate. She'd just seen a dancer who exuded what Tree labeled, for lack of a better term, *masculine* power. Now, she was supposed to dance with *feminine* power – but she didn't know how to begin.

Suddenly the obvious came to light: *It is not a matter of knowing, it is a matter of being.* The key to dancing authentically was not in anticipating the right moves to perform. The key was to wholly *be*, and let the breath move the body, become the spirit made flesh. Then the dance would arise not from preconception and convention, but artlessly, from her own essence.

Tree returned to the rhythm of her breathing and fell again into the pleasure of life circulating in her body. She gave herself to that pleasure physically, starting with her head, allowing the vital energy to move through her throat and face. To her surprise, she opened her mouth wide and sang out a single, clear note. Then another note followed, and another, and a melody of vibrant tones, each the length of an out-breath, rang forth from the well of her soul. The song unfolded as a moving energy, first inside her nervous system, then outward through her whole body until she became a dancing musical instrument. In moments, now and again, she returned to just enough self-awareness to realize that the moves that swept her across the floor were exquisitely beautiful, the most evocative and genuine ballet she'd ever danced.

Tree didn't notice the dance coming to an end, or walking back to the couch where K'un-Chien had watched. K'un-Chien had shed so many tears the front of her kimono was damp. Tree looked at K'un-Chien's face, blotched slightly from the bee stings, a bandage wrapping her neck. In spite of it all, Second Wife was still a painting to behold – which proved to Tree there was nothing skin-deep about her beauty. K'un-Chien gazed back at her with Asian eyes and Tree suddenly recalled a quarry in Nanjing where she'd swum as a girl – she saw clear blue depths where she could never touch bottom. What Tree recognized in K'un-Chien's tears was love.

Tree took K'un-Chien's face in her hands and kissed her full soft lips. The rest of the world melted like hot butterscotch. Nothing remained but tasting the Perfume of Earth-Heaven.

A tapping on Tree's shoulder grew painfully insistent. Tree turned around and saw Yu Lin, the commander of the guard, looking thoroughly drunk. She wore only a loincloth. Her beefy torso glistened with sweat. A rough patch of scar tissue marked the site where her left breast had been sliced off to make it easier to shoot a bow.

'I want you, apricot,' Yu Lin said. 'Come with me. Let us couple.'

Tree was still wrapped in a blissful spell, and it took a few seconds for her to comprehend: Yu Lin was demanding to have sex with her.

'Her name is Tree,' K'un-Chien said. 'Cannot you see that she and I are together? The etiquette of Ho Ch'i is that no embrace be interrupted.'

'You!' Yu Lin growled. 'You dare to instuct me in etiquette? You were not supposed to be invited to the Ho Ch'i ceremony. Ever. You contaminate this ceremony with your disgrace.'

'Then are we dismissed from our obligation to attend?' Tree asked.

'She is dismissed,' Yu Lin said, jabbing a thick finger at K'un-Chien. 'I want her to leave here now.'

'K'un-Chien is my servant and I have asked her to escort me home. Therefore, I too will leave now.'

Yu Lin shook with rage. 'Get out of here,' she shouted. 'Begone. Both of you.'

K'un-Chien and Tree found Mason curled up on the bedroom floor, asleep. They woke him and he sat up, disheveled and exhausted from his ordeal with the emetic.

'Sorry, guess I konked out,' he said. 'You two okay?'

'We're fine,' Tree said.

'You sure?'

Tree smiled at K'un-Chien. 'I'm sure.'

Mason looked from Tree to K'un-Chien and back. 'Looks like I missed something. What happened at the love-temple?'

'Yes,' Tree said.

He stared at her. 'Yes?'

She laughed. 'What do you imagine happens at a temple devoted to making love? First I watched a solo dancer – the most erotic dance I've ever seen. Then it was my turn to dance.'

'Really? I love the way you dance.'

'It wasn't me dancing. I froze in front of everyone. Then this . . . river of life – like the mighty Amazon – moved through me. I couldn't have resisted it if I had tried.'

He looked between the two women again, and smiled gently. 'Something's in the air, Tree, and it ain't just perfume.'

She blushed. 'Let's get some water back into you. Your lips are parched.'

Tree managed to get Mason to drink four teacups of water to rehydrate him. He dropped asleep again between the last two cups. Then she and K'un-Chien stood him up and tugged off his pajama-like *dhoti* – a knee-length muslin shirt over loose pants – and walked him to the bath and into the step-down tub. They washed his torso and face and hair, wrapped him in a robe, steered him to the bed and flopped him down, hair still dripping wet.

Mason was already asleep when K'un-Chien carefully tucked him in. 'Rest well, good husband.'

Tree looked at her with topaz eyes and K'un-Chien smiled nervously. Then Tree laughed, and some of K'un-Chien's shyness vanished in the music of her laughter. They gathered up armfuls of pillows, a quilted blanket and satin sheets and stepped outside into the open courtyard in the center of the palace. K'un-Chien's father had once lived in this palace and she showed Tree a secret retreat she'd discovered while a girl. Halfway up a big banyan tree the junction of two wide branches formed a smooth broad platform, slightly indented, like a giant dove's nest. They folded the quilt and laid it in the nest for a bed and then lay down on their backs and gazed at a rare view of the stars through the woody canopy.

From the heart of the sky shone a billion diamonds.

'The Southern Cross,' Tree said, pointing.

'General Wu's Chariot,' K'un-Chien said.

The stars sifted slowly, slowly, down behind the rim of the valley like sparkling sand in a timing glass. K'un-Chien lay next to Tree, feeling, breathing her warmth, the aroma of her hair and skin, the residue of her wonderful dancing. She was hungry to undress Tree and then clothe her again with careful kisses head to toe; she wanted to make herself as small as an ant so she would not miss the tiniest morsel.

At the same time, in spite of her desire, K'un-Chien had never felt so completely at rest. Tree had already made a choice. *She is with me now; tonight belongs to us.* K'un-Chien would have been satisfied to lie beside Tree and watch the stars for all the hours left in the sky. Tree held her hand; that was enough happiness.

For a long time the pair drifted in the lighted sea of space. A tink frog sang an arm's length away – *tink tink tink tink* – and crickets ratcheted everywhere. Banyan leaves gossiped in rustling tongues. A broad cloud sailed in the moonwind like a multi-masted junk. K'un-Chien watched a horse leap over the Great Wall, a dragon change into a tiger; the tiger become a dragon.

'I remember the first time I made love with Mason,' Tree said. 'He was still a virgin. I was not, but the sex I had experienced had been more out of curiosity than desire or love. It was a full-moon night like this, with little puffs of salty breeze off the ocean, calm and bright as a mirror. We were in our special hideaway – I do not know the word for it in your language – a lighthouse.'

'A house built of light? How magical.'

K'un-Chien felt rather than saw Tree smile. She believed she could feel Tree's heartbeat, strong and full like her own.

'Not a house of light,' Tree said. 'A lighthouse is a tower with a powerful rotating beacon light, a signal to warn ships away from reefs.'

'That seems nearly as magical.'

'Mason and I were alone on the balcony of the lighthouse. So nervous. So thrilled. We were both trembling and weak as if we had gone too long without eating. We undressed each other slowly – he said it was like unveiling a masterwork. When I saw how huge he was I think I gasped; I'm not sure why – it was not his physical size that daunted me – it was the size of his desire, of my own passion. I had never felt sexual hunger that way. My appetite was deeper than the sea the lighthouse overlooked, I was submerged in it, breathing underwater. "So this is what all the poetry and drama is about," I told myself, and I knew, then, that my life would never be the same. But when I looked back at Mason, he had become shy . . . he had read my expression and now he felt he needed to hide his raw desire. He started to pull his pants back on while mumbling some apology.'

K'un-Chien turned to Tree, holding her breath, powerfully

aroused by the story of two lovers she loved so much herself.

'How could I explain to him that the emotion that overwhelmed me was unavoidable?' Tree said. 'It was the shock of discovery: I had suddenly awakened as a woman. I could not talk. I wanted him completely. I tugged off his pants and pulled him down on me. All night we floated on the wooden deck between the moon and the sea, feeding each other's souls with our bodies.'

Tree turned to K'un-Chien and the sky-glow lit her green eyes. 'Mason likes to quote a proverb: "The best sauce in the world is hunger."'

With a little cry, K'un-Chien grabbed Tree into her arms and kissed her eyes and mouth. Tree parted her lips and their tongues interplayed like necking swans. K'un-Chien felt she would die of a bursting heart but she couldn't stop kissing, tasting Tree's sweet breath. She opened Tree's robe and snuggled her face against the small breasts; breathing in the spirit-food Tree had talked about.

Tree moaned softly as K'un-Chien pressed her eyelids against her erect nipples, wetting them with warm tears. Then Tree drew open the curtain of K'un-Chien's kimono and her hands played over K'un-Chien's ample breasts like heat lightning. Two sets of nipples brushed together, satin on satin, and the pleasure that came from their shuddering made them shudder again. Their hearts pounded like one double-headed drum.

Tree's mouth moved down onto K'un-Chien's pink nipples, and she suckled strongly, as if gulping nourishment. K'un-Chien remembered that Tree had grown up motherless and she gathered Tree into her lap like a child. Tree curled up with eyes closed and nursed on a firm round breast while squeezing the other nipple between her fingers. K'un-Chien stroked Tree's hair and watched her lover's suckling mouth. Her nipples ached with pleasure. She felt that if her love was milk it might spew from her breasts and feed the world.

Tree pulled back from K'un-Chien's bosom, the nipples swollen from her strong sucking. 'I remembered my mother,' Tree said. 'Like a trace of fragrance in a vacant room. I never got to tell her I loved her . . .'

K'un-Chien cradled Tree's head against her bosom and rocked her, humming a classical Ming lullaby. It was her turn to feel tears splashing her skin.

Several troops of white-faced monkeys passed a raucous song back and forth; the loudest troop was encamped in a nearby banyan just beyond the palace's outer wall.

After a long cry, Tree became so relaxed K'un-Chien thought she might be sleeping, her face snuggled in K'un-Chien's cleavage.

K'un-Chien slipped Tree's silk robe the rest of the way off and began kissing her way downward, slowly, slowly, like a snail descending sacred Mount Meru, until she reached the curly delta mound. There she bowed, nudging her nose and mouth into Tree's slippery cup. Tree gasped and moaned. Everything was fragrance and flavor and heartbeat. *Wei dao le haoji.*

Then Tree tugged at the cummerbund on K'un-Chien's kimono and K'un-Chien panicked. Tree wanted her to turn around, to align their bodies toe to head, so that Tree could mirror her lovemaking. K'un-Chien's ironhard erection, tightly bound by a thick loin cloth, throbbed painfully for release. But if Tree were to discover her secret, how could Tree go on loving her?

She will be disgusted with my body, as my father was. I am so ugly – she will hate me.

'Tree, no.' K'un-Chien pushed her hand away.

'I want to taste you,' Tree said. 'You seduced me – why stop me now?'

'Please. Only let me pleasure you. I do not want you to reciprocate.'

Tree's eyebrows went up. 'You have your moon-blood? That is no shame. I would be a happy vampire.'

Tree reached down between K'un-Chien's thighs and K'un-Chien batted her hand away.

'No! You must not!' K'un-Chien leapt up, gulping for air. The dearest intimacy she had ever felt was splintering apart, all because of her freakish anatomy. She hung her head. 'I . . . I am sorry . . . it is my fault. I should not have brought you up here.'

'K'un-Chien, did I offend you?' Tree said, and laid a warm hand on K'un-Chien's shoulder.

At Tree's touch, K'un-Chien began to tremble. She shook her head, wanting to say, *You were wonderful,* but the lump in her throat was too tight to squeak out a whisper.

'Shhhh,' Tree held her closely. 'I do not understand, but it is all right.' Tree embraced her and their bare breasts cuddled. Tree's body heat pierced K'un-Chien's heart and she could not hold back her shame; she bawled with sputtering sobs.

'Oh, Tree . . .' she said, sniffling. 'Please, may I . . . please . . . ?' K'un-Chien could not bring herself to ask for what she desperately wanted: To seal the rift. To return to the embrace that had blended their souls.

'Come,' Tree said. 'I want you close again. Come to me.' Tree pulled K'un-Chien down on top of her. K'un-Chien kissed the firm curve of Tree's belly and burrowed her face between slippery petals of seashore.

Ecstasy. Heartdrum. Music of the blood.

Tree moaned and twisted her fingers in K'un-Chien's hair. Her breath came in heavy gasps and stops. Her belly tightened into a washboard; then she arched into a single band of trembling muscle, grinding against K'un-Chien's mouth. Tree muffled her screams by biting a satin pillow. In the next instant K'un-Chien was racked by a dual spasm of pleasure so intense it bordered on pain. She cried out too, fluttering inside her womb and spurting like a geyser.

In their bedroom of crickets, treefrogs and stars, the two wives lay panting in a shipwrecked heap, glistening inside and out. In the garden pool beneath the banyan tree, white lotuses were burning in moon flames, softly.

28

M ason awoke with head pain of nine on the tequila hang-
over scale. But he was grateful he at least no longer felt
nauseated. In fact, having thoroughly emptied his stomach
contents the night before, he now was famished. He sat up
in bed and saw Tree and K'un-Chien snuggled together on a
quilt spread over straw mats on the floor. *I thought something
was going on with those two.*

He examined the complex feelings that stirred in his body.
He wasn't sure what to name his sudden emotions, but was
relieved to find that jealousy was only a minor element in
the mix, like red pepper in a stew. Maybe he could remain
neutral about their budding love affair; maybe it was okay
– not something that required a reaction from him – so far,
anyway. He sighed. What he felt strongest was just plain envy.
He surely had missed out on something especially beautiful.

And the truth was, he was intrigued. He wondered at the
alchemy when a woman as passionate and sensual as Tree
combined with a woman as intense and ravishing as K'un-Chien:
bright fire and dark incense.

He wanted to ask Tree about the experience – or would she
consider the affair too private to discuss? He rehearsed for
that possibility: *Come on, Tree, you're my intimate friend, you*

can trust me with your feelings. K'un-Chien is my wife, for God's sake. You're both my wives.

Mason sighed again, reflecting on the comic absurdity of his situation. Here he was, married to two unreasonably beautiful women, who had now managed to fall in love with each other. So did that make the three of them a lusty trio, ready to make mysterious jazz between the sheets? Hell no. *Because I can't get it up.*

He forced a grim little laugh, then winced and clapped a hand to his head.

'May-Son?' K'un-Chien sat up. 'How do you feel this morning?'

'Like an elephant used me as a suppository.'

'Your head aches. It is caused by an imbalance in the Triple Burner. I can fix it.'

'Triple Burner?'

'One of the fourteen channels of *ch'i* through which energy circulates in the bodily vessel.'

The welts from her bee stings had subsided and faded to pale pink. The formula for that anti-inflammatory was just one facet of the medical knowledge Mason would like to pluck from her mind.

'I will show you, you will feel much better.' She climbed onto the bed and knelt behind him. The tension in his temples melted beneath her skilled fingers.

'I feel better already. Some of the pain is gone.'

'This is not the treatment. It is just to get you familiar with my touch so you can trust me and relax.'

'Well, I do trust you – completely.'

She climbed out of bed and sat on the floor in front of his feet. 'This will hurt at first, then you will be like new.' She lifted his right foot and pressed her thumb into a painful little knob on the instep of the sole.

'*Ouch!*' Mason shouted in a whisper. He didn't want to wake Tree. 'Feels like lightning, shooting straight into the core of my headache.'

K'un-Chien kept digging hard with her thumb. He pressed down on the top of his head with both hands to keep the bolt of pain from blasting a hole through the roof of his skull. Suddenly the pain began to drop away.

'Are you pressing as hard as you were?'

'I am applying even more pressure.'

His headache dissolved quickly now like salt in hot water. 'Gone,' Mason said, amazed. 'Vanished.'

'I pressed a *tsubo* that sent a messenger to open the gate of your Triple Burner. The meridian is now unblocked, restored to balance.'

He looked at her with unconcealed admiration. 'There are many aspects of the medical arts you practice that Western doctors such as myself have not even begun to imagine.'

She smiled. 'And can there be any doubt the reverse of your statement is also true? We could learn a great deal from each other.'

Mason wanted to ask the question on his mind but felt too bashful.

'Yes, husband. Ask me.'

'No . . . I . . . never mind. Thank you—'

'Do you want to know if I have a cure for male impotence?'

He gulped. 'Do you?'

She got up from the floor and sat on the bed beside him. 'Dear husband, you must understand – you are not impotent. I have seen you in the mornings – hard as teak.'

He sighed and hung his head. 'Yes, but . . .'

'But you are unable to manifest your manhood when loving Tree.'

'Exactly.'

'Listen. I have learned two things about you. The first is, you are a man of great and powerful feelings. The second thing I have observed is that you squeeze back your feelings, hold them down below your chest. You are afraid to feel the grief that lurks in you, and that is how you have given it power to rob your life and your manhood. With emotions as strong as yours, the effort to hide them away is exhausting.'

He sighed deeply. 'I think you have put it well.' And he reached up and ran his fingers through his black ringlets, amazed again at how K'un-Chien had erased his headache.

'Have you ever asked yourself how you hold your feelings down, how you keep yourself from encountering them?'

'Well. Tree and a few close friends have accused me of being numb. It is true that I often do not feel much – good or bad. Not like I used to.'

K'un-Chien nodded. 'You feel numb much of the time,' she said, 'but what I am asking is *how?* How do you manage to do that? What is the mechanism by which you make yourself numb if grief swells up?'

He shrugged. 'I don't know.'

'Of course you know. You are adept at it,' she said. 'Try it now. Think of something sad, and then make the feelings go away. Observe yourself closely and tell me exactly how you block your emotions.'

It was easy enough to think of something sad. Only a thin levee kept Mason partitioned from a sea of endless sorrow over Gib's death. Every day was a constant struggle to keep the flimsy levee in place, shore it up, stab his finger into any leaks. He was starting to see what she was talking about. He'd caught himself doing it just now. When the sorrow swelled, he pushed against the levee by tensing his muscles; his jaw, his chest, his gut; he locked the energy inside the tight box of meat that was his body. And he stopped breathing to deaden the seawaves, to stop the motion and the emotion and the life. No rhythm, no flow, no feelings.

'I guess I tighten my muscles against the . . . uh, I was going to say energy.'

'Yes. *Energy*. That's what emotions are – energy, life-force. They *flow*.'

'Right. And I hold my breath. That stops the flow.' He sighed. 'Makes sense. That is why I do not experience the heights or depths that I felt when I was younger.' He gave a crooked smile. 'I used to be quite the passionate man: poet, lover, idealist – all that volatile nonsense. Life has flattened out for me.'

'The Tao of the body and mind includes this simple principle: If we numb ourselves to pain, we numb ourselves also to pleasure. If we would feel joy, we must be open to sorrow.'

'Only two settings, eh? Open or closed. I know you are right, but how I wish it were not so.'

'What would happen if you let your feelings out? Let them express themselves without hindrance, without pinning them under your ribcage?'

'No. I could not.' Mason ran his hand through his hair. 'That would ... I could not do that.' He shivered. 'That would destroy me.'

'At what price do you cope? You are unable to make love to the person who means the most to you in the world. You say relaxing your grip on your emotions would destroy you – but *who* has survived?'

'A wax figure of Mason Drake.' He choked up and automatically squeezed his throat and chest tighter to trap the sadness inside. 'Since Vietnam, I feel like the biggest part of me has been dead.'

K'un-Chien put a strong and slender arm around his broad shoulders. 'Have you heard the Chinese proverb, "We learn by teaching"?'

'"*Homines dum docent discunt*" – "While they teach, men learn." Seneca, the Roman philosopher.'

She nodded. 'What I am saying to you is this: I seem to be an expert regarding your troubles because they duplicate my own. I, too, am adept at repressing emotions and I do it by the same method – by deadening my breath and stiffening my whole body. Caving in upon myself.' She gave his shoulder a squeeze. 'I do not mean to make you into an isolated example, husband.'

'I understand. And I thank you for the insight you have given me. But, to be honest, I am too afraid of my grief to set it free. I believe it would kill me.'

'We both have killed ourselves to keep our grief from laying its hands upon us. I did not realize it myself until last night. I have been unable to sleep, wondering what to do with this new wisdom.'

Mason nodded. 'I will be glad to listen to you, if you want to talk about it. Meng Po has told me about your brothers' deaths.'

'That would have been enough sorrow, but there is more to my woe than that.'

'Would it help to share it? What has hurt you so?'

She smiled crookedly. 'If I could tell the man I love, would I not be already healed?'

Mason's heart skipped a beat. 'I . . . I love you too, K'un-Chien. And I'm happy for you and Tree.'

K'un-Chien shook her head. 'You do not know my situation. Neither does Tree.' The tears in her eyes made them brighter blue. 'I would very much like to help you and Tree get back together. That is a love that was meant to be.'

Mason pursed his lips. 'She is better off without me. I would only drag her down. Something happened in my past, during a war far from home, and . . .' He gulped and shoved hard against the levee so it would not give way. 'If only I could go back and change my actions – ten minutes – five minutes. Just five minutes of one lifetime. That would make all the difference.'

'I believe I can help you,' K'un-Chien said, and took his hand. 'It is obvious that you feel a terrible guilt. And of course, you cannot change your past. But you can *revisit* the past. And by revisiting it, you can review it. See it again. Often a new perspective is all that is required to revise the whole dynamic of your karma. I can help you go back to your past.'

He shrugged. 'What do you mean, "go back"?'

'Ling-Chih,' she said. 'You can take the Sacred Mushroom. In a person whose orientation to the past is stronger than to the future, the journeys are always to the past.'

'But what good would that do? They are only drug-induced visions.'

'No. More than visions. You will have to make the journey yourself to understand the truth of what I am saying. It is much more than a dream or a vision.'

'Look, I do not mean to insult you, but if revisiting your past is so therapeutic, why have you not taken the Ling-Chih and healed your own unhappiness?'

'Because my karma leans toward the future. I have a destiny I was born to fulfill. I have used the mushroom only once and I saw what I was to become.'

'And what is that?'

She lowered her head. 'The very secret I cannot tell you or Tree.'

Mason blew out a long breath and fell back on the mattress, hands behind his head, his biceps bulging against the blue satin sheets. 'I do not want to revisit my past unless I can change it,' he said. 'I do not want to see what I did all over again.'

'But you already see your "crime" – every day. The Tao

requires that whatever you oppose be held always before you, like a hand in your face. You constantly repeat what you did; in your mind it never stops. That is your suffering. But if you could revise your view, see your actions again in a new light—'

Mason flashed upon Gib's mud-smeared face, raindrops spattering on open blue eyes. Gib's unblinking stare carried no accusation or acquittal – and no farewell.

'I killed my best friend. There is no better way to view it. I killed him. He's dead because of *me*.' Mason's face twitched as he clenched his jaw.

K'un-Chien lay down beside Mason and hugged him close, kissed his cheek. Her warm breasts beneath her thin robe pillowed against his ribs. Her tenderness only made it more difficult for him to shore up the straining levee that held back his hurt. The sea of his sorrow had never come so close to bursting through and drowning him.

29

Kiki ran to the bars and chattered excitedly, happy to see
Mason. Meng Po's eyes reflected the same joy.

'Welcome, welcome, Elder Brother,' Meng Po said. 'We're
glad to see you. A visit from you is like the sun burning away
the mists.'

'The sentiment is mutual. Indeed, I came today because I was
feeling sad and I knew you would cheer me up.'

'Shall we trade haiku, or paint?'

'Not today, Little Brother. I do not feel much like composing
poems or trying to create beauty while in an ugly mood.'

'Then shall we practice calligraphy? You are improving rap-
idly. You have nearly mastered Hsieh Ho's Six Principles. Next,
I will teach you the "slender gold" style of the Song emperor,
Hui Zong.'

'Ha. You make you fun of me. At this very moment Hsieh
Ho is bellowing in the Hall of the Ancestors: "Oh no! Not that
fool barbarian again! A cave fish – no eyes! no hands!—could
practice my principles with finer technique."'

Meng Po laughed. 'See, already you give me mirth. I have not
laughed all day.'

'Yeah, boss,' Mason said in a Southern black dialect. 'We
both got da blues.' And he began to sing *Sitting on the Dock of
the Bay*. Meng Po listened with rapt attention. Mason finished

the last verse and whistled the melody until it trailed away.

'A song can be sad and beautiful at the same time,' Meng Po said. 'Like a poem. Like life.'

'Look, I have brought you a gift.' Mason held out a disk he'd carefully whittled and sanded from a block of balsa wood. It looked like a large, very shallow bowl with beveled edges.

Meng Po smiled and took it. 'Thank you. I will treasure it.'

Mason laughed. 'I would wager that you do not know what the thing is that you intend to treasure.'

'A bowl, of course. Well made, but surely intended only for decor. It could not hold much food, and liquid would soak into the pores.'

'It is not a bowl. It is a flying toy.'

A smile tugged at Meng Po's lips. 'You are teasing me.'

'You can make it fly. Let me show you.'

Meng Po handed back the disk. Mason pointed and said, 'See that book sitting on top of the shelf against the far wall? Watch me.' He cocked his wrist and hurled the balsa disk. It soared fast to the bookshelf and knocked the book off onto the thickly carpeted floor. Kiki squealed and clapped his hands, then ran to fetch the balsa disk.

'Excellent,' Meng Po said. 'Can you show me?'

'Of course.' Mason took the disk from Kiki. 'This is called a Frisbee. Well, actually, this is just a balsa version of a Frisbee. A real Frisbee is a flying disk made of a material we call *plastic*.'

Meng Po furrowed his brow. 'Plastic?'

'Never mind, that does not matter,' Mason said. 'I have played with Frisbees for years. For some reason, I have always had a talent for throwing them well. Each year, there was a Frisbee Tournament at my college and one of the competitions was throwing at targets, both stationary and moving. We called it Frisbee Golf. I was the Frisbee Golf champion four years in a row, until I graduated.'

'Plastic?' Meng Po said. 'Is that what you call it? I thought they were plates.' He hopped up and Kiki tumbled from his lap. He hurried to the far side of the barred room and opened a deep wooden chest. He ran back with an armload of plastic Frisbees, bright neon and glow-in-the-dark colors. 'So these are Frisbees!' Meng Po said.

'Aha,' Mason said. 'So they were not destroyed. They came from the mountaintop workstation we called the Raft.'

'The soldiers brought them to me. I like to collect unusual things, and the strange material these "plates" are made of was fascinating. *Plastic*.' Meng Po bent a Frisbee in his hand and practiced the new word. '*Plastic*. Most odd. And beautiful colors.'

'I brought a few dozen with me to give to the Wawajero Indians that I work with each winter. A few years ago, I taught them to play with Frisbees and now they are wild about the sport.'

When Mason had first contacted the Wawajero tribe on his medical outreach program, the males were constantly showing up with strains, sprains and fractures from playing a violent stick-and-ball game similar to lacrosse, called *bunjarao*. First the players from both teams got tanked on cup after cup of a steaming black mud made from coffee and gotu-kola, which they guzzled until they puked. Then, with caffeine clanging through their nerves, they played the game like madmen for hours. Mason had decided they needed a non-violent alternative to *bunjarao*, so he'd introduced them to Ultimate Frisbee – a passing and running game like a cross between football and soccer. They had loved it instantly. The teams now got crazy on caffeine and smashed each other while playing Ultimate Frisbee; Mason ended up sewing and patching just as many crunched players as before.

'Show me again,' Meng Po said. 'Hit the back of that guard's helmet.' He pointed and giggled. 'Her name is Pa Kwo. She has the uncanny ability to sleep while standing up, leaning on her lance. See. You can tell by her even breathing that she is asleep right now.'

'Without doubt I could hit her helmet, but I do not want to make her lose face. I might make an enemy, and I do not need more enemies here.'

'You are wise, although Pa Kwo is the nicest guard who watches over me. She does not have a vicious temper like Commander Yu and some of the others. She tells me funny stories, thinks of things to do to keep me – to keep us both – from getting so bored we fall asleep on our feet. In fact, she's the one that brought me your Frisbees.'

'I am glad she did not keep them to use for food plates.'

'Actually, she did keep a few for that purpose.' Meng Po laughed. 'I have eaten from them as well.' He turned, eyes scanning the room. 'I know. Hit the stork in that painting on the wall. Can you? The fat one, flying on the left.'

'I think I could. But I do not want to damage your painting. It is my favorite. It is so . . . artless and innocent. I hope you will not misunderstand me when I say that it is primitive – and therein lies its beauty.'

'I understand you completely – that is exactly what I like about the painting. But it is not mine.'

'Whose? K'un-Chien's?'

Kiki hopped up and down and ran to the painting and slapped at it with a small black hand with long, thin fingers.

'Kiki answers your query.'

'What?' Mason eyes grew big. 'Now you are the one who is teasing.'

Meng Po shook his head, grinning. 'Kiki painted it.'

Mason felt stunned. 'Not possible,' he blurted.

'Oh yes. Kiki is quite an artist.'

'How . . . ? How smart *is* he?'

Kiki ran back to Meng Po's lap and the boy kissed the sage-monkey on his floppy white mustache. 'This little man will do just about anything if you rub his stomach or give him a fortune cookie. I recently trained him to write his own name.'

'Oh, please. I have got to see that with my own eyes.'

'Kiki, get your brush,' Meng Po said. The cinnamon-furred primate opened a narrow wooden box and took out a thick-handled calligraphy brush made of lacquered cherry wood with a pointed tuft of human hairs.

'I make the ink for him,' Meng Po said, 'he makes too big a mess.' The boy lifted the lid off his inkstone and added three water droplets. He ground a black inkstick on the wet stone and then added a pinch of powdered cinnabar to turn the puddle deep scarlet. Next he unrolled a blank linen paper scroll to shoulder-width and knelt before it.

'Kiki, here is your ink,' Meng Po said. 'Come write your name.'

The sage-monkey took his brush and dipped it in the scarlet ink. He made several quick, broad strokes that swooped over the paper like swallows. Then he flung a spatter of crimson droplets on top of the calligraphy.

Meng Po laughed. 'He always does that at the end. I tried to train him not to, but I have come to believe it is his personal signature – he likes it.'

'It reads' – Mason cocked his head to the left – ' "Kiki Sage-Monkey?"'

'Yes. All his characters slant to the left. It is the way he holds his brush.'

'I am utterly astounded. He is unlike any animal that any scientists from my world know of – or even dream of. Kiki is in a class all by himself.' Mason thought for a moment. 'Or maybe it is that we humans are *not* in a class all by ourselves. I think that is what is such a huge shock to me – to everything I have studied in school. We humans are not alone.'

'I am never alone when my friend Kiki is here.'

Kiki hopped over and took Mason's hand, searched it. It was empty.

'He wants you to give him a reward,' Meng Po said. 'Here. Give him one of these. He delights in them.'

Mason took a deep-fried pastry from the boy. 'A fortune cookie?'

'You have heard of them?'

'I have eaten them many times. But . . . I had always thought fortune cookies are not an authentic Chinese food.'

'Indeed. And I was told it was something my father invented. But clearly that was mistaken, because you have eaten them before.'

Kiki took the cookie from Mason and cracked the crisp pastry shell with sharp little teeth. He snatched out the slip of paper with his purple tongue and handed the fortune to Meng Po. The boy read the calligraphy.

'It says, "*Your life will be filled with marvels.*" ' Meng Po grinned. 'My father brought a lot of strange ideas with him from the land where he came. He claimed he had been looking for us for much of his life.'

Mason gasped. 'My God,' he blurted in English. Then in Mandarin, 'Do you know the name of his homeland?'

'Oh yes. Kiki, from where did father come?'

'Aah-maah-ree-kaah,' the sage-monkey said.

'America,' Meng Po echoed, and handed Kiki another cookie.

Mason sat down, feeling dizzy. *So that was it. The old man* had *made it to 'El Dorado' after all.*

Huxley Summerwood – Tree's father – was the father of K'un-Chien and Meng Po. Tree was their half-sister. That's why K'un-Chien's blue eyes reminded Mason so much of Gib. He had thought it was her intensity, her soul-fire, but that was only part of it – it was an actual physical resemblance. Gib and K'un-Chien had the same father. And Meng Po was another child prodigy – just like his half-brother, Gib. *How could Tree and I have missed it?* The Asian features of K'un-Chien's face and eyes, the exotic setting of Prayer Mat of the Body, had obscured the obviousness of the truth.

What's this going to do to Tree? She's falling into a love affair with her half-sister. He glanced around the palatial room with its Ming-style tile work and architecture. *Does it make any difference, now – here? Do the morals of Western civilization, so far away, apply in Jou P'u T'uan? Wouldn't it be better not to tell her?*

'May-Son, let me show you my collection of mysterious things and you can tell me what they are.'

'What?' Mason asked, still dazed.

'My things from the outside world. Will you tell me what they are?'

Mason nodded. 'Of course. Show me.'

Meng Po walked back to the large wooden chest. He lifted out a pair of battered binoculars and arched his eyebrows inquisitively.

'For seeing at a long distance,' Mason said.

'Ah so. I thought as much.'

'Have you not tried gazing through them?'

'Yes, but everything is blurred.'

Mason stood. 'Toss them here.'

Meng Po tossed the binoculars underhand and Mason caught them with his hands inside the bars. He looked through the eyepieces, but the internal lenses had broken off their mounts and the focusing mechanism was jammed.

'They are called *binoculars*,' Mason said. 'This pair is broken.' He rubbed at a rusted serial number plate; the fieldglasses were an antique Dutch military model, manufacturer's date: 1810. Must've belonged to some European adventurer who last century had added his genes to the daughters of the valley.

'Do you know the history, the owner?' Mason said.

'I was told they belonged to someone who lived here years ago, long before my father.' Meng Po's muffled voice came from halfway inside the deep trunk.

'I know what this is,' Meng Po said, straightening up holding a long metal flashlight. 'It is a magic torch that burns cool fire. But after it shined for one night and one day, the flame died out. Can you restore the magic?'

'The batteries – the energy storage cells – have been depleted. I cannot restore the . . . uh, magic.' Mason smiled, thinking that modern technology was often indistinguishable from magic, even for himself. He regarded his personal computer as nothing less than a box full of little miracles.

'What does this do?' Meng Po held up a silver pipe lighter and flicked its hinged cap open and shut.

'May I hold it?' Mason caught the lighter and turned it over in his hand. One side bore the raintree logo for Halcyon Pharmaceutical Corporation and the other side was engraved: Barry Levine, Ph.D., Director, H.A.R.V.E.S.T.

Mason flipped the striker and a butane-blue flame appeared.

'Wonderful!' Meng Po said.

'It is used for lighting the bowl of a pipe.'

'For smoking opium?'

'No. At least, not in this case – aromatic leaves, called *tobacco*. This lighter belonged to an old colleague.' Mason smiled sadly, remembering his bear-sized friend; there'd better be good smoke shops in the next world, or Barry would be less than pleased.

'Please keep it. I can see it holds sentimental value for you.'

'Yes, it does. Thank you.' Mason pocketed the lighter.

Meng Po held up a video camcorder. 'And what is this?'

'Oh. Bring that to me and I will show you something amazing.'

Mason aimed through the eyepiece at the boy and pressed RECORD. After a few seconds, he stopped taping, rewound for an instant, then beckoned Meng Po to stare into the eyepiece. Mason pressed PLAY and Meng Po jumped back. He looked at Mason with huge eyes.

'How did I get inside there? Is it my soul? Please let me out.'

'Sorry, I did not mean to scare you,' Mason said. 'You are not inside the box. It can only capture images of light. The same light waves that reflect from objects and travel through space to your eyes are recorded in the form of, uh . . .' *How do you say 'electrons' in Mandarin?*

Meng Po frowned and bit his lower lip.

'No, no, everything is fine,' Mason said. 'You see, a rolling tape inside this box is coated with . . . well, let us simply call the whole thing magic. Only your reflected-light image is recorded in the magic box. Your soul is safe and sound, Meng Po. Trust me.'

'I trust you,' Meng Po said, and swallowed hard.

'Here, I will erase your image in the box, then you will not have to worry.' Mason put the camera to his eye to erase the short recording. He rewound past it. What he saw in reverse mode made him lurch as Meng Po had done. The backs of Mason's knees bumped the love-seat and he slumped down.

'What is it?' Meng Po said. 'You look as pale as I must look.'

'I thought I saw something.' Mason rewound the videotape for a couple minutes till it stopped. He pressed PLAY. The video footage had been recorded at the Raft. The camera must have been lying on the floor – the scene tilted at a crazy angle. Lynda Loyola's head filled the upper half of the frame, inverted, as if she were suspended from the ceiling; a huge albino harpie eagle perched on her chest, round red eyes darting nervously. The built-in microphone recorded the jingle-jangle of talon bells as the raptor hacked dripping chunks of flesh from the dead woman's face and jerked back its beak to gulp them down. Mason watched the harpie swallow the ruined sack of an eyeball; its throat bulged as the food slid down whole. Mason fought down the bile that surged up in his throat.

Then a thrown object – it looked like a camera – hurtled

past the bird's head, slammed the wall with a metallic bang and bounced away on the aluminum floor. The all-white harpy took flight with a loud whuffling of broad wings.

After a horrible moment of staring at Lynda's ruined face, the camcorder lens caught Domino's boots and pantlegs stepping into and out of its wide-angle view. Mason stiffened and sat up. This was the part he'd seen before: Domino knelt on the floor and dumped out an armload of the Raft's four emergency transponders. Then he lifted a metal tool box over his head like a sledge and rammed it down, smashing the transmitters into junk. Domino disappeared from view. The next boots in the frame belonged to a dragon soldier.

The bastard. Mason clenched his jaw. He didn't know what it all meant, but one thing was clear: Domino had sabotaged their rescue. And even with Lynda's body lying nearby in a puddle of blood, Domino did his dirty work in an almost businesslike way – seemingly unafraid – as if he knew his own life was going to be spared.

'You are frightening me, May-Son,' Meng-Po said. 'What do you see in that demon box?'

Mason looked up from the camcorder. 'Meng Po, would you let me take this with me?'

'Please take it back. I despise it now.'

Mason pressed RECORD with his hand held over the lens. 'There. I have erased your image,' he said. 'Excuse me, Little Brother, I need to go consult with my colleague, Senor Cruz. I have a few questions for him.'

Mason spun and strode through the archway. This time he could not restrain himself from breaking into a run, so badly did he burn to kick down Domino's door and stomp the traitor's head in.

30

Domino was still asleep when Mason stormed into his bedroom. 'Get your ass up outta that bed, Domino. *Now!* We got a score to settle.'

Domino jumped up in alarm. He grabbed from a nightstand a pair of red pajama bottoms, tugged them on. Three of his wives scrambled naked from under purple satin sheets and darted from the room, terrified.

Domino held a pajama shirt in his hands. 'What's your fucking problem this early in the morning?'

'*This* is my problem.' Mason shoved the camcorder into Domino's gut. 'You're on Candid Camera, asshole. Why the hell did you smash the transponders?'

Domino's face turned pale. 'Look . . . I didn't know.'

Mason shoved him hard against the wall.

Domino whipped out a knife from beneath his bundled shirt and poked the tip against Mason's belly. 'I grew up on the streets, remember?' he hissed. 'Now back off, hombre, or I'll cut your plumbing. *Bueno.* Now sit your ass down. *Muy bueno.* Okay . . . just keep your ass glued to that chair and I'll try to tell you the way my mind was working that morning.'

Mason sat tensely in a lacquered ebony chair. 'All right, I'm listening. Start explaining.'

'Look, I didn't know what was going on. All I knew, Lynda was

205

dead. And the helicopter – *boom* – I'd already heard it explode. I thought I was on my own – I had no idea you and Tree were survivors – so first of all, I didn't do anything I thought would affect anybody other than me.'

'You smashed the transponders to screw any chance you might get *yourself* rescued off the mountain. That it? You wanted to just stay here and die?'

'No, of course not. I knew I wasn't going to die.'

'How?'

' 'Cause I got big *huevos*.' He grabbed his testicles. 'They need men in a society of Amazons, they don't kill men here. Unless they maybe fuck 'em to death.'

'But . . . how the hell did you know about the Amazons?'

'I didn't . . . I mean, not ahead of time, not until the shit hit the fan. Then I put it all together in my mind. You see, I'm mestizo – part Spanish, part Indian.' He nodded. 'Yeah, you talk to anybody in my family they'll all claim we're pure Castillanos – like we just sailed outta Madrid last summer. Funny thing. Millions of Indians in Venezuela but somehow everybody's managed to keep a pure Spanish bloodline down the centuries – nobody ever messed with no native women. Bullshit.

'Anyway, my grandmother was a Yanomamo – a servant girl, brought back to the city by some copper prospector or something, I never got the whole story. She used to tell me tales from her tribe and neighboring tribes she'd heard as a kid. Some of her stories scared the crap outta me – about shrunken heads and piranha and electric eels. I remember, she said, "In the jungle, there is one door into life, and ten thousand doors into death".'

'What's your point?'

'She told me all about this mountain region and its female warriors. Some Indians call them *brujas amarillas* – yellow witches – and others call them *Coniupuyara* – means something like *Grand Mistresses*.'

'You knew they were here? For chrissakes, why didn't you warn us?'

'You're not letting me finish. I didn't even think they were real, let alone on this very mountain. I had just heard the folklore – myths, you know – about yellow witches who would come down and steal male children from the Indian villages. To me, it just seemed like a sexual fantasy – a whole city of women so hard up for cock they had to kidnap jungle boys for a lifetime of stud service. Used to exercise my *glorioso* to the idea – you know, man.'

'But you never guessed the stories were true?'

'Hell, no. Like I said, to me it was all a fantasy. I never believed it until the harpie killed Lynda and I saw women soldiers coming over the ridge. Then I knew instantly – Amazons – and I knew what this place was ... They were coming to kidnap me, take me to paradise. I'd never felt so lucky.'

'So you smashed the transponders ... ?'

Domino took a breath. 'I'm sorry. Like I told you, I didn't know it would affect anyone else. Thought I was the sole survivor.'

'But ... I still don't get it. Why bother—?'

''Cause Barry had the damned things programmed to transmit an SOS if they weren't reset every twenty-four hours. I'm no good with electronics—'

'And you didn't want to be found, period.'

'What can I say? I got a weakness for pussy, a life of leisure – and as it turned out, this place is more luxurious than I'd imagined.'

Mason shook his head. He didn't know whether to slug Domino or feel sorry for him. Given that the man gripped a knife, he decided that pity was more prudent. Mason was sexually impotent, yet he felt he'd been given eyes to see the fullest beauty of women, and sex had always been only a part of that beauty for him; indispensable, like sugar in pie, but only an element of the whole recipe.

Domino was his opposite, his shadow. The man was potent, all right – several dozen of his wives were pregnant – but he had no sensitivity to the grace of the goddess; therefore, his manhood was corrupted.

'Okay,' Mason said, 'I think I understand now. You're no saboteur, you're just a guy who thinks with his dick.'

'Speak for yourself. You think too much, that's why your dick argues with you.'

'You know, for all your love of pussy, it seems to me you

hate women, or at least you don't know how to love them completely.'

'I love them from the waist down, amigo, pretty damn good.'

'What about the Empress? I mean, I'm curious – were you able to make love with her?'

'*Fantastico*. Gave her two or three orgasms, no lie. I rested a couple days before the ceremony, you know, so I stayed hard like *el toro* all night. She got a nice body – too bad about her face. I just concentrated, you know, didn't look into her eyes or nothing. I wouldn't be surprised if I made her pregnant.'

Mason shook his head. 'You're a real piece of work, Domino. That video footage . . . tell me the truth, didn't you give a damn about Lynda? Where was your big knife then, when she was getting killed?'

'Fuck you.' Domino flipped up his middle finger. 'I was below the Raft on the ground photographing some little shrew-like rodent – new species,' he said. 'Lynda was up in the lab taping another video-journal entry. I heard the chopper crash and explode. I never even saw the eagle attack. Lynda screamed and I came flying up the ladder. I threw my Nikon at the bird and it flew off, but I was too late, blood was everywhere, Lynda was dead. She'd knocked over the camera tripod, or maybe I did, dunno, I was freaking out, man. Guess it was still recording.'

'Okay, so she was already dead. But didn't you feel a twinge of emotion for the poor woman? Try to cover up her body or anything? In the footage she's just lying there—'

Domino shrugged. 'Dead is dead. What are you, a mystic?'

They turned their heads toward a clamoring in the hallway. A half-dozen soldiers burst through the bedroom door, swords drawn. The soldiers stopped and shot glances from Domino to Mason who both now sat in chairs, talking civilly.

'What is going on here, foreigner?' Yu Lin said, sticking the tip of her sword under Mason's chin so he had to stand up from his chair on tiptoe.

'So sorry,' Domino said, bowing and smiling. 'We were having a noisy argument before, most impolite. Everything is fine now.'

Mason stretched up on his toes and squeaked out, 'Please forgive us for upsetting the *fung shui* of the community this morning.'

'We offer our humblest apologies, Commander Yu,' Domino said. 'And to repair the harmony, I'll send a trio of my younger wives as ambassadors of good will to your bedchamber tonight.'

Yu Lin looked at Domino and withdrew her sword. Mason coughed and wiped at a spot of blood on his neck. Yu Lin grabbed Mason's arm and stuck her face close to his.

'I do not tolerate petty disturbances in my city, barbarian. You have shown once again that you have no manners. One more commotion and you will pay for it with far more than a nick on your throat.'

Mason bowed. 'Yes, Commander Yu. Understood.'

Yu Lin nodded to her soldiers and they sheathed their swords and strode out of the room. She paused in the doorway. 'See that you send to me your three youngest wives,' she told Domino.

Domino nodded. 'Of course.'

She spun on her heels and departed.

'Dyke bitch,' Domino whispered.

Mason stood to leave and Domino followed him to the door.

'Maybe I should apologize,' Mason said, 'for stomping in here the way I did – but goddamit, you really screwed things up. It just might cost Tree and me our lives, but hey, it was all for an endless supply of pussy, no?'

'There is a solution to your problem, amigo,' Domino said. 'Tree is supposed to get pregnant or they'll kill her. Send her to me. One night, man – if you really love her.' His black mustache curled around a broad-toothed smile. 'One night, I'll save her life. Then send the blue-eyed girl to me, I'll save her life too. I'm ready.'

Mason stammered. He felt his rage rekindled, but it was smothered by a blanket of shame. Truth was, he'd thought of the same solution himself and had been agonizing that it might come to that.

He turned and hurried out the door, feeling angry at everyone, himself most of all.

31

K 'un-Chien entered the steamy bathhouse and saw Mason
soaking in the hot water.

'Exit the door, check the weather; enter the door, check the
face,' she said. 'What is wrong? You look so forlorn.'

Mason sighed. 'In another six weeks Tree will be banished if
she is not made pregnant by me, and I will be castrated. But I
am unable to help her as a husband. In some ways I am already
a eunuch.'

K'un-Chien walked over to the edge of the large tub and began
to massage the thick muscles of his shoulders and neck. 'Have
you thought any more about the Ling-Chih?'

'I have thought about little else since our conversation. But
. . . just thinking about it makes me recoil with fear. My stomach
is twisted in knots.'

'So is your neck,' she said, kneading the muscles deeply.
'May-Son, remember how I told you that I could read your
troubles so well because they matched my own?'

He nodded.

'I was like a blind woman carrying a lantern. Its light was
real, but I could not see it.'

'Poetry runs in your family,' Mason said. As soon as he said
it, he remembered K'un-Chien was Tree's half-sister. Their love
affair was incestuous. *I won't be the one to tell them*. In this

exotic realm far removed from the conventions of Western society, two innocent sisters who wound up in each other's arms should not be told their love is a crime.

'Lately I have begun understanding the ways in which I have practiced hating myself, shackling my mind to the past,' K'un-Chien said. 'Now I am beginning to live the truth I spouted to you. I have confronted my pain for the first time, and so far it has stopped short of killing me,' she said. 'I realize now, the best way is to keep moving through it, do not stand still.'

Mason smiled at her, in spite of his gloomy mood. 'It is plain to see that you are in love, K'un-Chien. No other medicine in the world has that kind of soul-healing power. If doctors could bottle the hormones and energies circulating through people newly in love, one swig would do what Jesus did for Lazarus.'

'Who?'

'I forgot you have never heard of those two.'

'I feel like the phoenix,' she said. 'Loneliness burned me to ashes, but now I have hope that someday I will be reborn.'

'Yes, that is what I was saying.'

K'un-Chien continued to massage Mason's shoulders and neck. *Such strong hands.* He leaned his head back as she rubbed his temples and scalp with expert fingers. He sighed and closed his eyes.

A warm kiss on his lips made his eyelids pop open. His lips parted in surprise and K'un-Chien bent her head and covered his mouth with hers. Her long hair spilled forward into the tub and spread out upon the water in a black slick. Mason remembered himself as a little boy hiding in the umbrella-cave of a weeping willow, engulfed in redolent shadow.

He reached up and held K'un-Chien's face tenderly and eagerly returned her kisses. Her mouth poured nectar over the famished bee of his tongue. His lower body stirred and curved upward hard and thick as an ivory tusk.

Mason knew from interludes with other women after his divorce that he was impotent only with Tree. She'd been the third lightbeam of a three-rayed star – Mason and Gib and Tree – a triskelion of friendship that had been the sun of his life. After Vietnam, whenever he'd tried to make love with Tree memories of Gib tore at his mind and seemed to drain his body like a wound. But with other women, he'd managed to stay focused in the pleasure of the moment and that had sustained him.

Now he felt an almost violent strength of desire; he hadn't the slightest doubt he'd be able to make love with K'un-Chien. Yet he made himself pull back from the sweetness of her mouth.

'K'un-Chien . . . I . . . what about Tree? I have already hurt her enough. This is not fair.'

'Tree and I have talked about this. She loves you. She loves me. She told me she wanted us to be intimate with each other. Remember, I too must become pregnant.'

Mason's breath shook with inner trembling. For weeks he'd wanted to touch K'un-Chien, hold her close. But even now it seemed a dilemma. How could he let himself make love with K'un-Chien while he was unable to make love with Tree? Tree had given her blessings, but how would it make her feel, really?

Mason swallowed hard. K'un-Chien's kisses had made his blood feel hotter than the steaming bath. 'But . . . Tree will feel jealous.'

'She told me she wants this between us – she asked me to make love with you.'

'I feel . . . please do not take this wrong, K'un Chien, but . . . I only wish it could be her. I need to make her pregnant, or I will lose her to Domino.'

K'un-Chien shook her head. 'You could not lose her to another man, your heart is tattooed upon hers. And Mason – I want to get pregnant, too.'

Her hands played over his furry chest, fingers circling his brown nipples. He moaned softly. He wanted so badly to take her down, to immerse himself in her beauty.

He stood and turned. Water ran down his chest in strings of beads. He swept K'un-Chien off her feet and carried her to the futon bed. Mason felt the firm and supple curves of her breasts nestled against him. Neither of them moved. He wanted just to lie next to her for a long time, drinking in the moment. Not thinking. With his lips opened against hers, he breathed her sweet breath down into his belly again and again.

Wet hair fell across half her face and he gathered it in his fingers and gently lifted it away and splayed it across her back. Half-closed, her sapphire eyes exaggerated their Oriental upsweep. She nuzzled the dark curls on his chest, inhaling deeply; and at the same time, her fragrance, like warm butter and musk, stirred beneath his mind and took hold of his soul; his heart thumped faster.

'One moment,' K'un-Chien said, and stood and crossed the room. She padded back to the bed with two purple silk scarves. With one, she tied her long hair up in a turban. Then she folded the extra scarf several times lengthwise and began to tie it around his eyes as a blindfold.

Mason smiled, but pushed it away. 'I want to see you. You are so beautiful.'

'I insist. It is for my own modesty. Please? I will be more relaxed during first congress with my husband.'

In the flush of desire, Mason had forgotten that K'un-Chien was a virgin. Now that fact hit his belly like a deep swig of whiskey and took his breath away. He was already fully aroused, but the idea of being K'un-Chien's first male lover was both tremendously exciting and endearing. His cock became achingly stiff, bouncing with each heartbeat.

'Cover my eyes, then,' he said. 'Hurry. I want you so badly.'

With blindfold in place, Mason felt the mattress dip as K'un-Chien climbed into bed. Their bare skin touched with a shock of bliss. She slid up his chest until her fragrant mound was an inch from his mouth. Warm butter and musk.

He grabbed her hips and buried his face in her garden. Her moans covered his ears like moss. The pulse in his cock had turned into bodily throbs. He felt he might burst from his own male power. An impulse came to pin her shoulders against the mattress and drive himself in so deep he'd feel their pubic bones meshing; but she was a virgin and he chose to touch her as carefully as a child beginning piano.

Mason kissed and sucked K'un-Chien's breasts and she purred from deep in her throat. Her breasts seemed smaller to his mouth and hands than they had appeared to his eyes; she pressed taut nipples against his swirling tongue. His fingers dipped between her thighs and were drenched in a hot slippery flood. Now he felt her heart pounding against his own, their torsos shiny with sweat.

'K'un-Chien, I'm aching, let me take you now.' But he only moaned louder when she raised her hips to meet him as he slid inside. 'Shhhh. Stop. Do not move just yet,' he said. 'Let me catch my breath, or I will explode.'

They rested in deep union for a timeless moment. A purring sound hummed from her throat. After a few long breaths, his urgency had melted into a feeling of fullness.

'Oh, K'un-Chien, you smell so good, your fragrance perfumes the room.'

Mason began to move, slowly at first, like steam rising in lazy coils from the summer sea. Rising and circling in the rich, scented air. Gathering, thickening into clouds. Building to higher and higher altitudes of pleasure. A thunderhead expanding up and up from the sea. Hotter now. More fragrant. Two hearts pounding like thunder in the swelling sky. His whole body more and more dense with rain. He could feel a cloudburst approaching, a typhoon swirling over the heat of the sea, churning the warm waters. Crest and trough, crest and trough, rhythm of the sea beneath a building mountain of rain.

K'un-Chien shuddered and pushed forward with her pelvis, gyrating her hips, grinding their pubic mounds. Her gasps turned into loud cries: 'Oh, oh, oh, oh . . . *ohhhhhhhhh!*' She sucked in her breath and arched her back, muscles clenching him in rippling spasms. Then the storm erupted inside Mason, a gushing monsoon with terrific lightning that jolted his body, head to toe.

'Oh Mason, God, I love you so much . . . so much, so much . . .'

Mason recognized the voice and ripped off his blindfold. It was Tree who snuggled her face into his neck and wept.

'Tree,' he whispered hoarsely. He tugged off her turban and apricot curls tumbled free.

They had made love passionately, as in their torrid past. Mason's gratitude mixed with sorrow. The ruse of the blindfold, he knew, could never work again.

32

K'un-Chien and Tree stood inside a gold-domed stupa at the center of the round room. K'un-Chien had wanted to bring her here to show her the marvelous acoustics – like standing inside a bell. K'un-Chien carried a cloth-draped bundle under each arm.

The carpet on the floor was woven in an octagonal pattern depicting the eight primary trigrams of the *I Ching*, the Chinese book of oracles. Beyond the borders of the mandala, fanciful animals from Chinese mythology circled the carpet.

K'un-Chien knelt and placed her bundles on the floor. She unwrapped the raw silk cloth from a seven-stringed zither called a *qin*. Quartz markers inlaid the lacquered rosewood of the fingerboard to indicate finger positions. K'un-Chien took a small ceramic pitch pipe from the folds of her robe and sounded the 'Yellow Bell' – the fundamental note of the Chinese quarter-tone musical scale. The note hovered in the air like a floating seed.

'Now I see what you meant,' Tree said, then put her hand to her mouth when the echoes of her voice bombarded her ears. She whispered, 'I see what you meant about the acoustics in here.'

K'un-Chien turned wooden pegs and tuned the silk-wound gut strings. Like all important instruments, the zither had been given its own name: Wind in the Ten Thousand Ravines. K'un-Chien strummed several chords, satisfied the tuning was true.

'Sing the fisherman's song,' Tree said, 'the one Mason likes.'

'Alas, my poor voice is not for delicate ears,' K'un-Chien said, being properly modest. It was now proper etiquette for Tree to insist.

'Alas, my poor ears cannot tell a nightingale from a gecko,' Tree said. 'Please sing. I think your voice is quite lovely.'

'The Analects say that music is as important to human nourishment as food,' K'un-Chien said. 'It would be impolite of me to let you go hungry.'

Tree smiled. 'That is one of the few teachings of K'ung Fu Tse with which I wholeheartedly agree.'

K'un-Chien plucked the strings of the zither; her mezzo voice sang out, rich with vibrato, a plaintive melody about a fisherman on the Yangtze who catches a magic fish that turns into a maiden. The domed ceiling amplified and recirculated the sound so that the music took on a tangible presence in the room. From inside the second bundle on the carpet pure tones rang, resonating with K'un-Chien's voice.

K'un-Chien watched Tree's face and smiled when she read her surprise.

'What is in there?' Tree said.

'Unwrap it. It is a gift for you.'

Tree opened the bundle and removed a hollow-bodied wooden instrument that resembled a lute, but with a more bulging sound box. She looked to K'un-Chien.

'What kind of music makes a lute pregnant?' Tree asked.

K'un-Chien laughed. 'Lay it on the floor in front of you like my zither.'

Tree knelt before the instrument. Within its deep soundbox dangled neat rows of quartz crystals of graduated size. Tree plucked a thick bass string. The larger crystals vibrated sympathetically, emitting a pure bass tone. She plucked a high string and the small cystals sang along. Next she strummed a chord and the crystals replied with multi-layered harmonics. In the exquisite acoustics of the golden dome, K'un-Chien felt the notes play over her skin.

Tree glanced at K'un-Chien with a big grin. 'Beautiful. What is it called?'

'A crystal lute. I named this instrument Voice of the Mountain. I have played it since I was a little girl, it was my favorite.'

Tree's eyes met hers with an open look of love, at once strong and vulnerable. K'un-Chien swallowed. Tree had never looked so beautiful. She wore a crimson robe decorated with embroidered peaches; the blushed golden fruit was the very color of Tree's hair. K'un-Chien felt a sudden thrill of desire, and the energy passed between them like a shared breath.

Tree's eyebrows shot up and she put a hand to her mouth.

'What is it?' K'un-Chien said.

'My vision,' Tree said. 'The Ling-Chih. This was my vision, exactly.'

K'un-Chien nodded with her whole torso. 'Ah so.'

Tree looked shaken. 'It is so strange . . .'

'But why? For me, it is only strange to feel this happy.'

'But I tried . . .' Tree shook her head. 'How did the Ling-Chih make this happen?'

'The Ling-Chih did not make anything happen. It merely opened an eye onto your future.'

'But I tried to prevent it. How could it happen in spite of . . . ? I was cool toward you. I ran from you.'

'One often collides with the destiny one races to avoid.'

Tree swallowed hard. 'I did not want to fall in love with you. Not like this.' She leapt to her feet and hurried out under the archway of the stupa.

K'un-Chien watched her go. Tree's words hung in space like musical notes.

Tree is in love with me, K'un-Chien realized, and her heart sang in her chest like a trembling crystal.

33

Mason knelt on the floor of the palace alongside a rice-paper scroll, practicing the Slender Gold calligraphy style of the ancient Song Dynasty emperor, Hui Zong. Breathing evenly in coordination with each stroke of his brush, he tried to form flowing graceful characters as Meng Po had shown him. He sat back from his work and frowned at the stiff-looking ideograms that marched down the paper. Marched. Not danced. If calligraphy were music, his characters would sound as boxy as *Stars-and-Stripes Forever*. But Meng Po's calligraphy would sound as lively and fluid as Brazilian jazz.

He began again. The ideogram he practiced over and over was the Chinese word for *forgiveness*. It was formed with the character for *action* above the character for *heart*. Forgiveness was an act of the heart. He had chosen to practice writing the word as a meditation on its meaning. There was nothing passive about forgiveness, that much was clear. He would have to make the effort of his life to achieve the goal of forgiving himself. And he was trying. For everyone's sake. He tried.

Guilt and grief were smothering his life like wet sand smothered a fire. But how to go about moving on was the problem. Forgiveness required an act from the center of his emotion, because it was at the core that he blamed himself for Gib's death. And try as he might, he had not been able to make that leap. He couldn't get beyond his rational mind that told him, logically, that he was to blame. He had pulled the trigger. Gib had been cut down by the bullets. It was Mason's fault. How could he forget that?

Mason had felt closer to Gib than to his own brothers. Blood is thicker than water, but spirit runs deeper than blood. To find a friend whose soul magnifies your own – whose company somehow makes you bigger, brighter, better – is a rare and wonderful grace. Real conversation, not just shooting the shit about TV shows and sports and cars, that was the treasure of Gib. And when – abundance cubed – Mason had fallen in love with Gib's sister, the three-note harmony was supposed to play forever.

Mason carefully tore off the bottom portion of the rice-paper scroll. He crumpled the still-wet calligraphy and tossed it aside. The paper wad struck a pile of other rejections.

Mason closed his eyes and pictured Meng Po's effortless brush strokes. The boy looked serene as he worked, with a little smile as subtle as the Buddha's. Meng Po reminded him so much of a young Gib. Sometimes Mason even grew sad and had to excuse himself and leave before the lesson was finished. Lately Mason was beginning to sense the possibility of loving Meng Po and K'un-Chien as he had loved Gib and Tree. His chest tightened at the thought. He was terrified to get that close to anyone again. Dangerous. *What will happen to them if they get too close to me?*

Tree stormed into the room and Mason looked up. Her cheeks were streaked with tears. She flung herself onto the bed and sobbed quietly into a pillow.

Mason felt instantly sick inside. *Here it comes, another fight.* Should he say something? Go to her? Or just leave her alone?

He stood and walked to the bed, sat down and began rubbing her slender back. Tree said something into the pillow.

'I can't hear you,' he said.

She turned her wet face sideways. 'I said, we only have another month. If I'm not pregnant by then . . .'

'Tree, we've been over this. What do you want me to do?'

She sniffled. 'What do I want? I want you to make love with me like you did when you thought I was K'un-Chien. Make

219

love with me like that again. Every day, every night, until I'm pregnant.'

'Baby, as much as I would like to, I can't just make myself perform. We both know what happens. How many times have we tried now? I've lost count.'

'It never hurts to try.'

'Yes, it does. It hurts terribly, and you know it. It makes us both miserable.'

Her glare softened and then she looked away. 'That's true,' she said.

'Look,' Mason said, gently, 'We don't like it, but we both know what you have to do. Go to Domino.'

She shot him another glare. 'Yeah, well, "we" don't have to have sex with that pig.' She started crying again. 'I can't believe you just said that,' she sputtered. 'You, my knight. Do you know what that would be like for me? I'd be humiliated.'

'The samurai believed death was preferable to humiliation, but I didn't know you shared their sentiment.'

'For God's sake, Mason, I don't want to have his baby – I want *your* baby, *our* baby.'

He held up his hands in helplessness.

'Take the love-seeds again,' she said.

'That was a nightmare. I told you. It amplified *all* my emotions, including the worst ones. I had a panic attack, thought I was back in 'Nam. It's damn hard to have sex when I'm so freaked out I can't even catch my breath.'

'The goddam war is over, Mason. What will it take for you to come home to me? You're still wandering around over there in the jungle, lost.'

Mason stood up, angry. 'You can't know what it was like. You were hanging around Harvard Square strumming your guitar, doing yoga, eating sprouts. I was over there jamming my thumb into a hole in some guy's heart to keep his life from pumping out in squirts. You don't just walk away from that shit and go have a Coke, watch a sitcom. It haunts your ass. It stomps your ass.'

Tree sat up and grabbed Mason's hand. 'I'm sorry, baby, sorry. Come on. Let's not argue. Lie down here with me. Please. Let me hold you. Hold me.'

Mason smiled grimly. 'You saying, "Make love, not war"?

Wish I'd taken that option when I was a gung-ho kid. Gone to Vancouver like Mack and John. But no, I had to go wherever Gib went. Christ. Then I sent him someplace where I can't follow.'

Tree frowned, sniffling. 'What do you mean?'

'Forget it,' Mason turned away.

Tree clung to his arm and stood up to face him. 'Mason. What do you mean, you sent Gib someplace you can't follow?'

Mason clenched his jaw. 'Don't.' He shook his head.

'This is the secret, isn't it? This is your secret.'

'Don't, Tree. You don't want to know.'

'Mason. Tell me. I've got to know. It's eating you hollow.'

'I'm asking you to just . . . let it be.'

'What happened to Gib? You were there. How did he get killed?'

'For God's sake, Tree, why are you doing this?'

'Tell me, so there won't be anything left to hide. Then you can throw down your shield. No more terrible secret. I'll know the truth, and you can be naked with me again.'

'I can't.' His voice choked. 'I need you. I need your love, Tree. I can't lose you too.'

'*Lose* me? Baby, here I am – I'm stuck on you. I'm here to stay. If you'll only be *with* me, open up to me, share your pain with me.'

'No!' He peeled her hands off his arms. 'Let go, I can't breathe. Let me go.' He turned and started toward the door, bent over and wheezing.

'Mason, turn around, you can't run away from this. We have to talk. It's time to go through this with me, not stop part-way.'

He kept walking. His chest felt so tight he thought it might implode.

'Mason!' Tree shouted. 'All right, I'll go to Domino. If this is how it's gonna be. I'll go to him. Do you hear? I'll go tonight.'

When he reached the round doorway he doubled over with gut pain. He stepped out into the rain and ran, stumbling. *If I'd told her the truth, she'd hate me; but if I don't tell her, I'm going to lose her anyway.* In either case, he was damned. He'd now nearly finished the destruction of all that was most beautiful to him. *I'm a madman pouring weedkiller on a rose garden.*

221

The black clouds sagged opened like a purse and dumped cold rain in torrents. Every part of the world was weeping at once. But Mason could not risk shedding a single tear. If he let just one teardrop escape and roll down, it would crack the dyke of his heart and the bitter sea would drown him.

He stopped in the middle of a boulevard and sank to his knees in a shallow puddle, overwhelmed by the bodily struggle to hold back his pain.

K'un-Chien, where are you? Please. I'll take the mushroom. Just help me. Help me to live again. I want to be with Tree. I want her. God have mercy, I want her with all my soul.

34

K'un-Chien gave Mason hot green tea in a black crackled-glaze cup. He was wrapped up in two robes and, although he was no longer cold, he shivered through the silk.

'I am not sure if I am doing the right thing,' he said. 'What if it does not work? No, that is not my fear,' he confessed. 'What if it *works*? What if I really *do* go back to Vietnam? I do not know how to face my past.'

'You do not know how to face your past now, sitting on the bed in this room. But when you travel back to your past, you'll find that you *are* facing it. That will be the reality. You will really be there, not here.'

'It was hell. The last thing in the world I want to do is to go back and relive that.'

'But you will be returning to your past with a wiser soul. You will not be the inexperienced young man that you were the first time. You will see with older eyes. You will see your actions anew.'

'What will happen to me then?'

'There is no certain outcome. The only certainty is that the Ling Chih will open a window. What you see . . . that has to do with your own eyes.'

Mason reached up and caught K'un-Chien's hands in both of his. 'I feel afraid.'

'I understand. That is why you must revisit your earlier life. To face the trauma that wounded you.'

'Will you hold me for a while?'

She gathered Mason into her arms and he let himself fall into the warmth of her body. If he could only rest in such safety forever, abide in the stirring of her breath against his cheek. But he had to go back to the war that had killed his soul. He had to go back to the one jungle night he most hated and feared. *The only way out is through.*

After a moment, Mason lay down on his back on the futon. K'un-Chien popped the lid off the mushroom container made from a fat joint of green bamboo. A pungent, sweet smell escaped. With a copper spoon she dipped up a blob of bright yellow slime.

'Remember, it will feel like a burning, a melting. It is only pain-ful for a few breaths. Relax into it. Let the dissolution happen.'

He took a deep breath. 'I am ready.'

K'un-Chien coated his chest over his heart with the chromium-yellow slime. Within seconds Mason tasted the dank earthy flavor of mushrooms on his tongue. K'un-Chien lifted his head and cradled it in her lap, soothing his temples with her fingertips. Mason closed his eyes as his head grew light and it seemed his body began to float off the mattress.

He jerked his head when flames ignited in the center of his brain. The fire felt physically hot.

'Relax now,' K'un-Chien said softly. 'It will begin to melt your thoughts. Allow the fiery light to burn away all your boundaries.'

From red through orange to yellow, then blue, the blaze grew in intensity. A blue morning glory flower of light expanded, sparkling at its edges, then shattering into a complex geometric symmetry like a kaleidoscope turned upon a fireworks sky. Mason had the strange sensation that he was not *inside* a body in any sense at all, but rather, his body was inside his expanded awareness.

Then suddenly he could no longer find his body at all. The release from the tension of his physical form was like yanking off a tight boot – his soul leapt and soared, and the fiery radiance outshone his mind completely.

Next came a feeling of traveling inward, receding toward some far-off inner point at incredible velocity. Then, suddenly, a whole lucid vision:

Dark moonless night rain jungle. Mason's medical kit was rubbing a blister against his right shoulder blade. He stopped in the middle of the trail through the former French colonial rubber plantation. Slid off the backpack. Tried for the third time to pad the sore spot with a folded T-shirt. Gib, the platoon leader, sauntered back to see if he was okay. When Gib stooped to help Mason put his pack back on, the blackness was lit to daylight brightness, as if someone had thrown a light switch on a nearby rubber tree. A vicious blastwave punched Mason's face, and he reeled backward and splatted in mud, his eyebrows seared off. A man in the mud near him tried to scream; it sounded like gargling.

Mason scrambled to his feet and was instantly knocked down again, this time by an invisible hammer that slammed him in the left shoulder and spun him a half-turn so that he fell on that side in the slime. It took him a few seconds to realize he'd been hit by enemy rifle fire along with a lot of the other men in his platoon. They were caught in a Viet Cong ambush. As a medic, Mason carried no weapons.

The light from the enemy flare was fading as Mason jumped up again, in time to see a shape in black pajamas running out of the trees straight at him, blazing star-shaped bursts of automatic rifle fire. Mason watched his attacker's head disappear in a dark wet spray. Gib suddenly appeared at Mason's side, firing burst after burst of bullets at the moving figures charging between the trees. Shell casings, splinters of wood, chunks of mud flew in all directions. The black night was a solid mass of noise.

'Mace! Pick up Bobby's rifle!' Gib shouted above the chaos. 'Get the rifle!'

'I'm a medic!' Mason shouted.

'Grab the fucking rifle. That's an order. I need firepower – *now* – or there won't be anyone left to patch up.'

Mason spun where he lay in the mud and squirmed toward Bobby Smith; the man was still loudly gargling blood. Mason fumbled with the M-16, trying to take the rifle away, but Bobby wouldn't ease his death grip on it. Mason pried open the fingers and yanked away the rifle just as the gargling stopped.

Mason leapt to his feet with the M-16, not sure how to fire it. As a conscientious objector, he'd had no weapons training. He looked down and cocked the spring. A whizzing chunk of bark smashed his nose. Tears gushed out, blurring his vision. He blinked and shook his head, slinging blood from his nostrils onto his cheeks.

He squeezed the trigger and cut a rubber tree in half. He squeezed the trigger again and heard a scream and saw a figure in black pajamas lurch backward and drop. A mortar shell went off to his left and a sheet of lava flashed red across his vision. When he recovered his senses, he was kneeling in the mud. The black pajamas kept coming. Mason fired his automatic rifle from a kneeling position and saw two more figures fall. His mouth filled with blood draining from his nasal pharynx but he felt no physical pain. He'd never been more scared.

At some point in the black downpour, the clatter and crump of rifles and grenades ceased. Monkeys and parrots and men screamed and cried. Everything smelled like gunpowder, rain and blood. The monsoon rain did not slow down.

Mason gathered his medical kit and dragged himself around to the few survivors, jabbing morphine shots through blood-soaked khakis. Tommy was radioing in a helicopter med-evac, holding the handset in his one remaining hand. After Mason tied a tourniquet at the wrist and stabbed Tommy with two hits of morphine, he went back to check on Gib.

Gib's right cheek was split and burned to the bone; his mouth sagged and a string of blood leaked onto his chin. 'I'm all right,' Gib said. 'See to the others.'

'I already did. Only Tommy, Clark and Frog are still alive.'

'Fuck.' Gib coughed. 'Fuck this shit.'

Mason peeled open Gib's fatigue shirt and saw a shoulder and arm wound that looked non-critical. 'You lucky fuck, you're gonna be all right. But you'll definitely go home on this. Looks like you'll have to learn to paint with your left hand.'

Gib smiled crookedly. 'You're going back with me, buddy.

That's not a bullethole in your shoulder, that's a ticket to Frisco.'

'Yeah. Ticket's starting to burn like a sonufabitch.' Mason shot a dose of morphine into Gib's arm and injected a second syringe into himself.

After a minute Gib sighed, looking woozy. 'Ah, Mace, you're a great medic, but a lousy rifleman.'

'Thank God for that,' Mason said. As the painkiller kicked in he moaned softly with relief.

'Man, you look like hell,' Gib said. 'Good thing Tree loves you for your charm.'

As Gib reached the end of his sentence, a Viet Cong jumped up from a nearby heap of bodies among the shattered rubber trees. The enemy staggered their way, firing his wavering rifle at them. From a kneeling position, Mason whipped up his rifle to return fire. Gib sat up, firing his weapon from the waist. A bullet nailed Mason in the right shoulder and he reeled backward in the mud, still squeezing the trigger as he fell.

Gib grunted loudly.

When Mason got himself up, the attacker was dead and so was Gib. Mason had shot Gib with two or three rounds at near point-blank range.

'*Gib!*' Mason screamed. Gib's chest gaped open, a wet cavern of muscle and lung. Raindrops spattered blue eyes. Mason recoiled violently inside himself as if to withdraw his soul a million miles away from the fact of his friend lying dead.

Then Mason tasted a damp-earth flavor on his tongue and remembered the Ling Chih, and suddenly – in a pause between heartbeats – a window opened; Mason's mind swam through. He felt himself poised on a fulcrum of possible futures, with multiple paths leading onward from this moment in the jungle downpour.

He could blame himself for Gib's death. He'd have to shut down all his feelings at their root in his heart and remain numb for the rest his life in order to cope with such guilt. He already knew the consequences of that path: he'd chosen it before.

Now Mason saw an alternative path. He accepted that he'd been clumsy with the rifle because he'd been trained to be a healer, a non-combatant. He had shot and killed Gib. But what had happened was about war – not about himself – and he was not obliged to take it personally. In war, young men die in countless tragic ways – some are even killed by their best friends.

For the first time, Mason felt a profound compassion toward himself. For whom was mercy meant if not for the broken-hearted?

Abruptly, he returned to his wounded body coated with mud. He burst into sobs, pressing Gib's forehead against his own, kissing his brother for the last time. Mason tilted his face to the moonless sky and called out Gib's name.

'I'll never forget you!' he cried.

With a violent wrenching, the dam in Mason's chest tore to smithereens and his heart flooded back to life, a shoreless sea.

Mason's tears and the pebbles of rain splashed down upon the bosom of Gibraltar Edward Summerwood as if to wash the body for burial.

35

A servant girl answered the door of Domino's palace and led Tree inside. The interior concave walls were a soft pearl; Tree had the sensation of entering a giant clam. Ming-style paintings and scrolls decorated the walls and porcelain vases and statues lined the room on ornate pedestals.

Domino sat barechested at a large table drinking rice wine straight from a white porcelain bottle. He wore a black loincloth with a belt holding a sheathed knife. A young girl stood nearby him in a crimson kimono, fanning him with a broad silk fan. Domino's head jerked up when Tree entered the room. He grinned with big white teeth beneath a coal-black mustache.

'Well, look who's here.' He wobbled slightly as he stood. He was stocky and slightly overweight, but with the kind of dense fat that rides solidly atop thick muscles and heavy bones. Around his neck hung a silver-dollar-sized pendant with a miniature erotic scene, crafted in cloisonné, in the style of Chinese pillow books, showing a prince dallying with three courtesans.

'Welcome.' Domino bowed at the waist, which caused him to step forward off balance. 'To what do I owe the pleasure of your visit?'

Tree looked him in the eyes. 'We both know why I'm here.'

'Oh, but my ears crave to hear you say it.'

She sighed. 'I need you to make me pregnant.'

'I see,' he said, 'Mason has failed you.'

'Let's leave him out of this. This is just between you and me. I need your help.'

He laughed with a booming bass. 'You need me?' He flopped back down on his seat at the table and swigged wine from the bottle, then offered the bottle to her. She shook her head.

'A beautiful gringa like you, from the United States of Privilege, needs the help of a barrio rat like me? How very strange. We are from – how shall I put it?—different sides of the river. Your side has a sewer. My side *is* a sewer. Yet you say you need me. What is this world coming to?'

'Why bring up our social backgrounds? I've never made a big deal out of such things. Have you ever experienced me being prejudiced toward you – toward anyone – because of class status?'

'Of course not, *gringa*. You don't need to be aware of such trivia. You have always lived at the tip of the pyramid,' he said. 'From where you sit, no one is above you. Women like you have always been unreachable for men like me.'

'I'm sorry you've struggled in your life. It's true, my father was wealthy. But we can't really choose the circumstances of our birth, can we?'

Domino swigged at the wine. 'I would like to hear you ask me for what you want.'

'I did. I already told you, I need you to make me pregnant.'

'Ah, but that's telling me. I want you to ask me – as for a favor.'

She sighed. 'Please, Domino – Senor Cruz – will you have sex with me?'

He shook his head. 'No.'

'What?'

'No, I will not have sex with you.'

'You want me to beg, is that what you'd like?'

'Not at all. I simply want to see a little passion. I don't enjoy making love with a puppet stuffed with cotton. Come back when you feel more alive and in the mood.' He waved her away with his hand.

'Why are you making this so hard for me? I need your help.

I'm *asking* for your help. I'm fertile now – this is my last chance. I'm going to be kicked out of this valley to die if I'm not pregnant by the next full moon.'

'Ah. You're angry. *Bueno*. At least that's brought a little heat and color to your face. Let's see some fire now below the waist.'

Tree shrugged. 'You want . . . what, I'm supposed to say, I love you?'

He laughed, white teeth flashing in his dark face. '*Love?* Love is no requisite for a good fuck. But without a little lust, why bother? Come back when you don't just need my services, but you *want* my cock.' He stood up from the table and walked toward the door to his bedroom.

'I can't come back,' Tree said. 'I'm fertile now.'

He kept walking.

She caught up to him and grabbed his shoulder. 'I'm ovulating. I need you now.'

He shrugged off her hand. 'Look, I have a harem of wives waiting for me. Some of them are also fertile now. They want to get pregnant too. There are lots of women here who want a piece of Domino. You'll have to get in line.'

'You arrogant little bastard.' Tree jumped in front of him and blocked the doorway. 'You're trying to take out your class anger on me.'

Domino tried to push past her. She shoved him hard and he staggered backward, laughing. 'Yeah! That's the spirit. Show me the cat in you.' He reached out and slapped her face. 'You like it rough?'

She started to punch him and he grabbed her wrist and twisted her arm behind her back. He pushed her through the doorway into the bedroom and drove her forward until she fell face down upon his big bed. He fell on top of her, pinning her down from behind.

'Ow, you're breaking my arm,' Tree yelled. 'Get off.'

'Now it's getting more interesting,' Domino said with his mouth close to her ear. His breath reeked of alcohol. 'Have you ever watched cats doing it?'

She squirmed beneath him and he shoved her shoulders and head down with his forearm.

'The tomcat takes the female from behind,' Domino said. 'He bites her neck, hard, she fights him all the way to the finish, hissing and screaming.'

Tree shoved backward against him. 'Get off, goddamit!'

'Why so upset, *gringa*? I thought this is what you wanted.'

'I've changed my mind, I'd rather die. Now get the hell off me.'

'Very good,' he said, huffing. 'Now that you don't want it, I want it. I'm gonna fuck you, Tree. I'm gonna fuck the cotton stuffing out of you. I'm gonna shove my cock so far in it makes you come alive and scream.'

'Get off me, you sick bastard.' She twisted her head to bite his face, but he kept out of reach. She squirmed furiously beneath him, but couldn't shake off his solid weight.

'Yeah, fight me, that's it. That's something I can't get my wives to do. These little girls, they don't understand. They submit to anything. But I like to take it the hard way – like you, eh?'

'When I tell Mason, he'll kill you.'

'For what? For saving your life? You were doomed with him. You both owe me.'

He had managed to yank off the sash of her robe and now he scooped the loose fabric up over the small of her back. Tree was naked underneath. Never had she felt so exposed and vulnerable.

'Okay, princess, I'm gonna give you the whole *chili* now. Feel how deep *senor chili* goes.'

Tree felt him penetrate her from behind. She cried out, not from pain, but from rage and humiliation. Tears burned her eyes. She grunted from her struggle to twist out from beneath him.

'Ride that mare, *guacaro*!' Domino shouted and laughed.

Tree lurched to the side and lunged forward. Domino slipped from inside her. She struggled to scoot out from under him but he threw his weight over her shoulders and flattened her into the mattress and penetrated her again. Domino pumped his body violently against hers, so that his pelvis slapped her buttocks. She buried her face in the futon and cried, feeling helpless and violated. The mattress smelled like cotton dust.

I'll live through this, she told herself. *I'll live through it.*

Then she heard an outraged shout that equaled the anger she felt inside. For a strange instant, she thought the sound had boiled up from her own lungs. Then she recognized Mason's thunderous voice.

'Domino! Get off her, goddamit!' Mason yelled.

Domino's head snapped sideways from the force of Mason's kick and he tumbled off the bed onto the floor.

Tree hopped off the mattress and hugged her kimono tightly around her body.

Mason scooped a hand under Domino's neck, jerked him to his feet and hammered his big fist into Domino's face, fracturing the nose bridge with a sound like cracking a lobster shell.

Domino staggered backward against the wall, blood draining from his nostrils in twin flumes. He slapped at the sheath at his waist and whipped out his knife, but in the same instant, Mason kicked furiously at Domino's groin and his heel rammed its target with a jellied thud. The knife clattered onto the hardwood floor and Domino crumpled forward in a curled-up ball, groaning and retching.

Mason grabbed Tree's hand and escorted her outside into the evening's cool fog. Then he turned her to him and tenderly kissed her, his gray eyes blazing in a pure language her eyes completely understood.

36

Mason carried Tree down the limestone steps into the bath still wearing his dhoti. He removed her robe and gently, lovingly, bathed her whole body with jasmine soap and a soft washcloth. His caring touch helped to wash away the tension and trauma of the ugly scene with Domino. He asked her not a word about it, which was exactly how much she wanted to say. He was acting like the old Mason, reading her heart, doing all the right things. After he shampooed her hair, he suggested she might like to be alone.

'No, I like being with you the way you're with me now,' she said. 'What's happened to you, Mason? Your eyes are so alive.'

He took a deep breath. 'Tree, there's something I need to tell you. My secret.'

'Yes, baby, you do need to tell me,' she said, 'for your sake.' She stroked his cheek with the backs of her fingers and he grabbed her hand and kissed it and began to cry. *Mason was crying!* Tree felt like the sun had come out inside her heart. She kissed his tears as they flowed down. Salt water had never tasted so sweet.

'The night Gib died,' he began in a whisper, then stopped. He opened his brimming eyes, and gazed at her, trembling. 'Look, this is going to be heavy for you. No matter how you feel about this, I want you to know I love you. So much, Tree. I can *feel* again. I'm not just remembering how I used to feel about you. I love you now. And if you . . . if you . . . Look, I want you to be angry with me, I want you to beat me, beat me with your fists – just don't . . . please don't hate me.'

'I'm not going to hate you, you loon.' Tree was crying now. 'I could never hate you. You're my brother, too. Don't you think I already figured out your secret long ago?'

'You know?'

'I don't know anything. I don't know what happened. Gib died and you think it's your fault. The worse thing that could have happened is that you somehow caused his death. You killed him. That's the worse thing I can imagine, and I think that must be it. Only a tragedy like that could break a heart like yours.'

Mason stared at her for a long moment, tears streaming down. In a faltering voice, he told her about the black night in the monsoon rain when he had cradled her brother in his lap. 'Oh Tree! I loved him so much. I never got a chance to say goodbye.'

Tree sobbed against Mason's neck. 'I'm so sorry, baby, so sorry.'

'I was afraid . . . if you found out . . .' He squeezed her so hard it forced air from her lungs. 'I couldn't bear to lose you.'

'Shhh. Sweetheart. It's not something to hate you for, it's something that pulls my heart out of me, tears it into tatters for you. I'm so sorry for you, Mason, so sorry you had to experience that.'

'Please just say . . . you . . . forgive me.'

'I never blamed you,' she said, and kissed his black curls. 'But yes, I forgive you. Look at me Mason, look up at me.' She searched his eyes. 'I forgive you, my love. Do you hear?'

'But . . . ?' He seemed surprised.

'Mason, what if it'd been me? What if I'd killed Gib in a car wreck? Would you hate me?'

He shook his head, grays eyes big and shiny wet.

'Listen to the truth: Mason Drake is an innocent soul,' she said. '*No one blames you*. Least of all Gib. He loves you, same as always.'

Mason pressed his face against her bosom and wept loudly

with deep masculine sobs. After a while his whole body relaxed and he grew quiet. Tree uncoiled the thick ringlets of his hair with her fingers and kissed his head and thanked the universe her beloved was alive again.

He tilted his face up and kissed her mouth passionately. 'Oh,' her lips said. Her heart and soul said it at the same time: *Oh*.

Mason swept Tree up out of the bath and carried her into the bedroom. He laid her down on the bed, water dripping from her blonde waves. He wore soaking wet dhotis; the center of his baggy pants bulged stiffly outward like a tall-masted sail.

They made love, as love made them. *Hunger is the best sauce.* Tree and Mason transported each other, blissfully famished, to a paradise of appetite.

Tree slept soundly, the soft hills of her breasts rising and falling in the dark. Mason lay awake on his back on rumpled sheets, savoring the glory of the evening and his victory over sorrow. No, not a *victory* over sorrow, but the abandonment of his war with sorrow. He'd accepted Gib's death at last, and was wholly at peace: muscles, bones and marrow at rest in the present moment. Outside, the night choir of forest creatures and distant waterfall sang in the hall of the valley.

Lying next to Tree again in this way, in the aftermath of passion, was the sweetest feeling – in its own way it seemed to him as intimate as their lovemaking. He'd had sex with a half-dozen women in the eight years since his divorce from Tree, but he'd never *slept* with any of them; he'd always gotten up and gone home to his own bed.

Sleeping with Tree had meant sharing his dream space with her. Cuddling on cold nights like a set of camping spoons, or on muggy nights just touching fingertips; their sleeping bodies had enriched each other. Now he could savor repose with his lover again.

Mason slid his hand over the smooth curve of Tree's belly until it nested in curly fur, still damp from their lovefest. Very gently his fingers combed her curls. Tree smiled and snuggled closer.

'You're so beautiful, baby,' he whispered, 'so soft.'

He remembered the scientific name for the small cushion of

fat over the pubic bone: *mons veneris* – 'mound of Venus' –
after the goddess of erotic love. Perfect. But why did the early
anatomists stop with that bit of poetry? They'd given such drab
labels to other lovely features.

Vagina. Means *sheath* in Latin; either way, a clunky word for
something so slippery, soft and friendly. A Spanish slang word
for vagina was *la papaya.* That made good poetic sense, given
the resemblance of a woman's sex to an opened papaya: pink
flesh glistening like tropical fruit; and the fragrance and flavor
of papayas and women belonged to the same aromatic family.

Bartholin's glands. Bleak label for the tiny glands of a woman's
sex that make her slickly wet when aroused. Kaspar Bartholin,
a Danish anatomist, named the structures after himself. The
nerd. Why couldn't he have called them something romantic,
mythical? Anything but *Bartholin's.* Oh well, at least his name
wasn't Lipschitz.

Mason's mind roamed and he thought about many things;
memories of Gib no longer troubled him and it was a joy to
recall the good times again.

As he pictured Gib he had an odd recognition. No one
had ever closely reminded him of Gib – until he'd met K'un-
Chien.

Yes, Meng Po was intellectually and artistically brilliant
like Gib. And Tree was sensual and emotional like Gib. But
K'un-Chien captured – what? It was as if she exuded a manly
quality. It seemed strange to pursue that thought. But try as
he might, he could not discount it. It rang true. K'un-Chien was
pretty. But she was also handsome. She definitely had a strong
masculine element – and that was how she reminded him of
Gib. Was that weird?

Was it because she was tall and hard-muscled that he saw her
as masculine, or because she was brave? If so, his thinking was
false. As if there could be no petite, courageous women. Joan of
Arc was only four-foot-ten. He'd seen Vietnamese mothers the
size of elementary school kids carrying two children on their
backs, fleeing burning villages.

No. It wasn't K'un-Chien's stature or physique. In fact, Tree
was a bit taller, and naturally athletic – and Tree was as
female as a dark cave scooped in the bed of the sea. Whereas

K'un-Chien seemed somehow masculine in spirit and intensity, a bright tower.

Then again, her intensity didn't cancel her womanliness at all. K'un-Chien was more curvaceous than Tree, and she could be slinky, svelte, sultry, swishy, a real vamp.

Mason smiled at a comparison that came to mind. K'un-Chien was like a dolphin.

Some animals came across to him as feminine. Cats, for example. Even male cats seemed feminine. The word *feline* had come to mean sleekly graceful, womanly.

Other animals seemed masculine. Dogs, even female dogs, were boyish and butch.

But dolphins – male or female – were nature's androgynes. Each incorporated the qualities of both genders.

Mason smiled again at the image. It fit for him. Dolphins were like K'un-Chien.

He admitted to himself he was in love with her. He'd already decided he'd better talk to Tree about it sometime. *Very* diplomatically. Obviously Tree came first. And it wasn't that he was needing more than Tree; one sensual lover like Tree was earthy abundance.

It was just that . . . well . . . to know K'un-Chien was to love her. She was like a priceless violin that had never been out of its case, waiting to hear its own music.

'May-Son?' K'un-Chien whispered in the darkness, standing at the foot of the bed.

'K'un-Chien, I was just thinking about you.'

'May I . . . ?' She hesitated. 'Not to remove my clothes. Just to sleep next to my husband?'

He flung down the covers and K'un-Chien climbed into the wide bed and cuddled against him. Her hair was redolent with cinnamon oil; her skin smelled like freshly stripped maize. Mason smiled in the spicebox darkness; his body between his two wives, his mind between waking and dreaming, his heart between love and desire.

37

The Empress Fang-Shih stared up at the volcanic rim of the valley from near the base of the Southern Face. Wind moaned softly through the tall crags with the mournful tones of a bamboo flute. The morning's sad music and chilly drizzle made her mood darker than usual. Everything smelled like wet cold rock – even the pale sun.

The doubt that had circled her head for months seemed to have finally made its nest: Had her bitter sacrifice been for naught?

From the time of her earliest memories, she recalled being praised for her physical loveliness. The other children had kept at a subtle distance, a footstep or two that acknowledged that she, Fang-Shih, was especially enchanting, and one day surely would be chosen to be the sacrificial Mother-of-Sons. For this she had been honored above all others in Jou P'u T'uan.

Then, when she was seventeen, one year before the selection ceremony, the remarkable barbarian, Huxley Summerwood, had arrived in Jou P'u T'uan. The foreigner spoke their language and knew their ways perfectly. He had even entered the Debate of the Two Schools and publicly argued against the cult of the Lung-Hu.

Huxley had fallen in love with her on first sight; that was when her face still belonged in classical paintings. And in spite of his foreignness – or partly because of it – she had fallen in love with him. Her love-play with the dragon-women could not match the intensity of desire and pleasure she felt with Huxley – her *ta heng*, great stalk.

Then she had been chosen to be the new Empress.

Standing in the drizzle now, Fang-Shih flinched at the unbidden memory of scissor-teeth fish slicing her face like gnashing razors. In a flurry of heartbeats, her life as a matchless beauty had been torn apart. But through that dreadful offering she had been empowered to give birth to sons and was again honored above all others in Jou P'u T'uan, this time for the gifts of her womb.

After her sacrifice Huxley had been openly repulsed, his former love gagging in his throat. Nevertheless, they had carried out their duty and she had become pregnant. She ate the Ling-Chih mushroom and received the revelation that the Holy Hermaphrodite was destined to be born through her; further reason for her husband to feel alienated.

She had believed the Lung-Hu would be her own child, but it had not come to pass.

First, she had given birth – most inauspiciously – to a mere daughter. Superfluous. Every tiger-woman in the city was capable of making girls.

Then she had birthed three sons in four years. But it was a burst of light that preceded blackness, as when a lamp flares as its last drops of oil are burned. On the same gruesome day her husband was killed and her two oldest sons drowned.

Now it was too late to begin anew. She felt exhausted, too old to have more babies. Even the goat-man, Domino, had failed to make her pregnant. Her days as Empress were at a close.

As a girl there had been power in her beauty, but as Empress she had never found the beauty in her power. No joy in ruling a society of women who desperately envied her ability to birth sons but who cringed in her presence, silently thanking the ancestors they could not see her visage behind the mask.

Along with the end of her beauty had come the end of all possibility of being loved. Even when her sons were infants they had been frightened by her ruined face, so she had always worn a mask. But how sweet it had been to feed her babies at her breasts – in moments such as those all her karma had seemed worth it.

By the spirits of all who lived before, how I miss my sons!

She had never dared take off the mask around Huxley. He had depended on a handful of love-seeds to inflame his lust before they copulated. Even so he would avert his eyes whenever her gaze met his through the eyehole. The thin porcelain separated their souls by ten thousand leagues.

Imprisoned behind a false face, her heart felt suffocatingly lonely. Yet many times over the years she had been glad for the mask, for it hid her tears.

Fang-Shih sighed as a tear rolled down now.

K'ung Fu Tse, the Great Tutor, had commented in his Analects that physical beauty was merely a surface feature; appearances did not penetrate below the depth of the skin. But he did not have his face replaced by scars. Was beauty only skin-deep? How, then, had its slashing cut out her heart?

'Is something troubling you, Empress?' Yu Lin asked. 'You don't seem to be enjoying the hunt.'

'I am fine.' The Empress lifted her head and watched two harpy eagles circling over the cliff, searching for prey. It was easy to spot her bird – charcoal-and-white bars on wings and tail; blue-gray head and white torso. Yu Lin's eagle was entirely white, an albino.

'All morning your gaze has polished your boots,' Yu Lin said.

'I confess I am adrift in reveries today like a rudderless ship.'

'It is known throughout the city that the barbarian's seed did not take root in you,' Yu Lin said. 'You must try again, perhaps with the bigger man, May-Son.'

'Yes,' the Empress said, wearily. 'I should try a few days hence, when I'm fertile.'

The Empress watched the hunting eagles soar alongside the rocky face with wingtips nearly touching the crannies of the upper ledges. 'The barbarian, May-Son,' she said, 'he seems restless, untamed, like a newly snared harpy.'

'Indeed. Perhaps one could use the same methods to gentle the man: Tie a leash on his leg and keep him in a darkened room, never let him eat but from your own hand, and always keep a hood over his eyes until he is ready to perform.' Yu Lin laughed at her joke.

'I had begun to believe the rumors that he could *not* perform,' the Empress said. 'Now his First Wife is with child.'

'Do you believe she could actually give birth to a son?'

The Empress shot a glance at her. 'If such power is so easily obtained, then why my sacrifice?' She lifted her mask. 'Is this mere decoration?'

Yu Lin averted her eyes. 'My apologies, Mother-of-Sons. I will give the order that May-Son be brought to your bedchamber, bathed and perfumed, his black hair oiled, and prepared with enough love-seeds to keep him impassioned from night to dawn to noon. If his great size bears any relation to his virility, he could fill a barren womb with twins.'

The Empress replaced the mask but continued to glare. 'Do you imply my womb is now barren?'

'I said nothing of the kind. I only made a joke about his man-size. I would wager there is not a well in this city where he could not touch bottom.'

'The Tao provides, yin for yang. Both his wives are tall pots to accommodate deep roots.'

The Empress pictured K'un-Chien and the girl's beauty haunted her, reminding her of her loss. If anything, her daughter was more lovely than she herself had been. K'un-Chien's blue eyes had come from her father, but they were much darker blue, like sky-ink.

When Huxley told her their baby was a girl the Empress had felt humiliated. But she had not hated K'un-Chien. A daughter was simply without value to a Mother-of-Sons. She allowed Huxley to raise the girl in private and for years she gave the embarrassing matter as little thought as possible. But since the grim day when her daughter had survived while her sons drowned, her aloofness had turned to loathing.

How strange. It now seemed inevitable that K'un-Chien would become the new Empress. Fang-Shih's faith that she would be the mother of the Lung-Hu had crumbled. She had decided the meaning of her revelation must be that the Lung-Hu would be born through her daughter – thus, indirectly, through her.

'Then shall I give the order?' Yu Lin asked.

'What?'

'To have the man brought to you when you become fertile.'

The Empress looked down and did not answer.

'Empress?'

'No,' the Empress said. 'No. I have decided, this very moment, against it,' she said. 'The time is nigh for a new Empress.'

'You are ready to call for a new selection?'

'I have been ready,' the Empress said. 'Now K'un-Chien is ready.'

Yu Lin frowned. 'What? . . . to be the new Empress?'

'See for yourself if there is one more beautiful.'

Yu Lin hesitated. 'But . . .'

'She is my daughter. Therefore it falls to her, for it must be her destiny to give birth to the Lung-Hu.'

A piercing staccato *kak-kak-kak-kak-kak* drew their eyes over the cliff. The two harpies had flushed a covey of gray doves and were closing fast upon the fleeing birds. The eagles rocketed straight into the flock and each snatched a gray dove in its talons.

The charcoal-and-white eagle immediately swerved and headed back toward the Empress's gloved fist with its catch, but the albino eagle dropped its first victim and killed a second dove, let it fall, and killed again and again. It knocked down six doves before the flock managed to escape by diving into a thicket of eucalyptus. Gray feathers spun down from the air like autumn leaves.

The Empress raised her leather-gloved fist to shoulder level and propped up her arm with a special walking stick. Her eagle homed in above her, dropped its prey to the gravel, braked with broad wings and alighted on the glove. A servant ran to the dove and quickly sliced the body into several strips of meat. The Empress fed her harpy on the glove; it clung to its perch with an iron grip.

The albino harpy flew to Yu Lin's leather glove. It had not brought back a kill and it greedily eyed the dove meat the Empress hand-fed her eagle. The albino was a female, and therefore a third larger than the Empress's charcoal-and-white male.

'White Blade kills for sport, as usual,' the Empress said. 'That is not a good trait, you should train her from that habit.'

'Why? Indeed it was I who trained her to it.'

'If every eagle killed so savagely they would soon find they had no prey left for food.'

'But every eagle is not the same as mine. Look at yours – content with a beakful of dove.'

'As it should be – such is the natural order. Those who are not satisfied with the order of things, Commander Yu, are dangerous.'

'White Blade seeks more than a bit of songbird for breakfast,' Yu Lin said, and stroked the eagle's tufted crest. White feathers radiated like petals from its facial corona surrounding darting red eyes and a colorless beak. From a pouch Yu Lin fed the raptor a dried chunk of meat from a two-toed tree sloth, a harpy's main diet.

Yu Lin smiled at her pet. 'She knows she is Empress of the sky; she wants all other eagles to acknowledge it.'

'And this ambition – did you train her to that as well?'

Yu Lin stared at the Empress. 'She was born to it. Look at her size. Look at her fiery gaze.'

'Yes, I see well with one eye,' the Empress said. 'You once remarked there are only two classes of creatures—'

Yu Lin nodded. 'Predators and prey. Is this not so?'

'Tell me, then. What happens when two predators meet?'

'Then one finds there are two classes of predators,' Yu Lin said. 'The stronger and the weaker.'

Yu Lin flipped her gloved fist, launching White Blade into the air with a burst of power. The albino harpy screeched and chased the Empress's eagle off the glove. They climbed quickly over the cliff, the larger albino pursuing the smaller eagle out of sight over the lip of the valley.

38

On the morning of the selection ceremony cool mists shrouded the fields beyond the city's stone walls. Tree's robe clung damply to her skin and her bright blonde tresses curled in the fog like gold-plated springs.

Nearly the whole population of Prayer Mat of the Body had gathered on a large rock-strewn plain outside the city's walls. A pavilion had been erected on a small hilltop at the front of the crowd. Tree and Mason and K'un-Chien stood near the pavilion so they could visit with Meng Po who had been allowed outside his cage for the first time in six years.

'May-Son, I had forgotten how beautiful the world is,' Meng Po said. 'The textures, the flavors, the smells. I had tried every day, with paintings and poetry, to hold on to it, but now I see how foolish were my efforts. How could I capture something so boundless within the box of memory?'

'It is so good to see you out here enjoying yourself,' Mason said. 'I am very happy for you.'

Tree worried about K'un-Chien. There was no doubt in her mind that K'un-Chien was the most beautiful woman in the city – a powerful statement considering the throng of lovely women who now crowded the rocky field. K'un-Chien stood out like a rare blue diamond on a rough cloth heaped with gems.

Mason stood in the center of the trio, holding the hands of his two wives.

'I'm scared, Mason,' Tree said in English.

'Me too, baby. But remember, beauty is in the eye of the beholder and no one else loves K'un-Chien as we do.'

The last few weeks had been a blissful time of reunion for Tree and Mason. She'd gotten pregnant, which had bought them more precious time to engineer an escape. Mason had asked Tree to marry him again and Tree had told him that she'd never divorced him from her heart. 'You've always been the the only man for me,' she'd said, and Mason had cried, because his heart was now alive and well.

'These past few days, I've realized truths that will carry me along for the rest of my life,' Mason had told her one evening after he'd returned from a long walk. 'For years I'd been struggling to make love safe, but love can never be safe. Love is the wound, not the scar tissue. Love is a tear in the membrane of our independent lives that lets in the world – joy and pain. The wound can't heal and still be love. The cure for vulnerability is numbness and death. As soon as I let my heart break fully, not saving myself from life, it was as if I was reborn.'

He'd held her close then and whispered into her mouth between kisses. 'But now I'm defenseless around you. Dissolved. You could drink me like wine.'

'Mmmm,' she'd said, 'is that your poetic way of asking?' And she'd parted his robe as she slid down onto her knees.

Now that they were making love again Tree wondered how she'd sustained herself so long without his man-smell, like warm dough rising; his weight pressing her down; his gray eyes caressing her, making her wetter. In the climax of passion, Mason wore a face of pleasure she knew mirrored her own – like an angel in pain. She loved that face, his and hers, the same one. She had waited to see that look of ecstasy for eight years.

Tree squeezed Mason's hand now, feeling grateful.

But she hadn't forgotten the danger of her vow to the Empress: *I, too, am a Mother-of-Sons.* Her baby must be a boy, or its life and her own would be ended on its birthday.

It was ironic. Years ago, before Vietnam, when she and Mason had first talked about having kids someday they'd decided they didn't want to undergo sonogram testing to learn the baby's gender. They liked the idea of being surprised. Now she'd kiss a sonogram machine if only she could know.

She and Mason had managed to joke about the folklore methods of foretelling a baby's gender. If a pendulum rotates around the belly, it's a boy; if the pendulum swings in line, it's a girl. If the mother's belly is more pointed, it's a boy; if more rounded, a girl. Any such prediction was right half the time.

Medical guesswork proved more reliable. Mason had told her the best clue is the baby's heart rate: the normal range is 120 to 160 beats per minute; babies with lower heart rates, 120 to 130, tended to be boys; babies with higher rates, 150 to 160, tended to be girls. 'It's accurate in maybe seventy percent of cases,' he'd said. 'Trouble is, without a stethoscope I won't be able to hear the baby's heartbeat until about thirty weeks. By then, your belly will be so big it'll slow us down if we need to escape.'

They'd both tried to pinpoint the moment of lovemaking when she'd gotten pregnant, because a baby's gender could be predicted with high accuracy based on the conditions at conception: Boys are most often conceived during sex at ovulation, with deep penetration at ejaculation, accompanied by a female orgasm; girls are more likely to be made during sex a few days before ovulation, with shallow penetration at ejaculation, and without a female orgasm. But they'd made love so many times, ending up on the straw floor mats, in the hot bath, in the banyan tree, sprawled in the courtyard grass – panting, laughing, drunk on sexual energy – who could say when fertilization had occurred?

The factors did seem to stack up in favor of a baby boy: Tree had felt the pinch of ovulation on her left side the day they'd first made love; she'd had multiple orgasms that shivered her timbers; and, with Mason, there was no such thing as shallow penetration.

Tree laid a warm hand now over the new life in her womb. Chances were probably excellent she and Mason had made a son. But of course they couldn't gamble on it. Time was running out. They'd have to find a way out of the valley. And soon.

Tree glanced across Mason at K'un-Chien. She wished the woman's beauty did not sing out so loudly.

The night in the banyan with K'un-Chien had been very sweet – more than that; it had been true communion. K'un-Chien's love-desire was raw and soulful, and Tree still felt with her an inexplicable polarity, much like a male-female magnetism.

But since Mason and Tree had been reunited, the trio's dynamic had changed. K'un-Chien had drifted to a polite distance emotionally. She seemed genuinely happy for the two of them, but couldn't keep her loneliness from showing. Tree felt K'un-Chien hurting and even brought up to Mason the notion of including Second Wife at times in their lovemaking, but neither of them felt ready for such intimate company.

Today K'un-Chien wore an unbleached silk robe that buttoned up the front to a high mandarin collar. Her hair gushed down the plain cloth like an avalanche of obsidian. Porcelain-smooth skin. Brilliant blue eyes. Face a blend of East and West. Tree gulped. What could save K'un-Chien from being chosen to be the next Empress?

Whoever was selected today would undergo the sacrifice at the next full moon; in a few ragged seconds her physical beauty would be reduced to a broth in the guts of fishes.

'*Mis amigos.*'

The three turned and saw Domino weaving his way toward them through the crowd. His broken nose had healed larger and flatter than before, bent slightly to one side.

'Oh shit,' Mason said, bristling. 'Here comes my ulcer.'

K'un-Chien took a step toward Tree, protectively.

'What the hell do you want?' Mason said. 'I can't believe you've got the nerve to show your face to any of us.'

'I need to talk to a couple scientists about a matter of science,' Domino said. 'But first, Tree, allow me to apologize—'

'Don't you dare,' Tree said.

'I was very drunk, you know that.'

'That's no excuse.'

'I'm sorry, honestly. I sincerely regret it.'

'Just skip it. Never mention it again.'

'Agreed. Let's forget about it. It never happened.'

'To hell with that,' Tree said. 'It happened. I'll never forget it – I just don't want to talk about it. You got that?'

Domino held up his hands. 'I understand.'

'I doubt that's possible.'

Mason glared at Domino. 'Look, man, say your piece and leave.'

'Okay. It's about these monkeys.' He nodded toward the U-shaped chair where Kiki sat in Meng Po's lap. 'Have you had a good look at them?'

Mason nodded. 'What about them?'

'What about them?—*Mi Dio*, they're the most startling thing since Darwin's theory.'

'A new species,' Mason said.

'That's the least of it,' Domino said. 'Not just a new primate species – that would be good enough, but this is staggering. Have you looked at the hands? Those are fingernails, not claws.'

'Like pottos and lorises,' Mason said, 'they've got finger-nails.'

'True, but pottos and lorises have opposing thumbs and opposing big toes for climbing trees. Here, take a closer look at these hands and feet.' Domino took a step toward Kiki, and the sage-monkey scrambled up onto Meng Po's head to get away.

'So sorry,' Meng Po said in Mandarin. 'Kiki is shy around strangers.'

Tree could see Kiki's hands and feet resembled those of a human child.

'That's no tree dweller,' Domino said. 'It doesn't have a tail. All new world monkeys have grasping tails. Only the Old World chimpanzee, gorilla and orang-utan are tail-less. This little guy walks on the forest floor like a chimpanzee,' Domino said. 'Now watch how he walks.'

Domino dug into his pocket and held out a handul of raisins, but Kiki wouldn't budge from Meng Po's crown.

'We've seen him walk,' Mason said. 'Make your point.'

'All the great apes waddle from side to side as they walk,' Domino said. 'Only humans have the pelvic structure to walk straight ahead without rocking. These sage-monkeys walk like us.'

Tree was fascinated by Kiki but she didn't like the fact that Domino shared her interest.

'And they're far smarter than chimps or gorillas,' Domino said.

'Obviously this one is intelligent,' Tree said. 'He doesn't trust you.'

'I've been doing a lot of thinking about this,' Domino said. 'Look, we humans share a common ancestor with the Old World apes – both humans and apes evolved from some lemur-like primate about forty million years ago. Then the ape and human evolutionary lines split and went separate ways about six million years ago.

'Even so, gibbons, orang-utans, gorillas and chimpanzees are still our closest animal cousins. Ninety-nine percent of a chimp's genetic material is identical to our own. They're even closer to humans, genetically, than they are to most apes.'

'Okay. So what're you getting at?' Mason said.

'You've heard of Lucy?' Domino said.

Mason nodded. 'Supposed to be our common mother?'

'Yes. *Australopithecus afarensis*,' Domino said. 'She was about the same size and had the same brain-power as a chimp. Not any smarter. The only thing that made her more human than a chimp is that she walked straight ahead *without rocking side to side*. But these sage-monkeys walk like humans *and* they're fuckin' geniuses,' Domino said. 'One of my wives told me this one can write his name.'

Domino grinned. 'But that's not the most remarkable thing.'

'What then?' Mason said.

'*Fire*. They use fire in the wild,' Domino said. 'In the *wild*. They didn't learn it from humans. The colonists spotted campfires at night in the forests and investigated – that's how they discovered the sage-monkeys. They fucking use fire!'

Tree was stunned. 'I didn't know that.'

'I didn't either,' Mason said.

'One of my wives told me,' Domino said. 'She has an old female named Guan Yin.'

Kiki made a soft mewing, like a kitten, at the sound of his mother's name. Tree noticed, but didn't point it out to Domino.

'What are you trying to say?' Mason asked. 'You think Kiki is some kind of missing link?'

'Not so much a missing link, but a third and unknown branch of the primate line. Apes, humans, and these little whiz kids. Three types,' Domino said. 'I'm naming the species *Proto hominidae cruzanus*.'

'Oh, barf,' Tree said.

'Apparently the species is totally endemic to this valley,' Domino said. 'My wives told me there are only a handful of the sage-monkeys left alive, none in the wild.'

'That's terrible,' Mason said. 'I wonder how we can help?'

Tree saw the Empress approaching and stiffened involuntarily. She poked Mason's ribs.

'I'm outta here,' Domino said. 'Don't want her to see me.' He slunk into the crowd.

The Empress strode to a small pavilion at the center of the hill and faced the gathering. She wore a crimson lacquered mask, with red hair that spread over her shoulders. On cue, the entire assembly kowtowed to the gravel.

The Empress clapped once and everyone rose and shouted, 'Mother of Sons!'

39

The Empress paused in dramatic silence before she spoke: 'Twenty suns ago, in the Year of the Snake, standing in this very field, I was selected for the highest honor conferred on a tiger-woman of Jou P'u T'uan. I became a Vessel of Sons.

'As I am now too old to birth more sons it has become my duty to select the next Empress, to replace me. Therefore, in this Year of the Dog, I now call all tiger-women to assemble in rows of twelve before this pavilion, to await my selection.'

The tiger-women nervously arranged themselves in rows. On stage, a *sheng* quartet began to play; each musician blew into and sucked air from a bamboo mouth organ consisting of a reed chamber joined to seventeen pipes. The multi-chorded melody, accompanied by clashing cymbals, drums and bells, sounded to Tree like two carloads of bagpipes in a head-on collision.

A young woman with a severe limp hobbled past Tree, yawning. But none of the other women looked nonchalant as they jostled each other to get in line. A few sharp words were exchanged when three friends refused to be separated; all three were very pretty teenage girls who seemed terrified; stuck together. Tree gave K'un-Chien a hug before she stepped away to join the others.

About three hundred tiger-women, ranging in age from early teens to mid-twenties, lined up in ranks and files, like troops awaiting inspection. The Empress and her first-in-command, Yu Lin, and four dragon-women soldiers moved down from the hill. The Empress carried a single red lotus blossom, in full bloom. She walked slowly among the women, pausing now and then to examine a particular face and figure before moving on. Several times the Empress held a woman by the jaw and turned her face this way and that as if scrutinizing a fine porcelain vase for tiny cracks. At a nod from the Empress the soldiers separated women from the ranks and those finalists went and stood in a group to themselves, looking at once proud and frightened.

The entourage came to K'un-Chien and Tree held her breath. Without hesitation Yu Lin grabbed K'un-Chien by the sleeve and yanked her out of line. K'un-Chien went to stand with the other finalists, but they shifted as a group away from her.

K'un-Chien stood alone, looking brave and dignified, Tree thought.

And all too beautiful.

The selection process continued until the finalists had grown to a huddle of about twenty women. Now they were arranged in two files, and the Empress and Yu Lin paused before each candidate, studying her minutely. Each girl trembled as she was examined by the woman who had once been the most lovely girl in the city, but who now hid her ruined face behind a mask.

K'un-Chien, standing off by herself, was the last to be scrutinized. She did not appear afraid, but defiant. She stood a head taller than the others, and in Tree's mind, K'un-Chien was the most resplendent – alarmingly so. Tree hoped the distinction that trumpeted so loudly in her brain did not blare to the Empress, K'un-Chien's mother and judge.

Most of the women were cut from the group and fled back to the crowd, wilting with relief. Only four women remained standing out in front. Among them, K'un-Chien.

'Mason,' Tree whispered and bit her lower lip.

'Just hold on.' He squeezed her hand. 'We have to wait and see.'

The Empress stood back and took them all in with a sweep of her head, then reduced the finalists to two: K'un-Chien and one other.

The woman next to K'un-Chien was younger, perhaps only

fourteen to K'un-Chien's nineteen years. She was classically beautiful, like a Ming Dynasty courtesan: pale skin, black hair in an elaborate hair sculpture decorated with colorful combs and tassels, shiny eyes so black Tree could not see the border of iris and pupil, tiny mouth with deep red lips. Her body was a harmony of sensual curves, like sculpted music.

Tree looked from the young girl to K'un-Chien and pressed a hand to her sickened gut. The scissor fish were set to destroy one beautiful face or the other.

The Empress stared at the two women for what seemed like ten minutes. Finally, she dismissed the other woman with a flip of her hand. She held out the red lotus to K'un-Chien.

K'un-Chien closed her eyes and reached for it.

40

'Stop!' Tree shouted, and stepped forward.

Yu Lin blocked her way.

'K'un-Chien cannot be the new Empress,' Tree said. 'Her beauty is flawed.'

The Empress frowned. 'Let her approach.'

K'un-Chien glared at Tree, but stepped aside.

'Your opinion had not been called upon, barbarian,' the Empress said. 'But now that you have voiced it, why do you say her beauty is flawed?'

'Make her unbutton her collar,' Tree said. 'You will see what I mean. She has an ugly scar on her throat.'

The Empress nodded at K'un-Chien.

K'un-Chien unbuttoned her mandarin collar.

'Spread the cloth, let me see,' the Empress said.

K'un-Chien bared her throat. A nickel-sized pink scar stood out on her smooth skin.

The Empress stepped back, shaken. 'This cannot be. Something is wrong.'

'I am forced to agree with the unmannered barbarian,' Yu Lin said. 'K'un-Chien is not fit to be the new Empress, her beauty is marred. The sacrifice would not be pure, the gods would be cheated.'

'But ... this is not possible,' the Empress said. 'My vision showed the Lung-Hu will be born through me. For years, I mistakenly thought it referred to me directly – my own womb. But such was not my karma. I am too old now. It is time for me to be replaced. Therefore the next Empress must be K'un-Chien, my only daughter. In that way, the Lung-Hu will be born, indirectly, through me. Any other woman cannot fulfill my vision.'

'Then the selection ceremony was only for show?' Tree asked. 'You knew all along you would pick K'un-Chien?'

'Shut up,' Yu Lin hissed. 'You barge ignorantly into others' affairs. None of this concerns you.'

Mason stepped forward and took Tree's hand. 'It concerns us when you select my Second Wife to be a sacrifice.'

A half-smile tugged at Yu Lin's mouth. 'Wait. There is a way, Empress. Your vision may still hold true. This barbarian has given us the solution to the puzzle. He is your son-in-law by virtue of his marriage to your daughter, K'un-Chien. And because he is also married to this woman – Tree – she is your daughter-in-law. Thus, she is a member of your household family, who owes obeisance to you. The Ling-Chih vision may refer to her, even though she is not of your blood.'

Tree saw the cruelty in Yu Lin's smile and her gut turned to ice. This wasn't what she had in mind.

The Empress gazed at Tree through a ceramic eyehole. 'Her beauty is indeed dramatic. Had I considered her a proper candidate, it would have come down to a choice between three: Tree, K'un-Chien, and the other girl.'

'Look at her hair,' Yu Lin said. 'Such coils of gold must catch the attention of the gods. And even her eyes equal the splendor of K'un-Chien's. To send the gods the gift of her beauty would perhaps be the greater sacrifice, after all.'

The Empress stood silently focusing on Tree. Time elongated. The golden buttons on the royal yellow robe depicted stallions fighting and, for an instant, the two horses seemed to rear and bite and neigh.

'So be it,' the Empress said, at last. 'My daughter-in-law with the apricot hair shall be Empress and new sacrifice.'

The Empress held out the red lotus blossom to Tree.

41

Mason stepped in front of Tree. 'The hell you say.'
In a flash two swords zinged out of their scabbards and pointed at his throat. He stood on tiptoes, his head tilted back.

'Permit me the immodesty to inform you that you are mistaken about First Wife,' K'un-Chien said in a calm voice. 'Have you forgotten where she hides her ugliness? Examine her breasts. They are dotted with brown flecks, like spatters of mud.'

'I remember now – our first encounter,' the Empress said. 'K'un-Chien is right.'

Yu Lin raked open Tree's kimono and saw the freckles that sprinkled her bosom. She frowned. 'Like pottery with a sloppy glaze.'

The Empress frowned. 'But we cannot choose K'un-Chien, her scar makes her imperfect also.'

'I have the best solution,' Meng Po said in a loud voice, and stepped down from the pavilion. He stood before them in a yellow satin robe, looking and sounding mature for his years. 'I will marry the woman whom you just passed over as second-best, the beautiful girl with the white skin and crimson mouth,' he said. 'That will make her your daughter-in-law, mother, a member of your lineage. So make her the new

Empress. Such actions will comply with your vision. My First Wife may be destined to birth the Lung-Hu.'

'Yes,' the Empress said. 'Wonderful. That is the best solution. You are most wise, my young son.'

'There is one condition, however,' Meng Po said. 'Though I have not yet become a man, from this day forth, I will no longer live in that cursed lonely cage. I will live freely in my palace with my bride, and I will be free to roam the valley, within and beyond the city's walls.'

The Empress hesistated. Meng Po crossed his arms. 'I have spoken,' he said in a regal tone.

'Granted,' the Empress said at last.

The soldiers withdrew their swordtips from Mason's throat. The young woman was called back out from the crowd.

'What is your name?' the Empress asked her.

'Hsiao Pi,' the girl said in a quaking voice.

'Hsiao Pi, you are to wed my son, the Emperor. This is my final command as your ruler. From this day forward, you yourself shall be Empress.' The woman in the mask held out the red lotus blossom. 'At the next full moon, you will become the new sacrifice. May the offering of your precious beauty be auspicious for us all.'

Hsiao Pi swallowed hard and took the flower with shaking fingers.

Its blood-red petals fluttered like Tree's heart.

42

Mason dashed across the grassy courtyard, hurtled a low bench and snagged the Frisbee an inch from the ground. Kiki squeaked like a rusty gate, the sound he made to express delight.

'Miserable throw, marvelous catch,' Meng Po said, applauding.

'Your throws are improving,' Mason said. 'But remember: Release the disk when your hand is straight out before you.'

Mason flung the bright orange Frisbee back to the boy. It hovered above Kiki and the sage-monkey jumped up and tried to grab it, then it suddenly curved down into Meng Po's hand; he caught it without moving his feet. Kiki squeaked again and turned a couple pirouettes.

'You are with Frisbees as K'un-Chien is with arrows,' Meng Po said, 'your aim is always true. But sent from my hands, arrow or Frisbee flits about like a butterfly.'

'Release the disk in a flat plane and it sails straight ahead,' Mason said. 'Tilt it, and it curves to the right or left in the direction of the tilt.'

'Yes, I believe you, but my fingers do not obey the authority of my will.'

Meng Po tossed the Frisbee and it swerved on its side in the air, dropped to the half-moon bridge and bounced into the pond with a splash.

Mason looked around for a long stick. 'Hmmm. What we need is a retriever.'

'A servant who retrieves?'

'A dog,' Mason said. 'Actually, a whole group of dog breeds that like to swim and can easily be taught to retrieve objects from water. My brother was an avid hunter and he bred and raised retriever dogs called Labradors to fetch ducks from ponds.'

'I have read about dogs and seen drawings,' Meng Po said. 'Here, we hunt ducks with eagles.'

Mason shuddered. 'I have seen your eagles in action.'

'Perhaps we can teach Kiki to retrieve.'

'Can he swim?'

'Sage-monkeys live by streams in the wild – they swim fast enough to catch fish.' Meng Po turned to the sage-monkey. 'Kiki. See the Frisbee? See it? Swim out and get it, bring it back to Mason.'

Kiki dove into the pond before Meng Po had finished his sentence. The primate swam with amazing agility, frog-kicking his legs and feet. He reached the Frisbee, clamped teeth upon it, and swam back to the near shore. Reddish fur plastered his frame like wet clay overlaid by the white beard. He scampered with his prize across the bridge to Mason and hopped excitedly at Mason's feet.

'Kiki, you want to learn how to throw a Frisbee?' Mason said in Mandarin.

Kiki squealed like a kid on a rollercoaster.

Mason laughed. 'I will take that as a yes.' He knelt beside the sage-monkey. Its fur smelled like wet dog. 'Here. Hold it like this. Good. Whoops. Get a better grip, it is a little heavy for you. Okay? Now do not let go. At first we are only going to practice the motion.' He held Kiki's arm and guided him several times through a sidearm toss and follow-through.

'This time, when your arm is straight out, let go,' Mason said. 'Ready?'

Kiki cocked his arm and swung it forward. 'Throw!' Mason shouted.

Kiki launched the Frisbee and it flew straight into the pond. Kiki dove off the bridge and retrieved it, brought it back to Mason.

'Next time get your arm up, up. See if you can throw it across the pond.'

Kiki tossed the Frisbee toward the pond and chased after it even before it splashed the water. He plunged in and retrieved it.

Meng Po laughed. 'He thinks the game is Fetch the Frisbee from the Water.'

Hsiao Pi came out of Meng Po's palace carrying a tray of jasmine tea. Meng Po looked at his wife with unconcealed affection. Mason crossed the bridge to join them.

'Thank you, Hsiao Pi,' Meng Po said, and passed a cup of tea to his guest. Meng Po took his own cup and sat down on a garden bench.

'Please sit down,' Meng Po said, gesturing to them both.

Mason sat next to him but Hsiao Pi remained standing. Kiki rubbed his wet fur against her kimono-clad legs like a cat.

'Please excuse me, so sorry, I must oversee the servants in the kitchen,' Hsiao Pi said, and turned and walked back into the palace.

'I am sure she hates me for making her the new Empress,' Meng Po said. 'And, of course, I do not blame her. But she does not know that I would never allow her to be sacrificed. We must devise a plan to sneak my bride to safety in your land.'

Mason leaned closer. 'I was hoping you would say that. It is my real reason for being here today.'

'So I had suspected, but I was waiting for the right moment to turn our buoyant morning to lead.'

Mason took the boy's hand. 'What about you? What will happen to you?'

'No harm will come to me, do not worry. I will be the only male left in the city. My life is most precious here – stiflingly so.'

'But Domino is here as well. He may try to wield his power – after all, you are still a boy.'

'No. Domino wants to leave with you.'

'He does? Since when?'

'He told me he had a frightening vision. He took the Ling-Chih to search into his future and what he saw has unnerved him. He wants to leave here to escape his fate.'

'What fate?'

'He would not explain. He was pale and shaken. But he made it clear he is anxious to go and he offered to help Hsiao Pi escape.'

'When did you have this conversation?'

'Yesterday afternoon, after the selection ceremony. He came to me in private and we talked in secret.'

'But ... how did he know you would want to save Hsiao Pi?'

Meng Po blushed. 'He said he read it in my eyes – the way I look at her. He gambled that I would feel this way.'

Mason nodded and put his arm around the boy's shoulders. 'Yes, it is easy to see that you are a loving man, Meng Po,' he said. 'It is Senor Cruz I worry about. I only hope he can be trusted.'

The two forgot their tea and talked intently about their predicament.

Guan Di – Gods of War – were larger than bumble-bees and more aggressive than hornets; in sufficient numbers their venom paralyzed the diaphragm, suffocating their victims in minutes. Therefore, the problem of escaping the valley was the problem of exterminating the bees who had built a massive hive in the valley's only exit to the jungle below.

'This has happened before,' Meng Po said. 'Eventually, the soldiers will smoke them out. It is a suicidal mission. It will be given to a dragon-woman who has been disgraced and is desperate to restore her face.'

'When? When will this happen?'

'I am afraid it will not be soon enough for us,' Meng Po said. 'From Yu Lin's point of view, there is no pressure to hurry: Most of Domino's wives are now with child. The soldiers will leave the bees alone until the time arrives for the dragon-women to raid the native villages again for boys. That could be many months from now.'

Mason frowned and blew out a heavy breath. Was there a way to smoke the little bastards out without getting oneself stung to death?

A memory popped into his mind. *Carbon dioxide.*

'My god, the fire extinguishers,' Mason blurted, in English.

Domino blinked, uncomprehending.

When Mason was a boy, his older brother had earned spare cash by gathering and selling hornets to a drug company that marketed anti-venom. His method was simple and effective: At night when the hornets had gathered in their big paper nests along Burnt Mill Creek, he'd go drifting downstream in his bass boat, equipped with a carbon dioxide-type fire extinguisher and a gallon glass jug with a big paper funnel. When he came upon a hornets' nest, he'd position the jug and funnel below the opening at its base and douse the nest with the fire extinguisher. The cold gas knocked out the hornets instantly and they'd tumble out of their nest into the glass jug. After he got home, he froze the hornets in sealable plastic bags, packed them in dry ice and shipped them to off to New Jersey. The pharmaceutical company paid him for the hornets by the pound. Mason had begged to go on hornet hunts with him, but his mother had never allowed it.

'There are supplies at the Raft – the station where Tree and I dwelled up above – that I believe would allow us to get past the bees,' Mason said. 'Could you send soldiers to bring them to you?'

'Certainly. I told you that they bring me artefacts – the Frisbees, the awful camera—'

'Yes, yes. Good. You must send them right away.'

'For what items?'

'They are called fire extinguishers. Bright yellow metal tanks topped with a black hose and nozzle. You spray the contents on a fire to smother the flames. Here, let me draw one for you.' Mason drew with his fingertip in the fine pea gravel at their feet.

Meng Po broke into a grin. 'It is not necessary to send the soldiers.' He stood up and disappeared into the palace. In a moment he returned with a waddling gait, clutching a large yellow fire extinguisher, half as tall as himself.

Mason leapt up and ran to him. 'Wonderful,' he said, taking the heavy aluminum canister. 'Any more of them?'

'Three more, I think. I meant to ask you their function.'

'Their function is to get us past the bees, to freedom. Tonight.' Mason inverted the tank, pointed the black nozzle over the pond and squeezed the handle. A cold white spray blasted outward twelve feet. A dragonfly dropped to the pond's surface and was gobbled up by an orange-and-blue koi.

Mason and the boy then gazed at each other, knowing that Mason's escape meant they would never see each other again.

Meng Po took Mason's hand. 'I long to go to with you, Elder Brother. But my duty lies here.'

Mason swallowed past a lump in his throat. 'Younger Brother, there is nothing I would like more than to take you with me to my homeland. But . . . I understand your position.' Mason sat down on the bench. 'Sit here beside me.'

With a sigh Meng Po plopped down.

'Now, please listen carefully,' Mason said, 'there are crucial facts you need to know. No maiden ever again needs to be sacrificed. You can have sons with all of your wives.'

Meng Po's eyebrows arched. 'All my wives can have sons?'

'Absolutely.'

Mason carefully explained to Meng Po the biology of sexual reproduction and of planned gender selection. And he emphasized the need for all pregnant women in Prayer Mat of the Body to eat the Ling-Chih fungus within the first six weeks of conception in order to correct the karma that had led to a city of Amazons.

43

Mason peered down cautiously into the cave entrance at the base of the Western Face. A fire extinguisher hung over his right shoulder in a rope harness, the black nozzle slung at arm's length. K'un-Chien and Tree each carried a fire extinguisher in a similar shoulder sling.

'K'un-Chien, did you say there were fourteen dragon lizards?' He referred to the Komodo dragons who nested in clawed-out dens in the cliff near the passageway to the jungle.

'Yes, fourteen.'

'Well, there can be no more than twelve now,' he said, and pointed to two large reptilian carcasses slumped together just inside the jagged mouth in the rock that dropped into blackness. One dragon was mostly skeleton, the other heap squirmed with white maggots in the torchlight.

'They must have tried to enter the cave to get warm,' K'un Chien said. 'The bees killed them.'

Domino groaned. '*Mierda.*'

'Oh god, be careful,' Tree said.

Hsiao Pi looked terrified.

'It will be all right, Hsiao Pi,' Mason said. 'We will get past the bees.'

'I do not want to leave Jou P'u T'uan,' Hsiao Pi said.

'Do you want to become a sacrifice and wear a mask the rest of your life?'

The girl shook her head.

'Listen, in the land where we are taking you there are as many boys as girls,' he said. 'Suitors will form lines at your door to ask to court you.'

'Meng Po told me that.' Then she looked sad and began to cry. 'I did not know how much he cared for me.'

Mason hugged Hsiao Pi and glanced over at Tree who stepped forward and took his place comforting the girl.

Mason lowered himself into the fissure and dropped to the first ledge, holding out his torch made of oil-soaked bundled straw. 'Ugh. I see another dead dragon, farther in. Oooh, make that two more.'

'That makes four,' Tree said. 'What about the bees?'

'No bees.'

'So far,' Tree said.

'Believe me, I'm all eyes and ears.'

The plan was for Mason to descend into the tunnel mouth, fire extinguisher ready, to hunt out the hive. If *Guan Di* were like other bees, they were dormant at night, and he could knock out the whole hive at once with cold blasts of CO_2. K'un-Chien would stick close behind to back him up. Hsiao Pi and Domino would follow K'un-Chien and Tree would bring up the rear with the last fire extinguisher, covering everyone's retreat.

Even after their first escape attempt a month ago, climbing again over the city's walls and trekking to the Western Face undetected had not been difficult. News of the beehive in the passageway to the jungle had been enough to eliminate the need for extra security by the city's guards. If anything, they were more lax, for as far as Yu Lin and the others were concerned, there could be no escape.

Mason scooted down to the next ledge and his boot squished a half-rotten dragon carcass; the sole sideslipped as if he'd stepped in wet cheese. 'Gross. Pyoo. These guys smell even worse when they're dead.' The greasy yellow torch flame flickered against irregular granite walls. 'Okay, K'un-Chien. Heading down now.'

K'un-Chien dropped onto the ledge behind him. 'I am following, May-Son.'

Mason walked ahead and paused until he heard the footsteps of the others behind K'un-Chien. Then the five moved single file slowly down the narrow tunnel that housed the deadly bees.

This better work, Mason thought as he shuffled in the lead down the steep slope. The yellow ball of torchlight projected only six or eight feet in front of him. *My kingdom for a powerful searchlight.*

He glanced back at K'un-Chien. 'How far?' he whispered.

'Another hundred paces,' K'un-Chien said. 'Beyond where the tunnel bends to the left.'

He moved forward uneasily. 'No bees so far,' his voice squeaked. He cleared his throat. 'No bees so far. Where is Tree?'

'Bringing up the rear,' Tree said, and she waved her torch.

Mason crept forward to the bend and stopped. 'Uh-oh. I hear buzzing.'

'*Caramba*, they're supposed to be *snoring*,' Domino hissed.

Mason took a deep breath. 'What do you think, Tree?'

'I say it's too late to turn back,' she whispered. 'Let's go for it.'

Mason aimed the fire extinguisher's black nozzle and gripped the trigger handle. 'Be ready, everyone,' Mason said, in Mandarin.

'I am with you,' K'un-Chien said, 'I am ready.'

'Here we go,' Mason said, and stepped around the corner. 'Oh *fuck*.' The hive was enormous it stretched a dozen feet from floor to ceiling and was twice as wide. A terrible buzzing vibrated its gray papery walls.

'Blast the hell out of it!' Mason took a step toward the hive and shot it with cold white fog. The frigid spray from K'un-Chien's fire extinguisher joined in. At once, bees swarmed from the bottom of the hive. The fog stopped most of the bees in mid-air and they plopped to the granite floor with a spattering sound like fat gumdrops.

A drone buried its stinger in Mason's forehead, another stabbed the back of his neck. 'Ouch,' he yelled, 'everybody remember – do not slap the bees.'

Domino and Hsiao Pi squatted on the floor of the cavern beneath a thick quilted blanket. 'Okay, just kill the little cunts,' Domino shouted with a muffled voice. 'They're stinging the piss out of us.'

Tree sprayed the quilt and a handful of bees dropped off. Thousands of thumb-sized black shapes littered the cavern floor. The three with fire extinguishers kept spraying the hive and a cold fog filled the cavern. Suddenly the firelight from Mason's torch sputtered and went out and the room was plunged into deep shadows.

'Oh shit!' he yelled. 'Stop spraying!'

He gave the order too late. Tree's torch died next and the cavern went nearly black except for a halo of light that flickered weakly at the crown of K'un-Chien's torch. In the next instant, the fog snuffed that flame too. Mason could not see the hive two feet away.

Hsiao Pi screamed from under the blanket.

'Shhh!' Mason said.

Hsiao Pi whimpered loudly.

'Domino, shut her up!' Tree said.

Mason held his breath to listen. Hsiao Pi was panting with fear.

'*Mierda*,' Domino muttered.

'Everybody be *silent*,' Mason hissed.

In the stillness, the *plip-plip* of dripping water – fog condensing on cave walls.

And from within the hive, a deep angry buzz.

44

Mason aimed his fire extinguisher nozzle toward the noise in the hive, squeezed the trigger and emptied its contents in a long cold blast.

He listened again in the blackness. The buzzing was still strong.

'Damn it,' he said. 'The bees deeper in the hive must be insulated from the cold.'

'What about the ones all over the floor?' Tree said. 'How long do they stay knocked out?'

'Anybody's guess,' Mason said. 'Turn around. We gotta go back, get the hell outta here.'

'May-Son, we can press forward,' K'un-Chien said. 'I know the way down.'

'In the dark?' Domino whined.

'Yes, even in the dark,' she said. 'The passage is steep in some places, but fairly straight all the way to the bottom of the mountain. The tunnel bends once to the left and, just before the exit, it bends again to the right.'

'Good,' Mason said. 'You lead the way. Use the rope from our slings to form a guide line to stay connected.'

'Great idea,' Tree said. 'Hurry.'

The three of them undid their slings and looped the ropes around their waists, then handed the ends along in the darkness until each person was tied in.

'Ow, a bee's stinging my back,' Tree said. '*Ow!*' she yelped. 'A bunch of bees, help!'

Mason reeled himself along the rope to Tree. 'Gimme your fire extinguisher,' he said.

'Take it, hurry.'

In the blackness Mason grabbed the heavy canister. His hand fumbled for the trigger handle and squeezed. 'I'm spraying, Tree. Where are you?'

'Here,' she said. 'Just keep spraying. Jesus. Okay, they're falling off.'

'You okay?' Mason said.

'I think so.'

'Let's hope those were new bees from deep inside the hive,' Mason said, 'and not these fuckers on the floor waking up.'

'We've squished a thousand of them under our feet,' Tree said. 'The attack signal in here must be thick as olive oil.'

'Spray the floor, K'un-Chien,' Mason said. 'Empty your canister. I am going to untie myself for a moment. Got an idea.'

'What're you gonna do, Mason?' Tree said.

Mason cut loose from the others. 'Everybody follow K'un-Chien. Start heading down.'

'Mason?' Tree said.

'Go. I'll catch up.'

He reached before him, swinging his arm until it touched the rough surface of the hive. It felt like soaking wet cardboard. He dropped to his knees, following the outline of the hive with his left hand, then slid onto his back and scooted underneath the hive, groping for the opening.

He found it. A round hole, the size of a saucer. A bee stung his fingers as he felt the opening. He squashed it in his fist. No need to be careful about that now. He jammed the nozzle of the fire extinguisher as far up into the hole as it would reach and then shoved until his whole arm was buried in the hive to his shoulder.

Sharp bolts of pain stung the entire length of his arm as he squeezed a long burst of carbon dioxide until the canister was drained.

Mason listened intently. All the buzzing had stopped but

he heard breathing in the cavern. 'Who's there? You were supposed to leave.'

'Not without you,' Tree said. 'We sent Domino on with Hsiao Pi.'

'Hurry, tie on your rope and follow us,' K'un-Chien said.

The three started down and soon caught up to the other two and K'un-Chien took the lead. Tied together like mountain climbers they descended in blackness, sliding their left hands along the cool damp rock of the tunnel. This time Mason brought up the rear. In spite of the dank chill, sweat trickled down his chest and back.

Somewhere ahead K'un Chien cried out with pain. 'Stoop and guard your head as you round the bend to your left,' she said. 'The ceiling juts down sharply.'

After what seemed like hours, the five of them sat down in a huddle on the rocky floor to rest. Tree took Mason's hand. Mason felt exhausted, more from emotional stress than physical exertion.

'Tree, how you holding up?'

'I'll make it.'

'Hsiao Pi?' Mason said. 'How are you feeling?'

He heard a sniffle in the blackness to his right and then Hsiao Pi began to cry.

'We are nearly there,' K'un-Chien said in a calming voice. 'Maybe another hour.'

'Just great,' Domino said. 'Another fucking hour in this tomb. My left eye is swollen shut, and it's so black in here, I can't tell if I can still see out of my right eye or not. And if I eat one more spiderweb, I'm gonna freak.'

'Hey, I haven't run into any webs,' Mason said. 'Thanks for knocking them out of my path for me.'

'Fuck you, *compadre*.'

'Say, Domino, what was it made you change your mind about leaving Prayer Mat of the Body?' Mason said. 'A month ago you were as smug as a roach in a jelly jar.'

'My future there didn't look so good.'

'You had a bad vision with the mushroom?'

'Yeah, you could say that – I foresaw my own death. I was going to be electrocuted if I stayed in the city. I saw it

271

clearly, felt the shock, everything.'

'Electrocution?' Tree said. 'But there's no electricity there.'

'I'm telling you what I saw and felt. Electrocution – maybe lightning or something. I was wet, like I was drowning in rain. My muscles stiffened, my lungs went hard as steel. My heart stopped.' Domino's voice broke. 'I had to get away.'

Meng Po was the only man left in the city, Mason thought sadly. No longer a fraternity of two. A hermitage of one.

'Let's move on,' K'un-Chien said, and stood.

Mason helped Hsiao Pi to her feet. 'If it makes you feel safer, you can hold my hand,' he whispered.

'Yes, I would like that,' Hsiao Pi said and placed her delicate hand in his calloused palm. 'Thank you.'

The tunnel was relatively straight. In a few places, however, it was very steep. K'un-Chien would turn to face the wall and scoot down first. Then she'd help the others climb down. After half an hour the slope of the path became much less treacherous. Mason untied Hsiao Pi's rope and carried her piggy-back.

After their long dark trek K'un-Chien announced she'd reached the last bend before the exit.

'Oh, finally,' Tree said.

The blackness gradually gave way to dim light, which abruptly brightened in the glow of the half-moon. Mason was out of the tunnel. He found himself standing on a ledge several hundred feet about the treetops. The half-moon hung in the sky, turning the canopy of the rainforest silvery green. A balmy breeze stirred the greenscape and it rolled like waves.

'Glorious,' Mason said. It felt so damn good to be out of the tunnel. He noticed the temperature was twenty or more degrees hotter here at the base of the tepui than high in the mountain's cloud forest. The tepui's plateau had smelled of crushed wet rock and mushrooms and rain; the valley floor had smelled of waterfall and banyan groves; the avenues of the city had smelled of women's hair and perfume. Here, the thick jungle air smelled of warm damp rot and feathers and fur.

The forest was alive with the songs of birds, frogs, insects. Mason heard the growl of a big cat hunting below.

'What was that?' Tree said.

'Jaguar, probably,' Mason said, 'or maybe a marcay.'

'Dangerous?' she said.

'Very, if you're traveling solo. With this many of us together, I'd say not.'

Domino scanned the impenetrable green mass that stretched to the horizon. 'K'un-Chien, which way to the closest river?' he asked.

'I do not know,' K'un-Chien said.

'You do not know?'

'I have never been off the mountain before,' she said.

'*Caramba.* I thought you said you knew the way down the tunnel.'

'Only dragon-women use the tunnel, to raid villages and kidnap boys. My father warned me I might someday need to know an escape route and he showed me a tunnel map he had drawn.'

Domino frowned. 'Fuck,' he said. He turned to Tree. 'Have *you* any idea where the hell we are?'

'Don't look at me,' Tree said. 'I'd be lost even with a map and a compass. Zero sense of direction.'

'I got a fairly good picture of this area in my head,' Mason said, 'from when we overflew it in the helicopter. There are two or three rivers to the west, which merge into a major waterway.' He pointed to the half-moon that hung in the sky like an ivory amulet. 'The moon is setting, so that way is westward. We follow the moon to the river.'

Domino adjusted the fat pack on his back. '*Vamanos,*' he said.

'Wait,' Mason said. 'Hsiao Pi is exhausted. We rest here till morning. We'll be safe here on this ledge.'

'Safe from the jaguars?' Tree said.

'I was thinking of the Yanomorduro.'

Domino's eyes grew wide and he grabbed Mason's arm. 'Yanomorduro? Are you shittin' me? They're headhunters, for chrissake.'

'Correct,' Mason said, gazing below at the undulating jungle. 'We're looking down on the roof of their home.'

45

As soon as it was light enough to see, the group started down from the ledge. Within an hour's trek westward, Mason's khaki shirt clung to his back like a wet skin. It felt as if the whole jungle was sweating: Moisture steamed up from the spongy compost below his boots; each fern and leaf and tree dripped with dew.

'Water break,' Mason called.

The group sat on soggy mulch and sipped from ceramic water jars. Each head had its own cloud of gnats. A macaw squawked in the foliage nearby and Domino stiffened with alarm.

'What're you so jumpy about?' Mason said.

'I don't know about you, man, but I don't want my head shrunk by no fucking Indians.'

'Actually, they don't shrink your whole head,' Mason said. 'They carefully peel the skin off your skull and then stitch it over the skull of a spider monkey. Then they shrink your skin taut over the little skull by boiling it for hours in a special solution.'

Domino looked disgusted and turned away.

Mason enjoyed torturing Domino. He hadn't forgiven him for assaulting Tree, nor did he expect to any millennium soon. 'Besides, your government has declared headhunting illegal,' he said. 'Tell them you're a cop, *Policia Especial*.'

'Screw you, amigo,' Domino said, 'as if you're not scared too.' He pulled off his canvas hat and slapped it on his knee. Sweat flew off in sprinkles, scattering his personal cloud of gnats.

'Enough, you two,' Tree said. 'Jesus. It's hot enough without you guys being on a slow burn.'

Mason looked at Tree. The humidity had defeated her curls and they hung limply on her sweaty forehead. 'Our biggest danger is not from headhunters,' he said, 'but from dehydration. At the rate we're losing fluids, we'd better make the river soon, or we're gonna be in serious trouble.'

'Hsiao Pi, are you ready to continue?' Tree asked the girl in Mandarin.

Hsiao Pi nodded.

K'un-Chien took Hsiao Pi's hand, stood and pulled the girl to her feet. 'Let us go,' she said.

With a machete that had been salvaged from the Raft, Mason hacked a tunnel through the entangled greenery. Progress was excruciatingly slow. By late afternoon, Mason guessed they had pierced no more than three miles of jungle since their dawn departure. Tree and K'un-Chien had begun taking turns carrying Hsiao Pi, while Domino toted the bows and quivers and a backpack of his personal supplies. Tepui-cameleon loomed behind them over the treetops, a giant dark pedestal with its grand secret hidden in a cool-misted valley.

Mason paused and wiped sweat from his eyes; blew his nose to get the salt water out of his nostrils. And with his next breath he smelled the river.

'I smell water,' Tree said in the same instant.

'Let's hope it's potable,' Mason said. 'Our canteens are nearly empty.' He chopped at the ferns and vines with renewed vigor, and after ten minutes the dense foliage suddenly broke open onto the muddy bank of a whiskey-colored river.

Mason licked his lips. 'The current is flowing fast,' he said. 'That's good – not stagnant. We can build a raft and the river will take us north to where we're going.'

'Shouldn't we boil the water?' Tree said.

'That would be the safest move,' Mason said, 'but you gotta be an Indian to light a fire in all this wetness. I've never been able to do it.'

'I'm going to drink it,' Domino said. 'If you can drink the water from my barrio, you can drink anything.' He took his bundle off and set it on the bank. He slid down the bank and splashed into the water.

'*Es frio!*' he shouted with a laugh. 'Must be running down off the mountain.'

'Cold?' Tree said. 'Here I come.'

The rest of the them scampered down the bank and plunged into the water, laughing, splashing. Mason gasped as the chill water sent a burst of delight up his spine. The pleasure of the release from the oppressive heat made his body swoon. He rolled in the shallow water over to Tree who held her head back, soaking up the chill into her brain. He kissed her and whispered, 'I think I just discovered a new kind of orgasm.'

She grinned. 'Remember that time with the ice cubes—?'

He laughed and looked into her eyes and kissed her again.

Then a weak small voice called his name.

They both looked up. Hsiao Pi was dunking her head underwater, then slinging her long hair like a whip. K'un-Chien and Domino were busy with their own water play.

Mason frowned at Tree.

'I heard it, too,' she said.

They both walked up the bank toward the supplies. The bundle that Domino had been carrying squirmed on the ground like a cocoon.

'Mmay-son. Mmay-son,' came the muffled voice from inside.

46

Mason's gut clenched. He hurriedly unwrapped the bundle and found Kiki, the sage-monkey. The little creature's fur was wet and matted with perspiration; its eyes lolled in its head.

'Mmay-son,' it moaned.

Mason spun his head and looked at Domino splashing in the river, laughing. 'That son-of-a-bitch, I'll kill him.'

Tree gripped his arm. 'Stop it. Take care of Kiki. He needs your help now.'

Mason looked down at Kiki. 'Get me some water, quick. Here, use this.' He handed her a canteen.

'Oh, little Kiki. I'm so sorry,' Tree said, and hurried off.

Mason pressed his ear to the blaze of white fur on Kiki's chest. The little heart was racing arhythmically. 'Hang in there, little fella. You're gonna be all right.'

You'd better be all right. You'd just goddam better be. Mason had never felt such rage in his life. It was as if someone had harmed his little son. He felt that he could rip Domino's head off and shrink it himself.

Tree reappeared at his side. 'I brought you water, Kiki,' she said in a kind voice. 'Here. Try to drink.'

Mason lifted the sage-monkey's head and Tree tilted the canteen to its lips. Water trickled over its purple tongue and

Kiki choked and spluttered.

K'un-Chien knelt beside her brother's companion. 'Oh no, poor Kiki.'

'He will not take the water,' Tree said.

'Sage-monkeys suck dew from leaves,' K'un-Chien said, and offered a thick strand of her dripping wet hair to Kiki's lips. 'Here. Take it, sweet Kiki. I love you. Meng Po loves you. Please take the water.'

At the sound of her brother's name, Kiki stirred.

'Yes, Meng Po loves you,' K'un-Chien said, 'Meng Po loves you, Kiki.'

The sage-monkey began to suck at the water dripping from her hair.

To Mason, Kiki appeared more than ever like a hundred-year-old man with a long white beard. The old sage nursed from the wet hair of a beautiful young maiden who gazed at him with utmost tenderness. Mason prayed such fairy-tale magic would bring Kiki back to life.

Tree began to cry softly. 'Is he going to be all right?'

'I don't know,' Mason said. 'God. He's been wrapped in that bundle in this stifling heat. *Damn.*' A voice in his head tore through every curse word known to an ex-Army corpsman. Domino was going to pay for this.

Mason held the canteen over K'un-Chien's head and trickled water onto her hair. It flowed down the strand that Kiki sucked upon. 'Meng Po loves you, Kiki,' K'un-Chien kept repeating, soothingly, like a mantra. Tree wet her hand with cool water and stroked Kiki's head. His black eyelids fluttered.

'I think he's coming around,' Mason said. 'Let's get him into the river and cool his body temperature down.'

When the cold water swirled around Kiki's body he opened his big amber eyes. 'Mmay-son,' he said. 'Taa-reee.'

'Oh, you little doll. We're here with you,' Tree said.

Mason turned and glared at Domino who stood to his waist in the river, hands on his hips.

'What?' Domino said, and raised his hands, palms up. 'Why you looking at me like that? I drugged the monkey. He's not hurt. Look, he's the most important find ever made in evolutionary biology – *ever* made, are you listening? Do you hear me? This is bigger than Darwin's *Origin of Species*. I mean it. It's gonna shake the whole world.'

'Your precious specimen almost died from heat stroke, you asshole,' Mason said.

'Yeah, well, so I admit I goofed,' Domino said. 'But come on, you're both scientists. Look at the big picture here. I did it for science.'

'Cut the bullshit, you did it for your own selfish gains,' Mason said. 'Kiki is Meng Po's best friend. Did you stop to consider that? You broke the boy's heart.'

'Hey, fuck the kid, okay? This is way more important than one person's hurt feelings.'

'That's it.' Mason took three plunging steps toward Domino and plowed headlong into his torso, tackling him in the river. He hauled Domino up from the water by his collar and punched him so hard it knocked the man loose from his grip. Domino reeled back into the river and Mason stooped over him and hauled him up again. Watery blood streaked Domino's chin. Mason cocked his arm back and Tree grabbed it from behind and spun him around.

'Cut it out, you'll kill him.'

'That's the idea,' Mason said, lungs heaving.

'Like that's gonna help things?' Tree said.

'Might cure my ulcer.'

'Let me go,' Domino said.

Mason shoved him hard and Domino sloshed backward into the river onto his butt. The water came to his chin and he dipped his head and rinsed blood from his mouth. A thin streak of red swirled away in the current.

'I had to make it worth my while to go back to the world,' Domino said, staring at the water. 'I didn't want to leave, I didn't want to.'

'So why did you?' Mason said. 'No one invited you this time.'

'I told you, the electrocution. If I stayed—'

'So why didn't you take some gold instead, a sack full of diamonds?' Mason said. 'That whole valley is one big jewelry box.'

'Diamonds only make you wealthy,' Domino said. 'Wealth is

not enough. I got a cousin who's wealthy, smuggling cocaine. He's from the same barrio as me. He's got money, sure, but he can't show his face in decent society. He's got no respect, no influence, beyond the ghetto rats he bosses around. I've been to college, I've worked hard for respect—'

'You've got respect in your field,' Mason said. 'Barry didn't hire amateurs for his team.'

Domino shook his head. 'Smalltime – tenure, publishing, speaking at conferences. I'm talking *big* time – being a name on high school exams, a part of history like Darwin. You can be in on it too, man. We all discovered the species together, right?'

'How'd you get Kiki away from Meng Po?' Tree said.

Domino shrugged. 'Easy. I told him his pet was sick. I'm a zoologist, I knew how to cure him.'

'You still don't get it, do you?' Mason said. 'You've ruined everything. I can't let you take Kiki. I'm going back.'

'Mason, what're you saying?' Tree said.

'I can't let Meng Po lose Kiki, I know what it's like to lose a best friend.'

'But you can't go back,' Tree said. 'The bees. Besides, if you made it back to the city, they'd kill you.'

Mason blew out a long breath. He had to admit she was right. He kicked the water viciously and splashed a wave in Domino's face.

K'un-Chien waded over to them, cradling Kiki against her bosom like a child.

'I cannot allow Kiki to be stolen from my brother,' she said. 'I must return with him.'

'I feel the same way,' Mason said. 'But have you forgotten the bees?'

'I can carry wood for fuel up the tunnel and smoke the bees out.'

'You will be killed as you are lighting the fire,' Tree said.

'Yes, probably,' K'un-Chien said. 'But Kiki is small and very nimble and fast. His fur is thick and I can make a heavy smock for him from my shirt. He can wait far back in the tunnel. After I light the fire and the smoke kills most of the bees, he can race through the passage. He knows the way home.'

'No, K'un-Chien. You must not,' Tree said. 'Mason, tell her. She can't go. She'll be killed.'

Mason sighed heavily. The masculine spirit that he saw in K'un-Chien – the quality that reminded him of Gib – was fully alive now, dauntless. She wasn't asking his permission, and there was no way he could tell K'un-Chien not to go. She was going back and he knew it. K'un-Chien was free.

The hardness in K'un-Chien's face softened. 'I confess I never intended to travel the full journey with you,' she said quietly. 'I am certain I do not belong in your land. I do not even belong in my own. So it is best this way. I can do something useful now, instead of just waiting behind to die.'

Mason glimpsed the sadness and the love brimming in K'un-Chien's eyes. She turned quickly and waded back to the bank.

Mason watched her go and felt a terrible stab of guilt. He realized that he and Tree had failed to understand how much their private love affair had hurt K'un-Chien. How could they have been so blind? K'un-Chien had no experience with monogamy or western morals. She could only perceive their exclusive sexual relationship as a rejection of her. Why hadn't they seen things from K'un-Chien's point of view? They should have invited her into their marital bed. *Right and wrong can go to hell. Love is love. Love is the only morality.* That was obvious to him now; he felt its truth with luminous clarity.

Tree took Mason's hand. She was crying. 'Baby, we blew it,' she said.

He swallowed past a lump in his throat. 'I know that now.'

'Do you love her?' Tree asked, sniffling.

He didn't know how to answer. His eyes followed K'un-Chien walking up the bank. Mysterious soul. He almost couldn't imagine their life without her. Over the past months his heart had healed and expanded and now there was ample room in its depths for both of them, but how could he explain that to Tree?

'It's okay. I know how you feel,' Tree said. 'I only just now realized how much I love her too.'

Mason and Tree waded onto the bank. 'K'un-Chien,' Mason said, 'You and Tree and I need to talk. Please. We both have something important to say to you.'

Behind them Domino suddenly yelped in pain.

Mason spun around. Domino leapt to his feet in the river and screamed again with pain and fear. 'Help me!'

Mason ran down the bank toward him. Domino lurched forward and then Mason saw the black watersnakes, three or four of them, churning around Domino's legs like long shiny ribbons. Domino grunted explosively and his whole body stiffened in a jerking seizure. His arms flung straight out to his sides, fingers splayed, and he tumbled backward into the water as rigid as a mannequin.

Mason's feet struck the water and he was instantly jolted by a powerful electric current. He stopped his momentum short and caught his balance, barely able to keep from plunging in. A dozen feet away, underwater, Domino's eyes bugged out of his face. His teeth were clenched in a macabre mask of death by electrocution.

Tree yanked Mason by his belt back onto the muddy bank. Mason curled over, hands on knees, breathing hard. They stared at the sunken body on the bed of the river.

'Not . . . snakes,' Mason said, panting. 'Electric eels.'

47

The current dragged at Domino's body; it rolled slowly downstream along the riverbed, limbs floppy.

'Jesus,' Mason said. He glanced back at Tree. 'What I said . . . about killing him. I didn't really mean it – I don't think.'

'Nothing you could've done,' Tree said, and took his hand.

Mason remembered what he'd read about *Electrophorus electricus*, the electric eel. The Amazon and Orinoco River basins were their only natural habitats. A single eel could generate electric fields up to 600 volts within a short radius – intense enough to stun a human. Several eels together had easily stopped Domino's heart.

He recalled the Chinese proverb: Often one finds destiny where one flees to avoid it.

'This mushroom-vision thing gives me the creeps,' Mason said. 'Domino saw this coming – but how? How the hell does it work? And what does that say about space and time?'

'Mason, sit down here with me.' Tree took both his hands. 'My vision has also come true. I saw that I would love K'un-Chien in a . . . well, in a sexual way, as with a lover. But it's not what you probably think.'

'I think I can understand. She's a beautiful woman, you two together are like sister swans—'

'No, that's just it – it's not a lesbian desire I feel for her.

Or, not exactly ... It's more like ...' Tree took another deep breath. 'I don't get it myself, but I feel for her a desire like I feel for you. I know that sounds strange. Have you ever experienced a masculine nature in K'un-Chien? I'm attracted to her as to a man.'

'Oh, but she can be so womanly. I'm definitely attracted to her as to a woman. On the other hand ... yeah, sure I've felt a masculine energy from her. Like just now. There's no stopping her from taking Kiki back.'

'But its not just her courage—'

'True. We both know courageous women, strong women.' Mason smiled. 'I'm looking at one. No, you're right, it's something more,' he said. 'I've been aware of it almost from the beginning.'

Tree shrugged. 'Call it maleness, no better word.'

'Yes, but femaleness, too. Or are you saying you don't notice her female energy?'

'Are you kidding? Look at her.'

K'un-Chien sat higher up the bank, rocking Kiki in her arms like a baby, singing to him softly; Hsiao Pi lay on her back with her head in K'un-Chien's lap.

'She's as womanly as any madonna or vamp I've ever known,' Tree said, 'but at the same time, she's as masculine—'

They both stopped talking and stared hard at K'un-Chien.

'Oh my god.' Tree gulped. Her eyes grew big and she grabbed her face in her hands.

'Holy shit,' Mason said. 'It just now hit me.'

'She's the Lung-Hu – K'un-Chien.'

'How did we miss it?' He felt dizzy as his mind tried to sort through a crowd of conflicting feelings.

Mason saw Kiki asleep, snuggled against K'un-Chien. He tried to imagine a penis down below that mothering bosom. And a vagina and womb. She could get pregnant; those breasts could become heavy and aching with milk-fullness. And she could make Tree pregnant. K'un-Chien was Hermes and Aphrodite in one. Now that he knew, it seemed as if it had been transparent all along – the dynamic blend of opposites. But how could the mind grasp such a phenomenon? K'un-Chien transcended human biology that had evolved over millions of years. The people of Prayer Mat of the Body awaited the Lung-Hu as a demi-god – and perhaps they were right.

'Tree, how . . . what . . .' He took a deep breath. 'How do you feel about this?'

'Confused . . . like someone stuck a spoon into my heart and stirred.'

'Me too.'

'And vulnerable. I'm afraid if I don't say or do the right thing now I'm going to get very hurt – along with you and K'un-Chien.'

'It seems so unreal,' Mason said. 'I'm thinking what folktale, what myth are we living out here?'

'Do you still love her?'

'She's a hermaphrodite, Tree. She – *he* – has a penis.'

'Do you still love her, Mason?'

'Do *you*?'

'I want you to answer first.'

Mason watched K'un-Chien singing her ancient Chinese lullaby to Kiki. The sage-monkey had fallen asleep against her bosom, wrapped in her slender muscular arms.

He swallowed hard. 'I'm afraid.'

'I didn't ask if you were afraid,' Tree said. 'I'm afraid too. You told me earlier that you loved her – I'm asking you if you still love her.'

'What does it mean if I say I do?'

'Do feelings have to wear a label?'

Mason watched K'un-Chien. She tenderly kissed Kiki's sleeping face. Then she raised her head and her eyes found his. *If eyes are the windows of the soul, her soul must be bathed in deep blue light.*

Mason put his hand to his heart to keep it from skipping beats. 'I love her,' he whispered, 'I can't help it. I love her.'

'Good,' Tree said. 'So do I.'

Mason looked down. 'Tree, there's something you need to know . . . Your father . . .' He hesitated.

'What about my father?'

'He made it, he found the colony. He lived in Prayer Mat of the Body until he was killed by bees, the day K'un-Chien's brothers drowned.' He looked up at her. 'Tree, the boys were his sons: K'un-Chien is his child.'

Tree's face blanched. 'K'un-Chien and Meng Po.'

He nodded. 'Your half-siblings.'

Tree stared at K'un-Chien. 'Why did you wait until now to tell me?'

Mason ran his hand through his hair. 'When I found out, you and K'un-Chien were already – you know . . . in love. Given our strange circumstances, I just didn't see how it could make much difference.'

'You mean those quaint old morals against incest needn't apply here?'

Mason shrugged, not knowing what to say.

'Does K'un-Chien know?'

Mason shook his head. 'Neither does Meng Po. Look, I'm sorry. I didn't know how to deal with the news. Maybe I should have told you earlier.'

'Gee, you think?'

'In Ming Dynasty culture – the only culture K'un-Chien has ever known – it was common for a husband to marry several sisters, and all shared the marital bed,' he said. 'Remember your dad's collection of pillow books?'

'Remember when he caught us peeking through them?'

'Picture the woodcuts from Secrets of the Jade Chamber – the women weren't just passive observers in lovemaking, they made love with each other along with their husband.'

'What're you saying, "When in Rome—?"'

'I'm saying you can look at this relationship through the lens of western morality, or choose to see it in another focus. Did you know that of the several thousand distinct cultures anthropologists have identified, more than four out of every five are polygamous, and about one in every fifty is polyandrous – one wife with two or more husbands, usually brothers.'

'Sure. Okay. It's not like I just stepped off the *Mayflower*. I'm no Puritan. But none of that tells me how to feel about all this.' Tree rubbed her forehead. 'K'un-Chien is my half-sister. For chrissake, Mason, anything else you holding back on me?'

Mason looked at K'un-Chien. She now cradled Kiki and Hsiao Pi side by side in her lap; they both slept while she stroked their heads, cinnamon and black.

'So what do we do, Tree?'

'Kiki has to be returned to Meng Po. We'll go back with K'un-Chien.'

'You nuts? You told me they'd kill me and you were right – they'll kill us all.'

'Are you ready to say goodbye to her? Are you willing for her to be killed by the bees? We've got to tell her we know her secret and we still love her.'

'Okay,' Mason said. 'I agree. Look. We'll go with her to help her smoke out the bees; we'll convince her to return with us to build a raft and float down the river toward the Wawajero lands.'

'Return with us? *Where?* To California?' Tree said. 'Think about it. Immigration. Paperwork. Physicals. Her secret would be out. The media would eat her alive.'

'So what are you saying?'

'Mason, I'm willing to stay here, in Prayer Mat of the Body, as long as I'm with you and K'un-Chien.'

'But – Yu Lin – she'll have us both killed. And Hsiao Pi will be sacrificed.'

'Meng Po is Emperor now. K'un-Chien is the long-awaited Lung-Hu. She can reveal her identity and I can reveal mine – as their half-sister. They won't harm us when the truth unfolds. And now that the Lung-Hu is here, Hsiao Pi won't need to be sacrificed.'

He held her shoulders, studied her face. 'You're willing to stay in Jou P'u T'uan the rest of your life?'

'Just found out I got family there.'

'Be serious.'

'I don't know about the rest of my life, I only know about today. Today I'm not ready to leave K'un-Chien. We can't just abandon her and let her run off and get herself killed.'

Mason looked over at K'un-Chien. Her eyes were closed and she was gently rocking her sleeping wards, tucked in her lap.

'One thing I know now with certainty,' he said, 'my home is where my heart is. I'm not going to leave you again, Tree. As long as you're with me, Jou P'u T'uan is Shangri-La.'

48

With eyes closed K'un-Chien allowed her thoughts and feelings to drift downstream in a half-sleep. She felt Kiki's heart beating in syncopation with Hsiao Pi's heart, a duet of little drums in rhythm with the drumming of her own breast. Kiki smelled like wet fur, his breath smelled like the wild grapes that were his main diet. Hsiao Pi smelled like sweat and ginger and jasmine.

Sadness and joy ran within her like tributaries that fed a single deep river of emotion. Resistance to pain, clinging to joy, formed dams in the river here and there. When she concentrated on the barriers they were gradually swept away in the current of paradox.

Tree, she would never stop loving. Mason, she would never forget. Even though they did not love her. Even though she would never see their homeland. She prayed they would be home again soon and live as long as the turtle god, making love, having many sons.

Unrequited love was terribly difficult but not impossible to cope with. The most important thing was to not stop loving, to not cave in to feeling sorry for herself. She had to make the conscious choice again and again to pour her feelings into 'I love them,' rather than to dwell on 'They don't love me.'

K'un-Chien was reminded of an old legend about a young

man who transcended the pain of unrequited love. He was a poor woodsman who fell in love with the Emperor's daughter when he came upon her bathing in a river. He declared his love to her with such passionate sincerity that she was moved to tears. 'Lover, it is only in the cemetery that I will one day be able to join with you,' she said, meaning that only in death can a princess and a woodsman become equals. But the young man, beside himself with adoration, took her words literally, and went to the cemetery to wait for the princess to appear. Day after day, as he waited, he thought of nothing but his beloved, contemplating her lovely form and qualities. This led him to feel grateful to her ancestors, who had made possible her birth, and to meditate on all the elements that supported her life. His appreciation expanded to include vaster spheres of being that gave life to the woman he loved, until, at last, it seemed to him that the One who was his Beloved was the very universe itself.

K'un-Chien decided she did not have the saintly inclinations of the young man in the fable, but she thanked the ancestors for Tree and Mason, and she kissed the life that had brought them to her.

Circumstances were working out for the best, she knew, and that gave her some sense of relief and peace. Tree and Mason would never have to learn she was Lung-Hu. Her last efforts would be for the good – to return Kiki to her brother, who was surely heartsick over his missing companion.

K'un-Chien opened her eyes and peeked at Tree and Mason, talking intently. She sighed. To bond with a lover as intimately as spirit weds flesh; to be not alone in the world. That would be utopia, wherever it occurred.

The Buddha taught that desire is suffering: Extinguish all longing and be free of misery. A true formula, but drier than the parchment it was written on.

K'un-Chien knew a sweeter truth, the truth of love-desire. It circulated everywhere in the world, in the tiniest veins of a leaf, in the golden veins of a mountain. It moistened the world and made it live. She had known this energy from the time she was an infant, long before she had any notion of sex and gender. Love-desire included man and woman, but it was so much more than human. It was Nature, the life-force of the universe itself. Life was unabashed in its erotic play. The living world made acts of love in the sky and earth that people would fear to do, afraid of pouring themselves out or ripping apart; afraid to feel without limit.

Stormclouds hang low in the sky building electric charge until the valley begins to want the sky, and the sky aches to discharge. Clouds thicken and darken, roiling over the thirsty fields. Then the wanting becomes so magnetic nothing can hold earth and sky apart. Desire surges up to heaven, and clouds kneel down, kiss the ground with fire. The rain loosens from the sky and makes its home in leaves and grass and gardens. And little girls of Jou P'u T'uan dance naked in the streets, splashing in puddles while their mothers laugh beneath the pouring eaves.

K'un-Chien felt this cosmic dance of polarity within her own body and mind, felt it all around her. But not until she had met Tree had there been a valley in which to pour her cloudburst; not until Mason had there been a mountain to deepen her.

Buddha had been right: Desire is pain. Love is a wound. But K'un-Chien smiled now as she savored the wine of sadness along with the ambrosia of joy. Poor Buddha-san had no tongue to taste at all.

K'un-Chien looked up as footsteps approached. Mason and Tree sat down on each side of her and kissed her cheeks.

'My dear wife,' Mason said softly, 'we need to speak with you.'

'Mason and I have something important to tell you,' Tree said.

K'un-Chien recognized love shining in their eyes and instantly her world tasted infinitely sweeter.

49

On the trek back to the mountain along the hacked-out trail, K'un-Chien felt like clapping her hands and dancing pirouettes like Kiki did when he was overjoyed. She felt so buoyant she glanced down to make sure her feet were contacting the ground.

Mason and Tree had confessed their hearts to her. They had said they loved her. And they wanted to stay in Prayer Mat of the Body to be with her. What is more, the two had uncovered her secret, and knowing who she was – what she was – they had not rejected her.

'I would be dishonest if I did not admit that I feel confused about my desire for you,' Mason had said. 'But this I promise: My love for you is unshakable. You belong to me, K'un-Chien, and I to you.'

Tree had talked less than Mason but the message in her eyes and touch had told K'un-Chien what she needed to know. Tree's love-desire for her was not in doubt. On the other hand, Tree seemed upset by the revelation that she and K'un-Chien had the same father – startling news that had brought more joy than ever to K'un-Chien. They were sisters married to the same man. How perfect.

The mission now was to make their way past the bees and then for K'un-Chien to announce herself to the soldiers as

Lung-Hu. She would stride into the city naked, if need be, to proclaim her identity as the Holy Hermaphrodite.

The fetid stink of rotten meat pricked her nose. K'un-Chien frowned and stopped in her tracks.

Mason sniffed the air. 'What the hell?'

'Quiet,' K'un-Chien warned. 'The dragons from above. We are being hunted.' She had been carrying Kiki, and she passed him back to Hsiao Pi. 'Tree, take care of them.'

Tree gathered up the girl and the monkey and stepped off the trail into the dense undergrowth.

K'un-Chien notched an arrow on her bowstring and looked up in time to see a leathery-skinned black dragon emerge from shadows on the path in front of her. It bared its fangs and hissed like steam as it charged, jaws wide in a triangular head. At close range K'un-Chien shot the arrow straight down its throat, and the giant reptile gagged and lurched onto its side, tearing at its neck with scythe-like claws until the meat tore loose in bloody ribbons.

Behind the first dragon, two more appeared. They charged.

'Shoot the one to your right,' Mason yelled from behind her, drawing his own bow.

Her iron-tipped arrow split the lizard's skull with a sharp crack. Mason's arrow whizzed high over his target's back. K'un-Chien sidestepped as the lizard dashed past her toward Mason. She notched an arrow by sense of touch without taking her eyes from the charging reptile. Mason gripped his bow like a club and batted at the dragon's powerful jaws; it snapped at Mason's legs and he jumped back and stumbled and fell. K'un-Chien shot her arrow between the dragon's shoulder blades, pinning it through its heart to the ground.

Mason scrambled to his feet. 'Look out,' he yelled. 'More of them.'

K'un-Chien turned her bow sideways and crouched low and shot a charging dragon through its gaping upper jaw into its brain. Its legs buckled and it nosedived into her, knocking her sprawling backwards. Its sagging tongue flopped onto her forearm like a slimy whip as she rolled the dead dragon off.

Mason rushed out in front and used a lance to impale another beast, screaming at it in his guttural language as he drove the spearhead in.

K'un-Chien struggled onto her feet and saw the first of the soldiers appear on the trail beyond Mason. Three soldiers in the lead each controlled a black dragon with a chain collar on a leather leash. Commander Yu followed behind, sword drawn, scowling.

The soldiers stopped and Yu Lin shoved past. Hard black leather armor clattered as she strode forward, elbowing Mason out of her path.

'I have orders from the Emperor to kill the traitor who stole his pet,' she bellowed in K'un-Chien's face. 'Where is Domino?'

'Domino is already dead,' K'un-Chien said. 'We were returning Kiki to my brother when you attacked us.'

'And how did you expect to get past the bees in the tunnel?' Yu Lin said. 'They killed two of my soldiers when we smoked them out.'

'K'un-Chien was willing to risk her life to do what was proper,' Mason said. 'Can you not see that?'

Yu Lin spun on him and struck him in the temple with the hilt of her sword. He winced and folded onto his knees. 'Shut up, foreigner. Where is Kiki? Let me see the little beast.'

Tree stepped out of the underbrush. 'I have him here,' she said. 'He is well.'

'And where is the new Empress?'

A rustling behind Tree produced Hsiao Pi. She stepped onto the narrow path. 'I am here, Commander Yu. I am unharmed.'

Yu Lin strode, clattering, to the teenage girl and loomed over her. 'Tell me the truth, Empress. Did they kidnap you, or did you flee the city?'

Hsiao Pi glanced at Mason with fright in her face.

'I took her away against her will,' Mason said. 'Hsiao Pi and the others had nothing to do with it.'

Yu Lin glared at him. 'Foreigner, I ordered you to keep still.' She raised her sword over her head. 'There is but one way to shut you up.'

'*Halt*.' K'un-Chien yelled. 'I am the Lung-Hu. All of you, look upon me now.' She flung open her sarong. 'I am the Dragon-Tiger,' she said, and stripped off her loin cloth. Her sexual organs formed a duality – male above, female below.

The soldiers gasped and stepped back, gawking. Yu Lin's eyes bulged.

'As a child I was taught to hide my identity,' K'un-Chien said, covering herself again with her sarong, 'but as an adult I have learned finally that one cannot escape one's fate. I am Lung-Hu, the Holy Hermaphrodite.'

The soldiers dropped to their knees and kowtowed.

'Get up, you fools,' Yu Lin roared at them. 'Get up and open your eyes. Look at what you are venerating – a pathetic monster.' She glared at K'un-Chien. 'There is no such thing as a *holy* hermaphrodite. A hermaphrodite is un-holy – an abomination. I, too, have long awaited your advent – for this purpose . . .' Yu Lin raised her sword above her head with both hands.

'I now release my society from its curse,' Yu Lin cried out, 'by striking dead this freak of nature.'

50

'*No!*' Mason and Tree screamed together.

At the height of the sword's arc, Yu Lin stiffened and the sword slid from her grasp and fell behind her. She turned her face toward Mason wearing a curious look of shock, slumped to the ground and caught her weight on hands and knees. She reached around her back and her fingers wrapped a cotton-plumed arrow that stuck between her shoulder blades.

'Yanomorduro!' Mason yelled. 'Ambush!'

A soldier landed face down next to Yu Lin. Another soldier yelped and plucked at a blowdart sticking in her shoulder as another dart struck her hand.

'Set the dragons on them,' Yu Lin bellowed. 'Hurry.'

Half a dozen natives armed with bows and blowguns leapt out of the jungle onto the path. Red pigment from crushed urucu seeds daubed their hair, faces and torsos. The lead warrior wore a crown of blue and yellow macaw feathers. He tilted a six-foot-long blowgun to his mouth. K'un-Chien's arrow punched his chest with a loud *hwak* and he grunted and pitched forward. Her next arrow struck a warrior in the throat; he twisted as he fell, the full length of the arrow's shaft jutting from the back of his neck. Two black dragons slammed into a third warrior, knocked him down and tore savagely at both his arms, ripping the limbs loose in opposite directions.

Hsiao Pi screamed as a Yanomorduro warrior grabbed her from behind and dragged her off the trail. Mason snatched up Yu Lin's sword and plunged headlong after them. He hacked down hard on the captor's back and brought the man down on top of Hsiao Pi. Then he stuck the sword tip into the man's neck at the base of the skull and twisted sharply, like pithing a frog. He rolled the body off Hsiao Pi and tugged her to her feet.

When they returned to the scene of the battle the Indians were fleeing. The Yanomorduros and Wawajeros shared the same linguistic roots, and Mason could make out two words the headhunters shouted: *tepui dsiju* – mountain witches.

Three soldiers sprawled dead on the ground near the bodies of five headhunters and as many giant reptiles. Yu Lin and eight soldiers and several dragons had survived along with Mason and his companions.

Yu Lin had plucked the arrow from her back and refused to let K'un-Chien or Mason examine the wound. She tore her tunic into wide strips and tightly bandaged her thick torso. Blood streaked the bandage but did not soak it, and from Yu Lin's demeanor Mason judged that the arrowhead had punctured only dense muscle; she would quickly recover.

The soldiers left their dead comrades behind. Yu Lin refused to be carried on a stretcher, so a soldier on either side bolstered her on the trek back to the city.

Night had fallen as they neared the round bamboo gate in the walls of Jou P'u T'uan.

K'un-Chien strode at the head of the group with a graceful, regal pace, befitting a demi-god returning to her domain to claim her destiny.

51

T he last day of the week-long festival continued far into the
night. Banners flapped and horns blared, cymbals clanged
and clashed as big kettle drums led the stomping feet and
clapping hands of the celebrating crowd. Rice wine mixed with
laughter mixed with more wine, which flowed into singing and
dancing in the streets. Meng Po and Kiki hugged and kissed
and danced and played with Hsiao Pi, Tree and Mason.

K'un-Chien's hair had been braided into a thousand black
cables and decorated with purple orchids, rainbow ribbons
and tiny silver bells. She wore a black satin robe studded with
quartz-crystal sequins and embellished with gold-outlined bro-
cade of red lotus blossoms. Over the chest, a white tiger circled
a green dragon inside a yin-yang emblem. It was simply the most
gorgeous article of clothing Mason had ever seen, grander than
anything to be found in a wardrobe museum behind glass and
guard. K'un-Chien and the robe glorified each other. The fabric
swept up into a high mandarin collar, encrusted with heavy
gold embroidery, then cut free at the shoulders, highlighting
her muscular arms, spangled with golden bracelets over biceps
and wrists.

Hsiao Pi took Meng Po's hand. Mason smiled as he watched
their eyes: in those dark windows their young love blazed as
the first fireworks flowered the sky.

Beneath the fireworks a procession filed to a placid lake in the midst of a sandalwood grove. The celebrants launched a flotilla of colorful paper lanterns on the black water; the lights drifted like luminous planets in space.

Meng Po offered a poem:

> *Moon on black water*
> *Floating with other lanterns*
> *Alone leaves no wake*

Mason watched the candlelit lanterns glide outward on a puff of breeze. One lantern suddenly filled with heated air and lifted a couple feet off the surface before it whooshed into flames and sank back to the lake with a sizzling hiss.

The sight reminded Mason of the hot-air balloon system on the Raft, and it gave him a new idea. The rips at the bottom of the balloon fabric meant that only the upper envelope could trap hot air; the lift would be too weak to carry the Raft aloft. But what if they didn't try to fly out on the whole barge? What if they cut the Raft loose and left it behind? The spherical paper lantern rising above the lake had triggered an image of the balloon floating up on its own without the heavy Raft dangling below. *Just a few passengers riding in the nylon netting – the damaged envelope might have enough lift to fly that payload.*

Tree put her arm around Mason's waist and drew him close. 'Hey, Sugarbabe,' she said huskily, 'what're you doing tonight after the ceremonies?'

'I'm with you all night. You tell me.'

'Guess.'

He shrugged, playing innocent.

Her eyelids half-closed. 'We're going to make love in ways you've never let yourself imagine.'

Her words spoke directly to his body as if she'd touched him between his legs. He adjusted his robe.

Each breath of breeze carried the heady fragrance of sandalwood from the grove. He watched K'un-Chien strolling as stately as the moon through the flowering trees, and he felt the mix of desire and taboo that had disturbed him since he'd realized her true nature.

'What about K'un-Chien?' Mason said. 'I just don't how I'm supposed to feel about her. I mean, as a man – her husband.'

'*Supposed* to? Forget about "supposed to." Stay with how you *actually* feel – that's what I'm trying to do, anyway.'

'I'm not sure how I feel. Confused – I feel a lot of things at once,' he said. 'I know I love her, as a person – no doubts about that. I hope she knows that at least.'

'She knows.'

'And I do feel we need to . . . include her . . .'

'We going to. We three have been sneaking longing looks at each other all week – the sexual charge is so built-up our eyes are shooting sparks. We've waited long enough. Tonight's the night.' Tree slipped her hand between the folds of his robe. 'Like I told you, we're going to make love tonight in ways you've never allowed yourself to imagine.'

52

Steam hung in the air of the palace's bath chamber. Mason and Tree and K'un-Chien sat on the ledge and dangled their feet in the hot water. Then, at an unspoken signal, the three peeled off their robes, like the skins of summer fruit, and stepped into the bath.

It had been Tree's idea to begin with a hot soak. Tree was intelligent in these matters – wise as a goddess of love, Mason thought. He was glad to be given this prelude to attune to the newness of the situation. Mason gazed at his wives; one scooped from cinnamon-sprinkled snow, the other carved from light mahogany. Prelude or not, he felt as shy as he'd felt when he was a virgin – that crazy shy-boldness that arises when vulnerability mixes with aggressive desire.

He was following Tree's advice, staying with his real feelings, dropping 'shoulds' and 'should nots' like dead leaves.

Tree turned to K'un-Chien and kissed her on the forehead. K'un-Chien closed her eyes to receive the benediction. Tree's lips then blessed her eyes, her nose, and came to anoint her lips. K'un-Chien pulled Tree closer until their breasts mashed together. Steam rising off the water swirled around their bodies. Mason took a deep breath and the humid air tingled his lungs.

Tree reached for him. And although his blood had begun to

beat in his ears, he whispered, 'Let me watch. I've never seen a masterpiece as it was being painted.' And for a while longer he gazed as the two bodies opened into each other like irises. Emotion magnified his vision until it seemed he could see each downy hair on K'un-Chien's arms, a pearl of saliva at the corner of Tree's parted mouth.

He reached out like the sun to embrace his twin earths.

Tree's face grew flushed with sexual heat. Mason became so rigid his pulsing rippled the water. And K'un-Chien embodied the full magic. Even in her eyes, Mason saw reflected his own masculinity, and below the waist she was as abundantly male as himself. And yet K'un-Chien was also a woman, as feminine and flowerlike as Tree.

Mason realized that K'un-Chien knew what both her partners were experiencing. He kissed her sinewy neck, her golden breasts. She smelled like balsam and warm dough. Two sets of hands explored him. He did not recall the three of them walking from the bath to the bed. Only the moment when they fell together on the satin sheets, in a perfect harmony of hunger and feast, and all three of them inexplicably began to cry softly.

Then they began a new ballet none had danced before.

As a boy Mason had been taught that the body was a lifeless husk that contained and was animated by a living soul, a ghost in the machine. But as their lovemaking progressed, his learning fell asunder. He melted into a deeper truth: The body is more than a husk, even more than a temple with an eternal lamp flickering at its core. The body lived *inside* the soul. No seam where spirit ended and flesh began. Spirit sang the whole body. Electric. Delicious. All its parts were good, from light to breath to blood and bone.

Mason heard such music and was compelled to dance. Though his know-how did not know how, he danced. Gently or aggressively he moved by a primal grace. With Tree and K'un-Chien, his soul's body shared itself in ways he would never be able to describe, not even to himself.

Dawn came and painted the nude figures of Mason and Tree with liquid light. K'un-Chien had not closed her eyes. She did not wish to fall asleep and thereby wake up from her lovely dream.

Over the past few months, K'un-Chien had been terrified that Mason and Tree would discover her secret and reject her in disgust. But instead they had found out who she was and had accepted her in the most profoundly intimate way. She looked upon them now with great devotion.

Last night, as she had stepped into the bathhouse hand in hand with Husband and First Wife, her heart had felt at once as fragile as a soap bubble and as indestructible as a diamond wand. A strong energy ran between their bodies, even before they had removed their robes and were naked together at last.

K'un-Chien studied Tree's sleeping face, remembering the blissful shock of Tree's mouth on hers. She touched her own forehead, eyes, mouth, where Tree had first kissed her. Like the Yellow Bell that contained the tuning note of the whole Chinese orchestra, those first kisses had contained in them all the pleasure that was to follow. K'un-Chien had parted her lips to taste, to eat those kisses. *Let there be flavor like this forever*, she had thought, *even if forever is only this one timeless moment.*

Then a muscular jolt of bliss had overcome her. No one had warned her that an orgasm could slay her, consumed in fire like a phoenix. And with each subsequent orgasm she had died again, unable to survive the intensity of the pleasure. After each death she had risen from her own ashes to revel in the sexual play that aroused and fused the male and female energies within her body.

At one moment, she remembered pinning Tree's shoulders to the mattress and taking her hungrily, pressing down deep; Tree began a long trembling crescendo of moans; then Mason had penetrated K'un-Chien from behind and she had learned how it felt to be Tree, filled by another. When Tree had stiffened and cried out and Mason jerked involuntarily and groaned, K'un-Chien had suddenly spilled over in a violent gush of ecstasy, twin orgasms in her own body at once, and she had passed beyond the world in a swoon of pure sensation.

The night had gone on and on like that. Slain by waves of joy, reborn to make love again.

'*Love is a wound, O Buddha-san.*' The aches from her lovers' kisses still took her breath away.

Nestled between Tree, creamy and soft, and Mason, furry and hard, K'un-Chien closed her eyes now to the dawn and slept.

Tree awoke feeling happy. K'un-Chien slept snuggled between her and Mason. Tree looked at the two of them with supreme honor and affection. She felt that something astonishing had happened to her overnight, as if she had awakened now to discover that she could suddenly play the tuba, speak Hindi – and fly. It took her a moment to realize what it was: She had fallen in true love-desire for the second time in her life; first with Mason, now with K'un-Chien.

What a dance we danced last night.

Tree had found out long ago that the varieties of sexual positions were, in themselves, not the key to wonderful love-making. They were not IT.

IT was energy; emotional force. When it was intense, a simple kiss was hotter than arranging bodies into tantric pretzels. On the other hand, energy *moves*, and when one gives in to it the wilder poses take form by themselves. The warm love-aches in her body echoed last night's music and dance.

She glanced out the bedroom's high windows. Nothing had changed in the macrocosm. The Earth was spinning on its orbit around the sun, around the pinwheeling galaxy. But a miracle had rocked her own orbit. The borders of her life had expanded to accommodate another human soul, which enlarged her heart by a magnitude of joy.

It was as if she had begun the night as a little bird singing in the cloud forest, and she had awoken as the whole cloud forest singing in a little bird.

53

An armor-clad soldier appeared at the archway that led into the bedroom and halted, looking flustered.

'Yes?' Tree said. In the bed beside her K'un-Chien raised her head.

'Madam, I am here to announce an urgent visit from Fang-Shih, the former Empress, Mother of the Lung-Hu.'

K'un-Chien rose quickly from the bed and pulled on a robe.

'Mason, get up, get dressed,' Tree said. 'We have a visitor.' Mason sat up, his thick hair tousled. He stood to pull on trousers and a shirt. The soldier stared at his morning erection.

Fang-Shih appeared in the doorframe behind the servant and pushed past into the room. She wore a royal yellow robe and a white ceramic mask.

'All three of you, listen to me,' Fang-Shih said, 'You do not have much time.'

'What is wrong?' Tree said.

'Yu Lin is on her way here with soldiers.'

K'un-Chien raced to the wall and grabbed down her bow and a quiver full of arrows.

'But why?' Mason said.

'Because she is Yu Lin,' Fang-Shih said. 'Because she hates the Lung-Hu, because she hates me. She intends to kill us both.'

'I do not understand,' Tree said. 'I thought the society had been waiting for the Dragon-Tiger for years.'

'Not everyone accepts me,' K'un-Chien said. 'Not everyone welcomes a society of hermaphrodites.'

'She is right,' Fang-Shih said. 'Yu Lin has taken command of a large number of soldiers in open rebellion. They are fighting in the streets with Meng Po's guards. There is no time to explain further. You have to escape here at once.'

'But . . . where can we go?' Tree said.

'Return with me to my palace. Those who are loyal—'

The *cling-clang* of swords and the shouts and grunts of soldiers skirmishing reached the front door of the palace. Fang-Shih's soldier turned and raced to join the fight.

'Too late, too late,' Fang-Shih said. 'It means my palace has been overrun. Some of my loyal guards are out front now but they cannot hold them off.'

'Quick, out through the courtyard,' Mason yelled. 'Then up the banyan and over the wall. Go.' He ran to K'un-Chien's medicine cabinet and began flinging herbal concoctions into a bag of woven bamboo grass. The Ling-Chih container was still wrapped and tied with banana leaves from his last aborted escape. He tossed in a couple plastic Frisbees for the Wawajerós he hoped to see soon. He slung the pack over his shoulder and hurried out after the others.

K'un-Chien was boosting Tree up to the lower branch of the banyan; from there the branches were as easy to scale as a ladder. Tree shuffled sideways along a branch, lowered herself down the wall on the far side of the courtyard and dropped to the ground.

'Fang-Shih, you next,' Mason said.

'I am staying here, son-in-law.'

'Mother, no,' K'un-Chien said. 'Please come with us.'

'To where? The country of barbarians? And how will they regard me – a woman with a hideous face – in a land where any woman can have sons?'

'Come with us,' Mason said. 'We have surgeons who can reconstruct your face.'

'Ha. And restore the beauty I was born with? No. This is where I belong. Go. Be well.'

K'un-Chien gazed at her mother.

'Flee now. Hurry,' Fang-Shih said.

K'un-Chien reached out to lift the ceramic mask. Her mother grabbed her wrists.

'Please,' K'un-Chien said. 'Allow me to look upon the face of my mother.'

Fang-Shih's hands trembled and relaxed their hold.

K'un-Chien removed the mask.

Teardrops were snaking down the ridges and ruts of gnarled tissue. K'un-Chien bent forward and kissed the tears that wet her mother's scars.

54

'Where the hell we going?' Tree yelled, running down a broad avenue.

'They expect us to flee to the jungle below,' Mason said. 'This time, we're going to the mountaintop.'

'You crazy?'

'Got an idea, a way to make the balloon work.'

'It's shredded.'

'The upper envelope's okay – I think.'

'But—'

'We can fly off the mountain. It's the only way, I'll explain when we get there.'

'*If* we get there. It's several miles – they'll be after us in minutes.'

'But they'll be hunting in the wrong place, it'll buy us time.'

The trio scaled the city's outer wall on the waterfall side of the valley. After fifteen minutes running along a green-canopied footpath they splashed across the shallow river beneath the cataract and raced into the huge cavern. The far side of the room narrowed into the tunnel angling upward to the mountaintop. Mason used Barry's pipe lighter to ignite three torches.

By midday, having pushed themselves at a brisk hiking pace for five hours, they mounted the crest of a hill and saw the portable inflatable field station, the Raft, only a few hundred yards distant. Panting and sweating, they ran the rest of the way to the ladder before they let themselves flop, heaving, on the ground to rest. But only for a moment.

'Tree, get up the ladder, check out the burners and propane tanks. I gotta re-rig these gondola lines.'

'How can I help?' K'un-Chien asked.

'I will show you once we are up the ladder,' Mason said. 'After you.'

The hub of the field station supported a fiberglass laboratory. Mason pushed through its sliding doors and climbed an aluminum ladder to the roof. He dragged the balloon out of its canvas sleeve and tossed the sleeve over the side.

'K'un-Chien. Go back inside and grab a hatchet from the far wall and start cutting away these lines. See? There and there and there – they keep going all the way around. Cut every one of them. I am going to rig a nylon net beneath the balloon to carry us. I do not want anything else attached to the balloon.'

K'un Chien reappeared. 'There is no hatchet on the wall.'

Shit. Meng Po's got that too.

'Then do whatever you have to do to cut those lines. The balloon can only carry the three of us.'

'K'un-Chien, here.' Tree poked her head out of the lab and handed K'un-Chien a plastic box of stainless steel dissection scalpels. K'un-Chien began sawing at the nylon shroud lines with the scalpels. They smoked and then popped loose one at a time.

Mason's heart sank when he spread the ballon to its 180-foot length, stretching three times from one side to the other of the octagonal Raft. Most of the rips were near the base of the envelope, but one tear stretched upward to within about 100 feet of the balloon's dome. The fabric might rip further when stressed with the pressure of inflation from the heated air. Either they'd never get aloft, or worse, the balloon would come apart in mid-air and they'd drop like a plumb bob. Over the sheer edge of the tepui the green canopy of the rainforest was 10,000 feet below.

Tree stepped out of the lab. 'Burners look good. We got two-hundred-twenty gallons of liquid propane, good for about four hours of flight. How you coming?'

Mason glanced down at the bag and back up at her.

She eyed the rip in the balloon.

'It'll work,' he said.

'What makes you so sure?'

'Today's our lucky day – it's our anniversary.'

'Our anniversary's in January.'

'I mean the anniversary of the first time I ever kissed you. I went home that night and had a wet dream. I marked it on the calendar. Every time I met you in the hall after that I had to carry my denim jacket over my crotch so I wouldn't embarrass myself.'

She laughed. 'You teasing me?'

'Sorta. About the calendar.'

K'un-Chien was nearly finished cutting the inflatable field station away from the balloon. Mason began to reattach the loose lines to the nylon netting that stretched between the neoprene pontoons.

'Tree, any more scalpel kits?' Mason said.

'Plenty.'

'Good. Bring one for each us.' He turned to K'un-Chien. 'Now we cut away the netting from the pontoons.'

The three of them set to work with the scalpels around the octagon and after a quarter hour of sawing lines the balloon and cargo net stood free as an independent unit from the rest of the structure. Mason secured the fraying ends of the nylon cords with a couple tight twists of duct tape.

Mason and K'un-Chien helped Tree position a large gas-powered fan near the base of the balloon. She yanked a cord and the engine kicked over sending a gale of wind toward the envelope.

'K'un-Chien, help me hold open the mouth of the envelope,' Mason said.

They stood on either side of the Dacron bag as it slowly began to inflate, mushy at first and then more firm and buoyant.

Tree attached the three propane burners on gimbal mounts on an aluminum bracket at the mouth of the bag.

'Stand clear,' she said.

She ignited the burners and three six-foot flames roared up into the envelope with a deafening *whooosh*. As heated air forced its way upward, the envelope reared up and began filling out, taking on the shape of a sphere.

Mason cheered. 'See? It's gonna—'

Skrrrrrrrrrrreeeek. The sound of ripping fabric cut Mason off.

'Shit. Bastard.' He spit the words.

'Thought Dacron was rip-proof,' Tree said.

'Rip-resistant. Nothing's rip-proof, not with a slash in it like that.'

'Look, it stopped.' Tree said. 'It can't rip past the loadline.'

The rip had halted at a horizontal seam reinforced with stitched leather, but only eighty feet from the crown of the bag. The balloon wobbled and began to inflate again. Its lift would now be greatly reduced.

Tree gawked upward at the gaping rip. 'If we could spill the air and collapse the bag, we could try patching the rip with duct tape.'

'Won't hold,' Mason said, 'Fabric's got a stress load of hundreds of pounds of air pressure per square inch. Besides, there's no time to spill it and fill it again.'

Tree groaned.

'Yeah, it's gonna be close,' Mason said, and flopped down on his butt and started peeling off his boots. 'Take off your boots. Ditch the extra propane tanks. Toss everything that isn't attached to you by tendons. I gotta readjust these lines and even us up.'

Tree untied and yanked off her hiking boots, and K'un-Chien threw overboard her heavy wooden bow and two quivers full of arrows. Mason dropped three aluminum fuel tanks over the side and then set about cutting and retying the lines from the balloon to the netting.

After a few minutes of blasting hot air into the envelope, the balloon started to buck at the ropes, tugging to fly aloft.

'You first, Tree. Get in.' Mason said. 'You next, K'un-Chien.' He climbed into the net after them and held on as Tree squeezed the burner trigger and shot a long yellow flame into the open mouth of the lopsided sphere.

The balloon surged upward and carried them twenty feet into the air, above the pillar-like boulders where the Raft had been parked. Mason cheered again, but the envelope shifted, spilling hot air, and the balloon rapidly settled toward the ground.

'Hang on, Tree, we're gonna bump,' Mason said and wrapped himself around her to cushion the impact as the balloon plowed into a tall granite monolith and then hovered alongside the rock a few feet off the ground.

Tree looked out at the horizon and her eyes clouded with fear. 'They're coming!'

Yu Lin had appeared at the crest of the nearby ridge, tree-like thighs pumping under an armored kilt, green tunic flopping on her broad shoulders and bulging belly as she ran, leading a platoon of charging dragon-women soldiers.

The balloon bobbed against the sheer rock face with a scritching sound like rubbing sandpaper. Tree jerked the gas valve wide and blasted ten-foot-long flames into the envelope. The balloon surged up over the granite wall, but sagged in mid-air and sank queasily down to within six feet of the gravel, where it drifted along lazily.

'Too much weight, it cannot lift all three of us,' K'un-Chien said, and without warning hopped over the side of the netting. As soon as her weight dropped away, the balloon popped upward forty-five feet into the air and floated there, drifting toward the mountain's edge.

'We are not leaving without you,' Tree called down.

'You must,' K'un-Chien shouted. 'Once again, I have made the mistake of thinking I could simply run away from my destiny. But even the very wind blows me back to my fate.'

Tree searched frantically for a way down. Mason grabbed her arm. 'Don't. You'll break your neck.'

Tears leapt from her eyes. 'Can't we lower a rope? Something? Anything?'

'We're too high – and we're climbing.'

K'un-Chien was unarmed. Mason and Tree could only watch helplessly, gliding in their aerial net as the killers rapidly approached below.

55

Yu Lin drew her sword and approached K'un-Chien slowly, almost casually. She held up a hand that was clothed in a heavy black-leather raptor's gauntlet. Her troops halted at a distance.

Yu Lin laughed gruffly. 'The master archer has no bow or arrows? Is this what becomes of a Dragon-Tiger with no wings or fangs? Are you now a mere mortal, hermaphrodite?'

'I am exactly what I am,' K'un-Chien answered. 'Such cannot be altered by your words or mine.'

'Ah so, a philosopher. Philosophers are reputed to die well.'

'I do not want to die, Commander Yu. Although there was a time when I would have welcomed death; for even as you despise me, so did I despise myself. But I have lived and loved, and I have learned.'

'Then before I slay you, monster Hsiang, why not benefit us with a death poem, or perhaps some jewel of your learning?'

'Very well,' K'un-Chien said. 'I have studied Sun Tzu's 'Art of War' and the Thirty-Six Stratagems. Master Sun recommended studying your enemy, waiting for the moment of supreme vulnerability, then attacking with surprise.'

Yu Lin huffed. 'Common sense.'

'And of the stratagems, do you know which is considered most useful?'

'Do teach me, scholar.'

'The last one, thirty-six.'

'Which is?'

'Outrunning your enemy.' K'un-Chien spun and sprinted with all her strength in the direction of a tall mound of jagged boulders.

Yu Lin chased directly after her. The soldiers split up and took off running in two directions to flank K'un-Chien.

K'un-Chien scrabbled to the top of the rock mound and slid over its crest onto a narrow ledge where she crouched and waited, listening for Yu Lin's pursuing footsteps.

Just before the commander came into view, K'un-Chien hefted a potato-sized granite rock and leapt to the top of the boulders. With sheathed sword Yu Lin clambered up the steep mound directly below her.

Yu Lin saw K'un-Chien. Her black eyes bulged with surprise; she struggled to grab at the precarious handholds with one hand and draw her sword with the other. That was her moment of supreme vulnerability.

K'un-Chien cocked her arm and hurled the rock at close range. It crashed into Yu Lin's upper chest, smashing her backward. Yu Lin flung her sword in the air as her arms windmilled to regain balance. The sword clattered and clanged down the rocky slope, followed by the thud and crash of the commander's tumbling weight. Yu Lin sprawled at the base of the boulder pile in black-leather armor, her neck twisted at an impossible angle.

K'un-Chien heard an army of footsteps approaching, crunching the gravel behind her. She took a deep breath and turned slowly around in resignation to face her death.

Meng Po was leading a troop of several dozen dragon-women, scaling the much flatter backside of the boulder pile, bow in hand.

'Victory, K'un-Chien!' he shouted. 'We won. Yu Lin's forces are defeated.'

K'un-Chien started down the rocks and met and embraced her brother – the Emperor, the archer – halfway.

'Look up,' he said, pointing. 'Our friends are flying!'

K'un-Chien looked up as Tree and Mason peered down from

the net where they rode as if sailing in a hammock a hundred feet above the ground.

All four waved. None spoke.

The balloon gained altitude and caught a river of wind that quickly carried it northward and off the very edge of K'un-Chien's world.

56

Mason held Tree as the tepui receded like a rust-streaked ship in a white sea. Tree cried softly against his neck. The balloon sailed on like a lifeboat among a fleet of summer clouds.

Mason stared in the direction of the mountain that hid Jou P'u T'uan and its people, the race the Indians called El Dorado. To the Spanish explorer Orellana they were Amazons. To Professor Summerwood they were Ming Dynasty utopians who'd colonized the New World before the Europeans. To Mason, they were Meng Po and Kiki, Hsiao Pi and the Empress. And The Golden herself was K'un-Chien.

The mission of the HARVEST eco-survey team – to explore Cameleon-tepui in order to discover flora and fauna that might prove useful in the development of medicines – had been a success beyond his wildest hopes. Into his bamboo-grass bag, Mason had tossed a stockpile of K'un-Chien's herbal drugs – a giant boon for modern western medicine. And the supreme prize was the miraculous mushroom, Ling-Chih.

If pharmaceutical scientists could learn to grow or synthesize the gene-stimulating substance in the fungus – Mason guessed it was some type of reo-virus – the benefits in the treatment of burn patients, amputees and others would be incalculable.

But the harvest had come with a tremendous human price

tag. The harpy that knocked down the helicopter had killed four of Mason's friends and colleagues. Another harpy killed Lynda. And Domino, too, had paid the ultimate price.

Yet the cost of the discovery had not been paid in full, Mason knew. As soon as he delivered the bounty to the labcoat guys at Halcyon, there were going to be questions. And the answers would lead to Prayer Mat of the Body. And then more research teams would descend on the mountain like a swarm of locusts, along with anthropologists, journalists, TV news crews, political delegates from Venezuela. Security police. Catholic missionaries. Crystal-eyed New Agers. *National Enquirer* headlines would blare: NOSTRADAMUS PREDICTED CITY'S LOCATION! Jou P'u T'uan would become the new Machu Picchu.

No, Mason realized, it would be even worse than he could envision.

'Tree, we can't take this stuff – the medicines – back with us. We just can't.'

'You read my mind,' she said.

Mason breathed a heavy sigh. 'Shit.' He opened the woven bag and took out the three Frisbees, then tossed the rest of the contents over the side.

'I'm sorry, world,' Mason said, as twigs, leaves and powders scattered on the breeze. 'Sorry. Hope I'm doing the right thing.' Black gummy balls from the bottom of the bag dropped through the clouds.

Tree laid a hand on his shoulder. 'It's best that she didn't come with us. Her arrival would have led to the same invasion of their world.'

'I know that now,' Mason said. 'Everything has worked out as well as it possibly could.'

He picked up the leaf-wrapped bamboo container that stored the Ling-Chih. 'What about this?' he said. 'It's not human-made like the mixed powders, the Phoenix Balls . . .'

'And?'

'Well, maybe we can just say we found the fungus *after* we got off the mountain.'

'But—'

'Think of the suffering it could relieve. A guy gets his arm crushed in a car wreck. Surgeons amputate the ruined tissue, and the guy grows a new limb. It's wonderful. And the money it would bring – I could do a lot of good work in the world with that kind of income.'

'But Mason, remember – it's not just a medicine. It's an oracle. You see your future . . .'

'Go on.'

'Name me ten people you know who could responsibly handle seeing their own destinies.'

Mason took a breath and smiled wryly.

'Name me just three,' she said.

'No, you're right. They'll make a drug from this and distribute it to millions of doctors worldwide. Soon, it'll hit the streets. Kids, criminals, nut-cases – society will go off its rocker.'

'Toss it. It doesn't belong outside of Jou P'u T'uan.'

Mason chucked the leaf bundle over the side.

'I'm down to what I started the trip with,' he said, and held up his stack of Frisbees. 'Me and my flying toys.'

'Plus me,' Tree said, and kissed him on the lips. 'Now you've got me again.'

He kissed her back. He had his whole heart again, alive and well.

The balloon crossed suddenly into a big gap in the clouds through which they could see all the way down to the canopy of the rainforest. Mason's stomach tightened involuntarily.

'Wow,' they both blurted at the same time.

'We still climbing?' Tree said.

'No, I don't think so. If anything, we're slowly descending. It's just that it looks a lot different staring down from here than when we were only a hundred feet or so above the mountain. You gotta remember, that tepui was ten thousand feet high.'

'I'd rather not focus on those figures right now, thank you.'

Mason took a compass from his pocket. 'We're still heading north. That's great. I can't gauge our velocity, but if we spot a major river, it's probably the Caroni. Runs past several Wawajero villages,' he said. 'We spill some lift, drop down as close to the river as we can. My friends will give us a dugout and food, help us get farther north to Ciudad Guayana – a radio and an airstrip.'

'We're awful high, Mason.'

'It's okay. This net will hold us,' he said, grabbing the nylon mesh with his hand. 'In fact, I think we need to shoot some more heat into the envelope. I don't know the terrain. But we damn sure don't wanna collide with any other tepuis.'

'If you say so,' Tree said, and started to reach for the flame trigger on the gas burner. A screech made them both jump.

Tree's eyes went huge. 'What was that?'

Mason looked up at the red, white and blue envelope. 'Shit, are we ripping again?'

They heard another screech. It came from high on their left, above the balloon. They craned their necks and saw it: a harpy, circling with gigantic outstretched wings. The sun flashed white on its albino feathers.

The eagle screeched a long angry war cry, braked in mid-air, tucked and dived.

It fell like a flashing white blade.

57

The harpy shot its talons forward in the instant before the strike. Mason ducked involuntarily. The eagle slammed the balloon and slashed a long gash in the envelope, then veered away, flapping.

'It got the bag where it was already damaged,' Mason shouted, 'I think we're okay.'

The harpy climbed high above and hovered for a moment, emitting ear-piercing screeches.

'I could learn to dislike this species,' Tree said.

The eagle dove again. The talons ripped into another section of the envelope and a big square of Dacron flapped down like a torn-out knee patch. The balloon lurched and started to descend.

'Go away! *Zu kai! Zu kai!* We're not in your damn territory,' Tree shouted, and grabbed up one of the scalpels, jabbing it toward the harpy who climbed in lazy spirals.

Mason searched around frantically for something – anything – to throw, some sort of weapon. But they'd tossed all extra cargo over the side. He grabbed a Frisbee. Useless. Then his stocking foot bumped against a scalpel kit. It gave him an idea.

'Tree, quick. The scalpels. Do what I'm doing. Make me a throwing weapon.'

Mason turned an orange plastic Frisbee upside down and poked its concave edge with a stainless steel scalpel, shoving the blade through the lip. He forced a scalpel blade through the opposite lip of the Frisbee, as counterbalance.

'Duct tape?' he said. 'Duct tape?'

'There, at your foot.'

He quickly secured the scalpels with the tape, and held up his makeshift throwing star: a Frisbee with two razor-sharp blades jutting two inches out from opposite sides.

'Right with you,' Tree said.

He tore off two lengths of tape. 'Here. Tape 'em tight.'

With a screech, the harpy divebombed the balloon. The talons severed the crown spill cable and one of the shroud lines supporting the net and the mesh sagged three feet downward on that side.

'Hang on,' Mason shouted, as they both slid toward the low side. One of the blades on the Frisbee dug deep into Mason's palm, but his heart was pounding in his ears and he hardly noticed the pain.

'Get the harpy, Mason.'

'Can't. It's climbing again.'

'We're losing altitude, fast,' she said, and poured on the flames. The balloon slowed its descent and sluggishly began to climb.

The harpy tucked its wings and pointed its big head down.

'Here he comes,' Mason said, tracking it with his eyes. 'I'm ready for you now, you fucker.'

Just as the raptor spun its heavy body to bring its talons to the attack, Mason whipped the Frisbee outward with a forearm-wrist throw. The razors twirled in a blur around the spinning disk. It caught the eagle just above its broad chest. The bird's head seemed to switch direction and shoot skyward while its body plummeted and landed on the nylon mesh with a *thunk*.

Tree cheered. 'Bird, you just met the Frisbee Golf ninja.'

Mason wiped bloodspray from his face and looked at the decapitated eagle; the wings bucked and flapped in a brief death spasm.

Mason sank down on the mesh, breathing hard.

'That's for Lynda.'

58

Twilight. Purplish rain clouds smudged the western horizon. Mason tried to gauge the balloon's velocity by estimating the distance to a landmark below, and timing how long it took to fly over it. But the landmarks kept blurring in his mind. Each green canopy looked like the next. The clouds were no help because they weren't fixed points. The bulging cottony clouds that drifted alongside them in the same wind current travelled at the very same speed and, therefore, did not seem to move at all. Other wispy strings of vapor ran along at altitudes above or below at differing speeds. A channel in the sky high above even conveyed its clouds at nearly right angles to the direction the balloon was heading, still northward.

One thing was certain – the balloon was steadily sinking; Mason could now hear the squawks of St Vincent parrots and hoots of howler monkeys less than a thousand feet below. No matter how much heat Tree shot into the damaged envelope, they were slowly going down. At their present rate of descent, within the next twenty minutes they would crash into the treetops of a vast and non-human world.

Mason craned his neck to spot a river. Any river, he thought. Doesn't have to be the Caroni. Just some sort of route to travel through the solid mass of green.

'There!' Tree shouted.

'Where? Oh, I see it,' he said. A wide silvery ribbon snaked through the rainforest; they were nearly on top of it before it became visible between the trees.

'Is it the Caroni?' Tree said.

'Don't know. It's our best hope. Quick, spill some air, get us down there.'

'Can't.' She held up the severed end of the spill line. The line normally led to a vent at the crown of the balloon that allowed the pilot to bleed off hot air for rapid descent.

'Shit. Now what?' he said, and glanced down at the approaching river.

'I'm thinking,' she said, looking up at the balloon.

'What if we slash the bag?' he said. 'High up, so the heated air will escape.'

'Slash it with what?'

He held up the other bladed Frisbee.

She shook her head. 'It's Dacron. Even if you could toss it high enough up through the mouth of the envelope, it won't make much of a hole.'

'Night's falling, Tree. If we don't get ourselves down near the river, fast . . . Wait, I got it. What if we light the envelope, catch it afire with the burner?'

'Dacron will melt, we'll come down in a big fireball.'

'And hit the water, the fire goes out.'

'And if we miss?'

He glanced down. 'We gotta do something. We're gonna cross the river in less than a minute.'

'Wait. I got it.' She flipped a knob and turned off the pilot light to the three burners. The flames snuffed out.

'*What?*'

'Hang on, I'm gonna shoot liquid propane up inside the envelope – it's freezing cold. It'll cool our lift and we'll come down fast. We land in the river. It's the only way.'

Mason stared down at the oncoming river shining through the trees. 'Tree, we must be two hundred feet up.'

'Look,' she said. 'I'd rather break my neck in a flash than be some jaguar's all-night snack.'

'You've got a way of putting things.'

They watched between their feet as the river snaked closer.

Now Mason was glad the balloon was steadily sinking. Anything to narrow the vertical gap between them and their dropzone. *Sink, baby, sink.*

The river looked wide. He hoped it was deep. They were still maybe a hundred feet above the treetops.

'Ready?' Tree said. 'Right before we cross the near bank.'

'Now!' they both shouted.

A long blast of frosty propane shot into the envelope. The frost licked up the inside of the balloon and the Dacron began to shrivel. For an instant, the balloon wobbled drunkenly on its wad of heated air; then it started to drop, slowly, then faster.

The river's surface rushed up at them and Mason saw reflected in it a falling giant beachball.

The impact gonged his skull. Then a glaze of peace spread over his brain and he blacked out.

He awoke on his back on the shore. A dark-skinned man bent over him, gazing into his eyes. The native wore a blue and yellow crown of macaw feathers and his nasal septum was pierced by a porcupine quill.

Mason raised his head. 'Tree?'

'I'm here, Mason,' Tree said, to his left.

Mason sighed with relief and turned to that side, wincing at a whiplash pain in his neck and shoulder. Tree bent over him, one whole side of her face caked with black mud.

'I know I look like hell, but I'm okay,' she said, and smiled.

'You're the vision of beauty. You survived.'

What mattered now was their Indian host. Was he a Wawajero or a Yanomorduro? Mason and Tree had brought no items for bribe or barter; if the man was a scout for a tribe of headhunters, they were as good as dead.

'Freesbee,' the Indian said, holding up a yellow plastic Frisbee from the river. 'Freesbee.'

'Wawajero?' Mason asked.

The man slapped his muscular chest and grinned. 'Wawajero.'

Mason let his head drop back on the riverbank and he laughed until he cried.

EPILOGUE

Mason knelt on the red oak floor of his living room alongside a long unfurled scroll of bleached linen paper, held open with a brass weight. China Diana Drake bent over her own scroll, concentrating on each black-ink line of her calligraphy. This morning, they practiced the Chinese word *t'ai*, meaning 'peace.'

'Nice,' Mason said, looking over at his daughter's work. 'Very nice. You're really getting the knack.'

She looked up at him with lit green eyes.

'My teacher was just eleven years old and already a master,' he said. 'He made it look easy. Watch your brush, hon, you're about to drip.'

'Oh.' China rested the foot-long wooden handle in a soap-stone brush holder carved in the shape of a boy riding a water buffalo.

'*T'ai*. I like the shape,' she said, 'reminds me of a Christmas tree.'

'Ha. Don't get started, it's not even Thanksgiving yet.'

Tree walked into the living room cradling a baby in one arm and managing two steaming cups of coffee in her free hand. Mason stood and took both cups, placed them on a coffee table. Samuel Gibraltar Drake was sleeping cuddled against Tree's bosom. His blond hair outclassed his father's in the

324

coiled tightness of its ringlets.

'We're writing *t'ai*,' China said. 'Peace.'

'I see,' Tree said. 'Looks good.'

'*T'ai* is a special word,' Mason said, painting the strokes of the ideogram with controlled sweeps. 'It incorporates the whole Taoist philosophy of *yin* and *yang*.'

'Honey, don't go over her head,' Tree said.

'I know those words,' China said. 'Yin is girl, yang is boy.'

'Right,' Mason said. 'Look here.' With shiny wet ink he drew a figure of six horizontal lines on his scroll; the hexagram was made up of three broken lines above and three unbroken lines beneath. 'This is the hexagram called *T'ai* from an ancient Chinese oracle, the *I Ching* – or Book of Changes.'

'Oracle?' China said.

'Means like fortune-telling,' Tree said. 'But the *I Ching* is much more than that. It talks about a whole way of life.'

'Okay.'

'See these broken lines?' Mason said. 'They represent the ultimate yin: they're called *k'un*, which means Earth, the Receptive,' he said. 'The solid lines are the ultimate yang: they're called *chien*, which means Heaven, the Creative.'

'Then why is Earth above and Heaven below?' China said.

'Good. Very perceptive,' Mason said. 'Earth is thought of as flowing downward, and Heaven is pictured as flowing upward. So arranged this way, they mix at the center, see?'

'Earth and Heaven mix, and that makes peace?'

'The *I Ching* says, 'Their influences meet and harmonize and all living things bloom and prosper.' But let me show you something else, something you'll recognize.'

He drew a six-sided star formed of two intersecting triangles, one upturned, the other downturned.

'The Star of David,' China said. 'Jewish.'

'Right, and the Hindus and Buddhists and Taoists also drew this symbol to show Heaven and Earth meeting at the heart and becoming whole.'

'Neat,' China said and yawned.

'Okay. Enough calligraphy for one day.'

'I'm going next door to play with Grandma,' China said, and left the room, skipping.

'This stuff's a little beyond her years, sweetie,' Tree said.

'Probably. But what the heck, she likes calligraphy. Look how well she's coming along.'

Samuel began rooting for a nipple through the brushed blue wool of Tree's nightgown. He whimpered with frustration and began to cry.

'Shhh. Sammy,' Tree said, 'I got your milk right here.' She unbuttoned the front of her gown and her son lunged at the rosy target of a nipple and latched on with his sucking mouth.

Tree closed her eyes for a moment in obvious pleasure.

'That must feel so good,' Mason said. 'I wish I knew how that felt.'

'As close to feeling like a goddess as I can imagine.'

'Of all the aspects of womanhood, I think that's the one I'd most like to experience.'

'Oh, so you'd skip the childbirth part?'

Mason laughed. He thought of K'un-Chien; how she, alone among humans, could experience the joys and pains of womanhood and manhood in one human body.

After a while Tree laid Samuel down in his crib, sleeping soundly.

'You've got that look in your eyes, Mason.'

He smiled. 'Yep.'

'Have you had breakfast?'

'Hunger is the best sauce.'

He took Tree's hand and led her into their sunlit bedroom.